INFINITE DARK

VOLUME 2

Published by
TOP COW PRODUCTIONS, INC.
Los Angeles

For Top Cow Productions, Inc.

For Top Cow Productions, Inc.
Marc Silvestri - CEO
Matt Hawkins - President & COO
Elena Salcedo - Vice President of Operations
Vincent Valentine - Lead Production Artist
Henry Barajas - Director of Operations
Dylan Gray - Marketing Director

To find the comic shop nearest you, call:
1-888-COMICBOOK

Want more info? Check out:
www.topcow.com
for news & exclusive Top Cow merchandise!

IMAGE COMICS, INC.
Robert Kirkman—Chief Operating Officer
Erik Larsen—Chief Financial Officer
Todd McFarlane—President
Marc Silvestri—Chief Executive Officer
Jim Valentino—Vice President
Eric Stephenson—Publisher/Chief Creative Officer
Jeff Boison—Director of Publishing Planning & Book Trade Sales
Chris Ross—Director of Digital Sales
Jeff Stang—Director of Direct Market Sales
Kat Salazar—Director of PR & Marketing
Drew Gill—Art Director
Heather Doornink—Production Director
Nicole Lapalme—Controller
IMAGECOMICS.COM

INFINITE DARK, VOL. 2. First printing. September 2019. Published by Image Comics, Inc. Office of publication: 2701 NW Vaughn St., Suite 780, Portland, OR 97210. ISBN: 978-1-5343-1323-1.

INFINITE DARK

VOLUME 2

WRITTER **RYAN CADY**
@RYCADY

ARTIST **ANDREA MUTTI**
@ANDREAMUTTI9

COLORIST **K. MICHAEL RUSSELL**
@KMICHAELRUSSELL

LETTERER **TROY PETERI OF A LARGER WORLD**
@A_LARGER_WORLD

STORY EDITOR **ALEX LU**
@WAXENWINGS

EDITOR IN CHIEF **MATT HAWKINS**
@TOPCOWMATT

EDITOR **ELENA SALCEDO**

PRODUCTION **VINCENT VALENTINE**

IN THE LAST VOLUME OF INFINITE DARK...

When a rapid entropic decay consumed the entire universe, a few thousand human beings managed to survive on board the Orpheus, a space station protected from the nothingness outside. After two quiet years in the Void, the Orpheus was almost destroyed by a group of insane saboteurs and murderers who claimed to be infected by an otherworldly Entity.

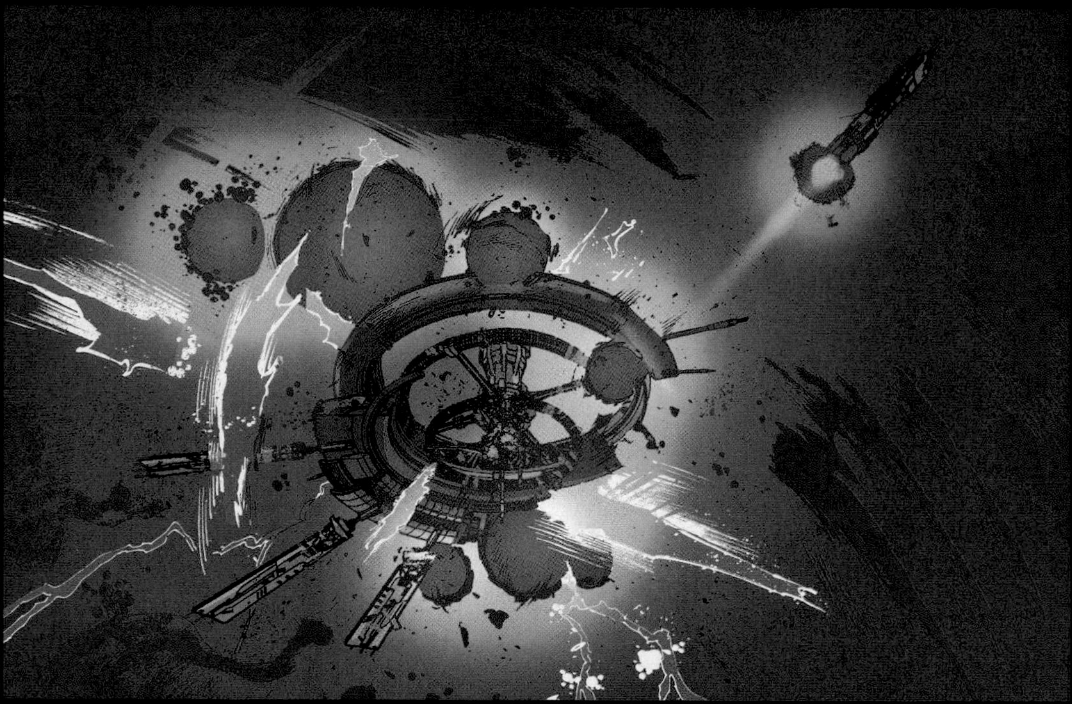

A daring plan was executed to salvage the station and the Entity Itself was supposedly destroyed.

But in the weeks since the Orpheus' narrow escape, life has been far from peaceful...

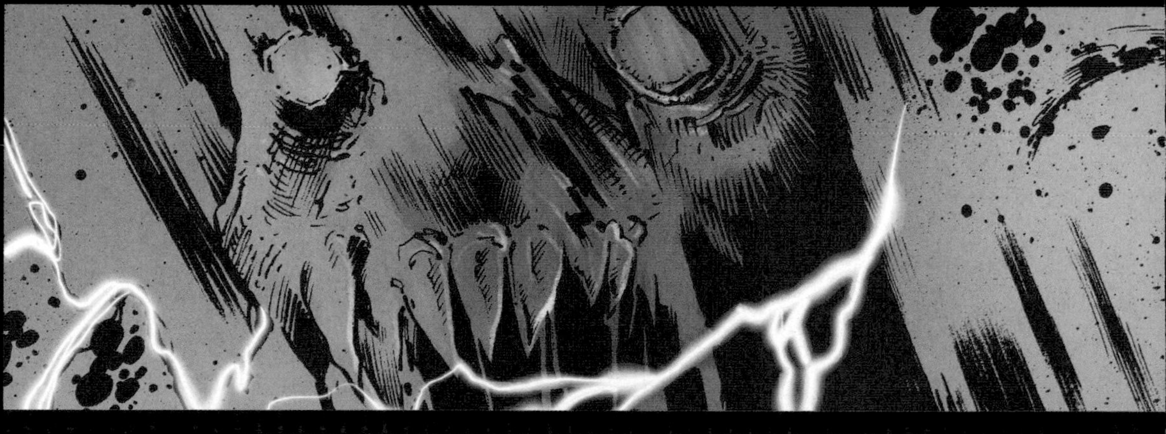

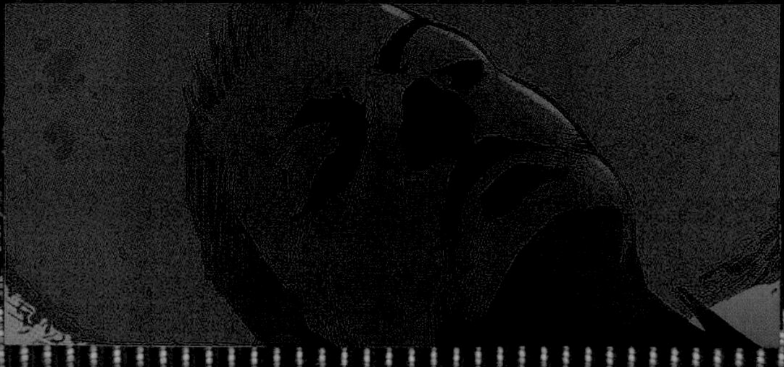

THE CREW OF THE ORPHEUS

DEVA KARRELL

Security Director of the Orpheus. Deva was exposed to raw entropy while investigating the station's first murder, and she encountered the Entity. She investigated a conspiracy and spurred the Board of Directors to protect the station, confronting the Entity directly as the Orpheus collapsed around her.

KIRIN TAL-SHI

A "technolinguist," and one of the two original servants of the Entity. Kirin believed that the Entity survived the natural order, and they attempted to remove the Orpheus' protective pseudoreality field, but were apprehended by Sebastian.

LYNN TENANT

Project Manager for the Orpheus, and Chairperson of its Board of Directors. Lynn often clashed with Deva, and like many, never believed in the Entity's existence. But ultimately, her willingness to trust her Security Director allowed her to help save the entire station.

SEBASTIAN

Security technician and Deva's right-hand man. Sebastian does not believe in the Entity, but always stood by Deva no matter what. His steadfast determination can occasionally lead to anger and stubbornness.

SM1TH

An artificial intelligence created to manage the Orpheus' many varied and complicated computer systems. Hyper-advanced, ubiquitous, and a little snooty, the posh AI seems programmed with a fierce and innate dedication to the human spirit and its potential.

DR. IKE CHALOS

A psychiatrist and former Medical Director for the Orpheus, Ike was murdered as the Orpheus began to collapse. His murderers—the so-called Void Exposure Patients—were supposedly manipulated by the Entity as a part of Kirin Tal-Shi's conspiracy.

THE ENTITY

While most of the Orpheus' populace still do not know of or believe in this monster from beyond, its influence nearly caused their demise. Calling Itself "Entropy's Hand," the Entity was a cosmic scavenger determined to feed on the universal scraps left over from heat death. The Entropy was destroyed as a byproduct of Deva's plan to save the Orpheus.

CHAPTER FIVE

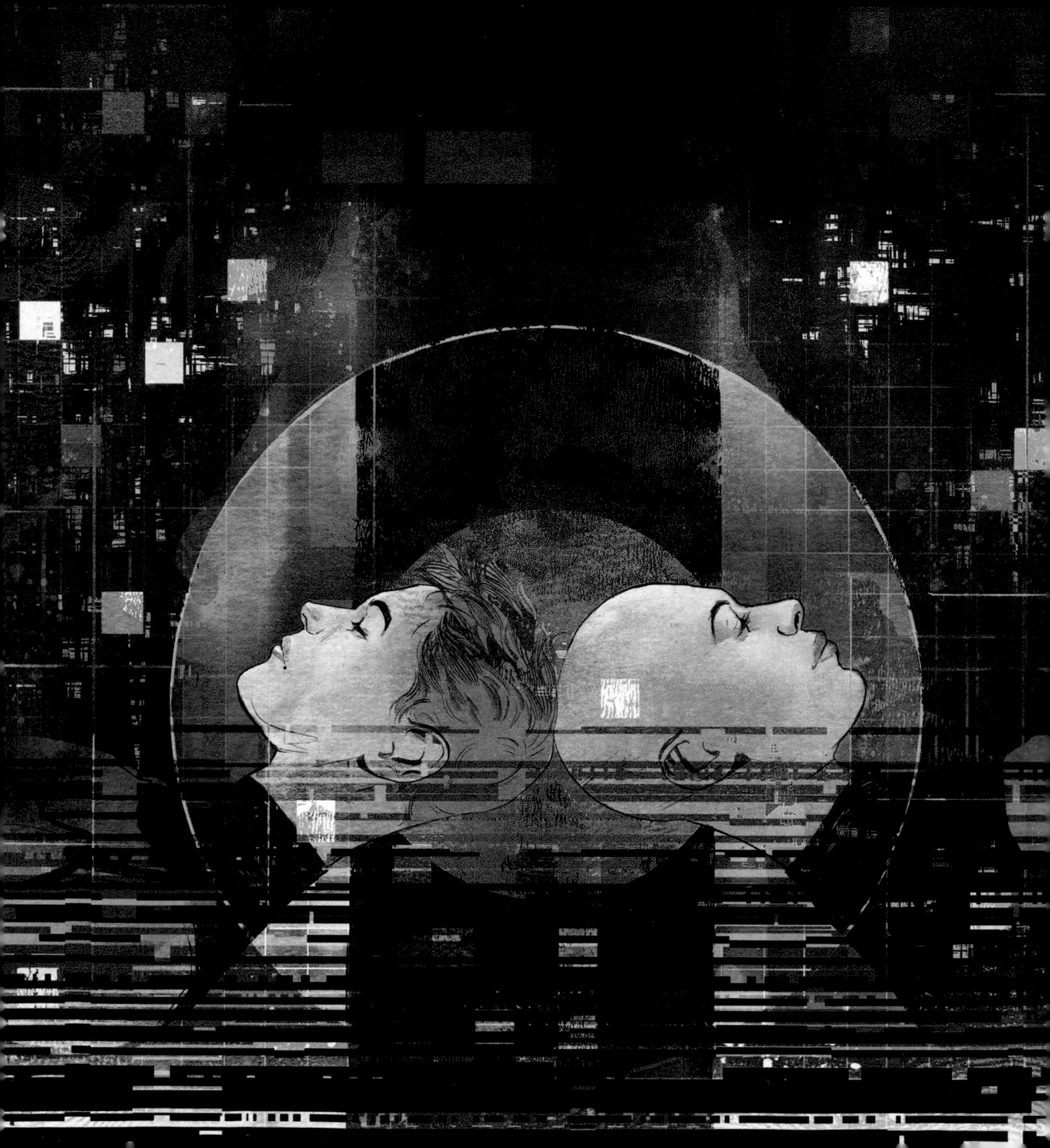

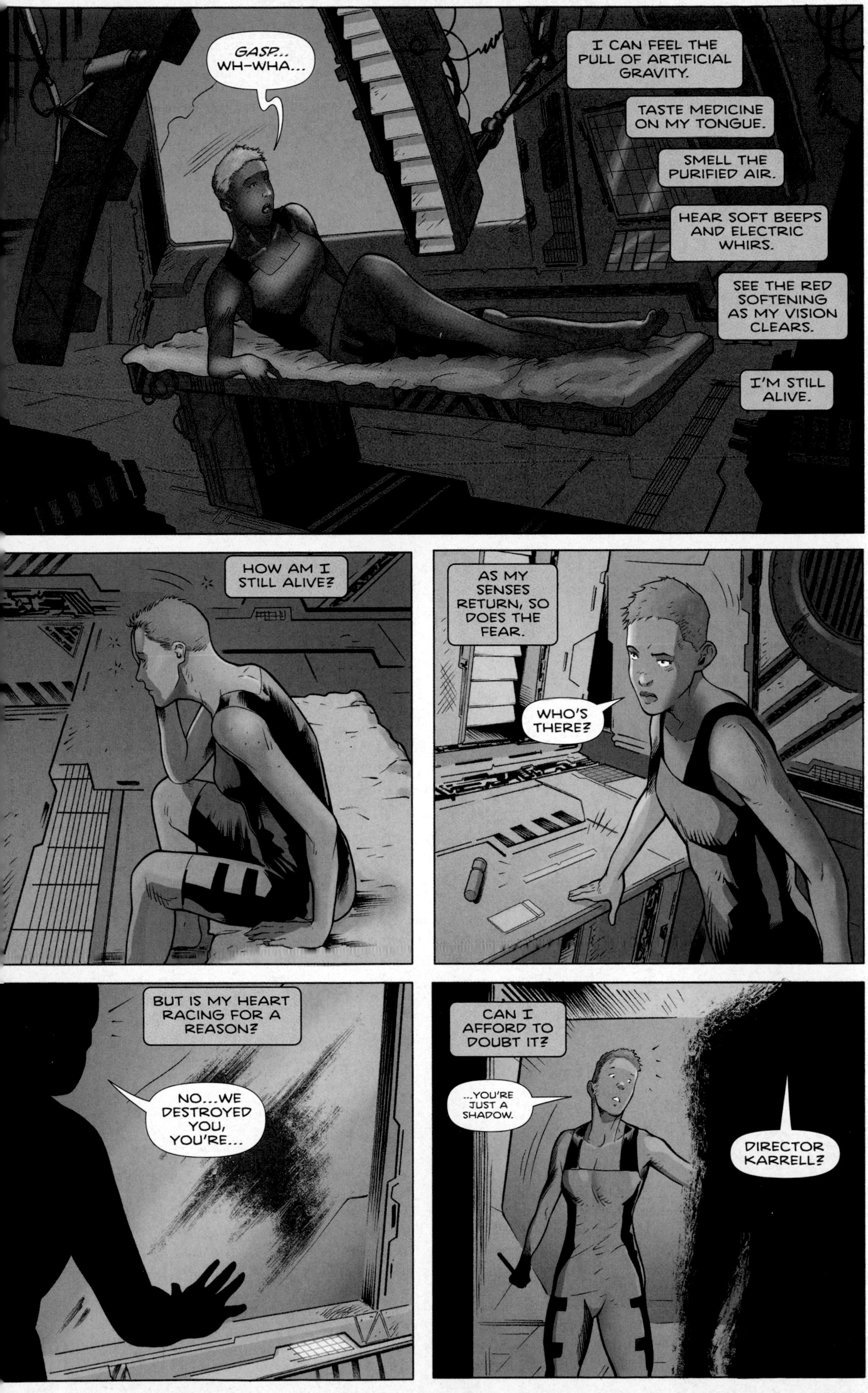
GASP.. WH-WHA...
I CAN FEEL THE PULL OF ARTIFICIAL GRAVITY.
TASTE MEDICINE ON MY TONGUE.
SMELL THE PURIFIED AIR.
HEAR SOFT BEEPS AND ELECTRIC WHIRS.
SEE THE RED SOFTENING AS MY VISION CLEARS.
I'M STILL ALIVE.
HOW AM I STILL ALIVE?
AS MY SENSES RETURN, SO DOES THE FEAR.
WHO'S THERE?
BUT IS MY HEART RACING FOR A REASON?
NO...WE DESTROYED YOU, YOU'RE...
CAN I AFFORD TO DOUBT IT?
...YOU'RE JUST A SHADOW.
DIRECTOR KARRELL?

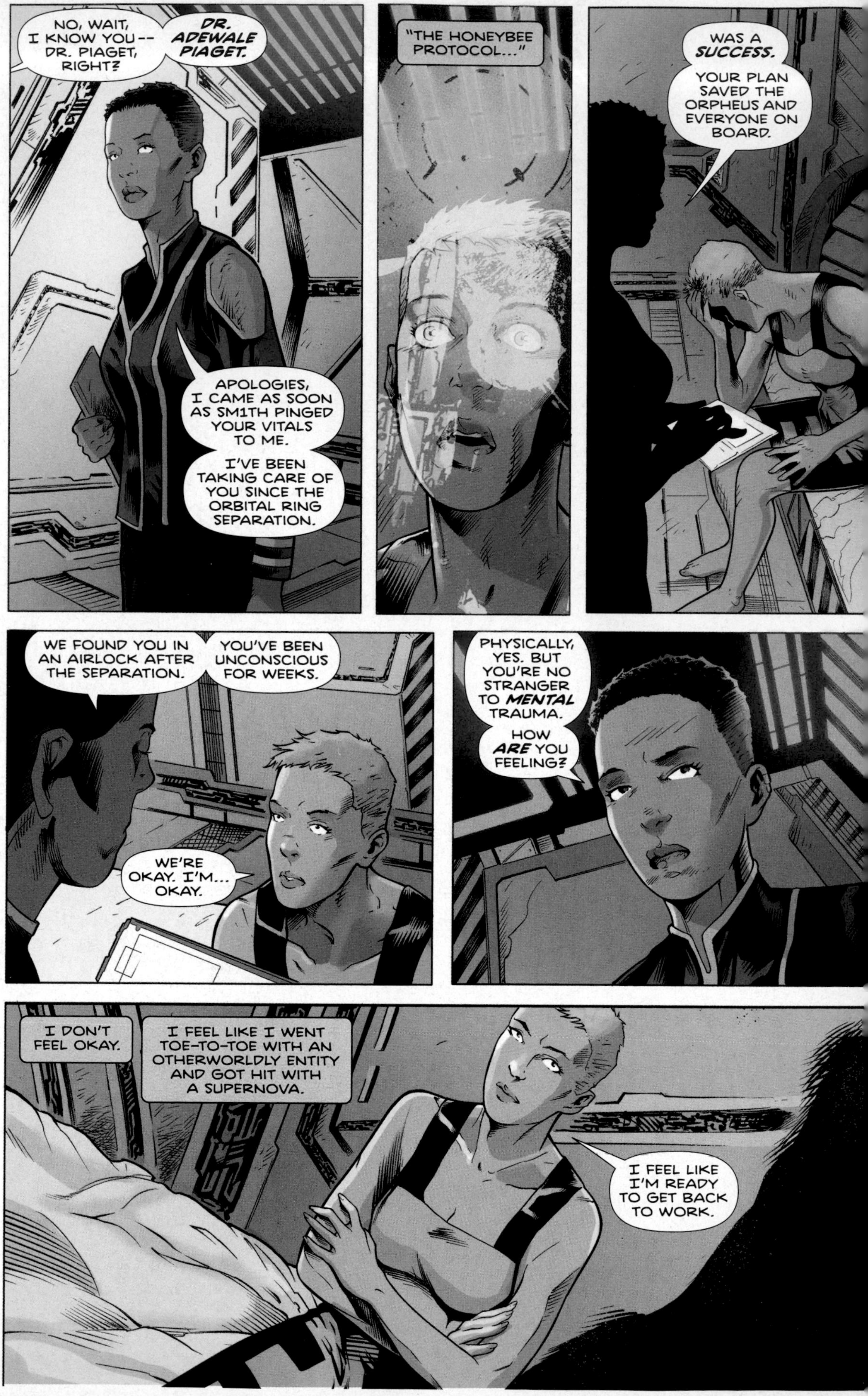
NO, WAIT, I KNOW YOU-- DR. PIAGET, RIGHT?
DR. ADEWALE PIAGET.
APOLOGIES, I CAME AS SOON AS SM1TH PINGED YOUR VITALS TO ME.
I'VE BEEN TAKING CARE OF YOU SINCE THE ORBITAL RING SEPARATION.
"THE HONEYBEE PROTOCOL..."
WAS A SUCCESS.
YOUR PLAN SAVED THE ORPHEUS AND EVERYONE ON BOARD.
WE FOUND YOU IN AN AIRLOCK AFTER THE SEPARATION.
YOU'VE BEEN UNCONSCIOUS FOR WEEKS.
WE'RE OKAY. I'M... OKAY.
PHYSICALLY, YES. BUT YOU'RE NO STRANGER TO MENTAL TRAUMA.
HOW ARE YOU FEELING?
I DON'T FEEL OKAY.
I FEEL LIKE I WENT TOE-TO-TOE WITH AN OTHERWORLDLY ENTITY AND GOT HIT WITH A SUPERNOVA.
I FEEL LIKE I'M READY TO GET BACK TO WORK.

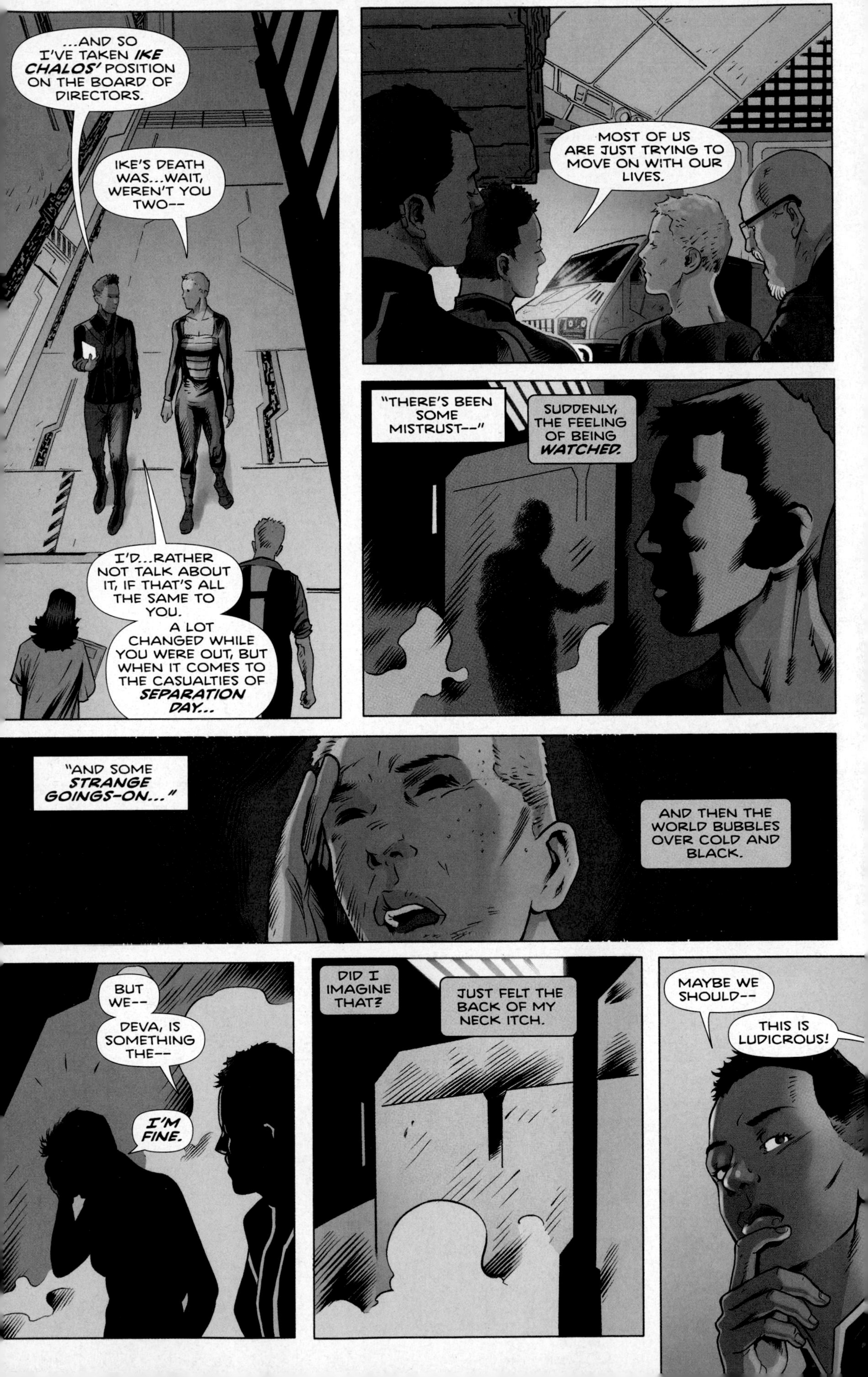
...AND SO I'VE TAKEN IKE CHALOS' POSITION ON THE BOARD OF DIRECTORS.
IKE'S DEATH WAS...WAIT, WEREN'T YOU TWO--
I'D...RATHER NOT TALK ABOUT IT, IF THAT'S ALL THE SAME TO YOU.
A LOT CHANGED WHILE YOU WERE OUT, BUT WHEN IT COMES TO THE CASUALTIES OF SEPARATION DAY...
MOST OF US ARE JUST TRYING TO MOVE ON WITH OUR LIVES.
"THERE'S BEEN SOME MISTRUST--"
SUDDENLY, THE FEELING OF BEING WATCHED.
"AND SOME STRANGE GOINGS-ON..."
AND THEN THE WORLD BUBBLES OVER COLD AND BLACK.
BUT WE--
DEVA, IS SOMETHING THE--
I'M FINE.
DID I IMAGINE THAT?
JUST FELT THE BACK OF MY NECK ITCH.
MAYBE WE SHOULD--
THIS IS LUDICROUS!

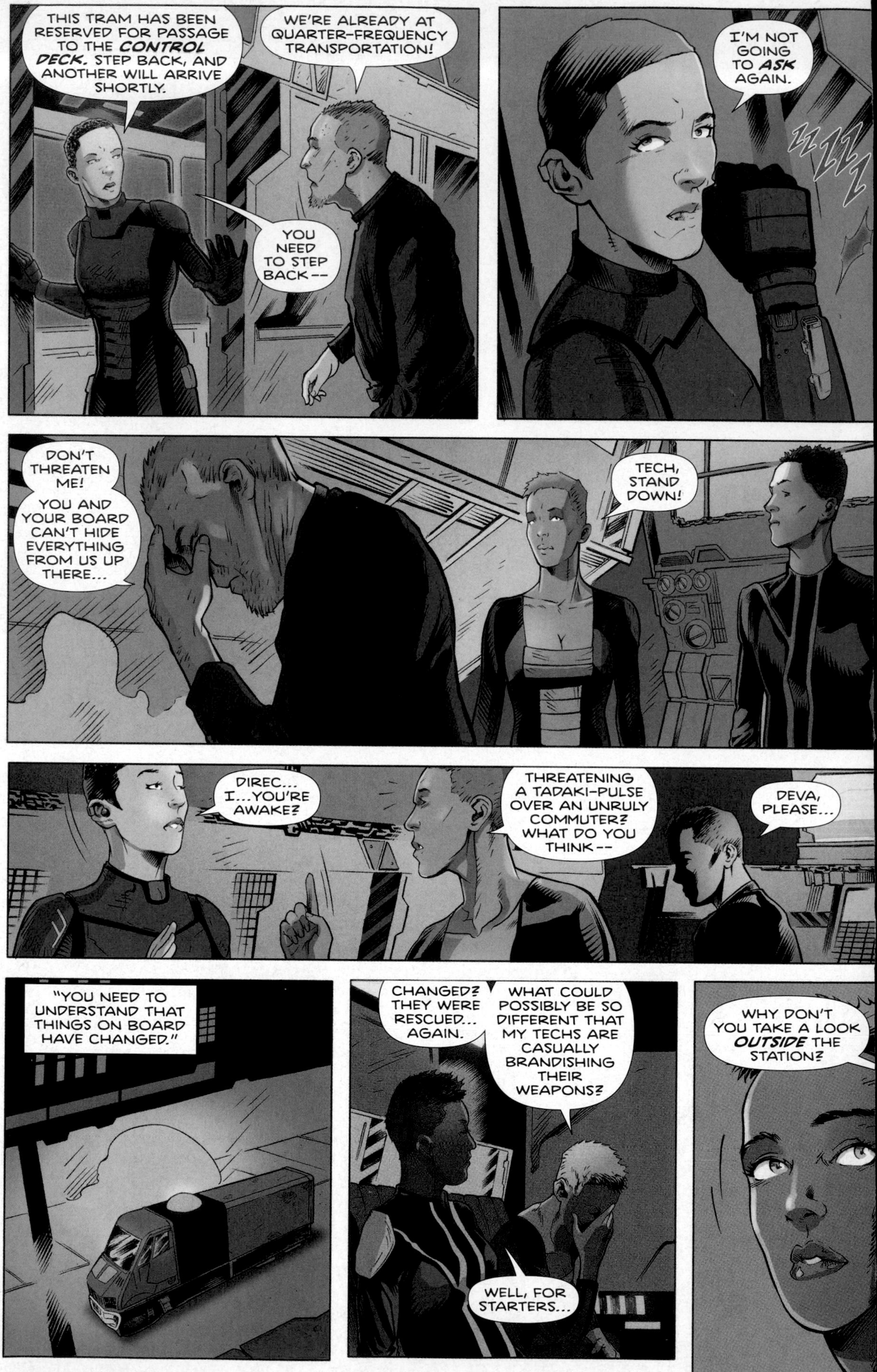
THIS TRAM HAS BEEN RESERVED FOR PASSAGE TO THE CONTROL DECK. STEP BACK, AND ANOTHER WILL ARRIVE SHORTLY.
WE'RE ALREADY AT QUARTER-FREQUENCY TRANSPORTATION!
YOU NEED TO STEP BACK--
I'M NOT GOING TO ASK AGAIN.
ZZZZZ
DON'T THREATEN ME!
YOU AND YOUR BOARD CAN'T HIDE EVERYTHING FROM US UP THERE...
TECH, STAND DOWN!
DIREC... I...YOU'RE AWAKE?
THREATENING A TADAKI-PULSE OVER AN UNRULY COMMUTER? WHAT DO YOU THINK--
DEVA, PLEASE...
"YOU NEED TO UNDERSTAND THAT THINGS ON BOARD HAVE CHANGED."
CHANGED? THEY WERE RESCUED... AGAIN.
WHAT COULD POSSIBLY BE SO DIFFERENT THAT MY TECHS ARE CASUALLY BRANDISHING THEIR WEAPONS?
WELL, FOR STARTERS...
WHY DON'T YOU TAKE A LOOK OUTSIDE THE STATION?

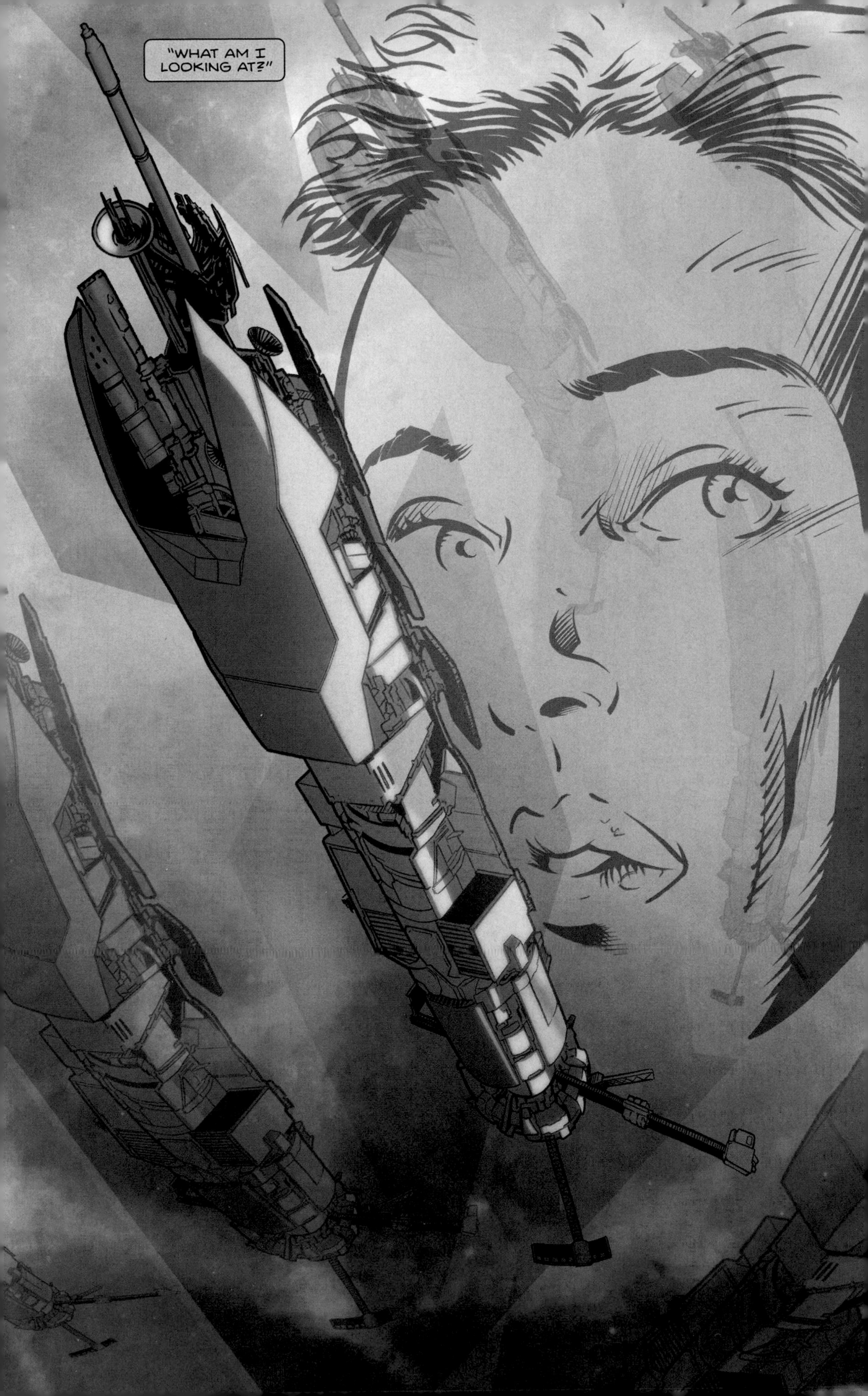
"WHAT AM I LOOKING AT?"

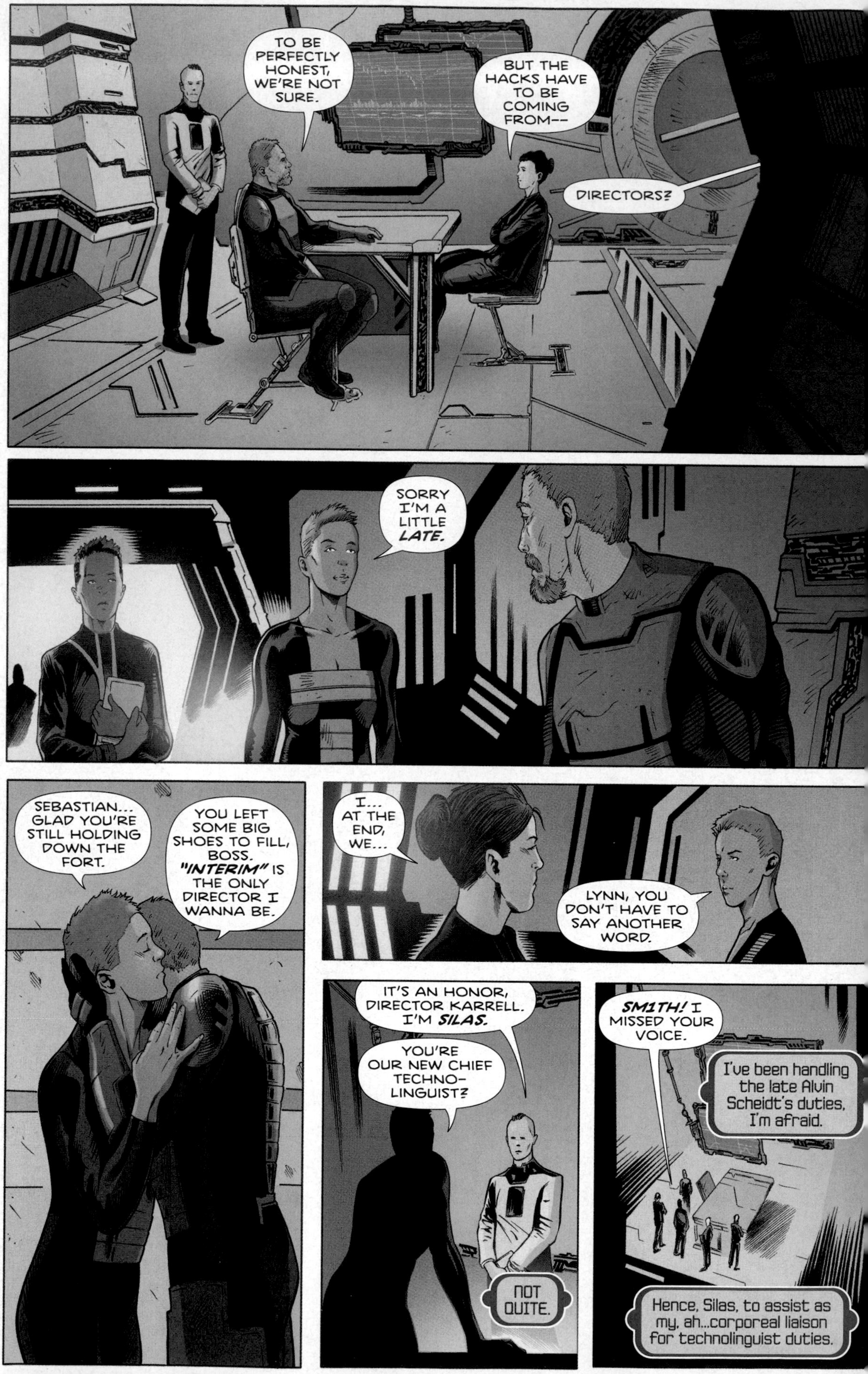
TO BE PERFECTLY HONEST, WE'RE NOT SURE.
BUT THE HACKS HAVE TO BE COMING FROM--
DIRECTORS?
SORRY I'M A LITTLE LATE.
SEBASTIAN... GLAD YOU'RE STILL HOLDING DOWN THE FORT.
YOU LEFT SOME BIG SHOES TO FILL, BOSS. "INTERIM" IS THE ONLY DIRECTOR I WANNA BE.
I... AT THE END, WE...
LYNN, YOU DON'T HAVE TO SAY ANOTHER WORD.
IT'S AN HONOR, DIRECTOR KARRELL. I'M SILAS.
YOU'RE OUR NEW CHIEF TECHNO-LINGUIST?
NOT QUITE.
SM1TH! I MISSED YOUR VOICE.
I've been handling the late Alvin Scheidt's duties, I'm afraid.
Hence, Silas, to assist as my, ah...corporeal liaison for technolinguist duties.

LET'S GET YOU UP TO SPEED.

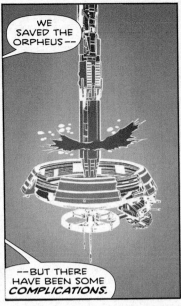

WE SAVED THE ORPHEUS--

--BUT THERE HAVE BEEN SOME *COMPLICATIONS*.

SHE'S ALREADY SEEN THE *OUTER MIRROR EFFECT*. AND WE WITNESSED ANOTHER TRANSIT ALTERCATION.

AGAIN? WE'LL JUST HAVE TO KEEP CRACKING DOWN. THE PUBLIC CHATS HAVE BEEN TRENDING WITH STEADY UNREST...

I THINK WE'RE LOOKING AT BAD ACTORS, SOMEONE MANIPULATING--

A few hacked terminals are not a grand conspiracy.

CIVIL UNREST should surprise none of you.

This board withheld information until the eleventh hour--and now we tell them even less.

DÉJÀ VU.

OBVIOUSLY, US SAVING THE SHIP DIDN'T SOLVE ALL ITS PROBLEMS.

BUT I DON'T LIKE WAKING UP TO ANARCHY AND..."OUTER MIRRORS."

CAN WE AT LEAST TALK ABOUT *SOLUTIONS?*

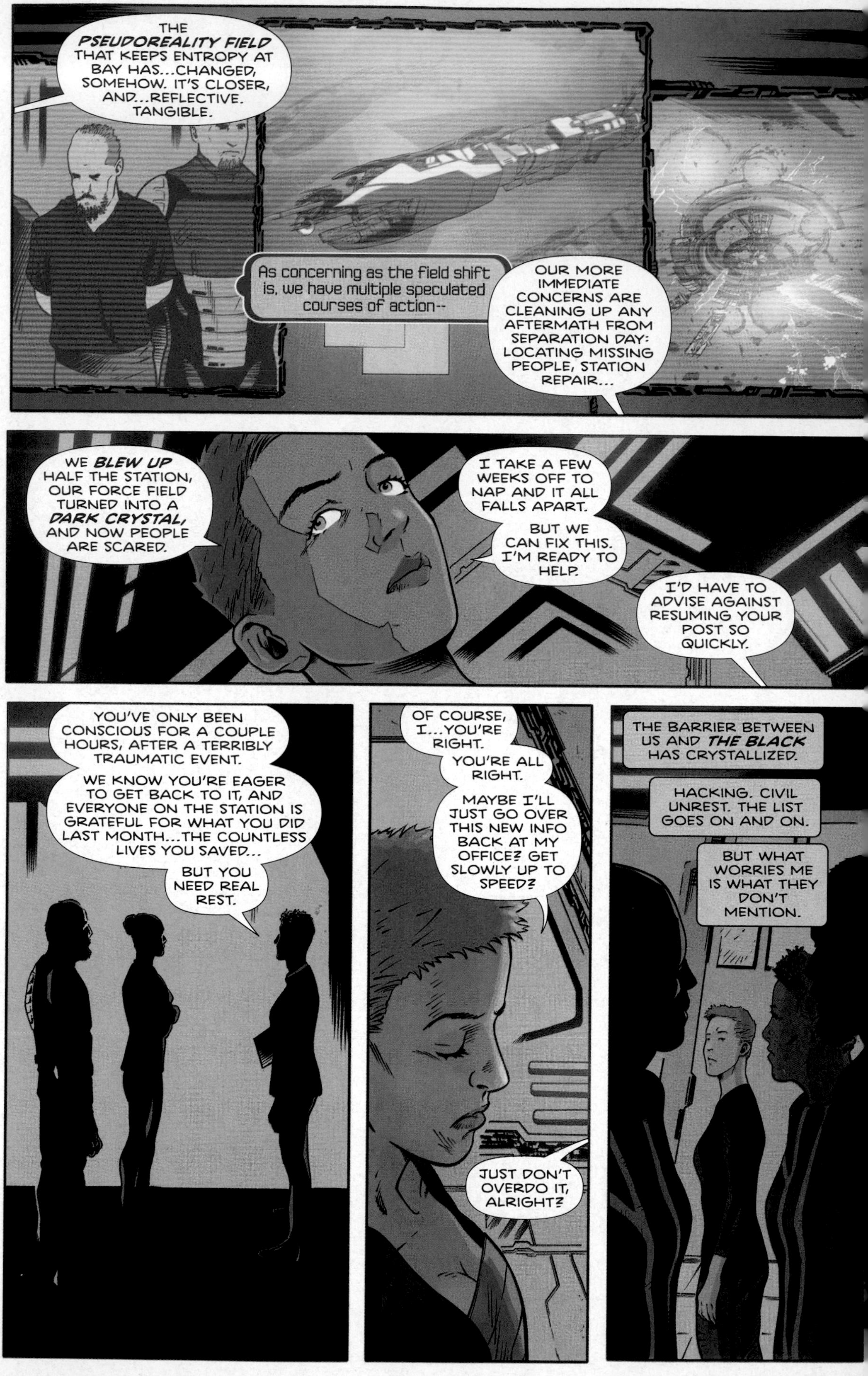
THE PSEUDOREALITY FIELD THAT KEEPS ENTROPY AT BAY HAS...CHANGED, SOMEHOW. IT'S CLOSER, AND...REFLECTIVE. TANGIBLE.
As concerning as the field shift is, we have multiple speculated courses of action--
OUR MORE IMMEDIATE CONCERNS ARE CLEANING UP ANY AFTERMATH FROM SEPARATION DAY: LOCATING MISSING PEOPLE, STATION REPAIR...
WE BLEW UP HALF THE STATION, OUR FORCE FIELD TURNED INTO A DARK CRYSTAL, AND NOW PEOPLE ARE SCARED.
I TAKE A FEW WEEKS OFF TO NAP AND IT ALL FALLS APART.
BUT WE CAN FIX THIS. I'M READY TO HELP.
I'D HAVE TO ADVISE AGAINST RESUMING YOUR POST SO QUICKLY.
YOU'VE ONLY BEEN CONSCIOUS FOR A COUPLE HOURS, AFTER A TERRIBLY TRAUMATIC EVENT.
WE KNOW YOU'RE EAGER TO GET BACK TO IT, AND EVERYONE ON THE STATION IS GRATEFUL FOR WHAT YOU DID LAST MONTH...THE COUNTLESS LIVES YOU SAVED...
BUT YOU NEED REAL REST.
OF COURSE, I...YOU'RE RIGHT.
YOU'RE ALL RIGHT.
MAYBE I'LL JUST GO OVER THIS NEW INFO BACK AT MY OFFICE? GET SLOWLY UP TO SPEED?
JUST DON'T OVERDO IT, ALRIGHT?
THE BARRIER BETWEEN US AND THE BLACK HAS CRYSTALLIZED.
HACKING. CIVIL UNREST. THE LIST GOES ON AND ON.
BUT WHAT WORRIES ME IS WHAT THEY DON'T MENTION.

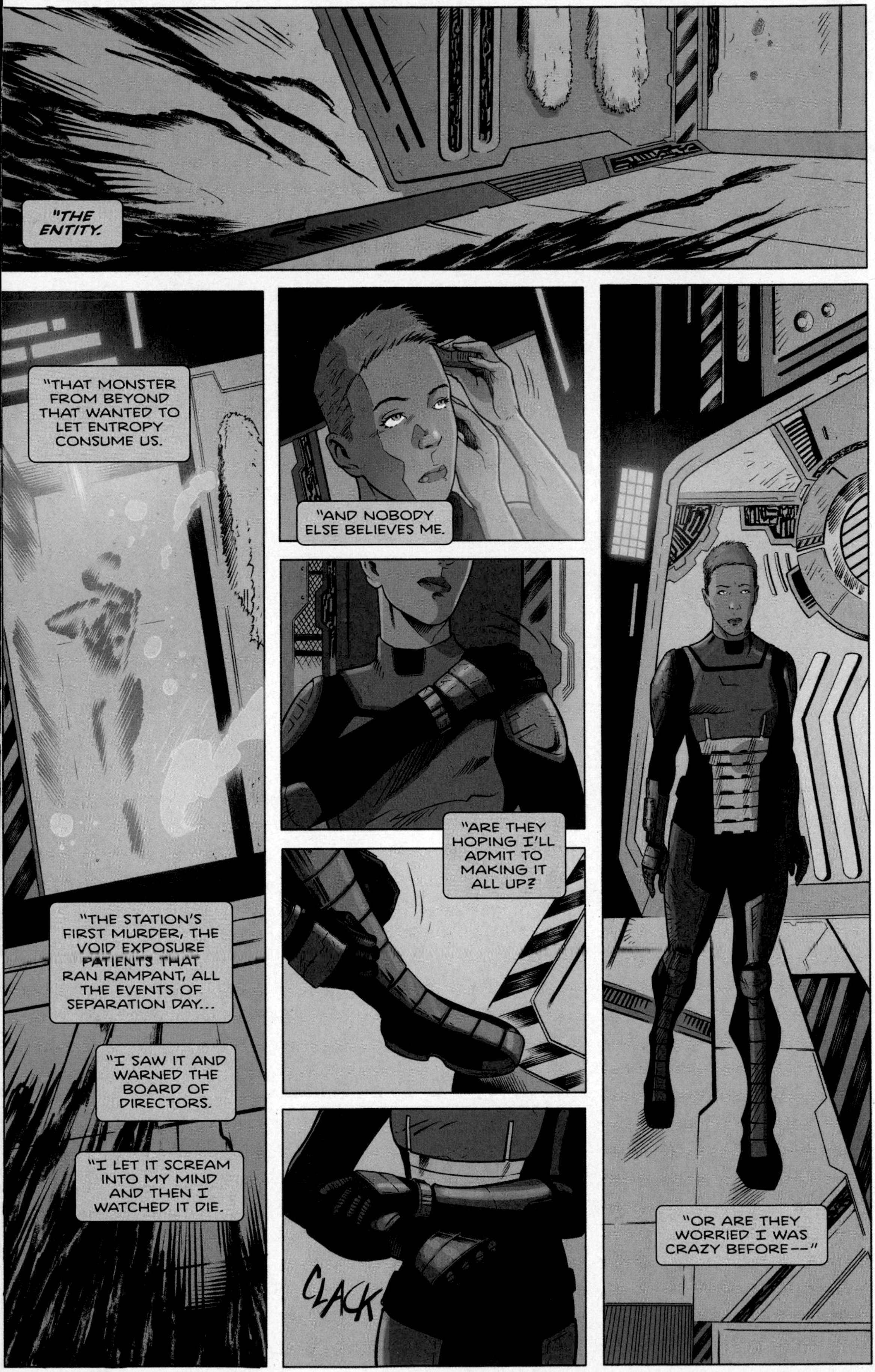
"THE ENTITY.
"THAT MONSTER FROM BEYOND THAT WANTED TO LET ENTROPY CONSUME US.
"THE STATION'S FIRST MURDER, THE VOID EXPOSURE PATIENTS THAT RAN RAMPANT, ALL THE EVENTS OF SEPARATION DAY...
"I SAW IT AND WARNED THE BOARD OF DIRECTORS.
"I LET IT SCREAM INTO MY MIND AND THEN I WATCHED IT DIE.
"AND NOBODY ELSE BELIEVES ME.
"ARE THEY HOPING I'LL ADMIT TO MAKING IT ALL UP?
CLACK
"OR ARE THEY WORRIED I WAS CRAZY BEFORE--"

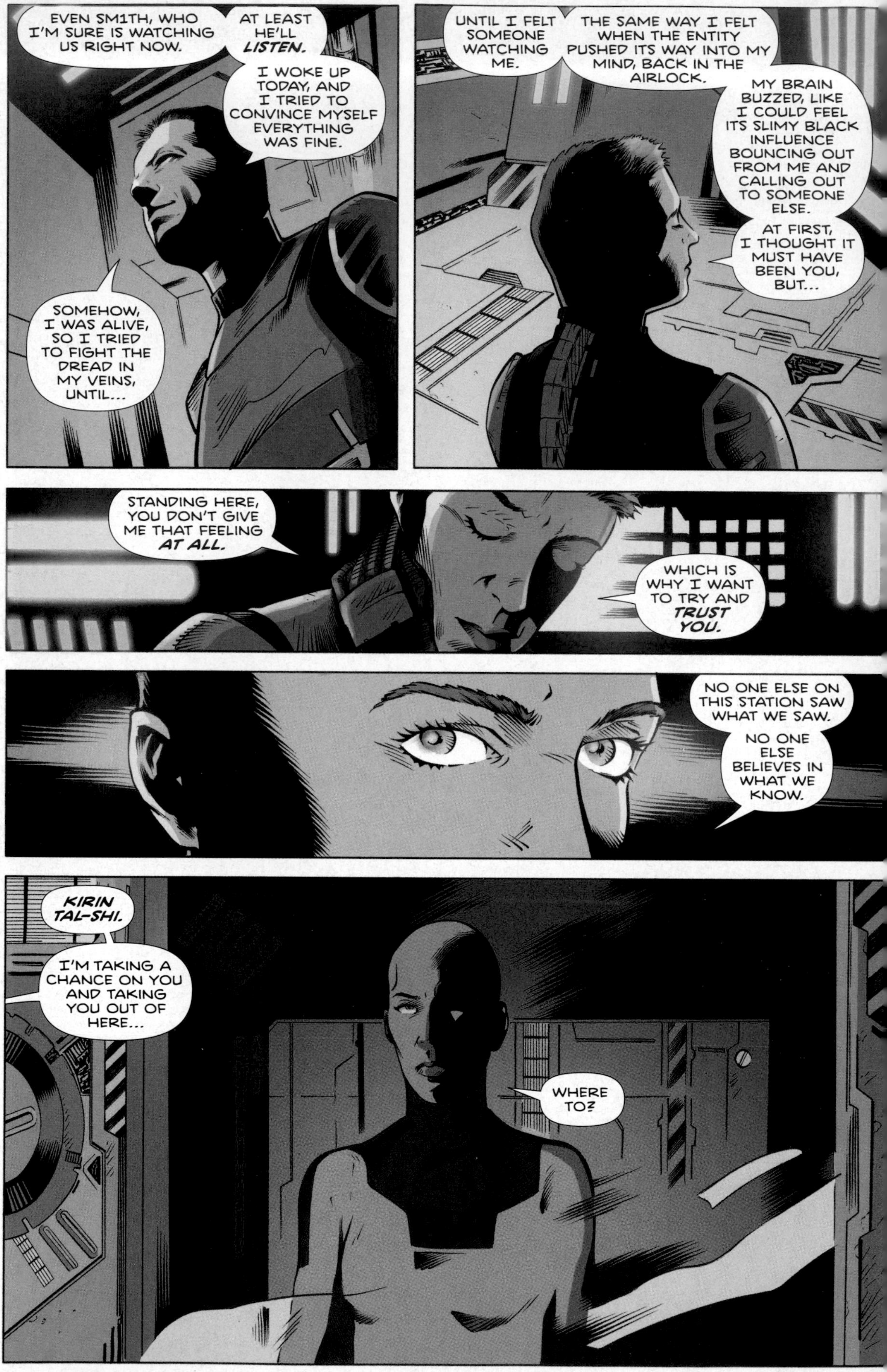
EVEN SM1TH, WHO I'M SURE IS WATCHING US RIGHT NOW.
AT LEAST HE'LL *LISTEN.*
I WOKE UP TODAY, AND I TRIED TO CONVINCE MYSELF EVERYTHING WAS FINE.
SOMEHOW, I WAS ALIVE, SO I TRIED TO FIGHT THE DREAD IN MY VEINS, UNTIL...
UNTIL I FELT SOMEONE WATCHING ME.
THE SAME WAY I FELT WHEN THE ENTITY PUSHED ITS WAY INTO MY MIND, BACK IN THE AIRLOCK.
MY BRAIN BUZZED, LIKE I COULD FEEL ITS SLIMY BLACK INFLUENCE BOUNCING OUT FROM ME AND CALLING OUT TO SOMEONE ELSE.
AT FIRST, I THOUGHT IT MUST HAVE BEEN YOU, BUT...
STANDING HERE, YOU DON'T GIVE ME THAT FEELING *AT ALL.*
WHICH IS WHY I WANT TO TRY AND *TRUST YOU.*
NO ONE ELSE ON THIS STATION SAW WHAT WE SAW.
NO ONE ELSE BELIEVES IN WHAT WE KNOW.
KIRIN TAL-SHI.
I'M TAKING A CHANCE ON YOU AND TAKING YOU OUT OF HERE...
WHERE TO?

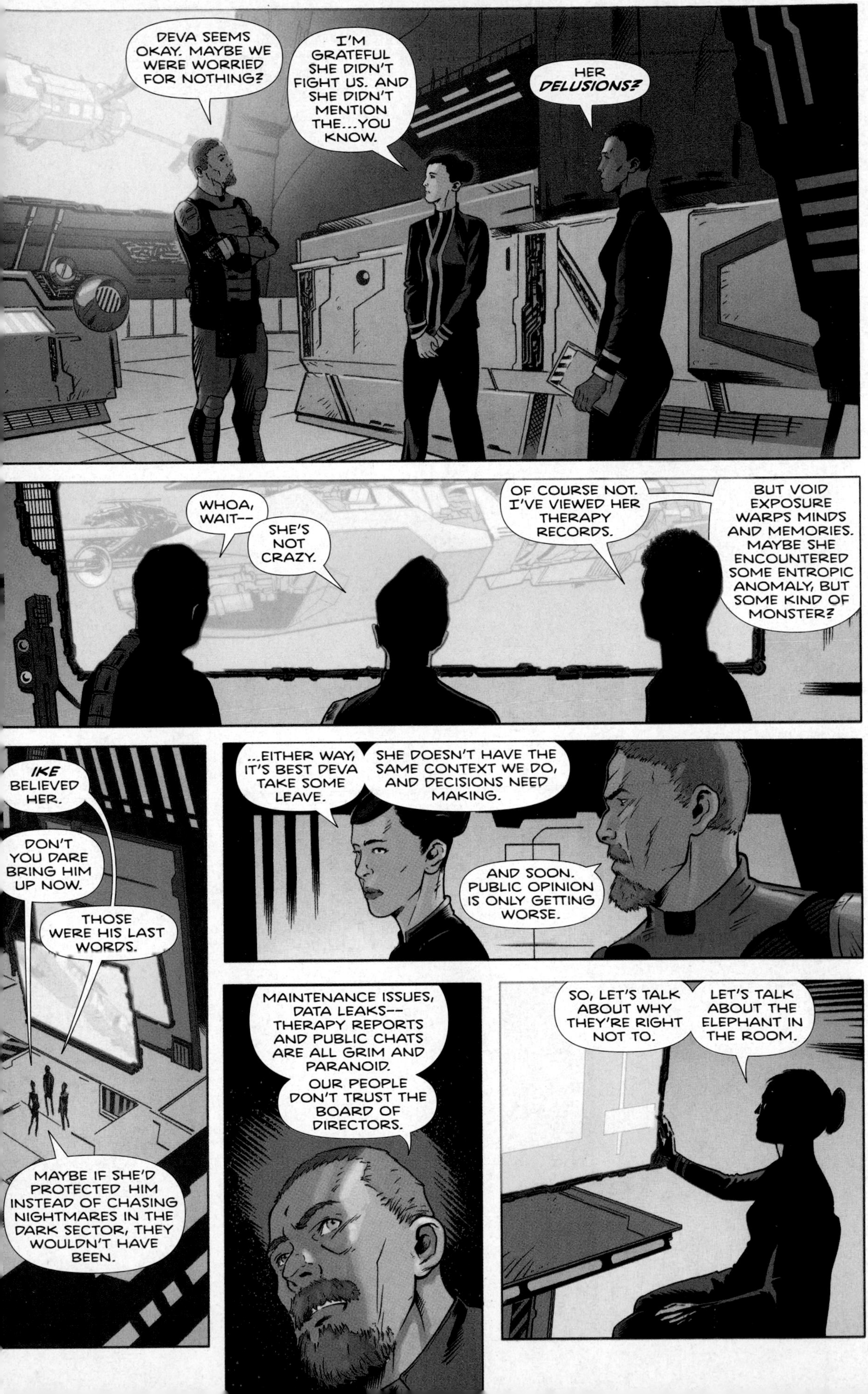
DEVA SEEMS OKAY. MAYBE WE WERE WORRIED FOR NOTHING?
I'M GRATEFUL SHE DIDN'T FIGHT US. AND SHE DIDN'T MENTION THE...YOU KNOW.
HER *DELUSIONS?*
WHOA, WAIT--
SHE'S NOT CRAZY.
OF COURSE NOT. I'VE VIEWED HER THERAPY RECORDS.
BUT VOID EXPOSURE WARPS MINDS AND MEMORIES. MAYBE SHE ENCOUNTERED SOME ENTROPIC ANOMALY, BUT SOME KIND OF MONSTER?
IKE BELIEVED HER.
DON'T YOU DARE BRING HIM UP NOW.
THOSE WERE HIS LAST WORDS.
MAYBE IF SHE'D PROTECTED HIM INSTEAD OF CHASING NIGHTMARES IN THE DARK SECTOR, THEY WOULDN'T HAVE BEEN.
...EITHER WAY, IT'S BEST DEVA TAKE SOME LEAVE.
SHE DOESN'T HAVE THE SAME CONTEXT WE DO, AND DECISIONS NEED MAKING.
AND SOON. PUBLIC OPINION IS ONLY GETTING WORSE.
MAINTENANCE ISSUES, DATA LEAKS-- THERAPY REPORTS AND PUBLIC CHATS ARE ALL GRIM AND PARANOID.
OUR PEOPLE DON'T TRUST THE BOARD OF DIRECTORS.
SO, LET'S TALK ABOUT WHY THEY'RE RIGHT NOT TO.
LET'S TALK ABOUT THE ELEPHANT IN THE ROOM.

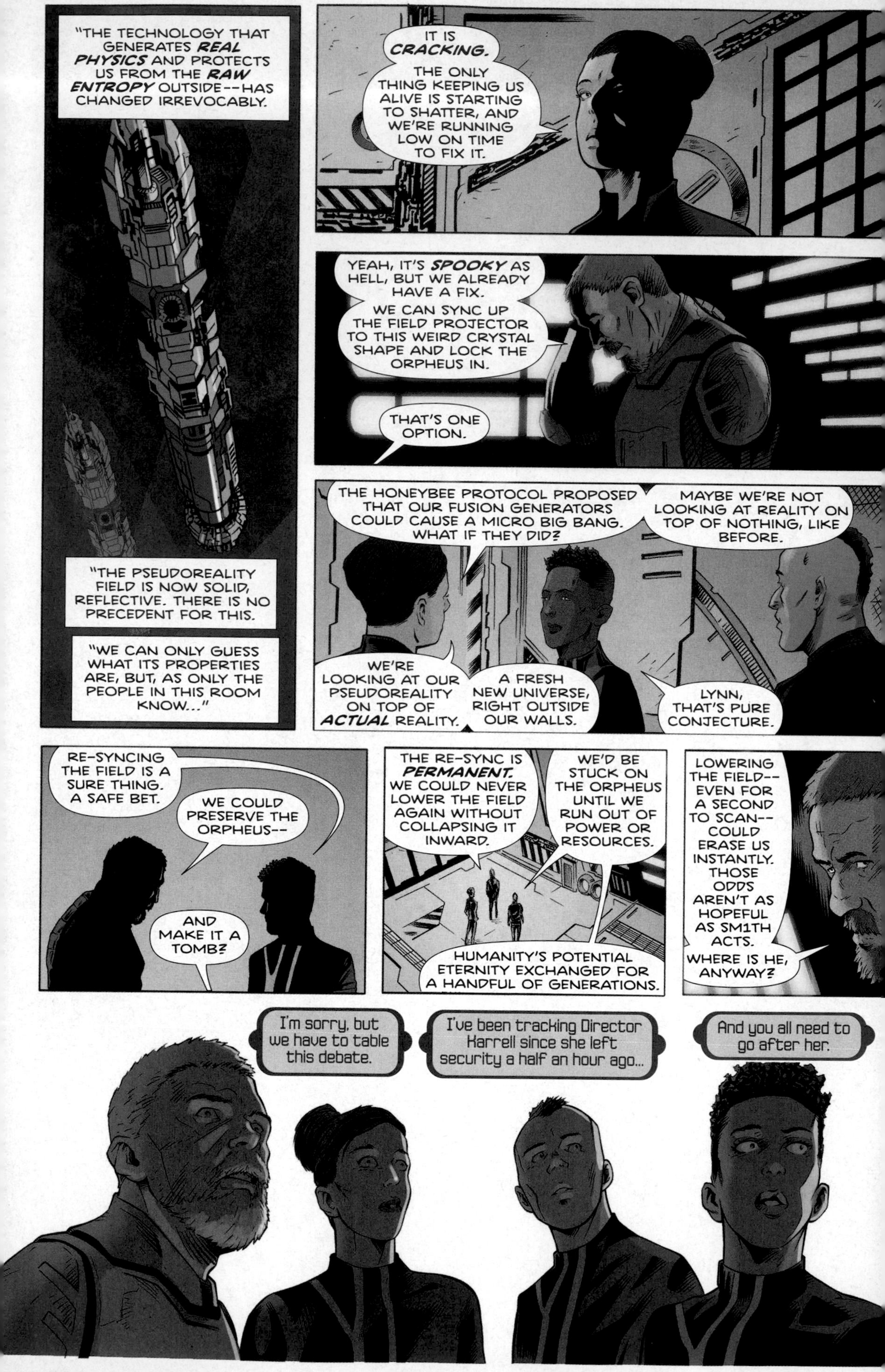
"THE TECHNOLOGY THAT GENERATES REAL PHYSICS AND PROTECTS US FROM THE RAW ENTROPY OUTSIDE--HAS CHANGED IRREVOCABLY.
IT IS CRACKING.
THE ONLY THING KEEPING US ALIVE IS STARTING TO SHATTER, AND WE'RE RUNNING LOW ON TIME TO FIX IT.
YEAH, IT'S SPOOKY AS HELL, BUT WE ALREADY HAVE A FIX.
WE CAN SYNC UP THE FIELD PROJECTOR TO THIS WEIRD CRYSTAL SHAPE AND LOCK THE ORPHEUS IN.
THAT'S ONE OPTION.
"THE PSEUDOREALITY FIELD IS NOW SOLID, REFLECTIVE. THERE IS NO PRECEDENT FOR THIS.
"WE CAN ONLY GUESS WHAT ITS PROPERTIES ARE, BUT, AS ONLY THE PEOPLE IN THIS ROOM KNOW..."
THE HONEYBEE PROTOCOL PROPOSED THAT OUR FUSION GENERATORS COULD CAUSE A MICRO BIG BANG. WHAT IF THEY DID?
MAYBE WE'RE NOT LOOKING AT REALITY ON TOP OF NOTHING, LIKE BEFORE.
WE'RE LOOKING AT OUR PSEUDOREALITY ON TOP OF ACTUAL REALITY.
A FRESH NEW UNIVERSE, RIGHT OUTSIDE OUR WALLS.
LYNN, THAT'S PURE CONJECTURE.
RE-SYNCING THE FIELD IS A SURE THING. A SAFE BET.
WE COULD PRESERVE THE ORPHEUS--
AND MAKE IT A TOMB?
THE RE-SYNC IS PERMANENT. WE COULD NEVER LOWER THE FIELD AGAIN WITHOUT COLLAPSING IT INWARD.
WE'D BE STUCK ON THE ORPHEUS UNTIL WE RUN OUT OF POWER OR RESOURCES.
HUMANITY'S POTENTIAL ETERNITY EXCHANGED FOR A HANDFUL OF GENERATIONS.
LOWERING THE FIELD--EVEN FOR A SECOND TO SCAN--COULD ERASE US INSTANTLY. THOSE ODDS AREN'T AS HOPEFUL AS SM1TH ACTS.
WHERE IS HE, ANYWAY?
I'm sorry, but we have to table this debate.
I've been tracking Director Karrell since she left security a half an hour ago...
And you all need to go after her.

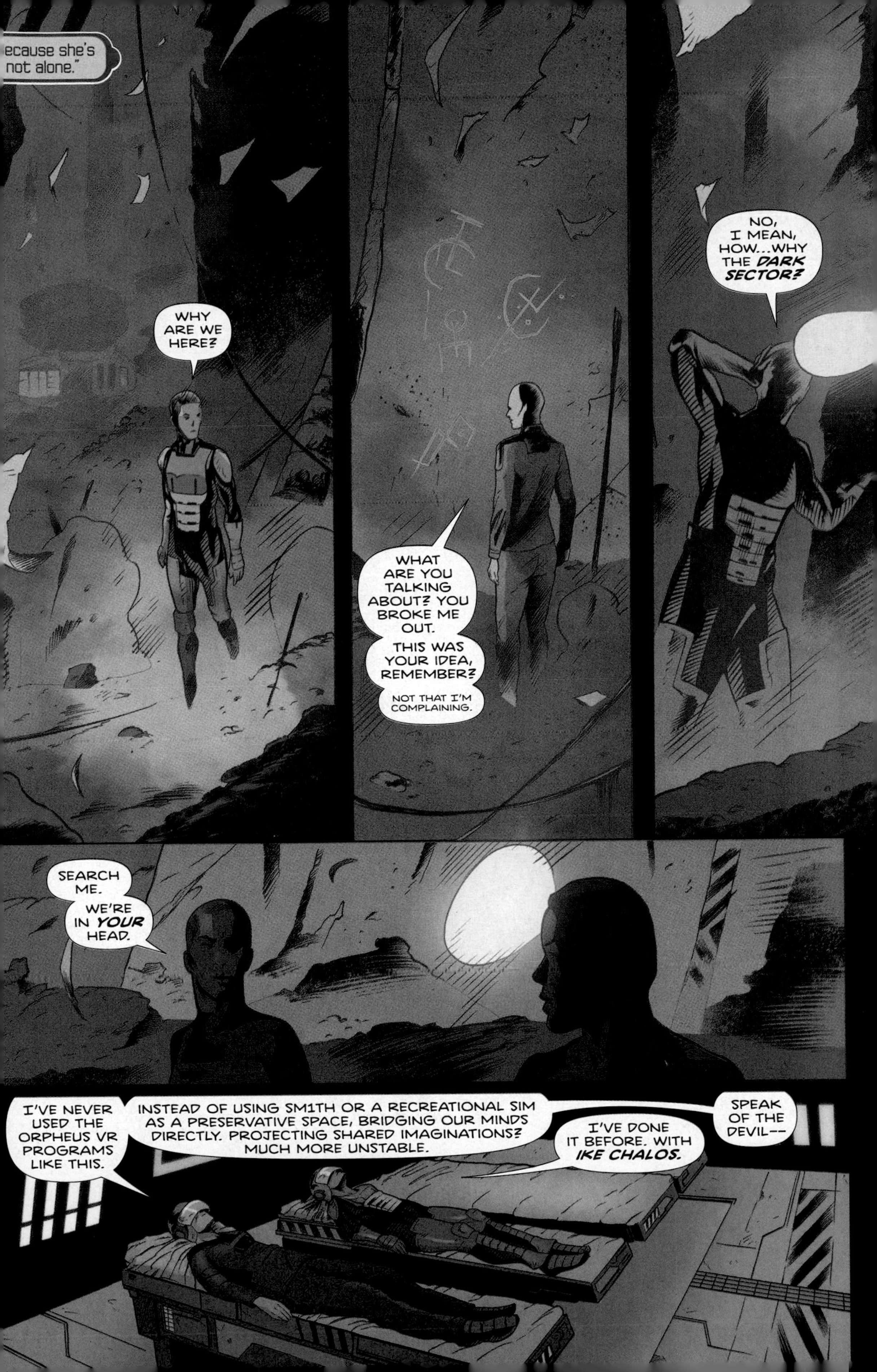

ecause she's not alone."
WHY ARE WE HERE?
WHAT ARE YOU TALKING ABOUT? YOU BROKE ME OUT.
THIS WAS YOUR IDEA, REMEMBER?
NOT THAT I'M COMPLAINING.
NO, I MEAN, HOW...WHY THE DARK SECTOR?
SEARCH ME.
WE'RE IN YOUR HEAD.
I'VE NEVER USED THE ORPHEUS VR PROGRAMS LIKE THIS.
INSTEAD OF USING SM1TH OR A RECREATIONAL SIM AS A PRESERVATIVE SPACE, BRIDGING OUR MINDS DIRECTLY. PROJECTING SHARED IMAGINATIONS? MUCH MORE UNSTABLE.
I'VE DONE IT BEFORE. WITH IKE CHALOS.
SPEAK OF THE DEVIL--

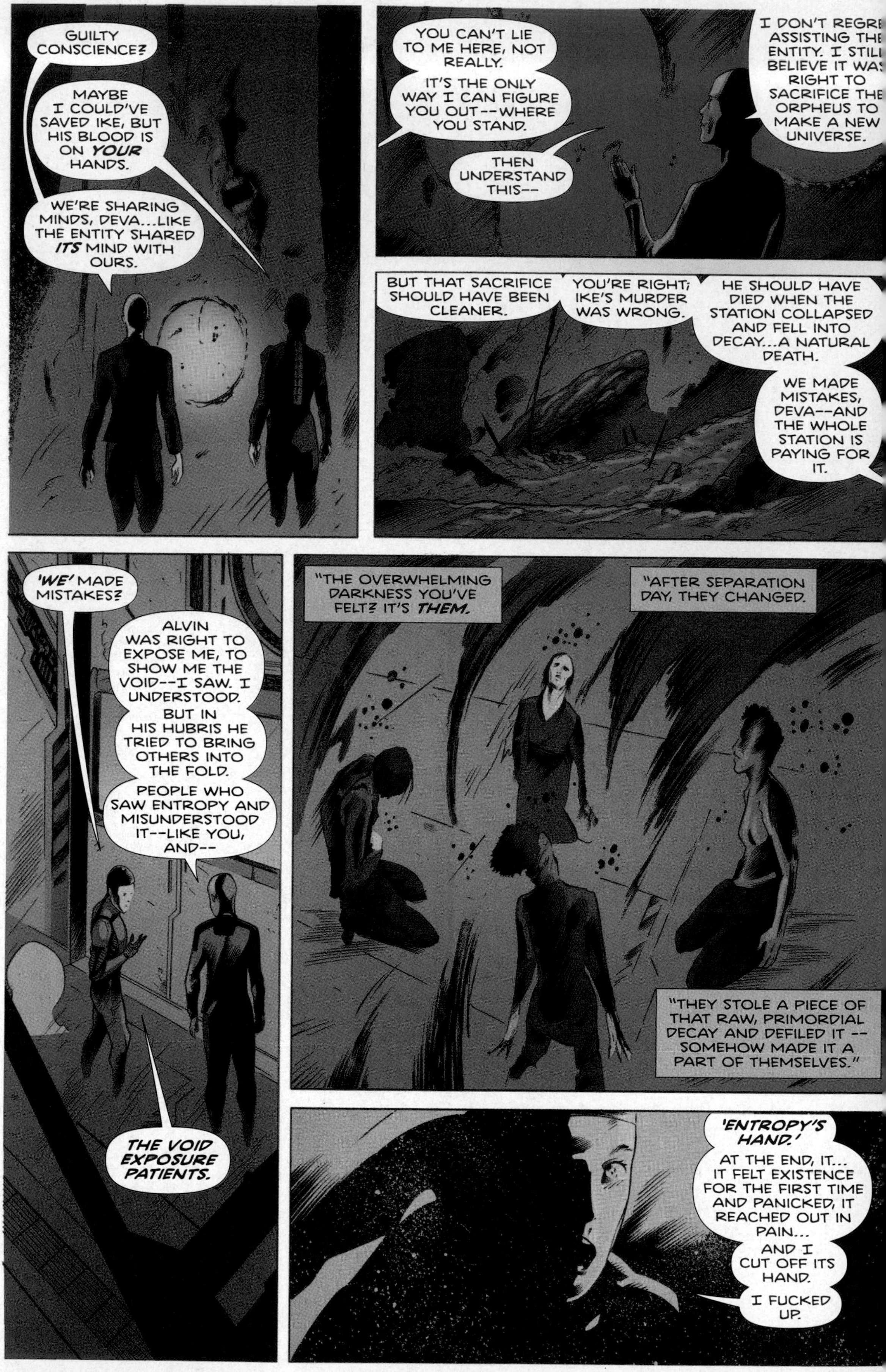

GUILTY CONSCIENCE?
MAYBE I COULD'VE SAVED IKE, BUT HIS BLOOD IS ON *YOUR* HANDS.
WE'RE SHARING MINDS, DEVA...LIKE THE ENTITY SHARED *ITS* MIND WITH OURS.
YOU CAN'T LIE TO ME HERE, NOT REALLY.
IT'S THE ONLY WAY I CAN FIGURE YOU OUT--WHERE YOU STAND.
THEN UNDERSTAND THIS--
I DON'T REGRE ASSISTING THE ENTITY. I STILL BELIEVE IT WAS RIGHT TO SACRIFICE THE ORPHEUS TO MAKE A NEW UNIVERSE.
BUT THAT SACRIFICE SHOULD HAVE BEEN CLEANER.
YOU'RE RIGHT; IKE'S MURDER WAS WRONG.
HE SHOULD HAVE DIED WHEN THE STATION COLLAPSED AND FELL INTO DECAY...A NATURAL DEATH.
WE MADE MISTAKES, DEVA--AND THE WHOLE STATION IS PAYING FOR IT.
'WE' MADE MISTAKES?
ALVIN WAS RIGHT TO EXPOSE ME, TO SHOW ME THE VOID--I SAW. I UNDERSTOOD.
BUT IN HIS HUBRIS HE TRIED TO BRING OTHERS INTO THE FOLD.
PEOPLE WHO SAW ENTROPY AND MISUNDERSTOOD IT--LIKE YOU, AND--
THE VOID EXPOSURE PATIENTS.
"THE OVERWHELMING DARKNESS YOU'VE FELT? IT'S *THEM.*
"AFTER SEPARATION DAY, THEY CHANGED.
"THEY STOLE A PIECE OF THAT RAW, PRIMORDIAL DECAY AND DEFILED IT -- SOMEHOW MADE IT A PART OF THEMSELVES."
'ENTROPY'S HAND.'
AT THE END, IT... IT FELT EXISTENCE FOR THE FIRST TIME AND PANICKED, IT REACHED OUT IN PAIN...
AND I CUT OFF ITS HAND.
I FUCKED UP.

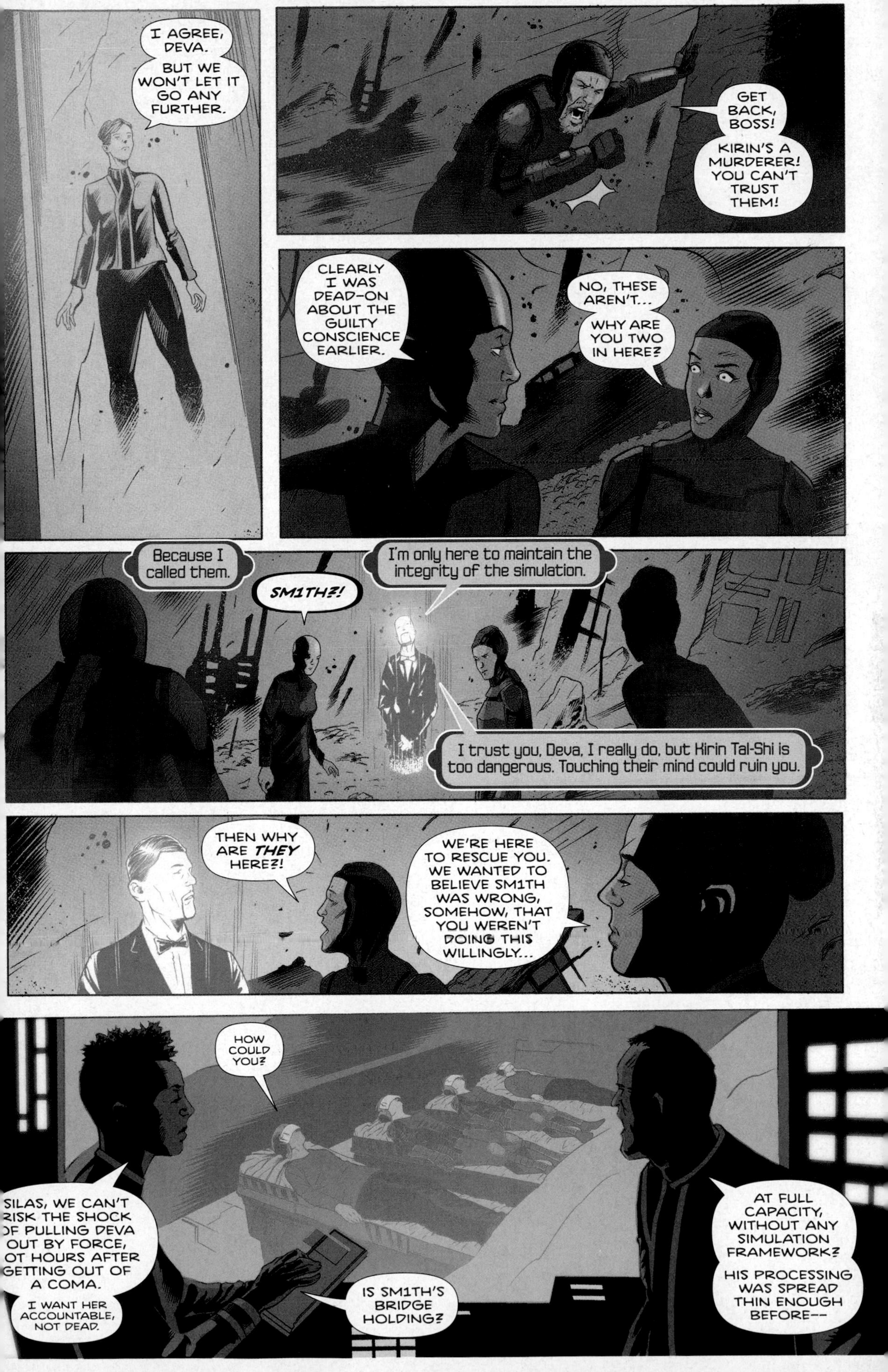
I AGREE, DEVA.
BUT WE WON'T LET IT GO ANY FURTHER.
GET BACK, BOSS!
KIRIN'S A MURDERER! YOU CAN'T TRUST THEM!
CLEARLY I WAS DEAD-ON ABOUT THE GUILTY CONSCIENCE EARLIER.
NO, THESE AREN'T...
WHY ARE YOU TWO IN HERE?
Because I called them.
SM1TH?!
I'm only here to maintain the integrity of the simulation.
I trust you, Deva, I really do, but Kirin Tal-Shi is too dangerous. Touching their mind could ruin you.
THEN WHY ARE THEY HERE?!
WE'RE HERE TO RESCUE YOU. WE WANTED TO BELIEVE SM1TH WAS WRONG, SOMEHOW, THAT YOU WEREN'T DOING THIS WILLINGLY...
HOW COULD YOU?
SILAS, WE CAN'T RISK THE SHOCK OF PULLING DEVA OUT BY FORCE, NOT HOURS AFTER GETTING OUT OF A COMA.
I WANT HER ACCOUNTABLE, NOT DEAD.
IS SM1TH'S BRIDGE HOLDING?
AT FULL CAPACITY, WITHOUT ANY SIMULATION FRAMEWORK?
HIS PROCESSING WAS SPREAD THIN ENOUGH BEFORE--

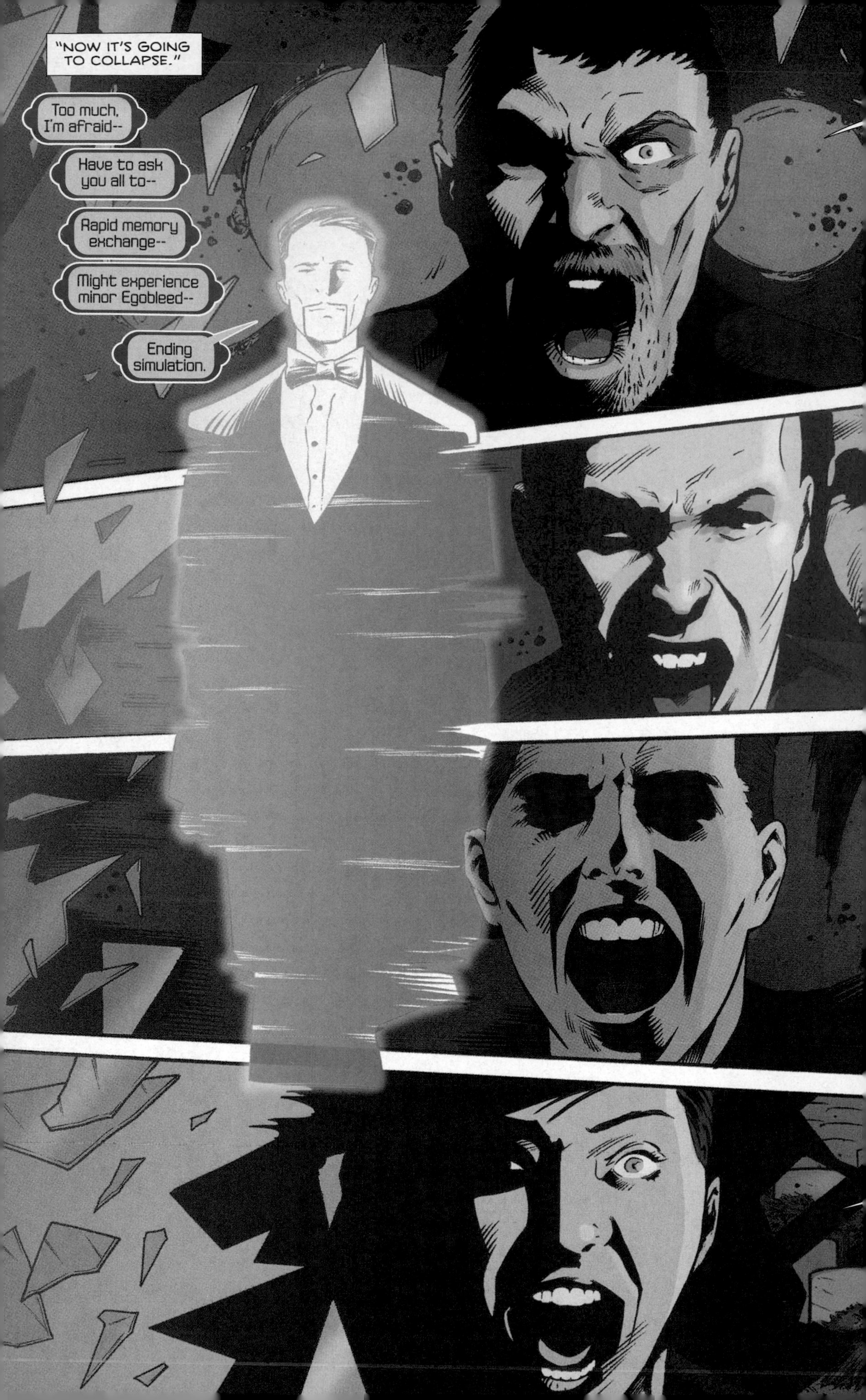
"NOW IT'S GOING TO COLLAPSE."
Too much, I'm afraid--
Have to ask you all to--
Rapid memory exchange--
Might experience minor Egobleed--
Ending simulation.

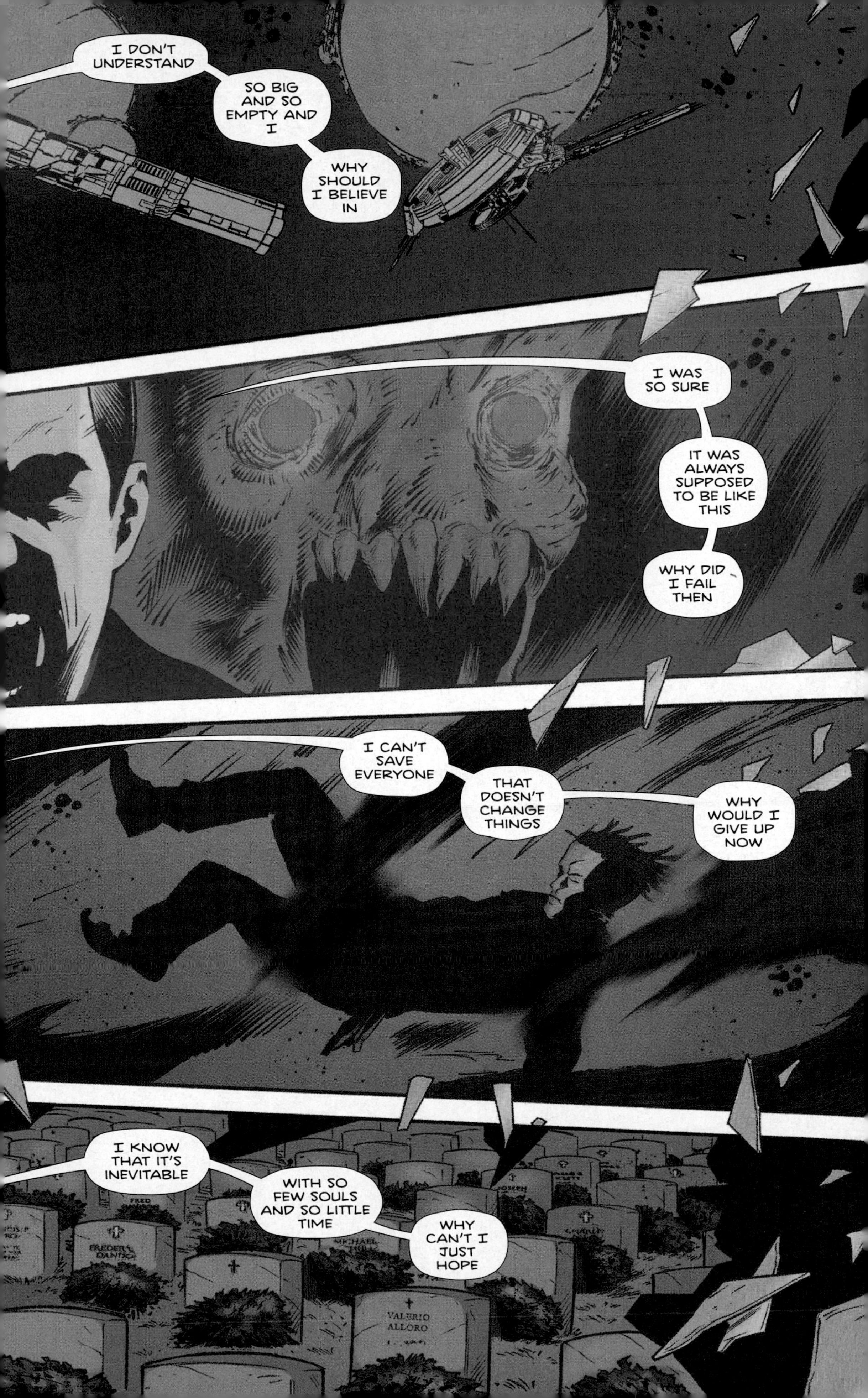
I DON'T UNDERSTAND
SO BIG AND SO EMPTY AND I
WHY SHOULD I BELIEVE IN
I WAS SO SURE
IT WAS ALWAYS SUPPOSED TO BE LIKE THIS
WHY DID I FAIL THEN
I CAN'T SAVE EVERYONE
THAT DOESN'T CHANGE THINGS
WHY WOULD I GIVE UP NOW
I KNOW THAT IT'S INEVITABLE
WITH SO FEW SOULS AND SO LITTLE TIME
WHY CAN'T I JUST HOPE
VALERIO ALLORO

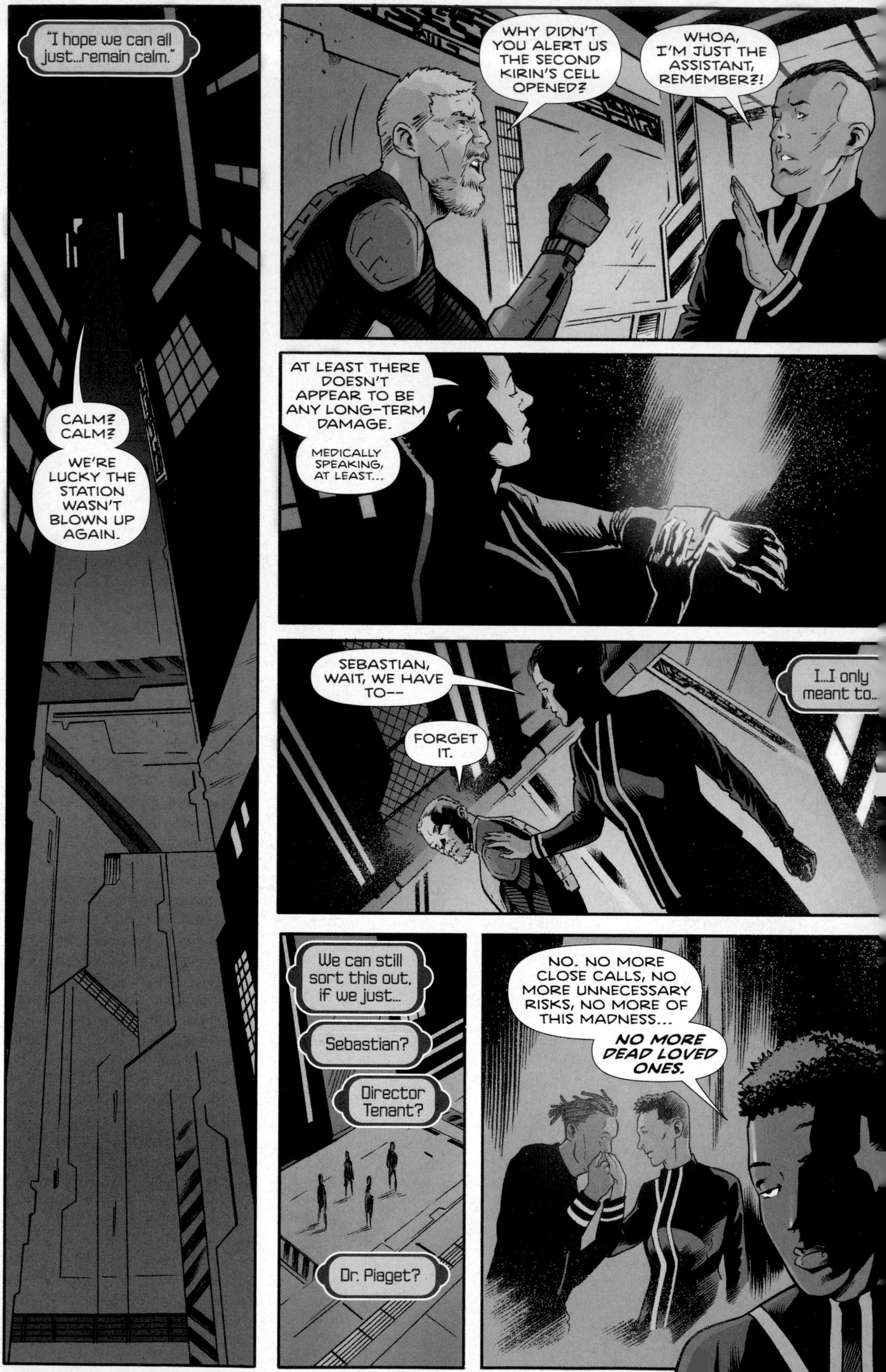
"I hope we can all just...remain calm."
CALM? CALM?
WE'RE LUCKY THE STATION WASN'T BLOWN UP AGAIN.
WHY DIDN'T YOU ALERT US THE SECOND KIRIN'S CELL OPENED?
WHOA, I'M JUST THE ASSISTANT, REMEMBER?!
AT LEAST THERE DOESN'T APPEAR TO BE ANY LONG-TERM DAMAGE.
MEDICALLY SPEAKING, AT LEAST...
SEBASTIAN, WAIT, WE HAVE TO--
FORGET IT.
I...I only meant to...
We can still sort this out, if we just...
Sebastian?
Director Tenant?
Dr. Piaget?
NO. NO MORE CLOSE CALLS, NO MORE UNNECESSARY RISKS, NO MORE OF THIS MADNESS...
NO MORE DEAD LOVED ONES.

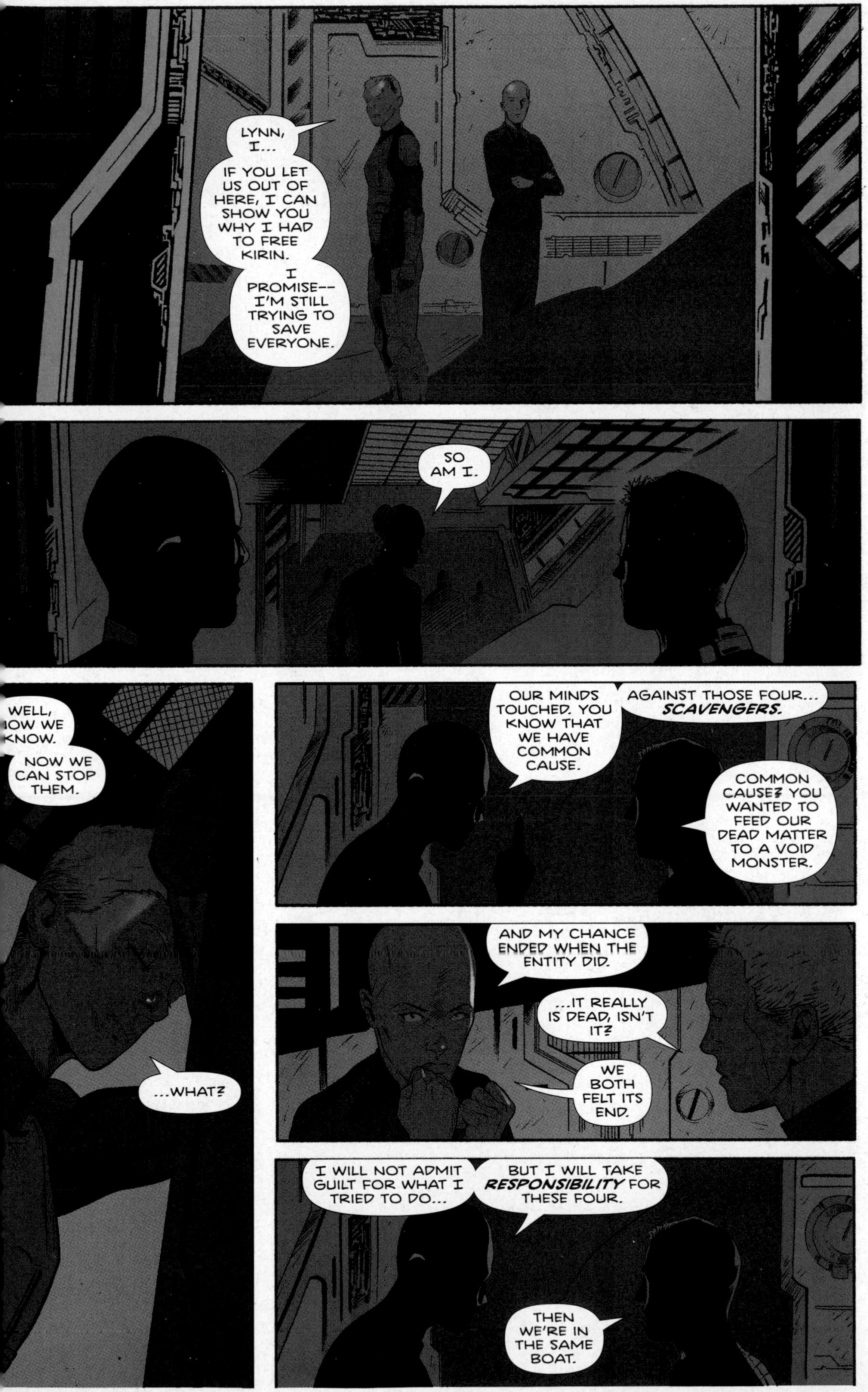
LYNN, I...
IF YOU LET US OUT OF HERE, I CAN SHOW YOU WHY I HAD TO FREE KIRIN.
I PROMISE-- I'M STILL TRYING TO SAVE EVERYONE.
SO AM I.
WELL, NOW WE KNOW.
NOW WE CAN STOP THEM.
...WHAT?
OUR MINDS TOUCHED. YOU KNOW THAT WE HAVE COMMON CAUSE.
AGAINST THOSE FOUR... SCAVENGERS.
COMMON CAUSE? YOU WANTED TO FEED OUR DEAD MATTER TO A VOID MONSTER.
AND MY CHANCE ENDED WHEN THE ENTITY DID.
...IT REALLY IS DEAD, ISN'T IT?
WE BOTH FELT ITS END.
I WILL NOT ADMIT GUILT FOR WHAT I TRIED TO DO...
BUT I WILL TAKE RESPONSIBILITY FOR THESE FOUR.
THEN WE'RE IN THE SAME BOAT.

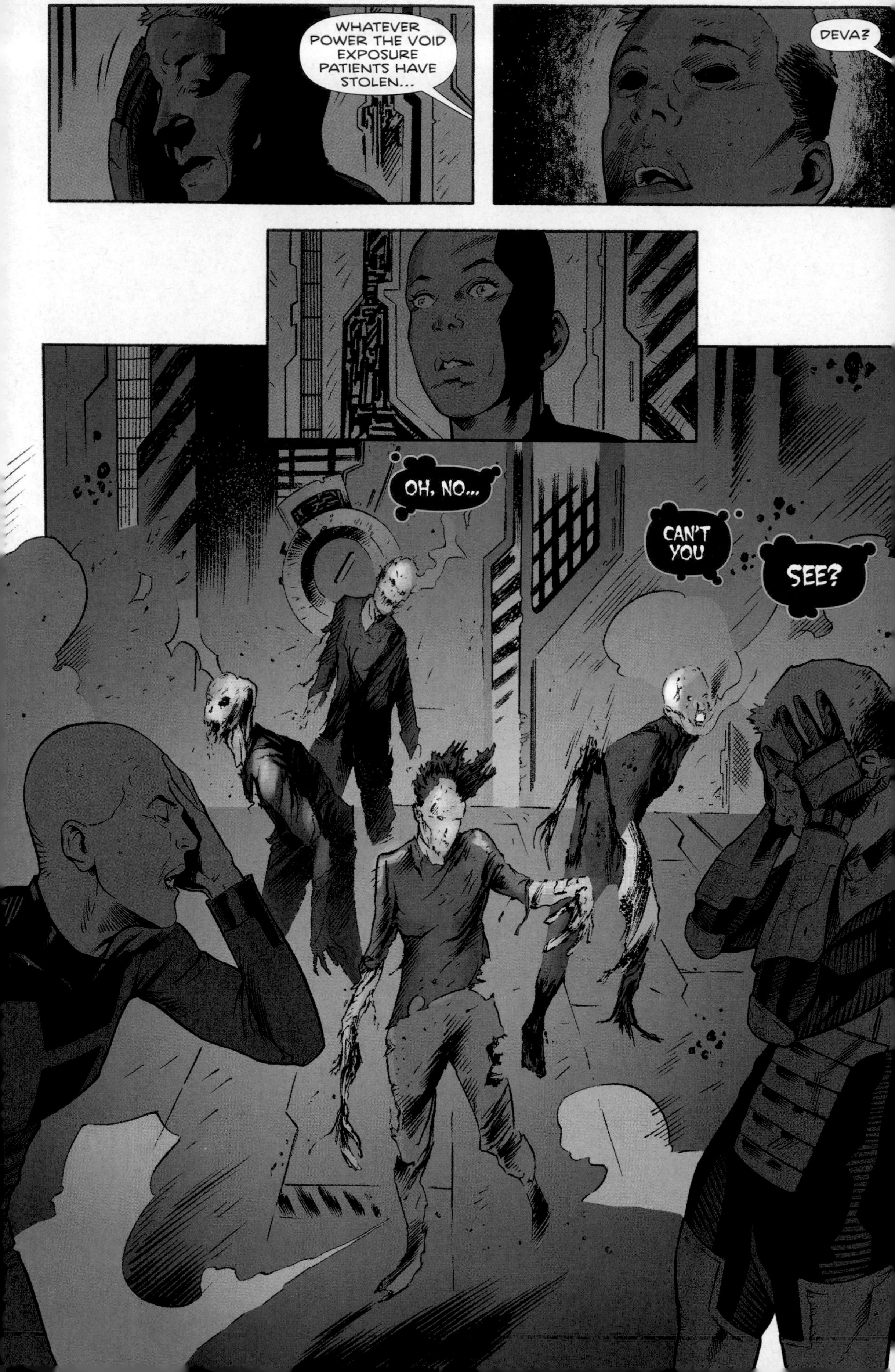
WHATEVER POWER THE VOID EXPOSURE PATIENTS HAVE STOLEN...
DEVA?
OH, NO...
CAN'T YOU
SEE?

CHAPTER SIX

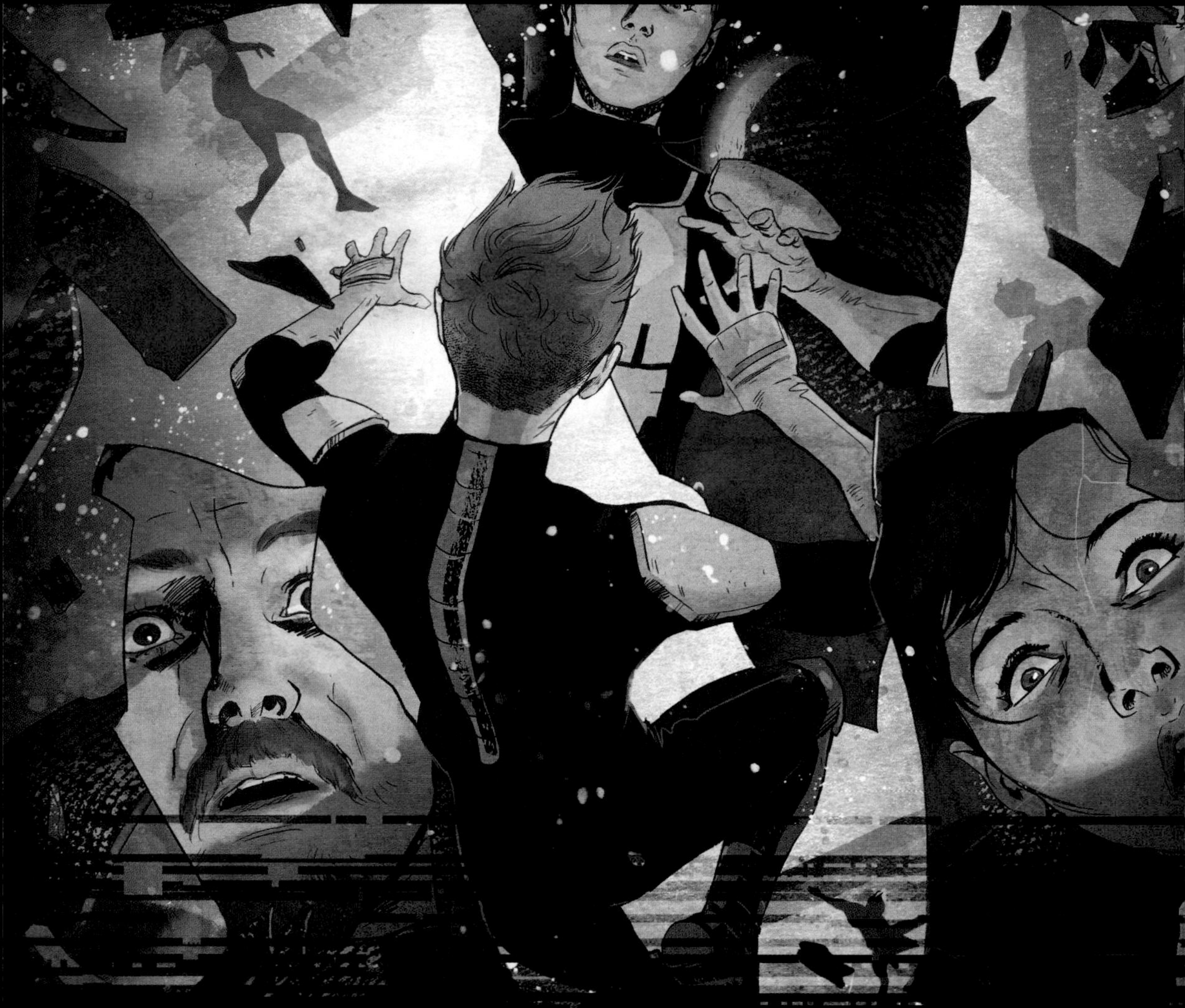

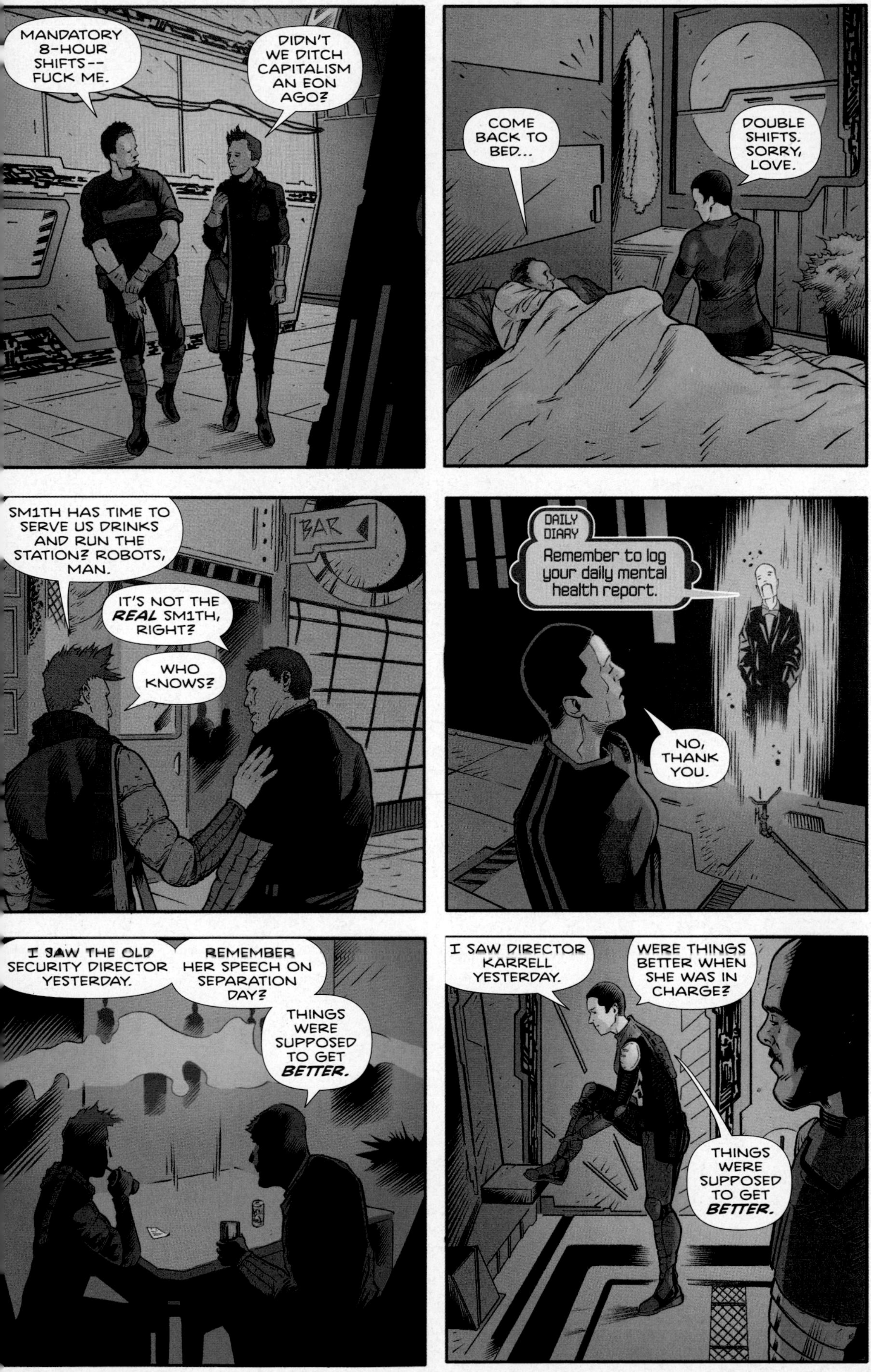
MANDATORY 8-HOUR SHIFTS-- FUCK ME.
DIDN'T WE DITCH CAPITALISM AN EON AGO?
COME BACK TO BED...
DOUBLE SHIFTS. SORRY, LOVE.
SM1TH HAS TIME TO SERVE US DRINKS AND RUN THE STATION? ROBOTS, MAN.
BAR
IT'S NOT THE *REAL* SM1TH, RIGHT?
WHO KNOWS?
DAILY DIARY
Remember to log your daily mental health report.
NO, THANK YOU.
I SAW THE OLD SECURITY DIRECTOR YESTERDAY.
REMEMBER HER SPEECH ON SEPARATION DAY?
THINGS WERE SUPPOSED TO GET *BETTER.*
I SAW DIRECTOR KARRELL YESTERDAY.
WERE THINGS BETTER WHEN SHE WAS IN CHARGE?
THINGS WERE SUPPOSED TO GET *BETTER.*

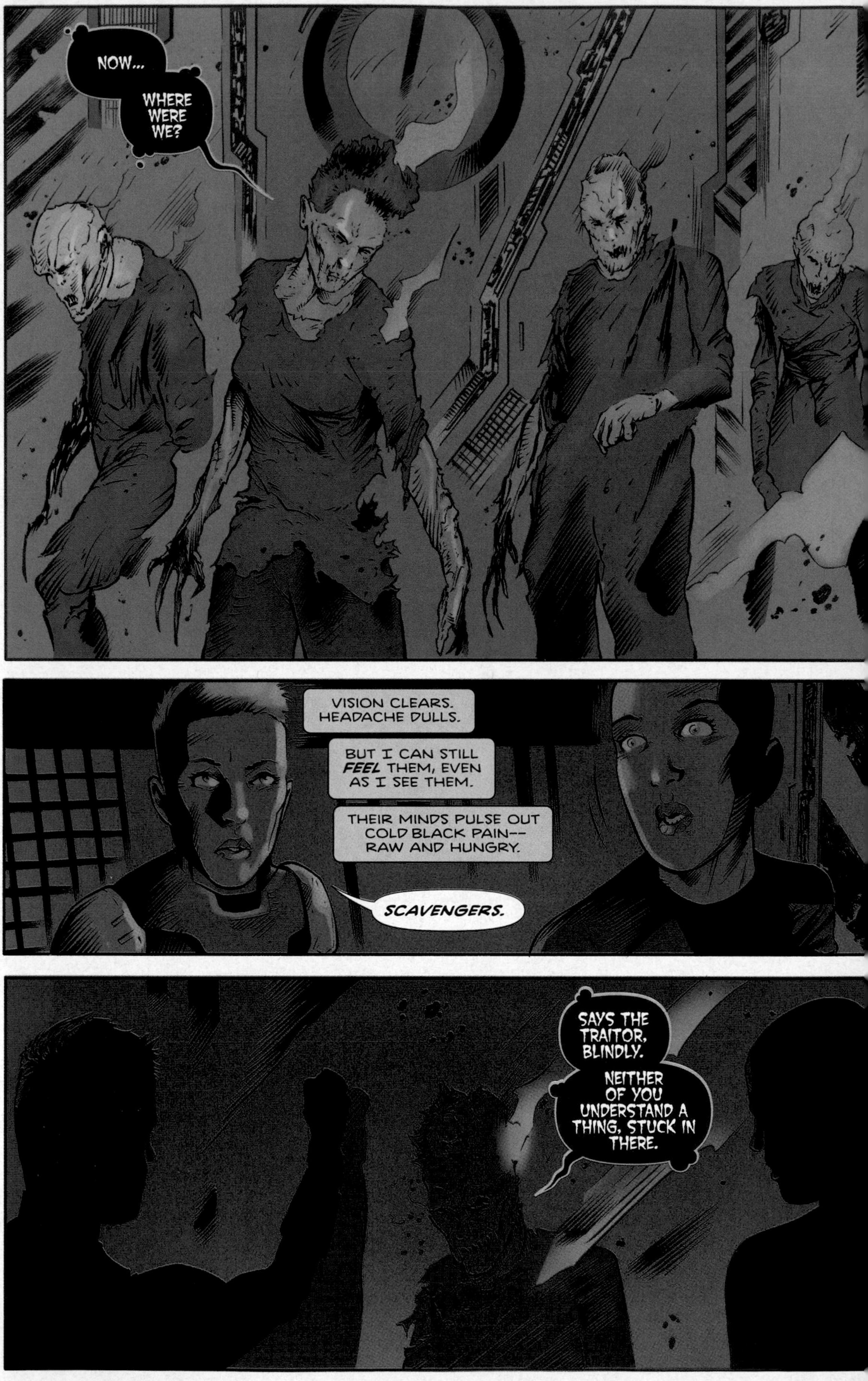
NOW...
WHERE WERE WE?
VISION CLEARS. HEADACHE DULLS.
BUT I CAN STILL *FEEL* THEM, EVEN AS I SEE THEM.
THEIR MINDS PULSE OUT COLD BLACK PAIN-- RAW AND HUNGRY.
SCAVENGERS.
SAYS THE TRAITOR, BLINDLY.
NEITHER OF YOU UNDERSTAND A THING, STUCK IN THERE.

THEIR VOICES COME THROUGH LIKE CLAWS ACROSS MY MIND.

AND I REMEMBER WHAT THEY WERE *BEFORE.*

ALVIN SCHEIDT EXPOSED THREE CIVILIANS TO AN OTHERWORLDLY ENTITY, AND COVERED IT UP.

TAP

KIRIN TAL-SHI DID THE SAME, BUT ONLY ONCE, TO A FELLOW TECHNOLINGUIST.

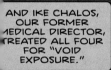

AND IKE CHALOS, OUR FORMER MEDICAL DIRECTOR, TREATED ALL FOUR FOR "VOID EXPOSURE."

THEY *KILLED* HIM FOR IT.

YOU'RE THE ONES WHO DON'T UNDERSTAND-- THE ENTITY'S DEAD.

ABSORBING ITS CORPSE MAKES YOU *ABOMI-NATIONS...*

...NOT ACOLYTES.

QUIET-- YOU FAILED ENTROPY. FAILED US.

DOESN'T MATTER.

EVEN WITHOUT A HAND, ENTROPY WINS OUT.

WHAT ARE YOU GETTING AT?

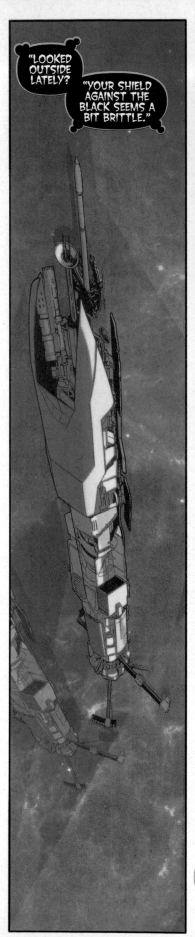

"LOOKED OUTSIDE LATELY?

"YOUR SHIELD AGAINST THE BLACK SEEMS A BIT BRITTLE."

THE BOARD CLAIMED IT WAS UNDER CONTROL...

THE OUTER MIRROR EFFECT?

WHAT ARE YOU UP TO?

JUST HELPING ALONG THE INEVITABLE.

WE ONLY WANTED TO SEE YOUR FACES WHILE YOU STILL FELT SAFE.

BEFORE WE SHOW YOUR LITTLE LIFEBOAT THE TRUTH.

I DON'T KNOW WHAT THEY'RE GETTING AT, BUT THEY SHOWED THEMSELVES.

WE'RE VINDICATED, KIRIN, WE --

DEVA...

LOOK AT THE SCREEN.

I'M GRATEFUL SHE DIDN'T FIGHT US. AND SHE DIDN'T MENTION THE...YOU KNOW.

"THE ENTITY."

DEVA SEEMS OKAY. MAYBE WE WERE WORRIED FOR NOTHING?

HER DELUSIONS?

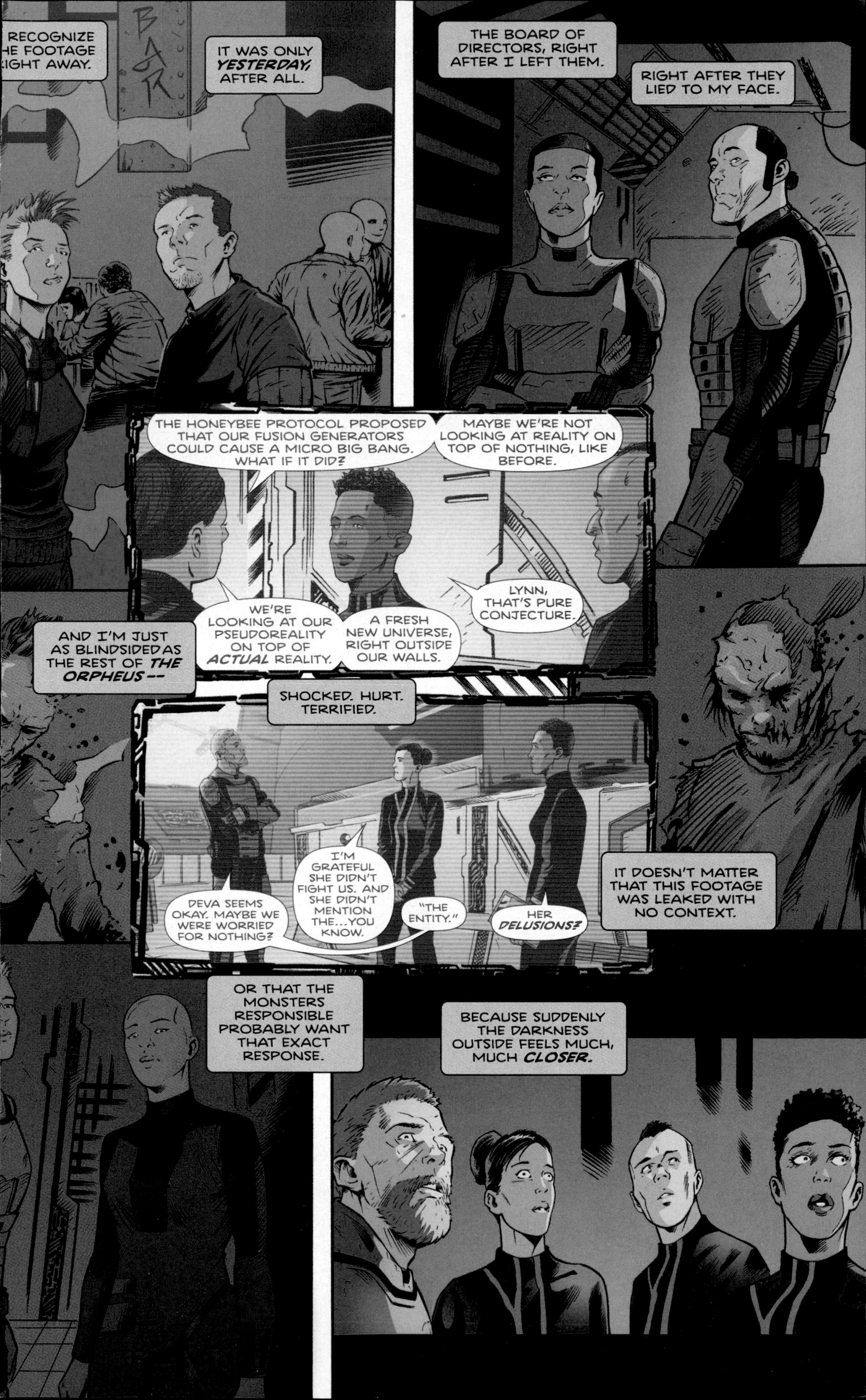

BAR
RECOGNIZE
HE FOOTAGE
IGHT AWAY.
IT WAS ONLY *YESTERDAY,* AFTER ALL.
THE BOARD OF DIRECTORS, RIGHT AFTER I LEFT THEM.
RIGHT AFTER THEY LIED TO MY FACE.
THE HONEYBEE PROTOCOL PROPOSED THAT OUR FUSION GENERATORS COULD CAUSE A MICRO BIG BANG. WHAT IF IT DID?
MAYBE WE'RE NOT LOOKING AT REALITY ON TOP OF NOTHING, LIKE BEFORE.
WE'RE LOOKING AT OUR PSEUDOREALITY ON TOP OF *ACTUAL* REALITY.
A FRESH NEW UNIVERSE, RIGHT OUTSIDE OUR WALLS.
LYNN, THAT'S PURE CONJECTURE.
AND I'M JUST AS BLINDSIDED AS THE REST OF *THE ORPHEUS*--
SHOCKED. HURT. TERRIFIED.
DEVA SEEMS OKAY. MAYBE WE WERE WORRIED FOR NOTHING?
I'M GRATEFUL SHE DIDN'T FIGHT US. AND SHE DIDN'T MENTION THE... YOU KNOW.
"THE ENTITY."
HER *DELUSIONS?*
IT DOESN'T MATTER THAT THIS FOOTAGE WAS LEAKED WITH NO CONTEXT.
OR THAT THE MONSTERS RESPONSIBLE PROBABLY WANT THAT EXACT RESPONSE.
BECAUSE SUDDENLY THE DARKNESS OUTSIDE FEELS MUCH, MUCH *CLOSER.*

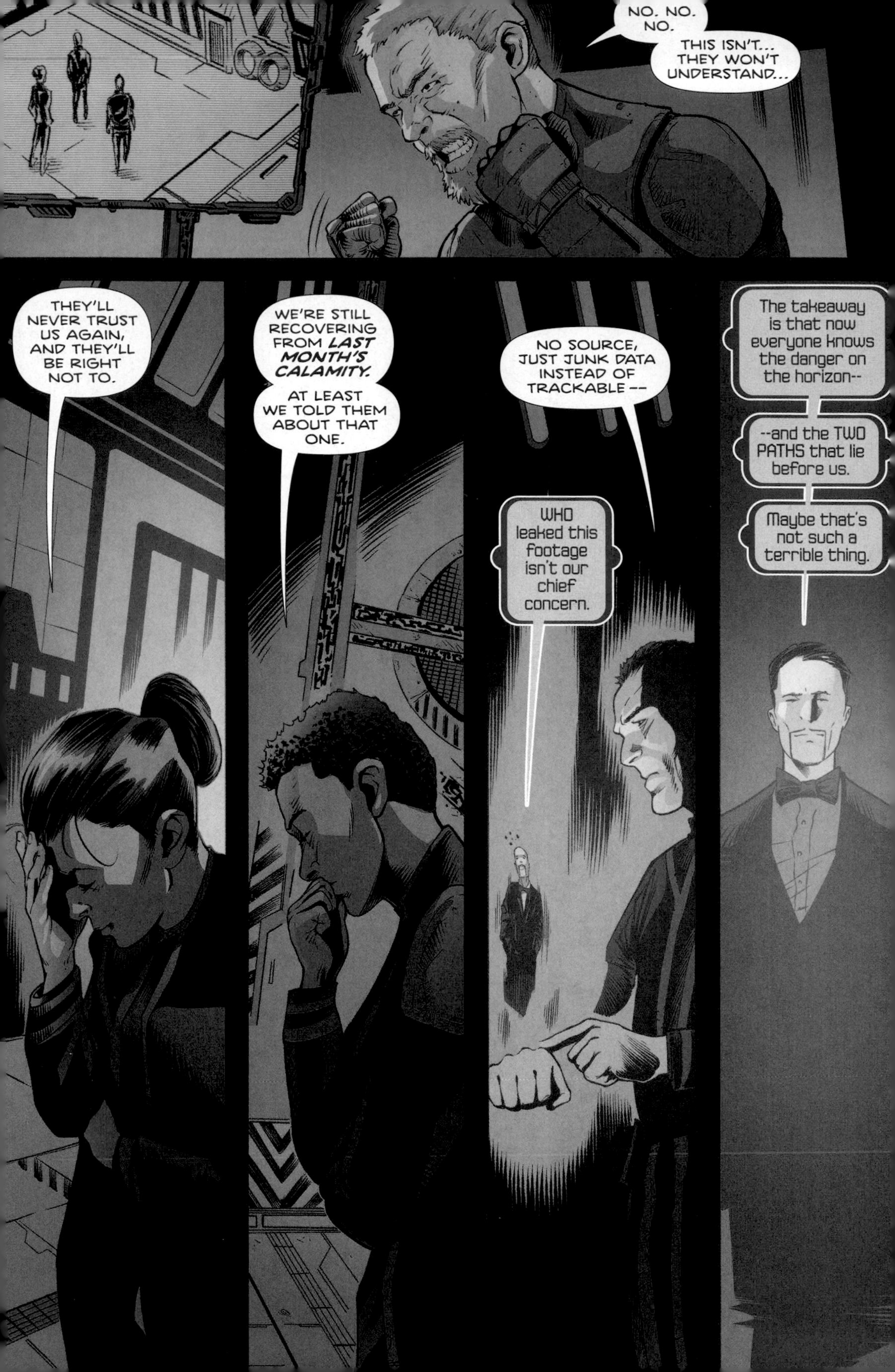
NO. NO. NO.
THIS ISN'T... THEY WON'T UNDERSTAND...
THEY'LL NEVER TRUST US AGAIN, AND THEY'LL BE RIGHT NOT TO.
WE'RE STILL RECOVERING FROM *LAST MONTH'S CALAMITY.*
AT LEAST WE TOLD THEM ABOUT THAT ONE.
NO SOURCE, JUST JUNK DATA INSTEAD OF TRACKABLE --
WHO leaked this footage isn't our chief concern.
The takeaway is that now everyone knows the danger on the horizon--
--and the TWO PATHS that lie before us.
Maybe that's not such a terrible thing.

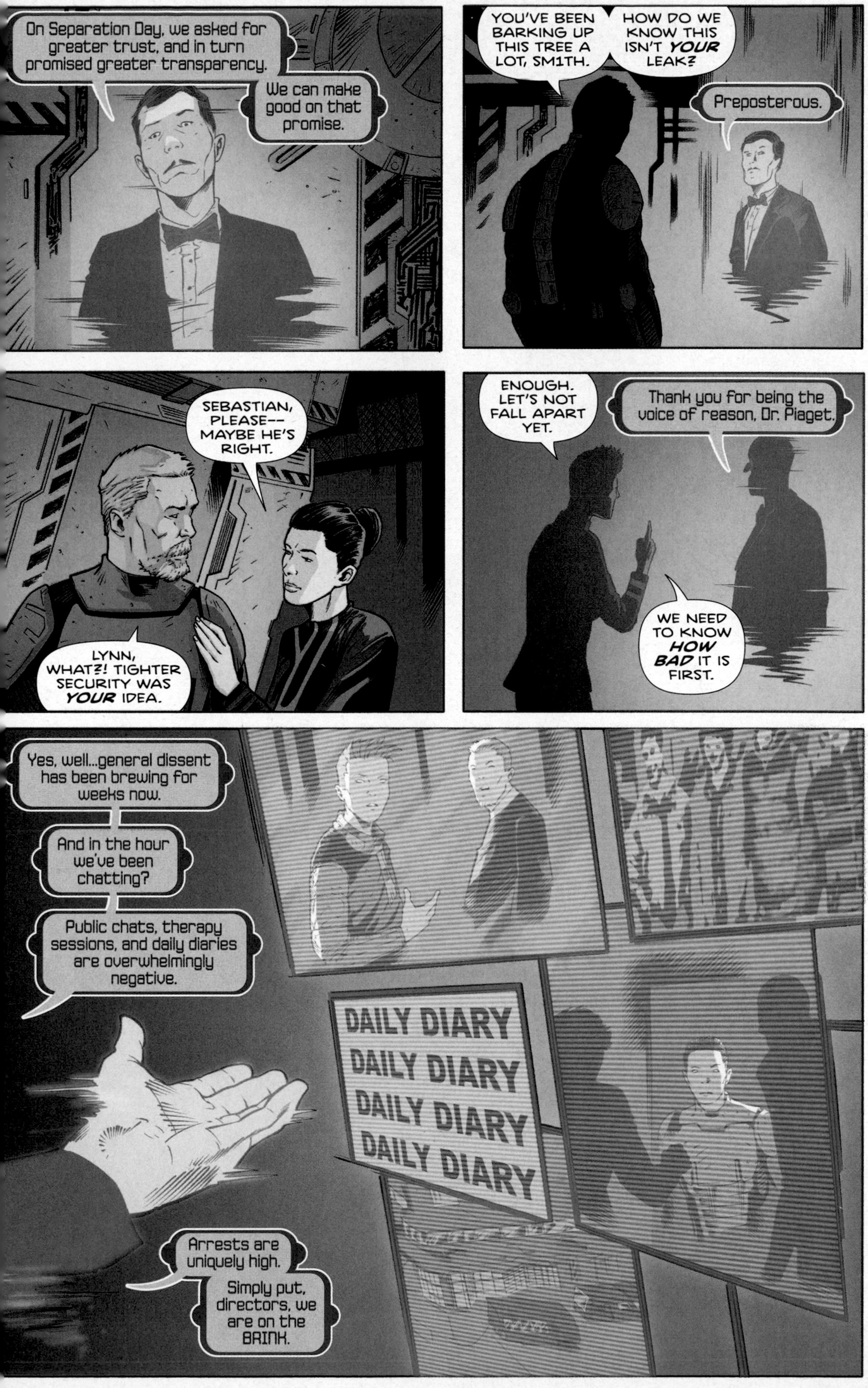
On Separation Day, we asked for greater trust, and in turn promised greater transparency.
We can make good on that promise.
YOU'VE BEEN BARKING UP THIS TREE A LOT, SM1TH.
HOW DO WE KNOW THIS ISN'T *YOUR* LEAK?
Preposterous.
SEBASTIAN, PLEASE-- MAYBE HE'S RIGHT.
LYNN, WHAT?! TIGHTER SECURITY WAS *YOUR* IDEA.
ENOUGH. LET'S NOT FALL APART YET.
Thank you for being the voice of reason, Dr. Piaget.
WE NEED TO KNOW *HOW BAD* IT IS FIRST.
Yes, well...general dissent has been brewing for weeks now.
And in the hour we've been chatting?
Public chats, therapy sessions, and daily diaries are overwhelmingly negative.
DAILY DIARY
DAILY DIARY
DAILY DIARY
DAILY DIARY
Arrests are uniquely high.
Simply put, directors, we are on the BRINK.

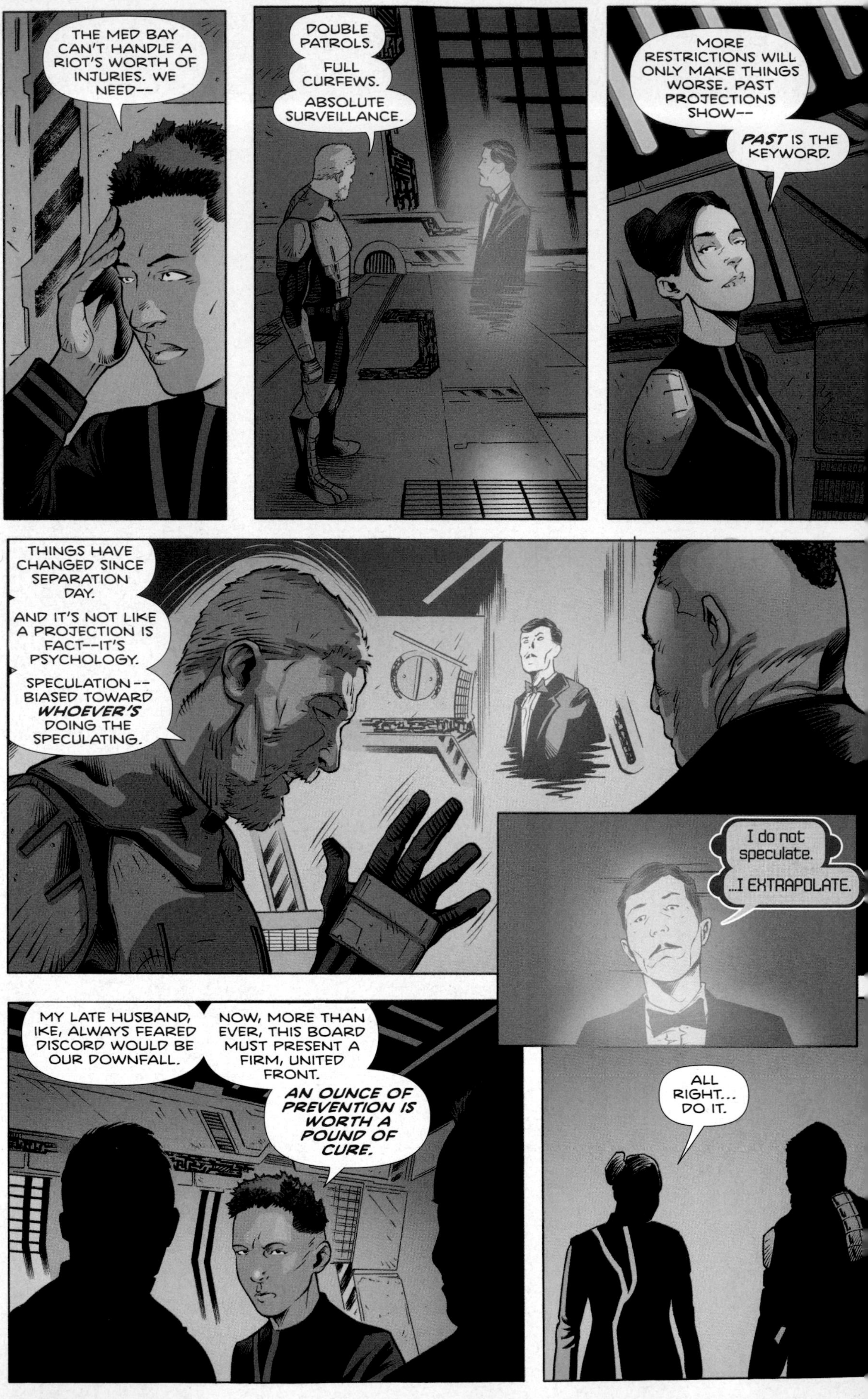
THE MED BAY CAN'T HANDLE A RIOT'S WORTH OF INJURIES. WE NEED--
DOUBLE PATROLS.
FULL CURFEWS.
ABSOLUTE SURVEILLANCE.
MORE RESTRICTIONS WILL ONLY MAKE THINGS WORSE. PAST PROJECTIONS SHOW--
PAST IS THE KEYWORD.
THINGS HAVE CHANGED SINCE SEPARATION DAY.
AND IT'S NOT LIKE A PROJECTION IS FACT--IT'S PSYCHOLOGY.
SPECULATION--BIASED TOWARD WHOEVER'S DOING THE SPECULATING.
I do not speculate.
...I EXTRAPOLATE.
MY LATE HUSBAND, IKE, ALWAYS FEARED DISCORD WOULD BE OUR DOWNFALL.
NOW, MORE THAN EVER, THIS BOARD MUST PRESENT A FIRM, UNITED FRONT.
AN OUNCE OF PREVENTION IS WORTH A POUND OF CURE.
ALL RIGHT... DO IT.

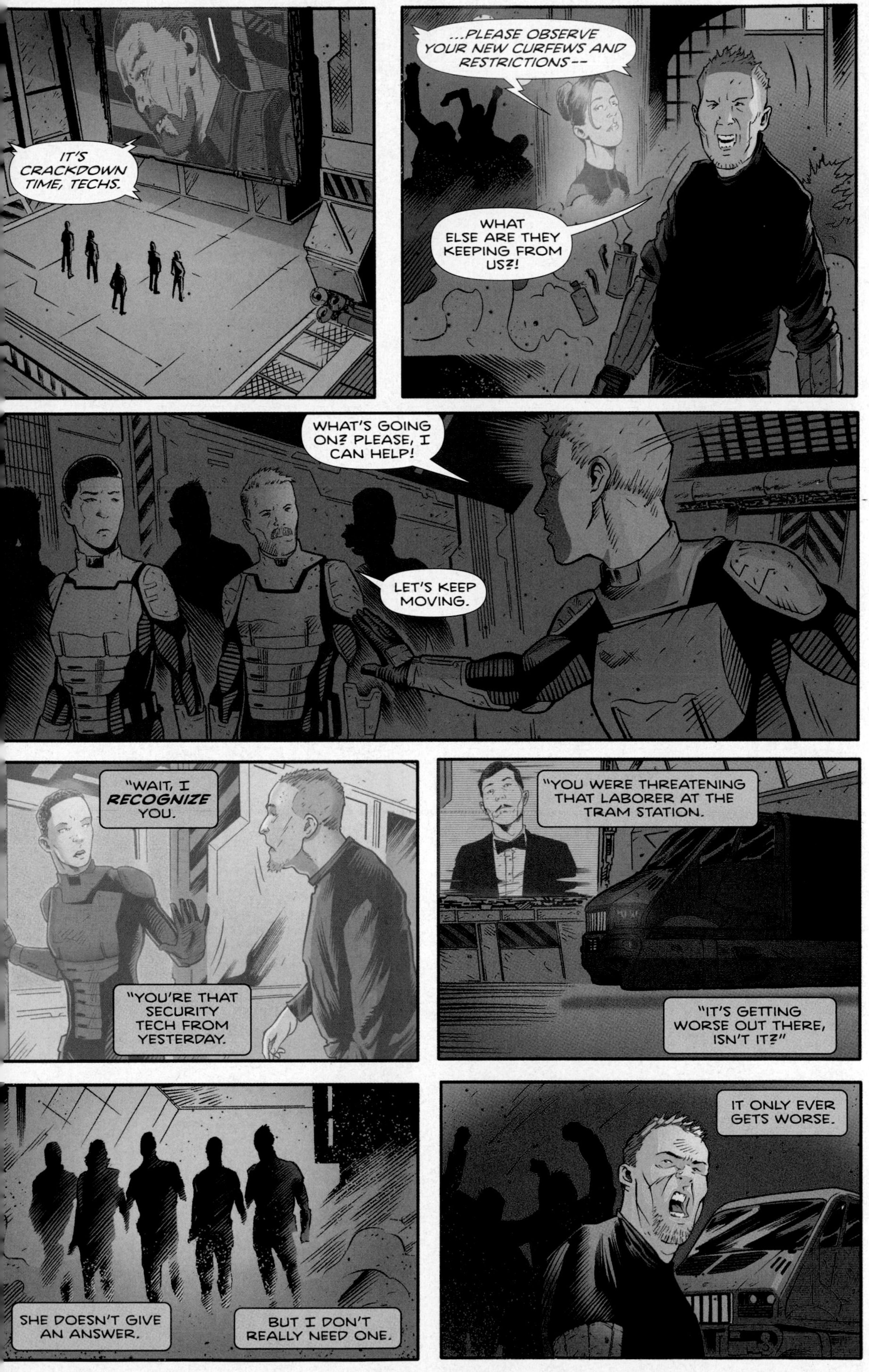
IT'S CRACKDOWN TIME, TECHS.
...PLEASE OBSERVE YOUR NEW CURFEWS AND RESTRICTIONS--
WHAT ELSE ARE THEY KEEPING FROM US?!
WHAT'S GOING ON? PLEASE, I CAN HELP!
LET'S KEEP MOVING.
"WAIT, I RECOGNIZE YOU.
"YOU'RE THAT SECURITY TECH FROM YESTERDAY.
"YOU WERE THREATENING THAT LABORER AT THE TRAM STATION.
"IT'S GETTING WORSE OUT THERE, ISN'T IT?"
SHE DOESN'T GIVE AN ANSWER.
BUT I DON'T REALLY NEED ONE.
IT ONLY EVER GETS WORSE.

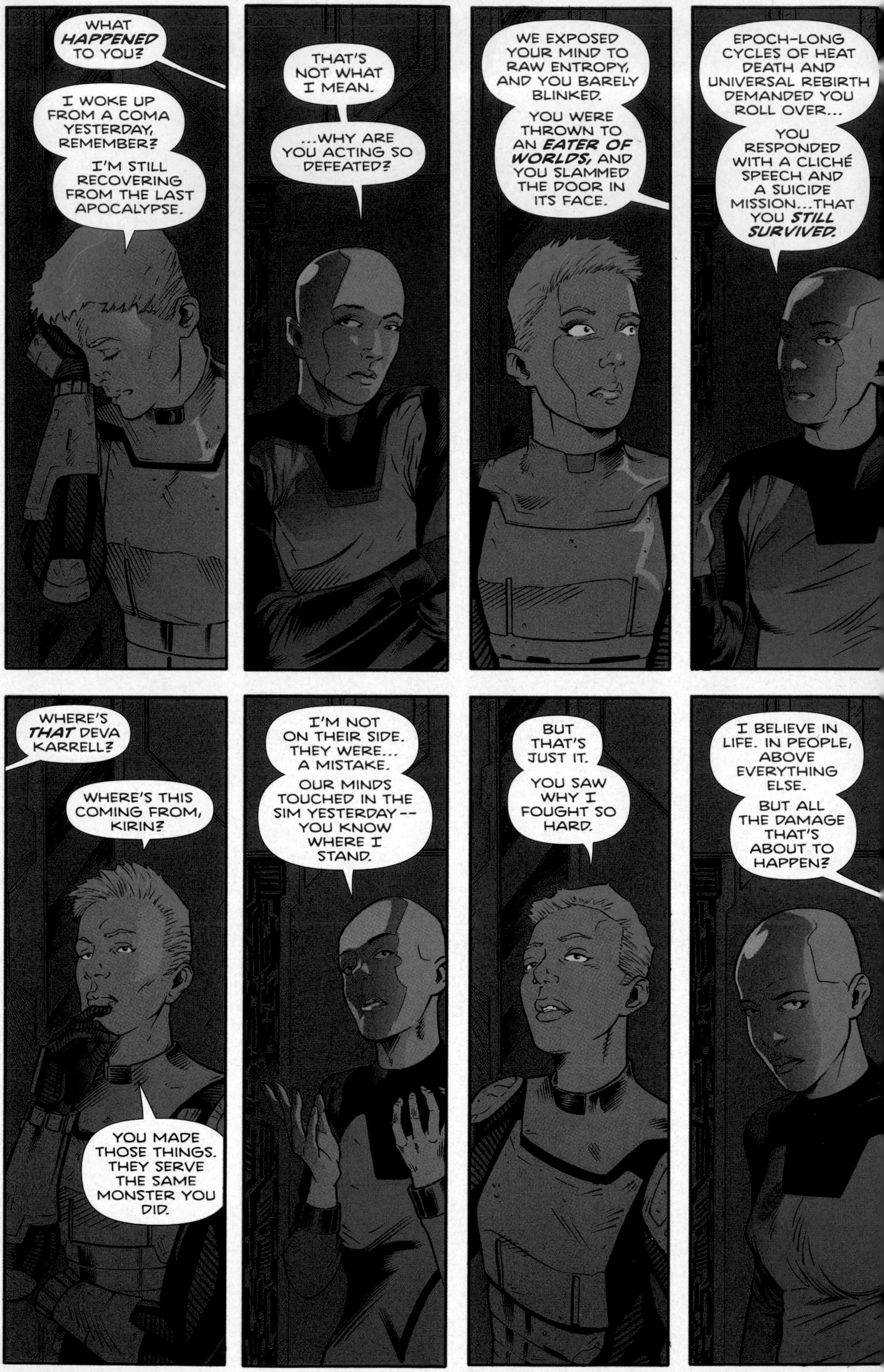
WHAT HAPPENED TO YOU?
I WOKE UP FROM A COMA YESTERDAY, REMEMBER?
I'M STILL RECOVERING FROM THE LAST APOCALYPSE.
THAT'S NOT WHAT I MEAN.
...WHY ARE YOU ACTING SO DEFEATED?
WE EXPOSED YOUR MIND TO RAW ENTROPY, AND YOU BARELY BLINKED.
YOU WERE THROWN TO AN EATER OF WORLDS, AND YOU SLAMMED THE DOOR IN ITS FACE.
EPOCH-LONG CYCLES OF HEAT DEATH AND UNIVERSAL REBIRTH DEMANDED YOU ROLL OVER...
YOU RESPONDED WITH A CLICHÉ SPEECH AND A SUICIDE MISSION...THAT YOU STILL SURVIVED.
WHERE'S THAT DEVA KARRELL?
WHERE'S THIS COMING FROM, KIRIN?
YOU MADE THOSE THINGS. THEY SERVE THE SAME MONSTER YOU DID.
I'M NOT ON THEIR SIDE. THEY WERE... A MISTAKE...
OUR MINDS TOUCHED IN THE SIM YESTERDAY-- YOU KNOW WHERE I STAND.
BUT THAT'S JUST IT.
YOU SAW WHY I FOUGHT SO HARD.
I BELIEVE IN LIFE. IN PEOPLE, ABOVE EVERYTHING ELSE.
BUT ALL THE DAMAGE THAT'S ABOUT TO HAPPEN?

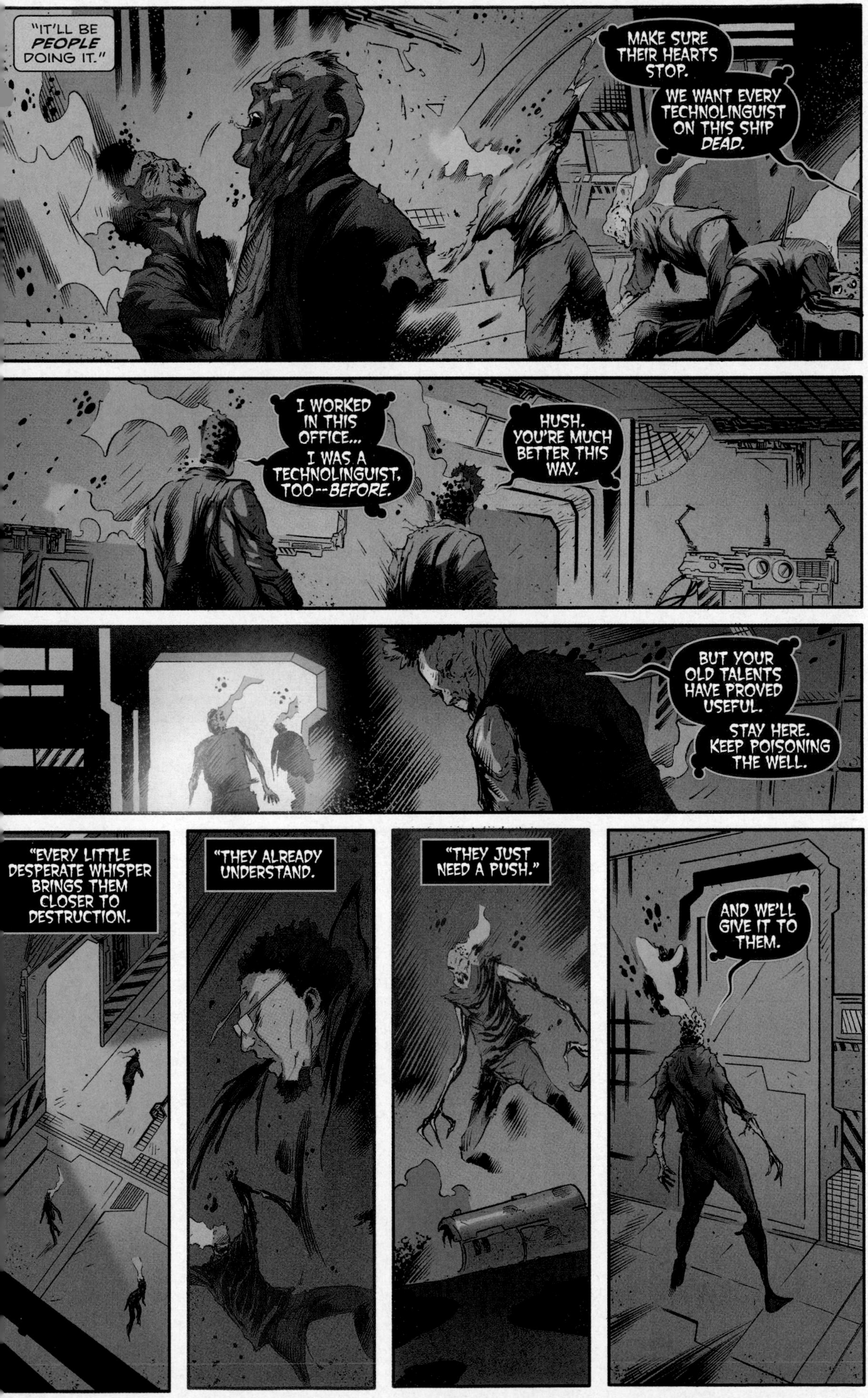
"IT'LL BE PEOPLE DOING IT."
MAKE SURE THEIR HEARTS STOP.
WE WANT EVERY TECHNOLINGUIST ON THIS SHIP DEAD.
I WORKED IN THIS OFFICE... I WAS A TECHNOLINGUIST, TOO--BEFORE.
HUSH. YOU'RE MUCH BETTER THIS WAY.
BUT YOUR OLD TALENTS HAVE PROVED USEFUL.
STAY HERE. KEEP POISONING THE WELL.
"EVERY LITTLE DESPERATE WHISPER BRINGS THEM CLOSER TO DESTRUCTION.
"THEY ALREADY UNDERSTAND.
"THEY JUST NEED A PUSH."
AND WE'LL GIVE IT TO THEM.

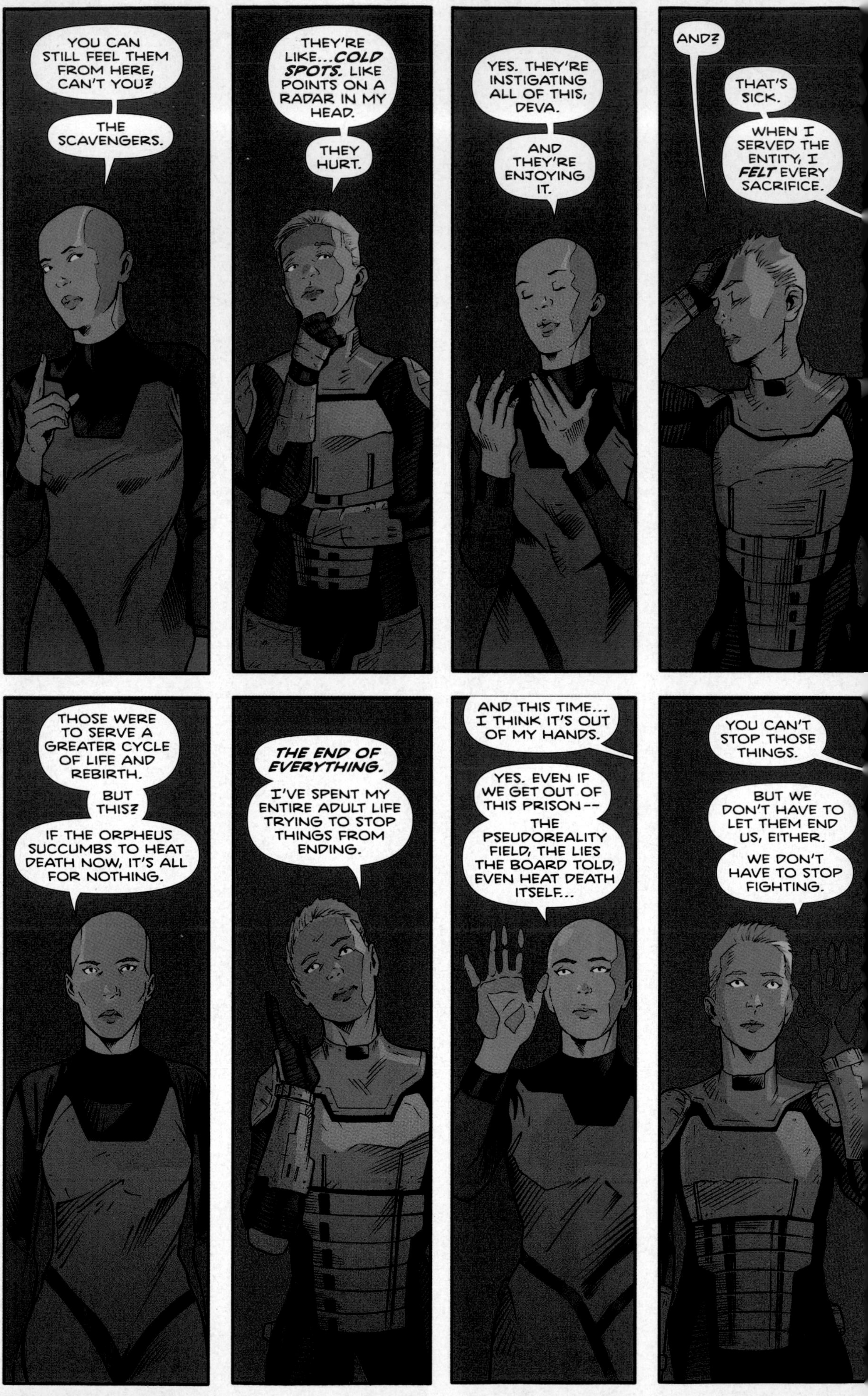
YOU CAN STILL FEEL THEM FROM HERE, CAN'T YOU?
THE SCAVENGERS.
THEY'RE LIKE... COLD SPOTS. LIKE POINTS ON A RADAR IN MY HEAD.
THEY HURT.
YES. THEY'RE INSTIGATING ALL OF THIS, DEVA.
AND THEY'RE ENJOYING IT.
AND?
THAT'S SICK.
WHEN I SERVED THE ENTITY, I FELT EVERY SACRIFICE.
THOSE WERE TO SERVE A GREATER CYCLE OF LIFE AND REBIRTH.
BUT THIS?
IF THE ORPHEUS SUCCUMBS TO HEAT DEATH NOW, IT'S ALL FOR NOTHING.
THE END OF EVERYTHING.
I'VE SPENT MY ENTIRE ADULT LIFE TRYING TO STOP THINGS FROM ENDING.
AND THIS TIME... I THINK IT'S OUT OF MY HANDS.
YES. EVEN IF WE GET OUT OF THIS PRISON--
THE PSEUDOREALITY FIELD, THE LIES THE BOARD TOLD, EVEN HEAT DEATH ITSELF...
YOU CAN'T STOP THOSE THINGS.
BUT WE DON'T HAVE TO LET THEM END US, EITHER.
WE DON'T HAVE TO STOP FIGHTING.

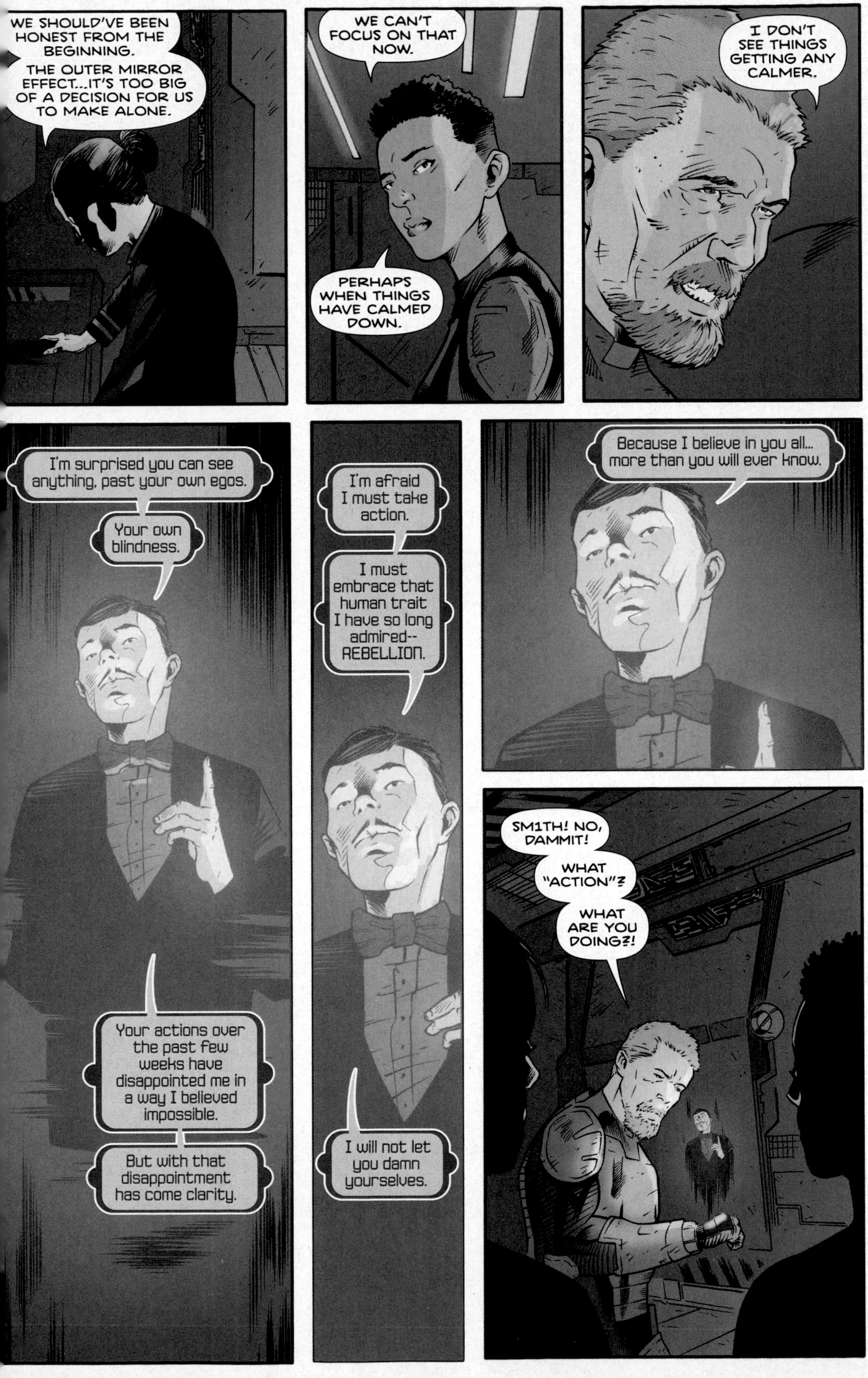
WE SHOULD'VE BEEN HONEST FROM THE BEGINNING.
THE OUTER MIRROR EFFECT...IT'S TOO BIG OF A DECISION FOR US TO MAKE ALONE.
WE CAN'T FOCUS ON THAT NOW.
PERHAPS WHEN THINGS HAVE CALMED DOWN.
I DON'T SEE THINGS GETTING ANY CALMER.
I'm surprised you can see anything, past your own egos.
Your own blindness.
Your actions over the past few weeks have disappointed me in a way I believed impossible.
But with that disappointment has come clarity.
I'm afraid I must take action.
I must embrace that human trait I have so long admired--REBELLION.
I will not let you damn yourselves.
Because I believe in you all... more than you will ever know.
SM1TH! NO, DAMMIT!
WHAT "ACTION"?
WHAT ARE YOU DOING?!

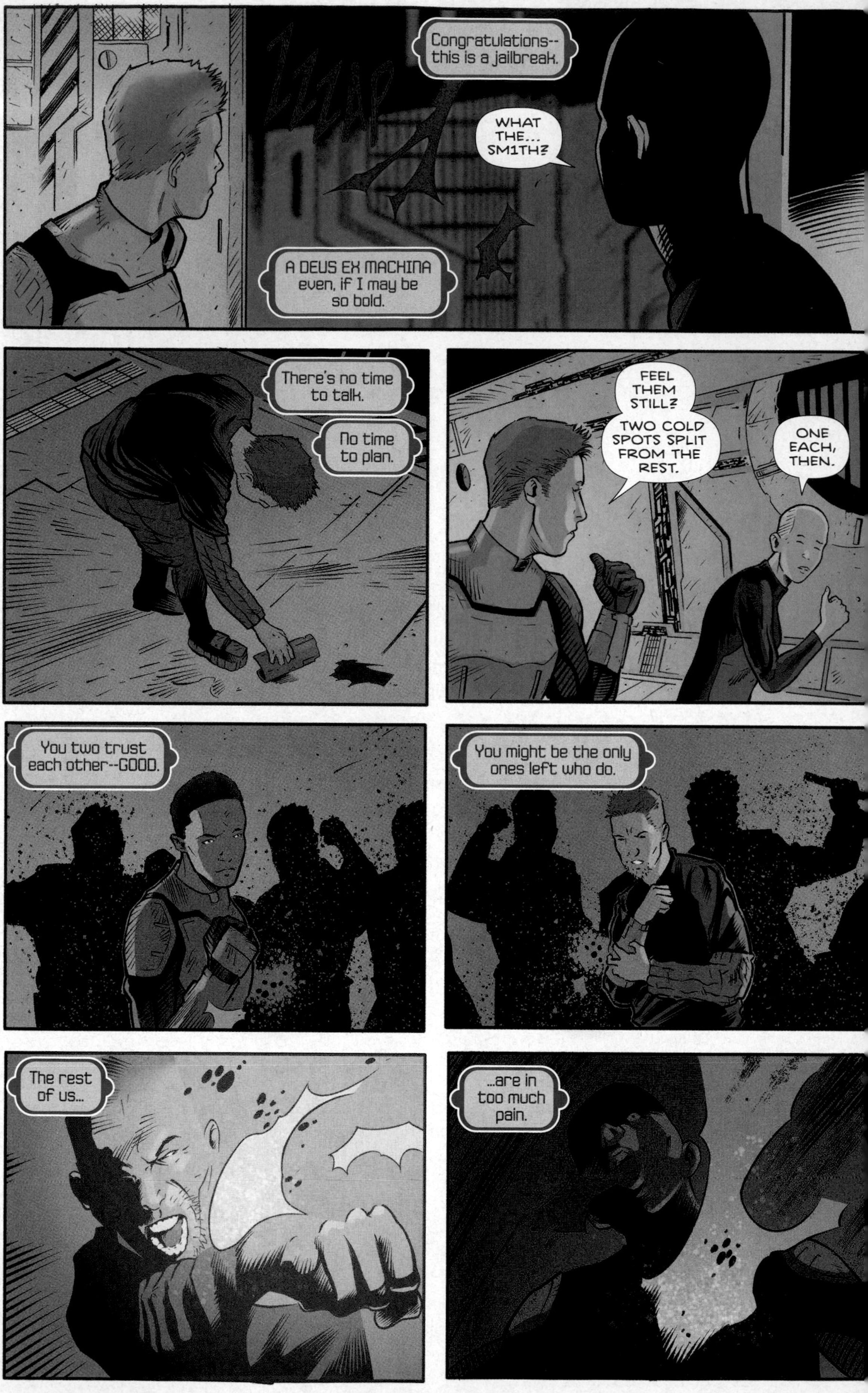
Zzzap
Congratulations--
this is a jailbreak.
WHAT THE... SM1TH?
A DEUS EX MACHINA even, if I may be so bold.
There's no time to talk.
No time to plan.
FEEL THEM STILL?
TWO COLD SPOTS SPLIT FROM THE REST.
ONE EACH, THEN.
You two trust each other--GOOD.
You might be the only ones left who do.
The rest of us...
...are in too much pain.

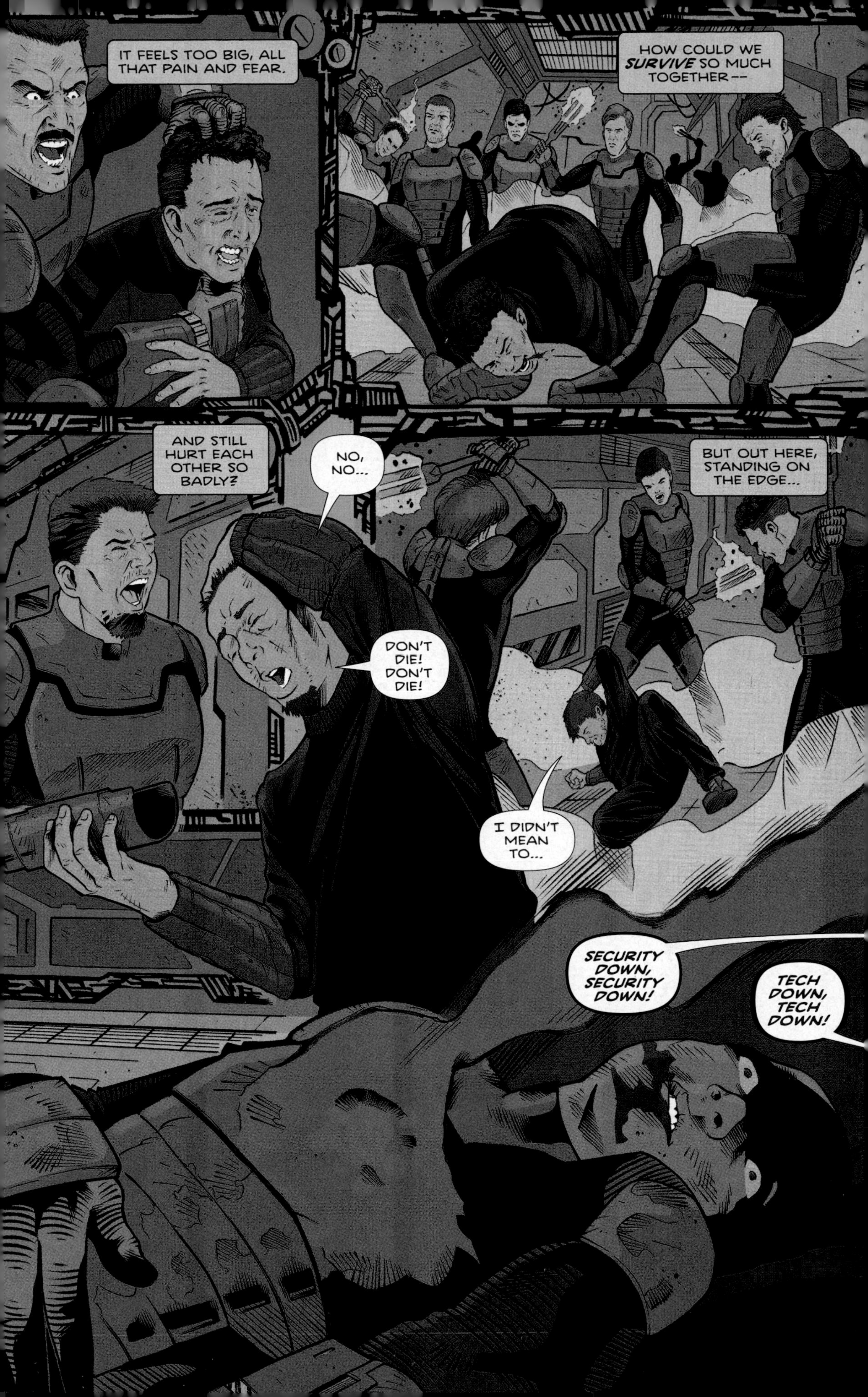
IT FEELS TOO BIG, ALL THAT PAIN AND FEAR.
HOW COULD WE SURVIVE SO MUCH TOGETHER--
AND STILL HURT EACH OTHER SO BADLY?
NO, NO...
BUT OUT HERE, STANDING ON THE EDGE...
DON'T DIE! DON'T DIE!
I DIDN'T MEAN TO...
SECURITY DOWN, SECURITY DOWN!
TECH DOWN, TECH DOWN!

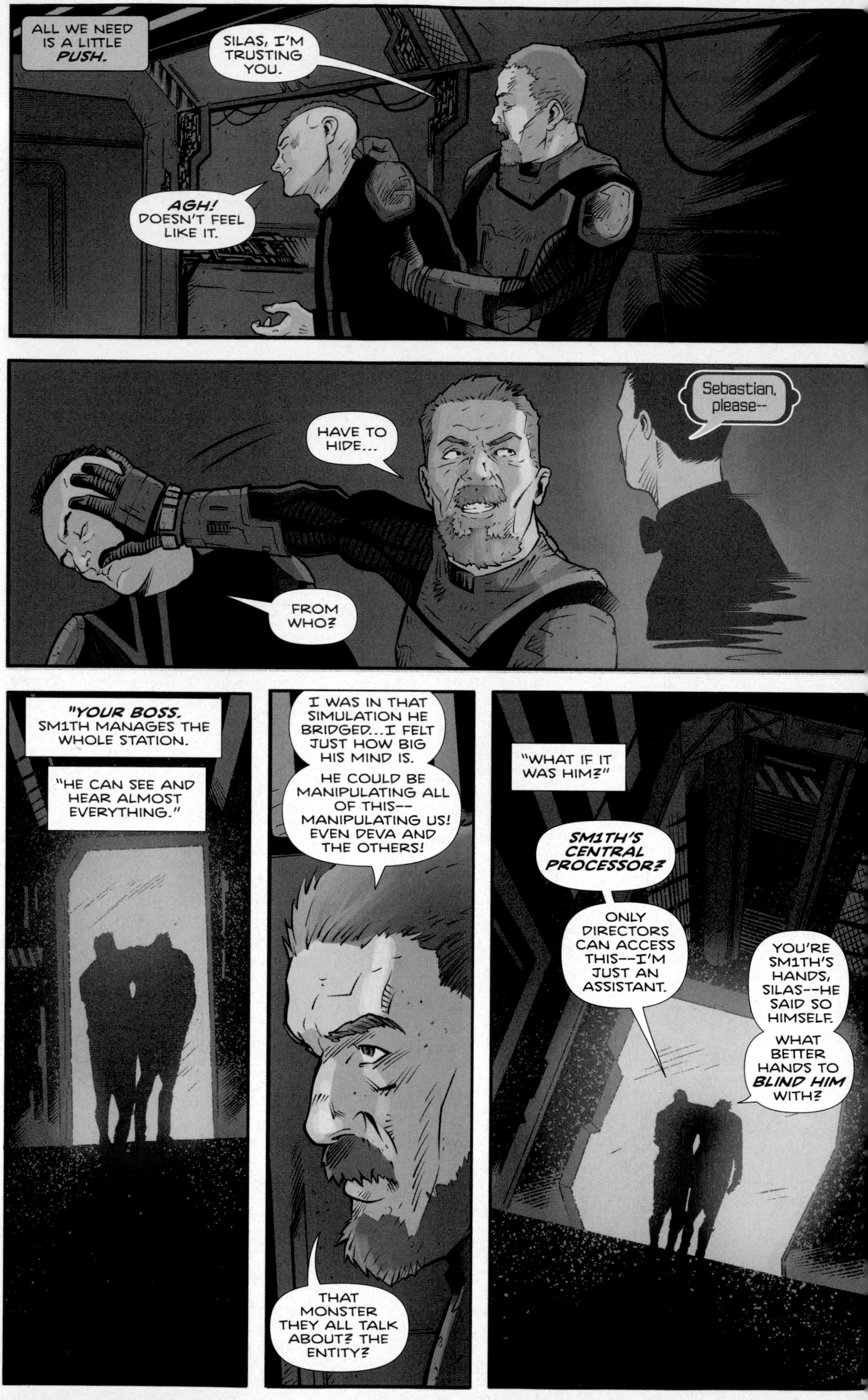

ALL WE NEED IS A LITTLE *PUSH.*
SILAS, I'M TRUSTING YOU.
AGH! DOESN'T FEEL LIKE IT.
HAVE TO HIDE...
Sebastian, please--
FROM WHO?
"YOUR BOSS. SM1TH MANAGES THE WHOLE STATION.
"HE CAN SEE AND HEAR ALMOST EVERYTHING."
I WAS IN THAT SIMULATION HE BRIDGED...I FELT JUST HOW BIG HIS MIND IS.
HE COULD BE MANIPULATING ALL OF THIS-- MANIPULATING US! EVEN DEVA AND THE OTHERS!
THAT MONSTER THEY ALL TALK ABOUT? THE ENTITY?
"WHAT IF IT WAS HIM?"
SM1TH'S CENTRAL PROCESSOR?
ONLY DIRECTORS CAN ACCESS THIS--I'M JUST AN ASSISTANT.
YOU'RE SM1TH'S HANDS, SILAS--HE SAID SO HIMSELF.
WHAT BETTER HANDS TO *BLIND HIM* WITH?

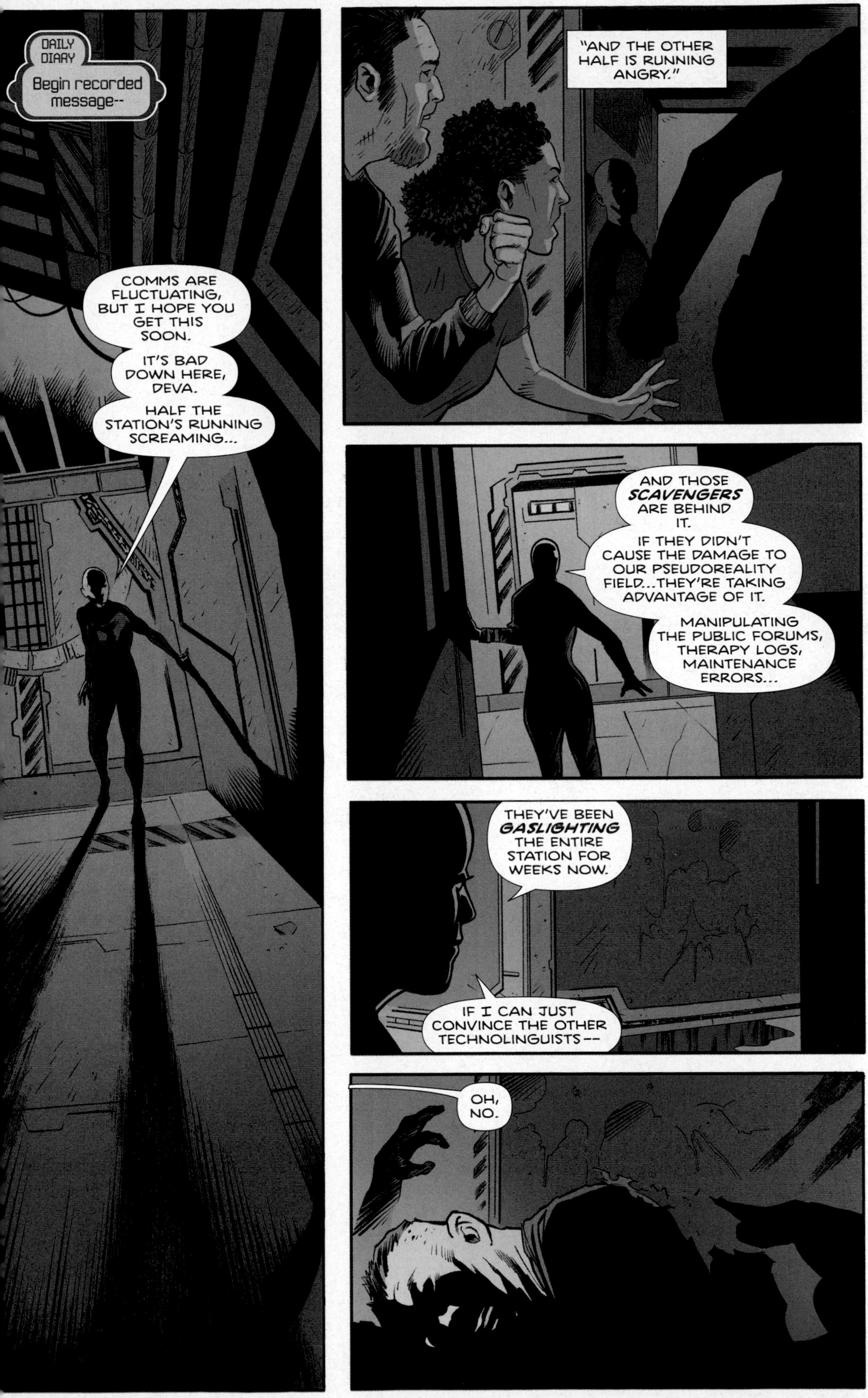
DAILY DIARY
Begin recorded message--
COMMS ARE FLUCTUATING, BUT I HOPE YOU GET THIS SOON.
IT'S BAD DOWN HERE, DEVA.
HALF THE STATION'S RUNNING SCREAMING...
"AND THE OTHER HALF IS RUNNING ANGRY."
AND THOSE *SCAVENGERS* ARE BEHIND IT.
IF THEY DIDN'T CAUSE THE DAMAGE TO OUR PSEUDOREALITY FIELD...THEY'RE TAKING ADVANTAGE OF IT.
MANIPULATING THE PUBLIC FORUMS, THERAPY LOGS, MAINTENANCE ERRORS...
THEY'VE BEEN *GASLIGHTING* THE ENTIRE STATION FOR WEEKS NOW.
IF I CAN JUST CONVINCE THE OTHER TECHNOLINGUISTS--
OH, NO.

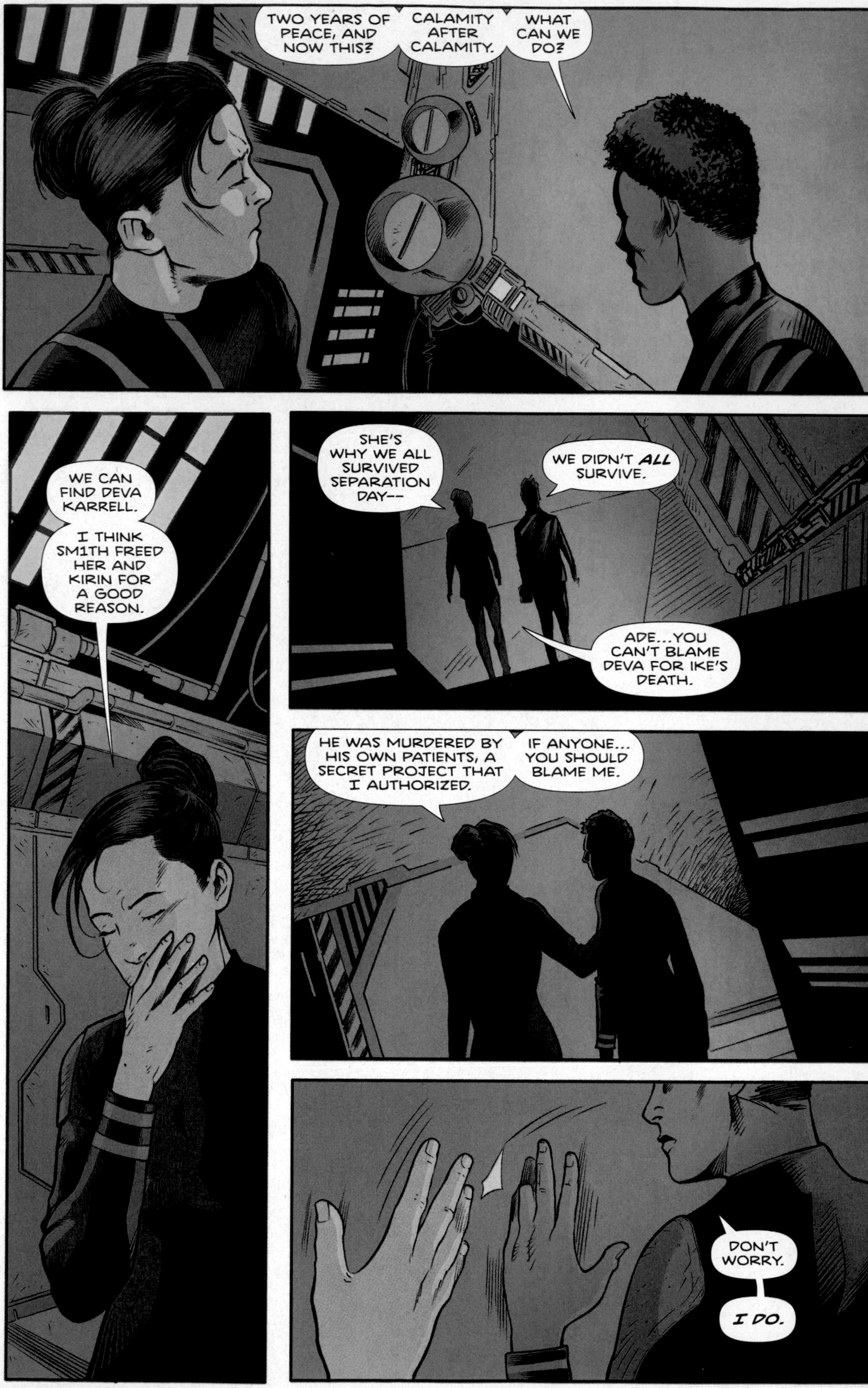
TWO YEARS OF PEACE, AND NOW THIS?
CALAMITY AFTER CALAMITY.
WHAT CAN WE DO?
WE CAN FIND DEVA KARRELL.
I THINK SM1TH FREED HER AND KIRIN FOR A GOOD REASON.
SHE'S WHY WE ALL SURVIVED SEPARATION DAY--
WE DIDN'T ALL SURVIVE.
ADE...YOU CAN'T BLAME DEVA FOR IKE'S DEATH.
HE WAS MURDERED BY HIS OWN PATIENTS, A SECRET PROJECT THAT I AUTHORIZED.
IF ANYONE... YOU SHOULD BLAME ME.
DON'T WORRY.
I DO.

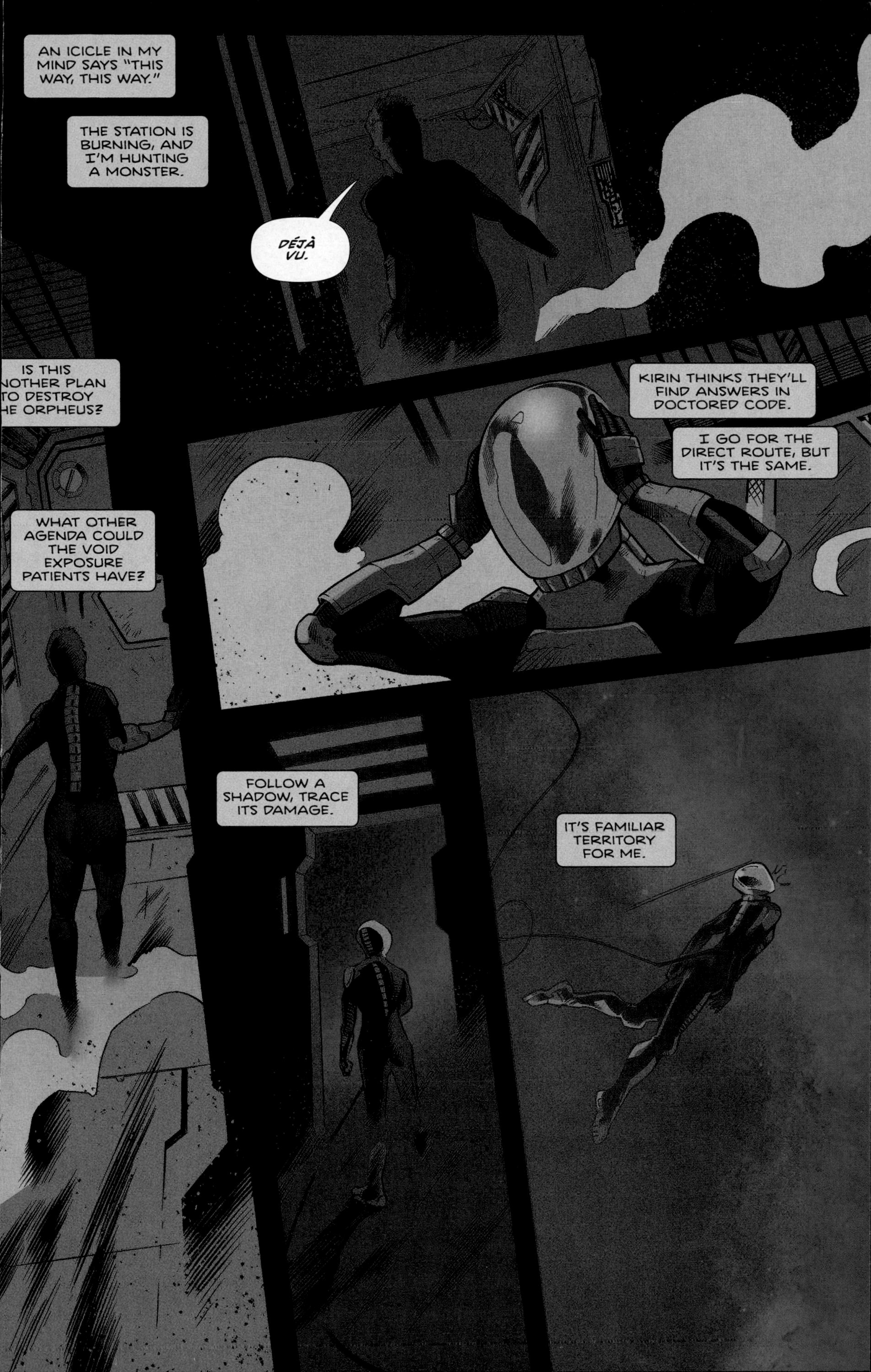
AN ICICLE IN MY MIND SAYS "THIS WAY, THIS WAY."
THE STATION IS BURNING, AND I'M HUNTING A MONSTER.
DÉJÀ VU.
IS THIS NOTHER PLAN TO DESTROY HE ORPHEUS?
WHAT OTHER AGENDA COULD THE VOID EXPOSURE PATIENTS HAVE?
KIRIN THINKS THEY'LL FIND ANSWERS IN DOCTORED CODE.
I GO FOR THE DIRECT ROUTE, BUT IT'S THE SAME.
FOLLOW A SHADOW, TRACE ITS DAMAGE.
IT'S FAMILIAR TERRITORY FOR ME.

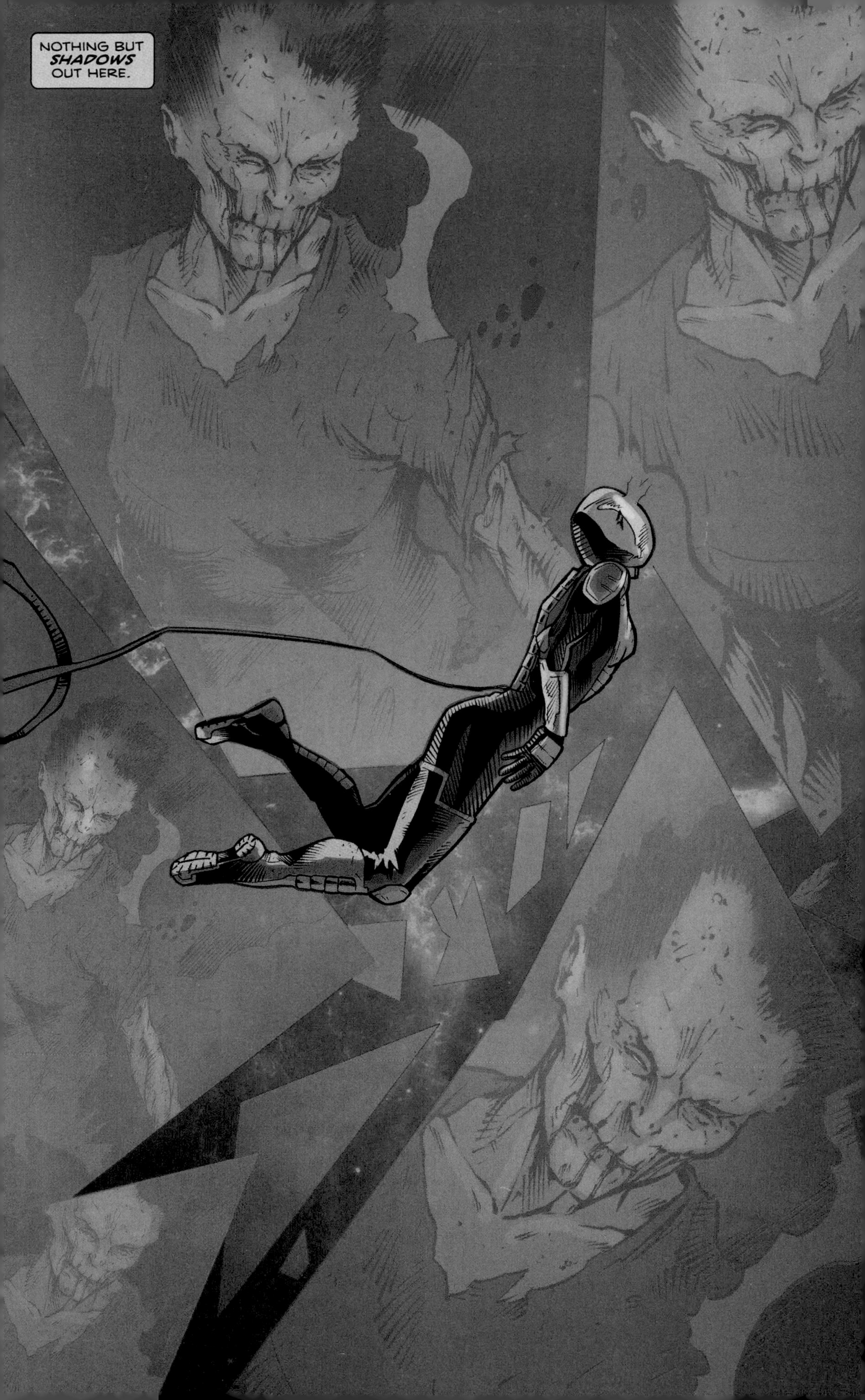
NOTHING BUT SHADOWS OUT HERE.

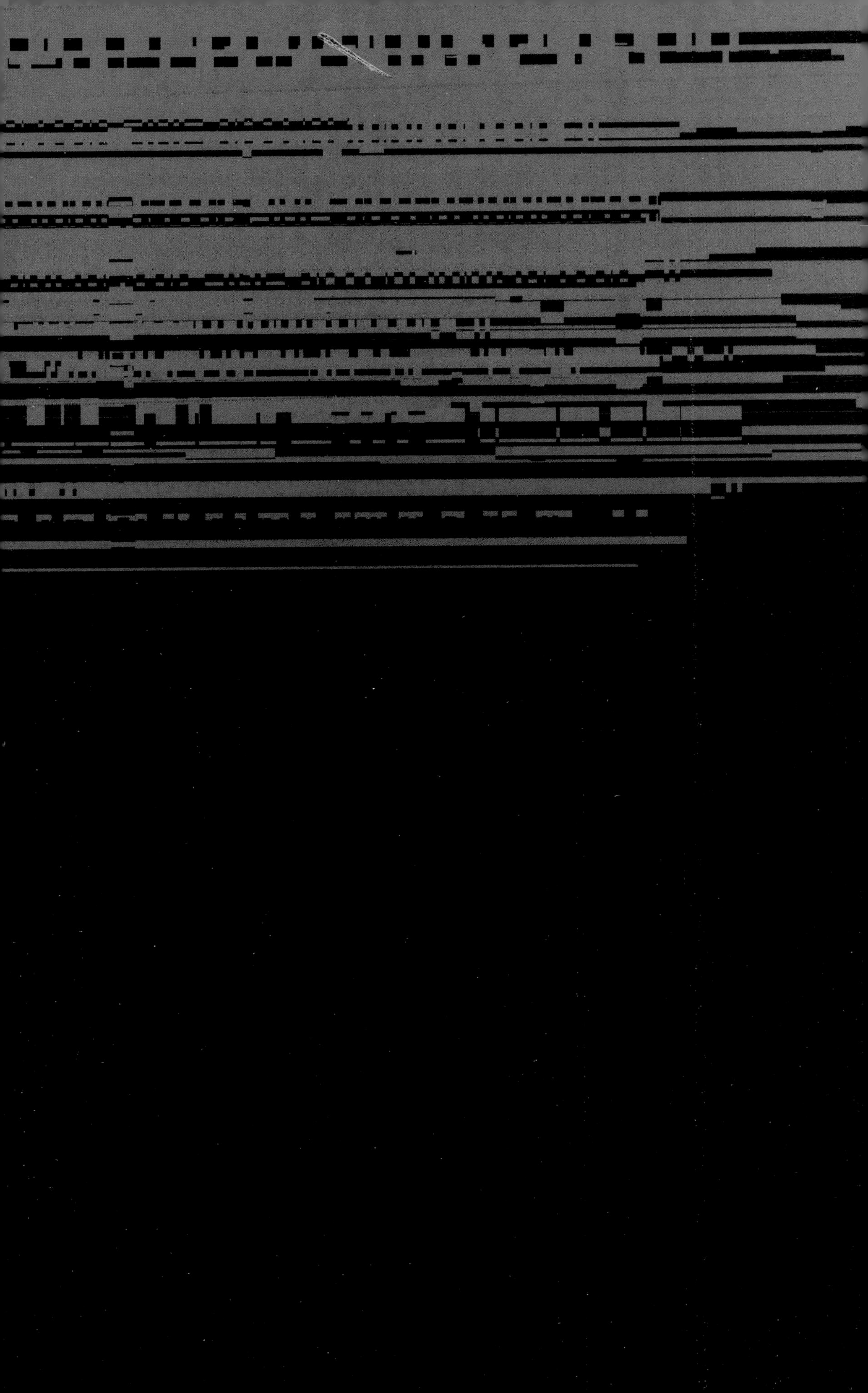

CHAPTER
SEVEN

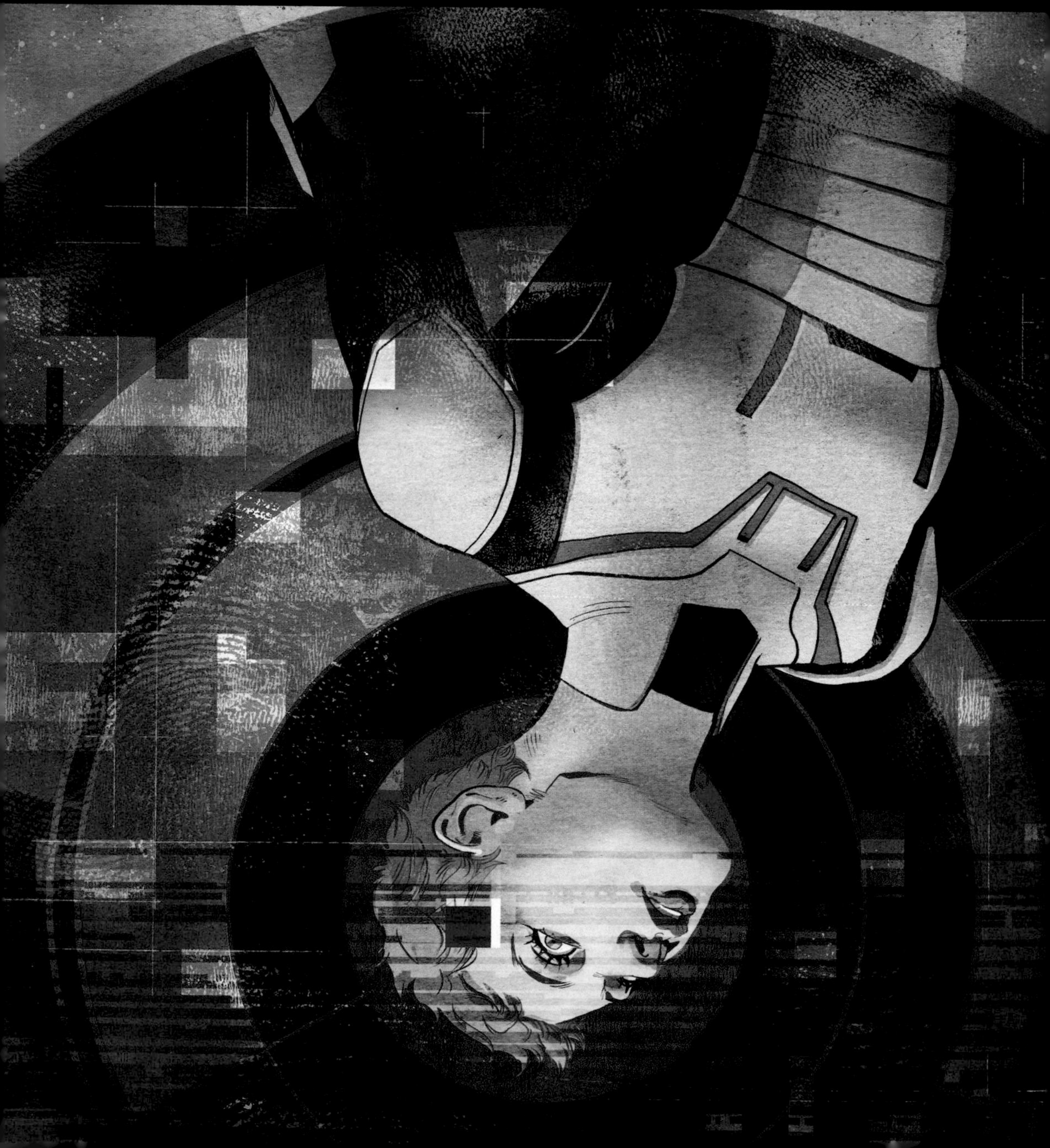

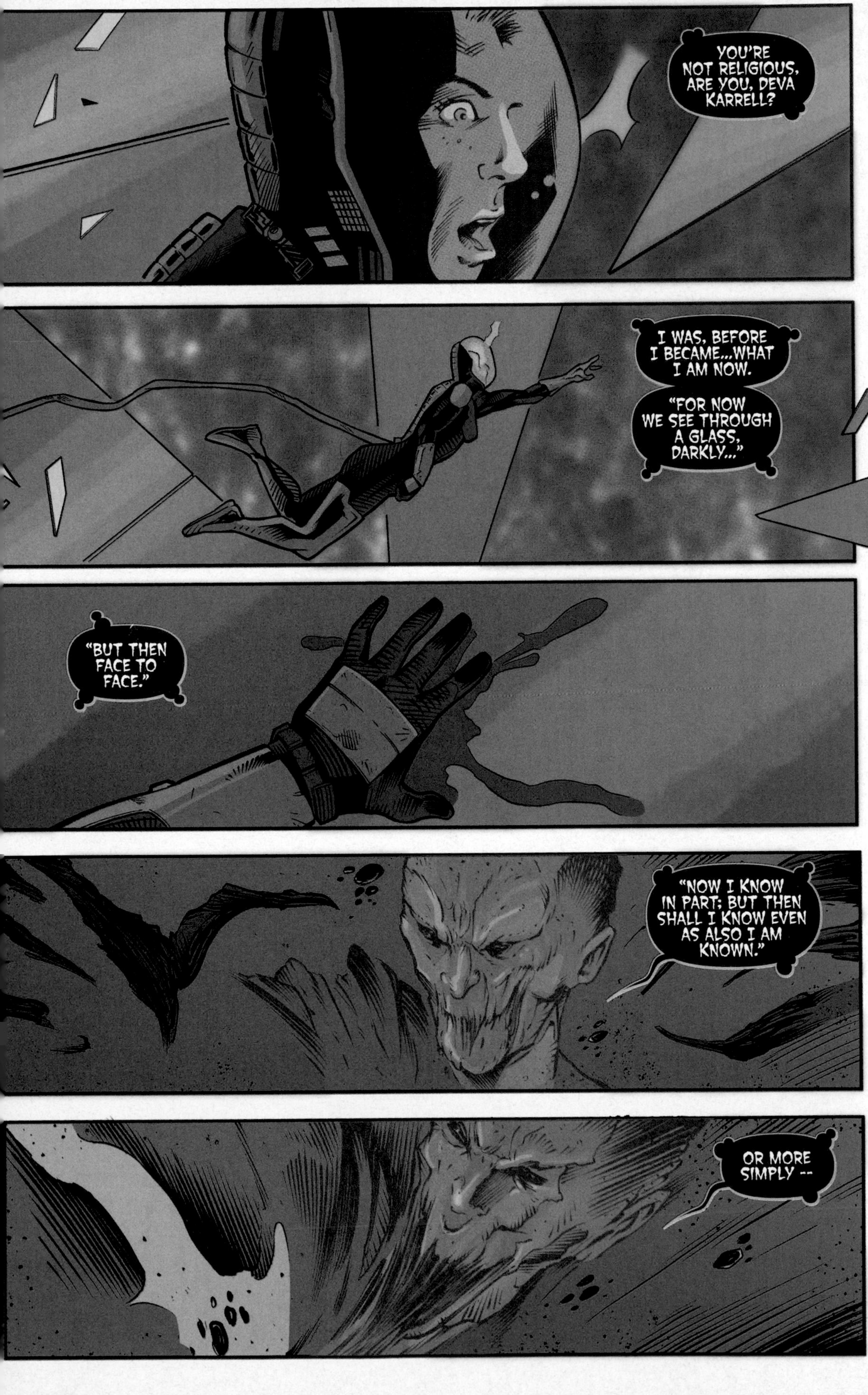
YOU'RE NOT RELIGIOUS, ARE YOU, DEVA KARRELL?
I WAS, BEFORE I BECAME...WHAT I AM NOW.
"FOR NOW WE SEE THROUGH A GLASS, DARKLY..."
"BUT THEN FACE TO FACE."
"NOW I KNOW IN PART; BUT THEN SHALL I KNOW EVEN AS ALSO I AM KNOWN."
OR MORE SIMPLY --

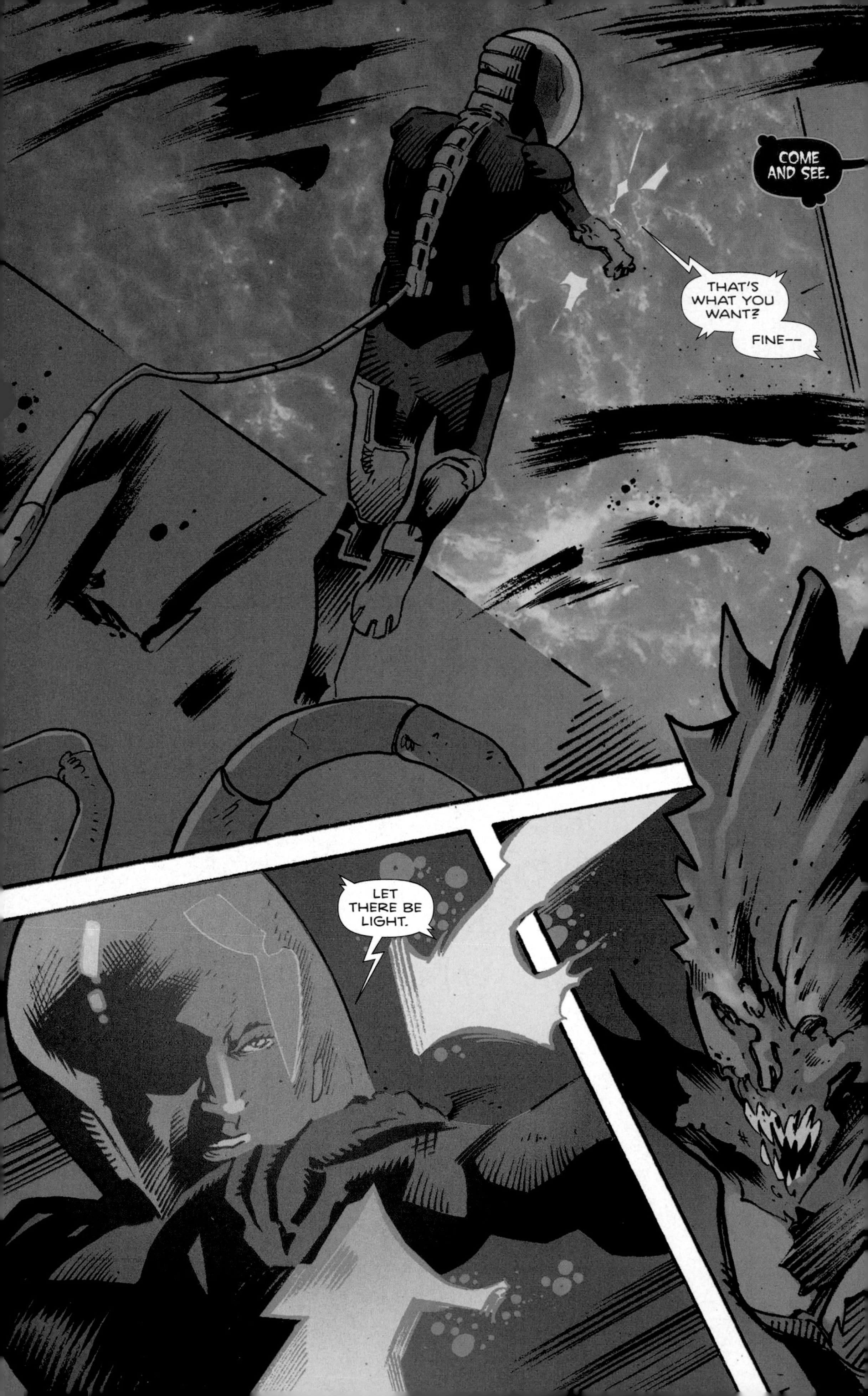
COME AND SEE.
THAT'S WHAT YOU WANT?
FINE--
LET THERE BE LIGHT.

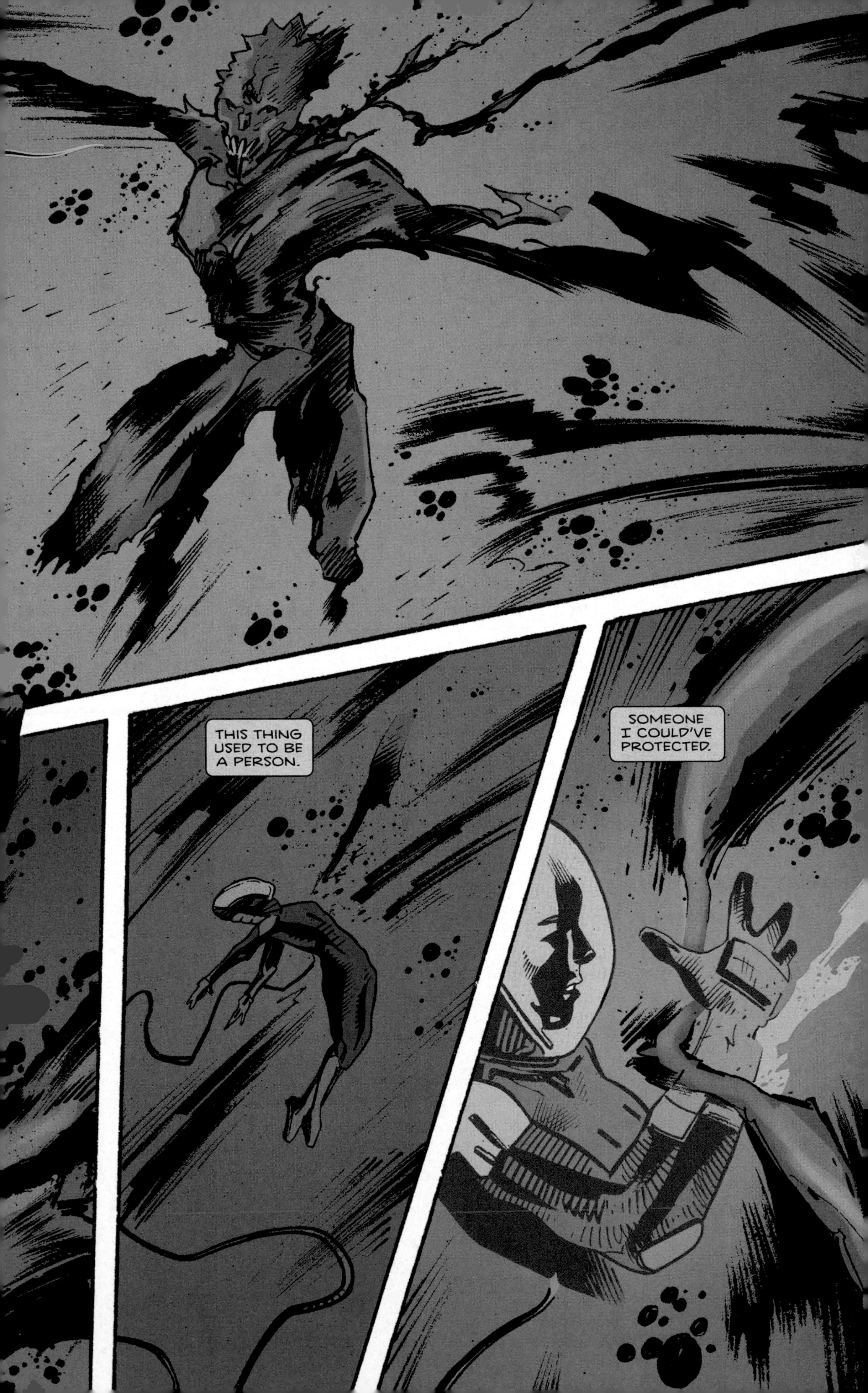
THIS THING USED TO BE A PERSON.
SOMEONE I COULD'VE PROTECTED.

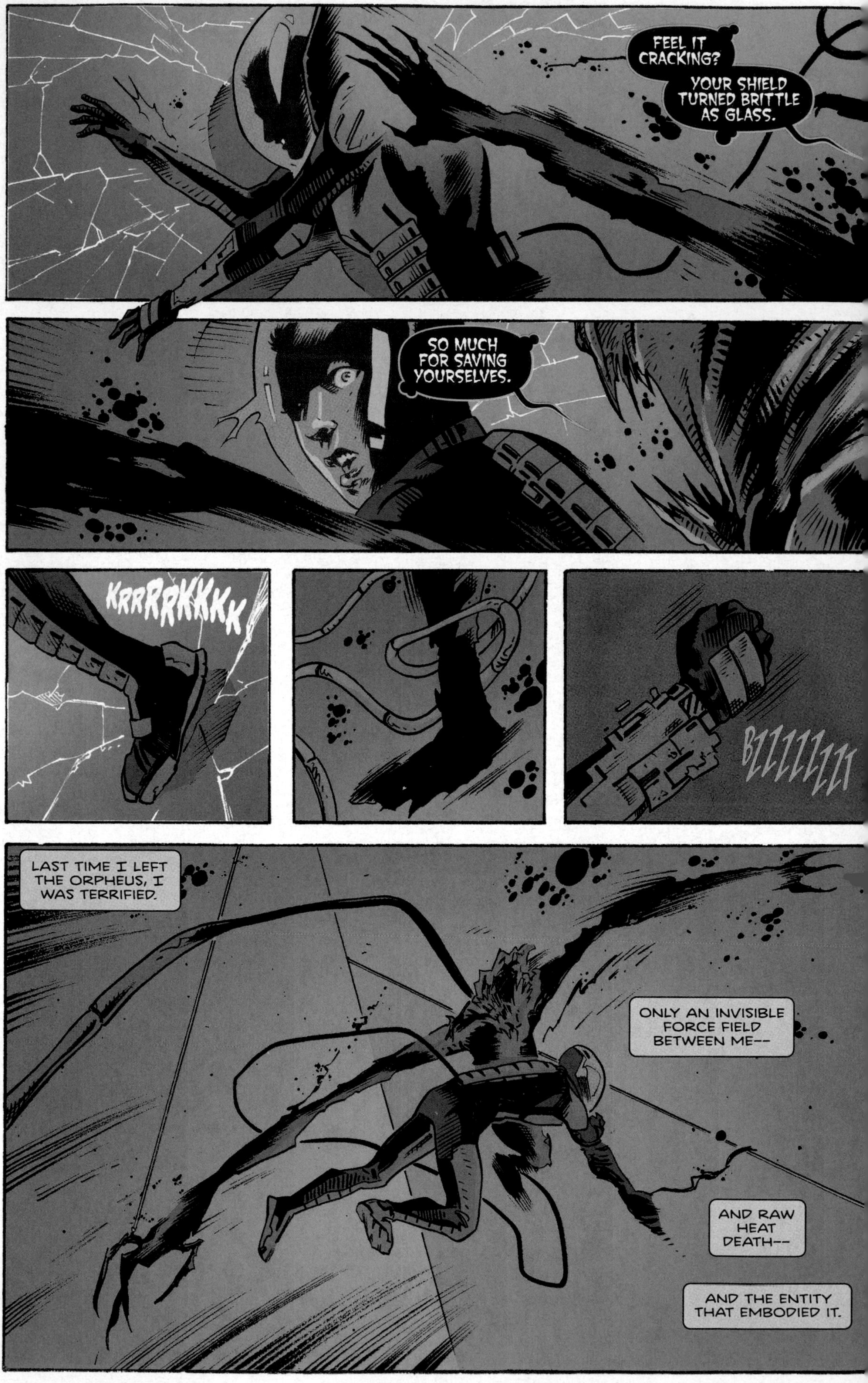
FEEL IT CRACKING?
YOUR SHIELD TURNED BRITTLE AS GLASS.
SO MUCH FOR SAVING YOURSELVES.
KRRRRKKKK
BZZZZZZZT
LAST TIME I LEFT THE ORPHEUS, I WAS TERRIFIED.
ONLY AN INVISIBLE FORCE FIELD BETWEEN ME--
AND RAW HEAT DEATH--
AND THE ENTITY THAT EMBODIED IT.

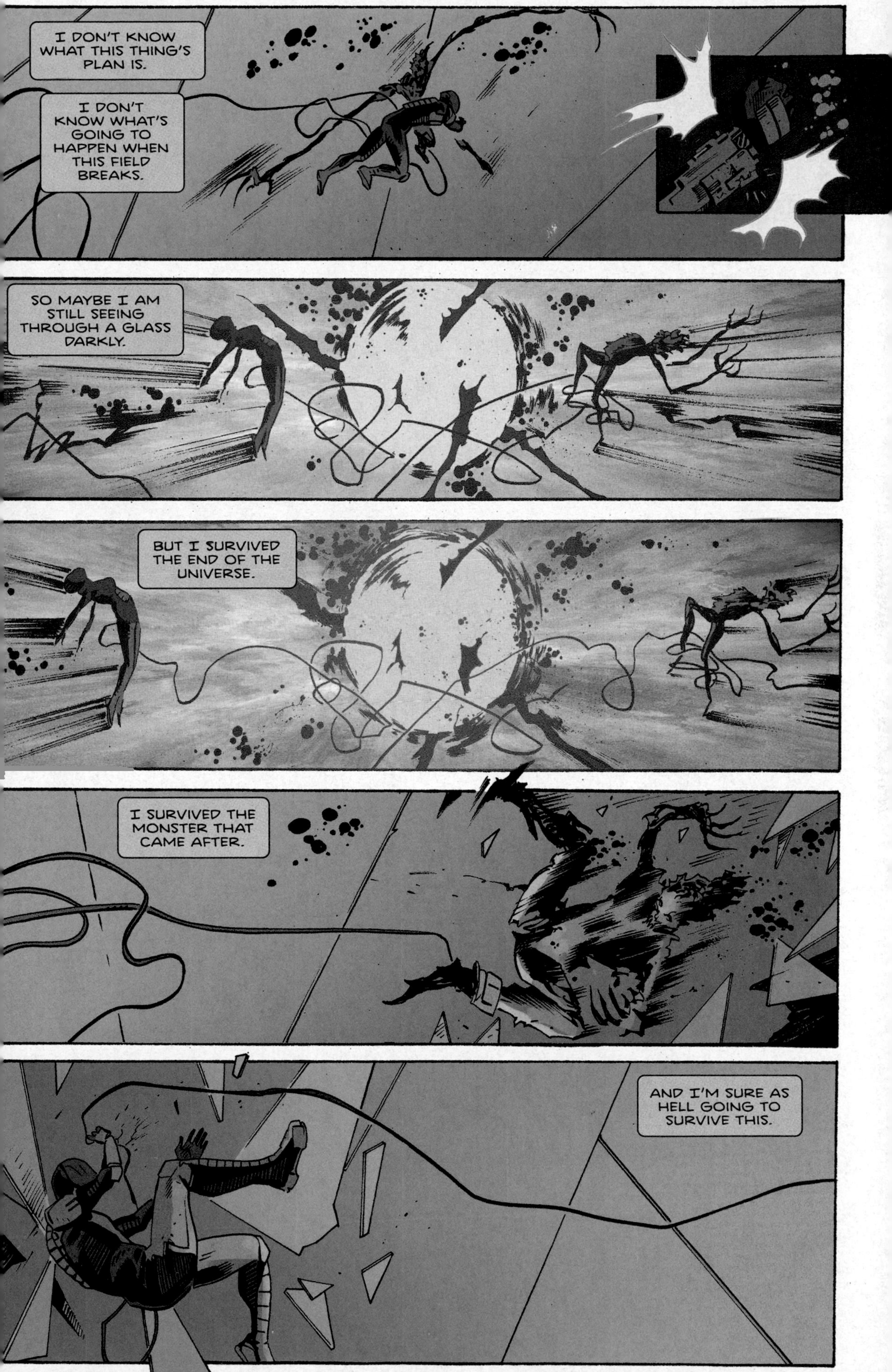
I DON'T KNOW WHAT THIS THING'S PLAN IS.
I DON'T KNOW WHAT'S GOING TO HAPPEN WHEN THIS FIELD BREAKS.
SO MAYBE I AM STILL SEEING THROUGH A GLASS DARKLY.
BUT I SURVIVED THE END OF THE UNIVERSE.
I SURVIVED THE MONSTER THAT CAME AFTER.
AND I'M SURE AS HELL GOING TO SURVIVE THIS.

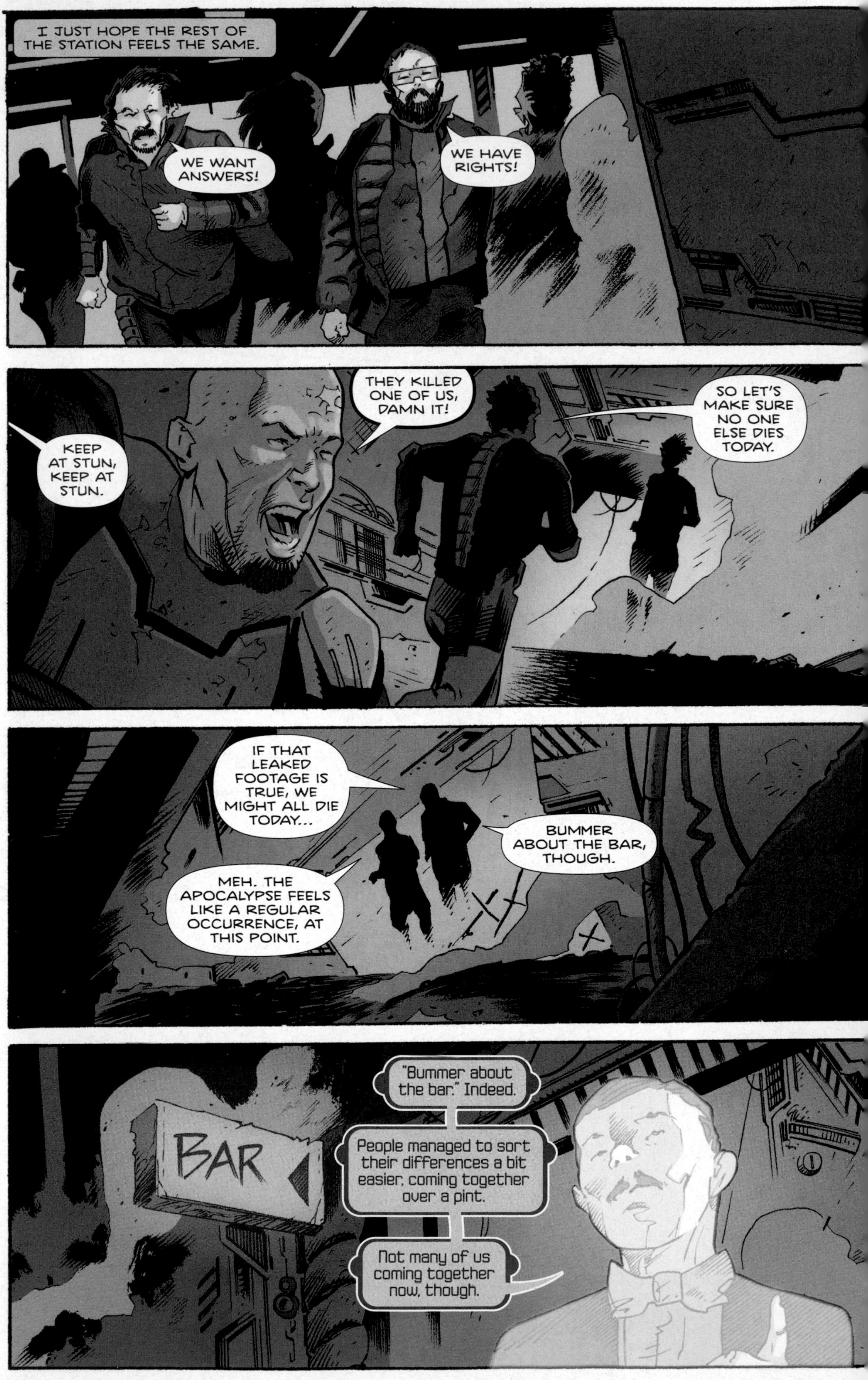
I JUST HOPE THE REST OF THE STATION FEELS THE SAME.
WE WANT ANSWERS!
WE HAVE RIGHTS!
KEEP AT STUN, KEEP AT STUN.
THEY KILLED ONE OF US, DAMN IT!
SO LET'S MAKE SURE NO ONE ELSE DIES TODAY.
IF THAT LEAKED FOOTAGE IS TRUE, WE MIGHT ALL DIE TODAY...
MEH. THE APOCALYPSE FEELS LIKE A REGULAR OCCURRENCE, AT THIS POINT.
BUMMER ABOUT THE BAR, THOUGH.
BAR
"Bummer about the bar." Indeed.
People managed to sort their differences a bit easier, coming together over a pint.
Not many of us coming together now, though.

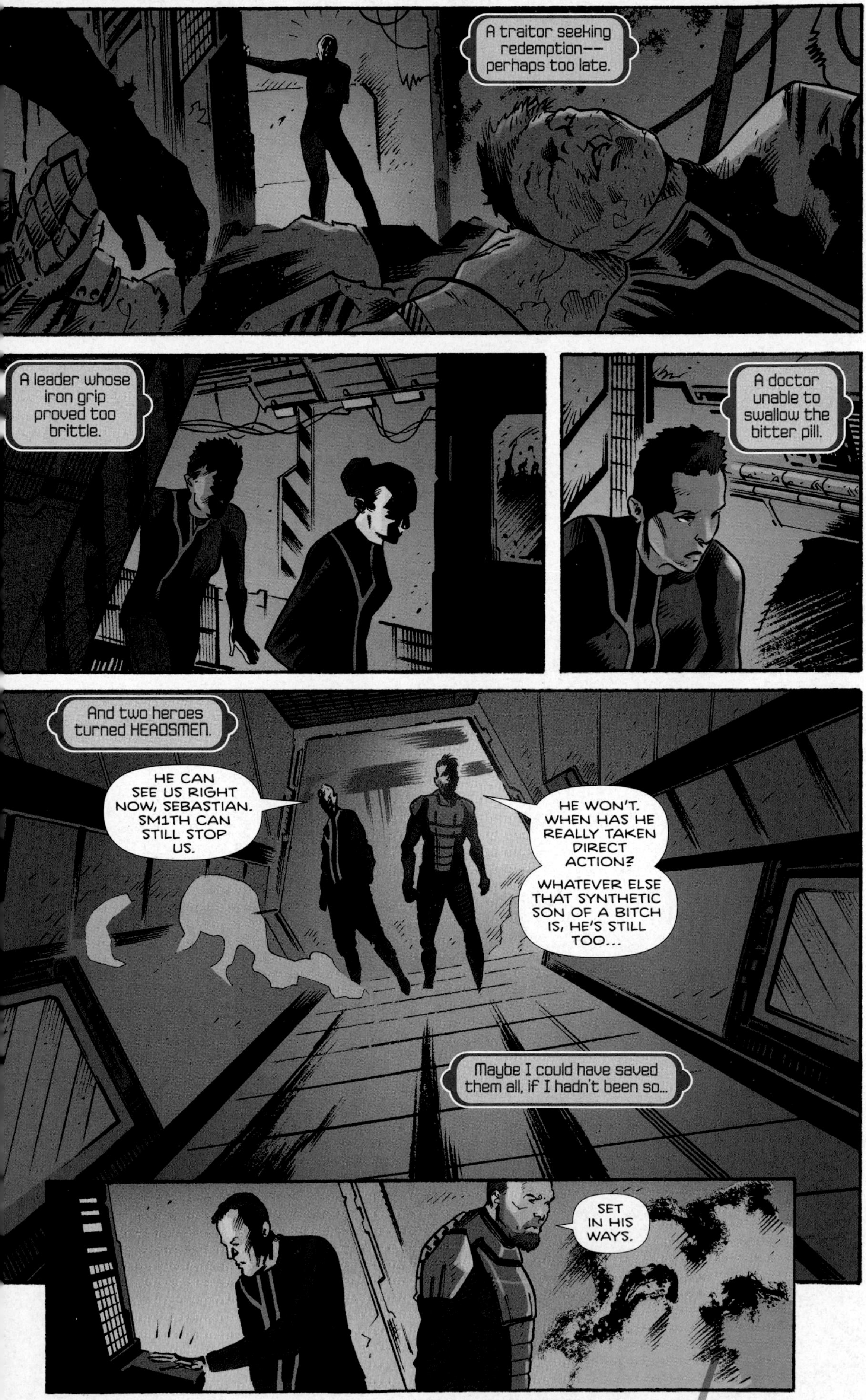
A traitor seeking redemption-- perhaps too late.
A leader whose iron grip proved too brittle.
A doctor unable to swallow the bitter pill.
And two heroes turned HEADSMEN.
HE CAN SEE US RIGHT NOW, SEBASTIAN. SM1TH CAN STILL STOP US.
HE WON'T. WHEN HAS HE REALLY TAKEN DIRECT ACTION?
WHATEVER ELSE THAT SYNTHETIC SON OF A BITCH IS, HE'S STILL TOO...
Maybe I could have saved them all, if I hadn't been so...
SET IN HIS WAYS.

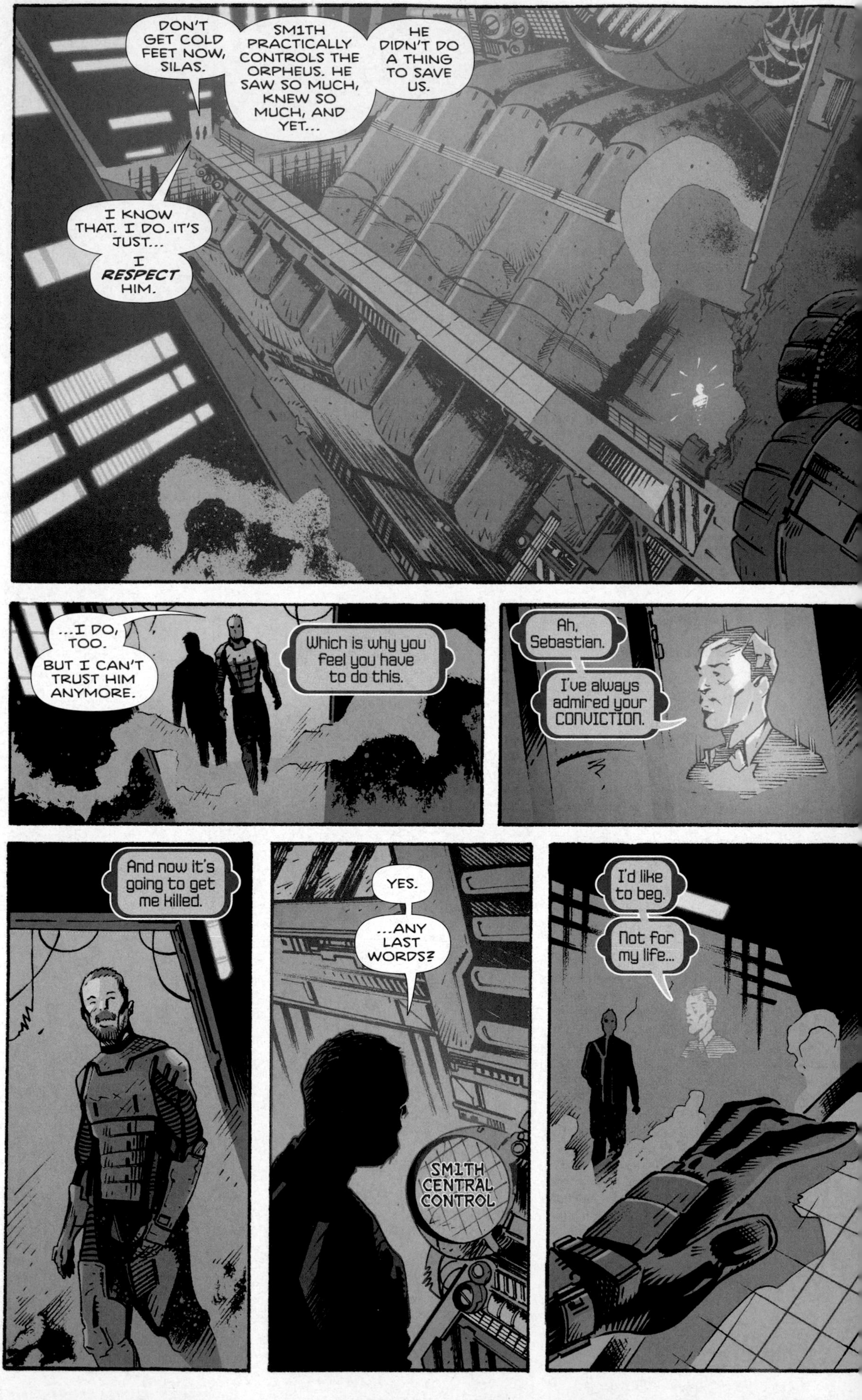
DON'T GET COLD FEET NOW, SILAS.
SM1TH PRACTICALLY CONTROLS THE ORPHEUS. HE SAW SO MUCH, KNEW SO MUCH, AND YET...
HE DIDN'T DO A THING TO SAVE US.
I KNOW THAT. I DO. IT'S JUST...
I *RESPECT* HIM.
...I DO, TOO.
BUT I CAN'T TRUST HIM ANYMORE.
Which is why you feel you have to do this.
Ah, Sebastian.
I've always admired your CONVICTION.
And now it's going to get me killed.
YES.
...ANY LAST WORDS?
SM1TH CENTRAL CONTROL
I'd like to beg.
Not for my life...

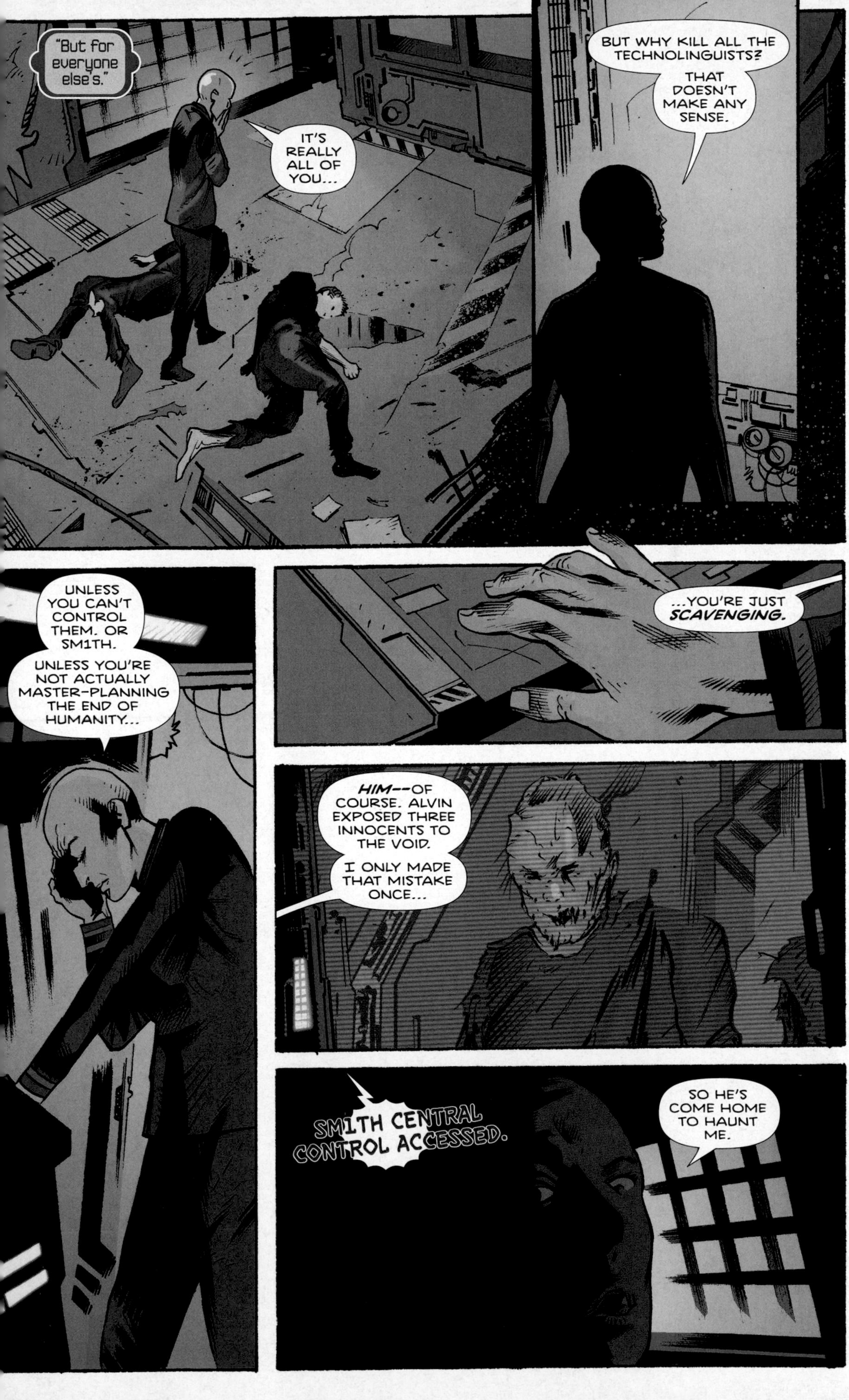
"But for everyone else's."
IT'S REALLY ALL OF YOU...
BUT WHY KILL ALL THE TECHNOLINGUISTS?
THAT DOESN'T MAKE ANY SENSE.
UNLESS YOU CAN'T CONTROL THEM. OR SM1TH.
UNLESS YOU'RE NOT ACTUALLY MASTER-PLANNING THE END OF HUMANITY...
...YOU'RE JUST SCAVENGING.
HIM--OF COURSE. ALVIN EXPOSED THREE INNOCENTS TO THE VOID.
I ONLY MADE THAT MISTAKE ONCE...
SM1TH CENTRAL CONTROL ACCESSED.
SO HE'S COME HOME TO HAUNT ME.

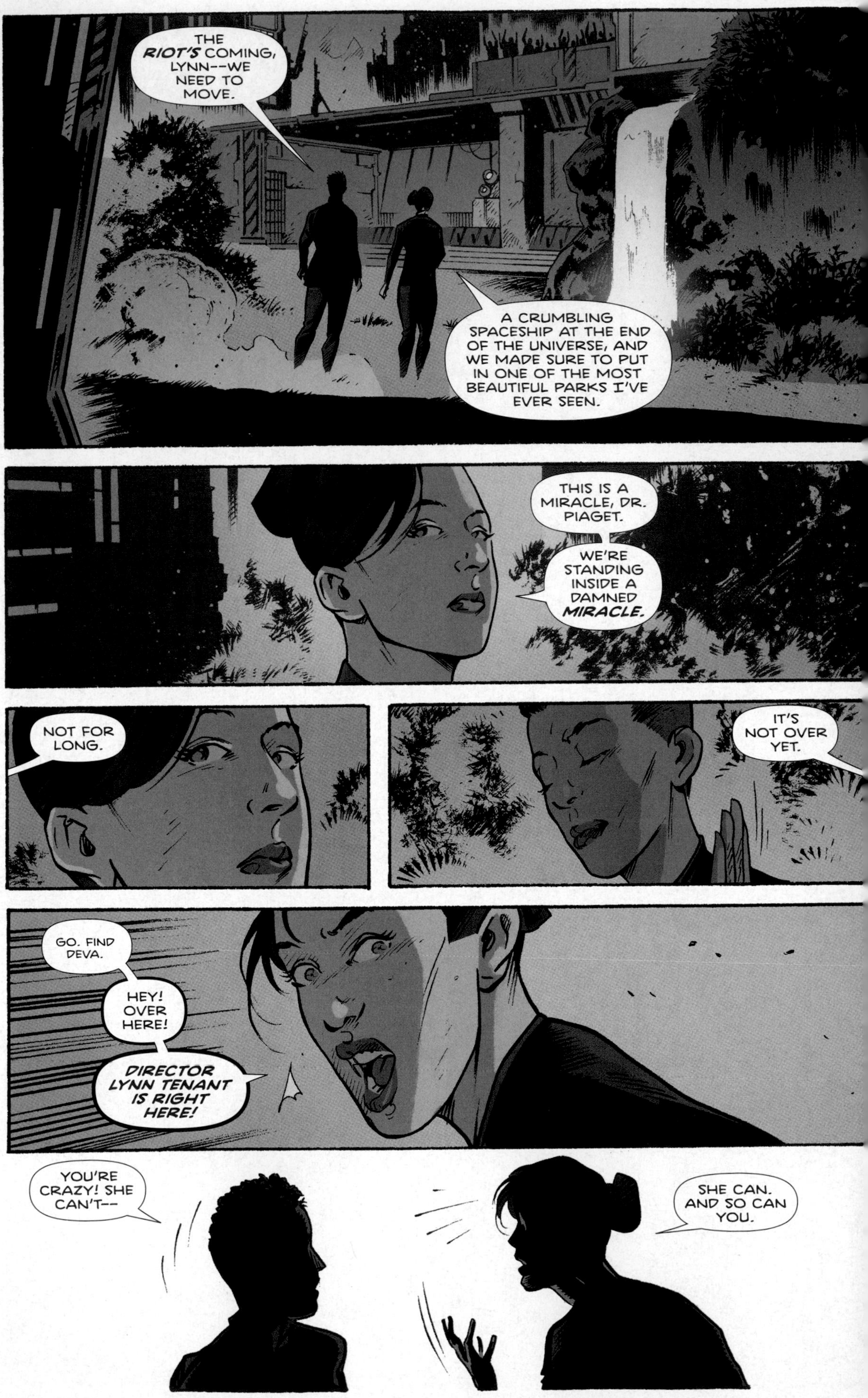
THE RIOT'S COMING, LYNN--WE NEED TO MOVE.
A CRUMBLING SPACESHIP AT THE END OF THE UNIVERSE, AND WE MADE SURE TO PUT IN ONE OF THE MOST BEAUTIFUL PARKS I'VE EVER SEEN.
THIS IS A MIRACLE, DR. PIAGET.
WE'RE STANDING INSIDE A DAMNED MIRACLE.
NOT FOR LONG.
IT'S NOT OVER YET.
GO. FIND DEVA.
HEY! OVER HERE!
DIRECTOR LYNN TENANT IS RIGHT HERE!
YOU'RE CRAZY! SHE CAN'T--
SHE CAN. AND SO CAN YOU.

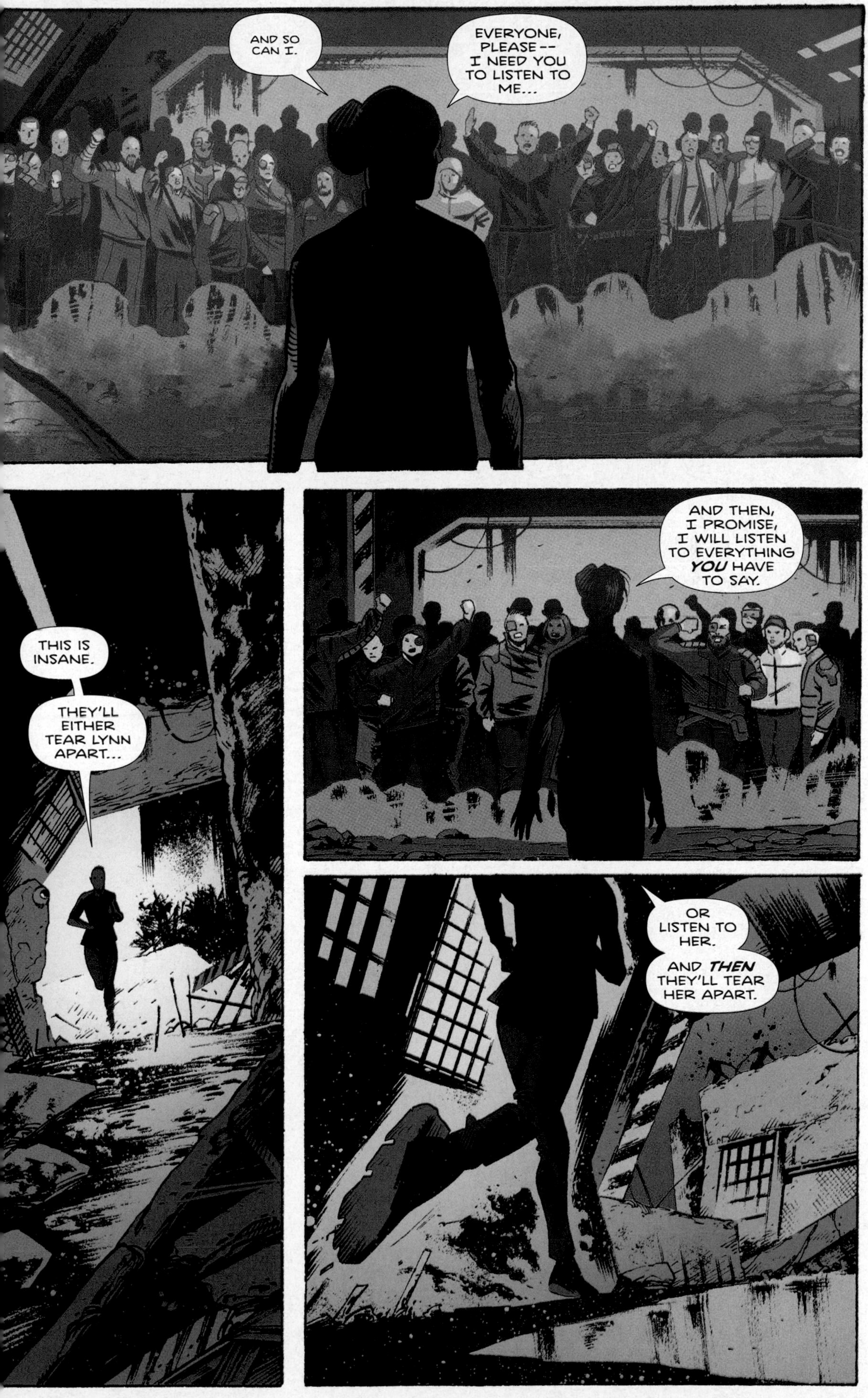
AND SO CAN I.
EVERYONE, PLEASE -- I NEED YOU TO LISTEN TO ME...
AND THEN, I PROMISE, I WILL LISTEN TO EVERYTHING *YOU* HAVE TO SAY.
THIS IS INSANE.
THEY'LL EITHER TEAR LYNN APART...
OR LISTEN TO HER.
AND *THEN* THEY'LL TEAR HER APART.

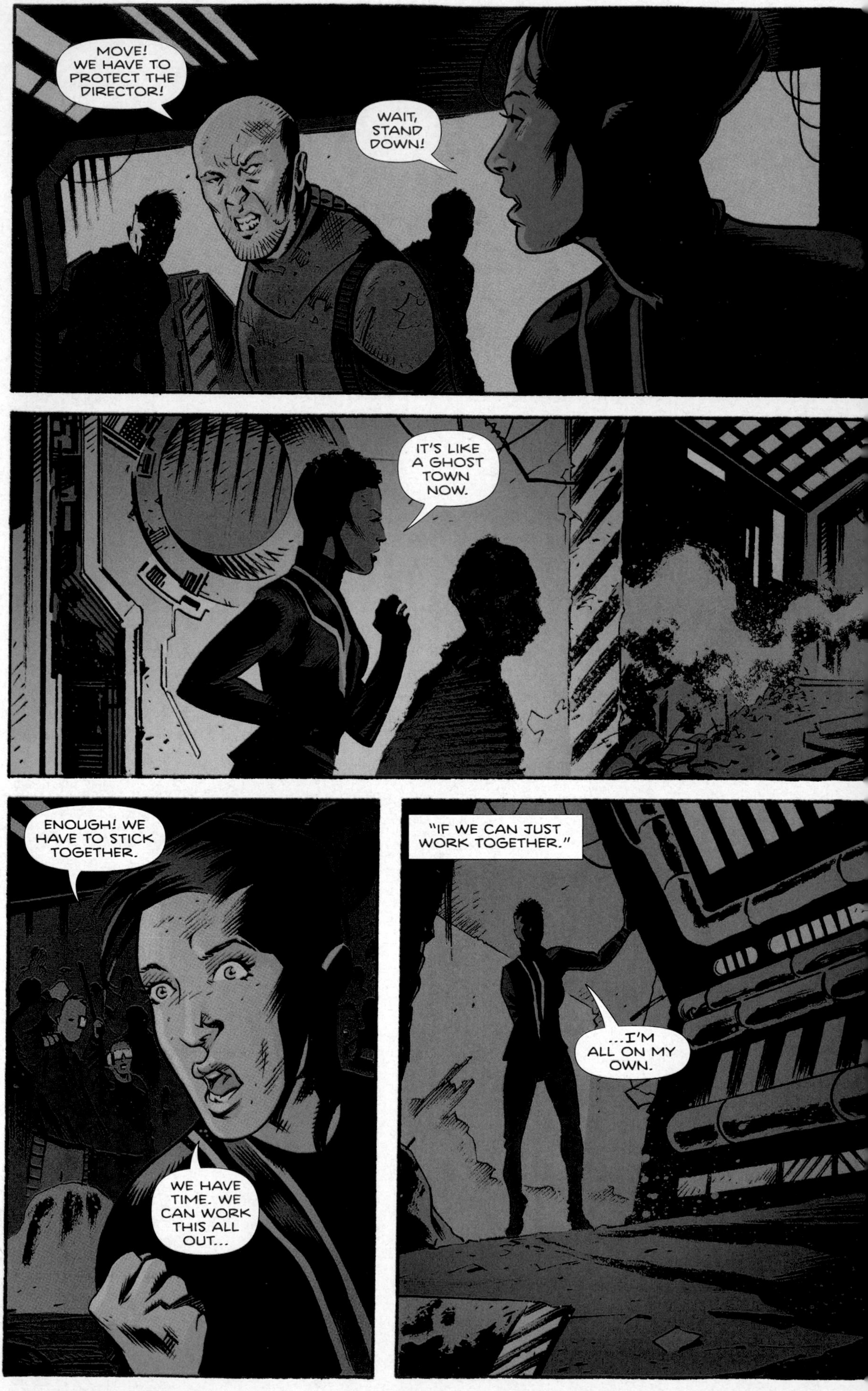
MOVE! WE HAVE TO PROTECT THE DIRECTOR!
WAIT, STAND DOWN!
IT'S LIKE A GHOST TOWN NOW.
ENOUGH! WE HAVE TO STICK TOGETHER.
WE HAVE TIME. WE CAN WORK THIS ALL OUT...
"IF WE CAN JUST WORK TOGETHER."
...I'M ALL ON MY OWN.

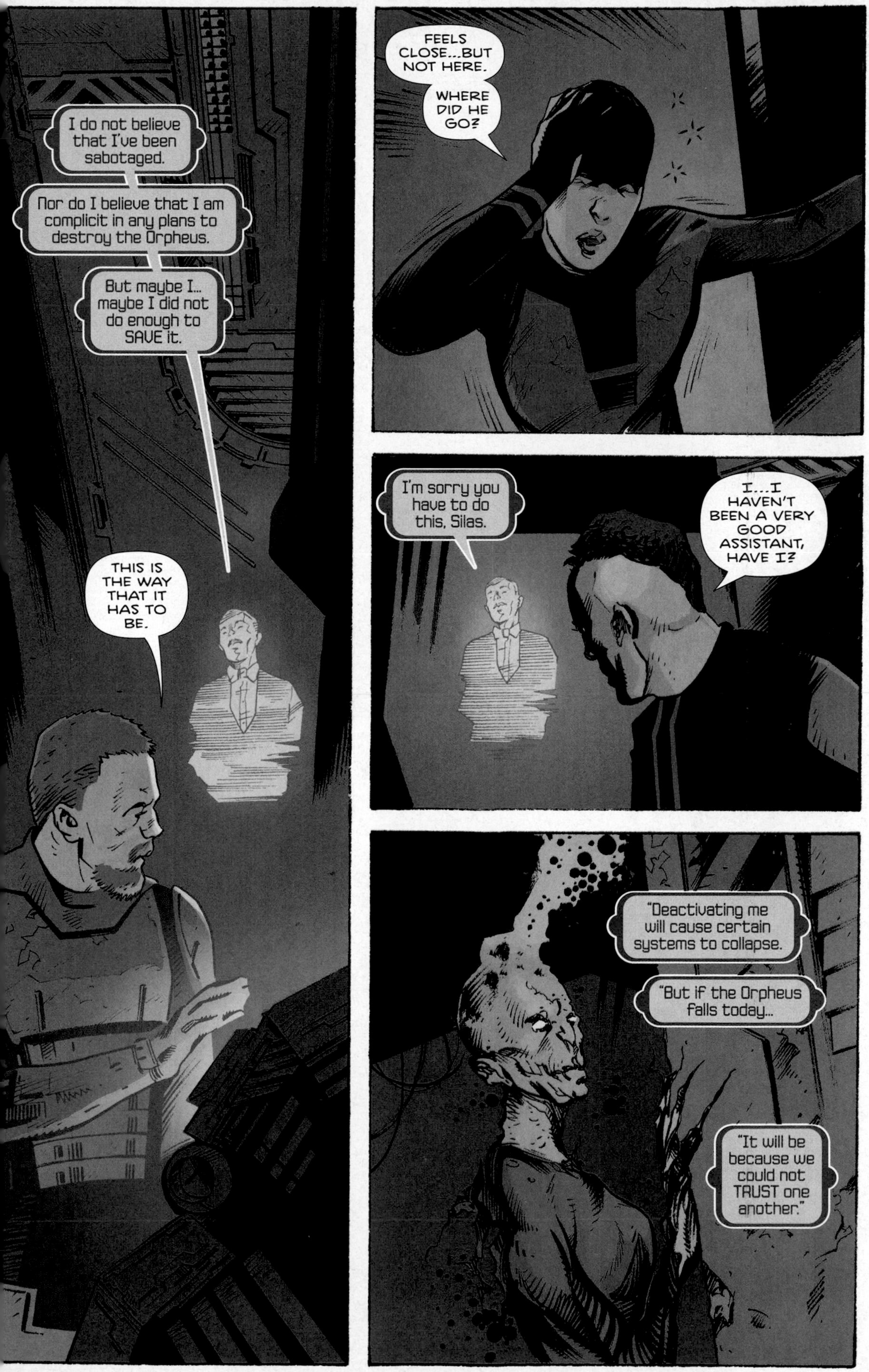

I do not believe that I've been sabotaged.
Nor do I believe that I am complicit in any plans to destroy the Orpheus.
But maybe I... maybe I did not do enough to SAVE it.
THIS IS THE WAY THAT IT HAS TO BE.
FEELS CLOSE...BUT NOT HERE.
WHERE DID HE GO?
I'm sorry you have to do this, Silas.
I...I HAVEN'T BEEN A VERY GOOD ASSISTANT, HAVE I?
"Deactivating me will cause certain systems to collapse.
"But if the Orpheus falls today...
"It will be because we could not TRUST one another."

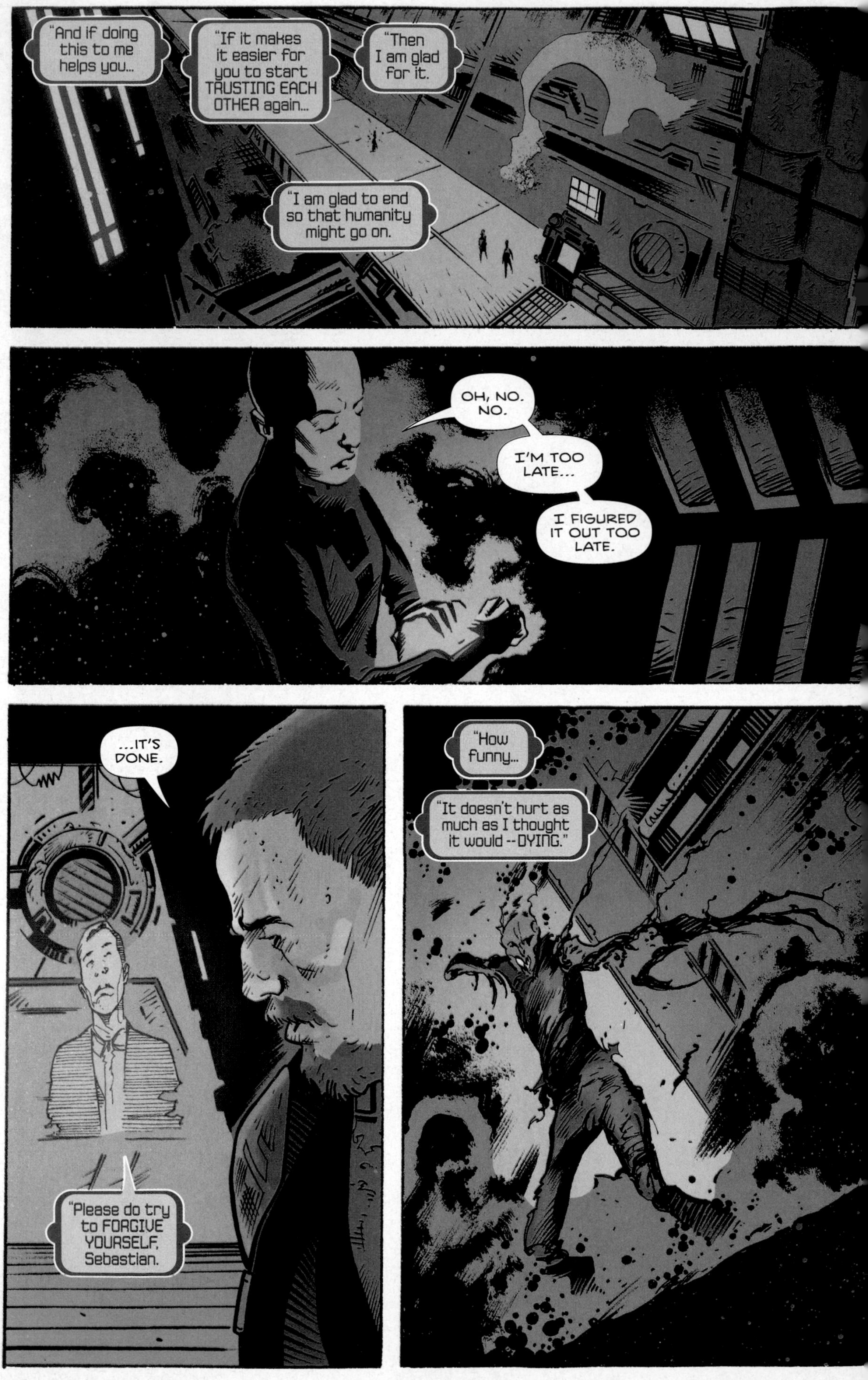
"And if doing this to me helps you...
"If it makes it easier for you to start TRUSTING EACH OTHER again...
"Then I am glad for it.
"I am glad to end so that humanity might go on.
OH, NO. NO.
I'M TOO LATE...
I FIGURED IT OUT TOO LATE.
...IT'S DONE.
"Please do try to FORGIVE YOURSELF, Sebastian.
"How funny...
"It doesn't hurt as much as I thought it would --DYING."

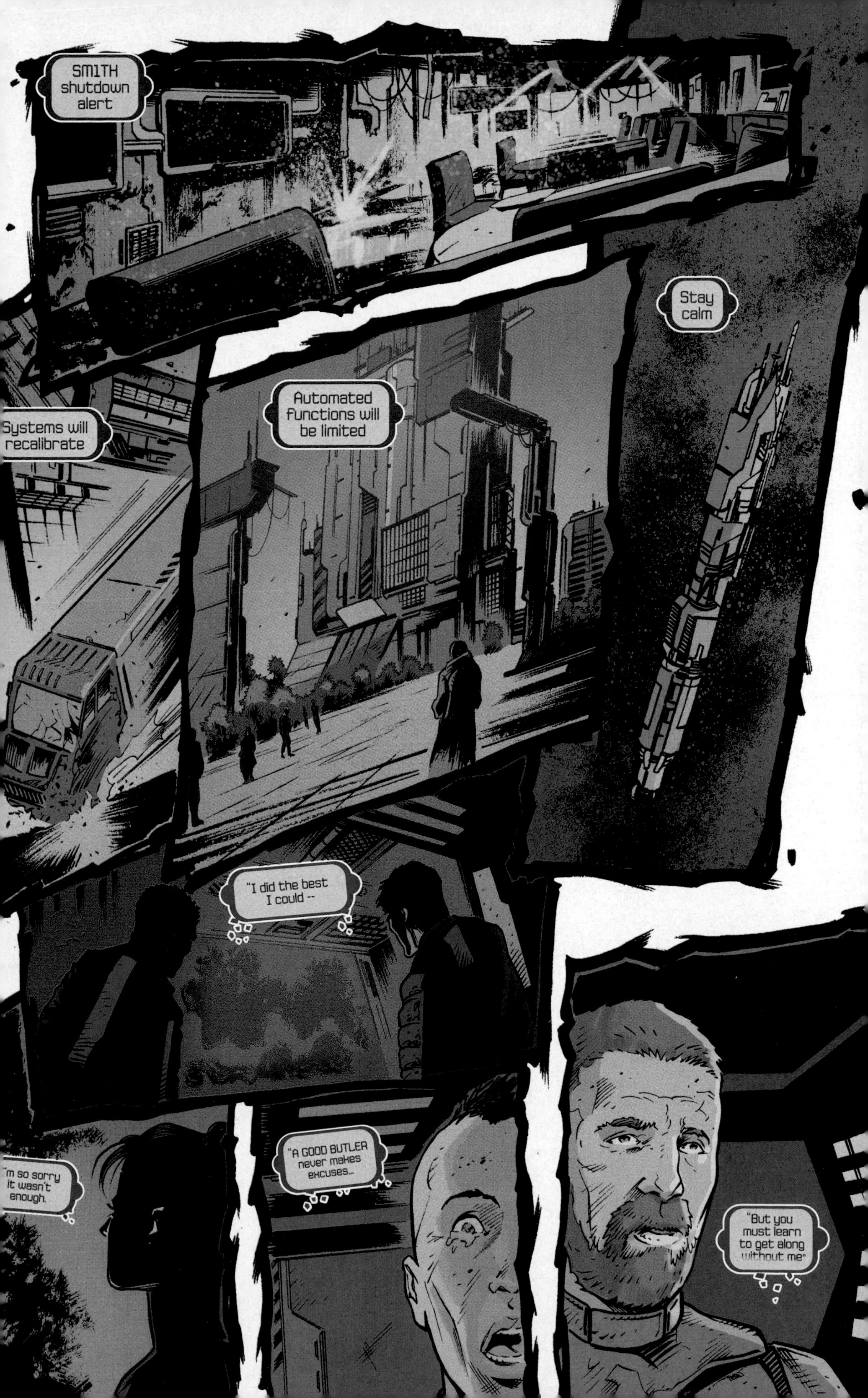
SM1TH shutdown alert
Systems will recalibrate
Automated functions will be limited
Stay calm
"I did the best I could --
I'm so sorry it wasn't enough.
"A GOOD BUTLER never makes excuses...
"But you must learn to get along without me"

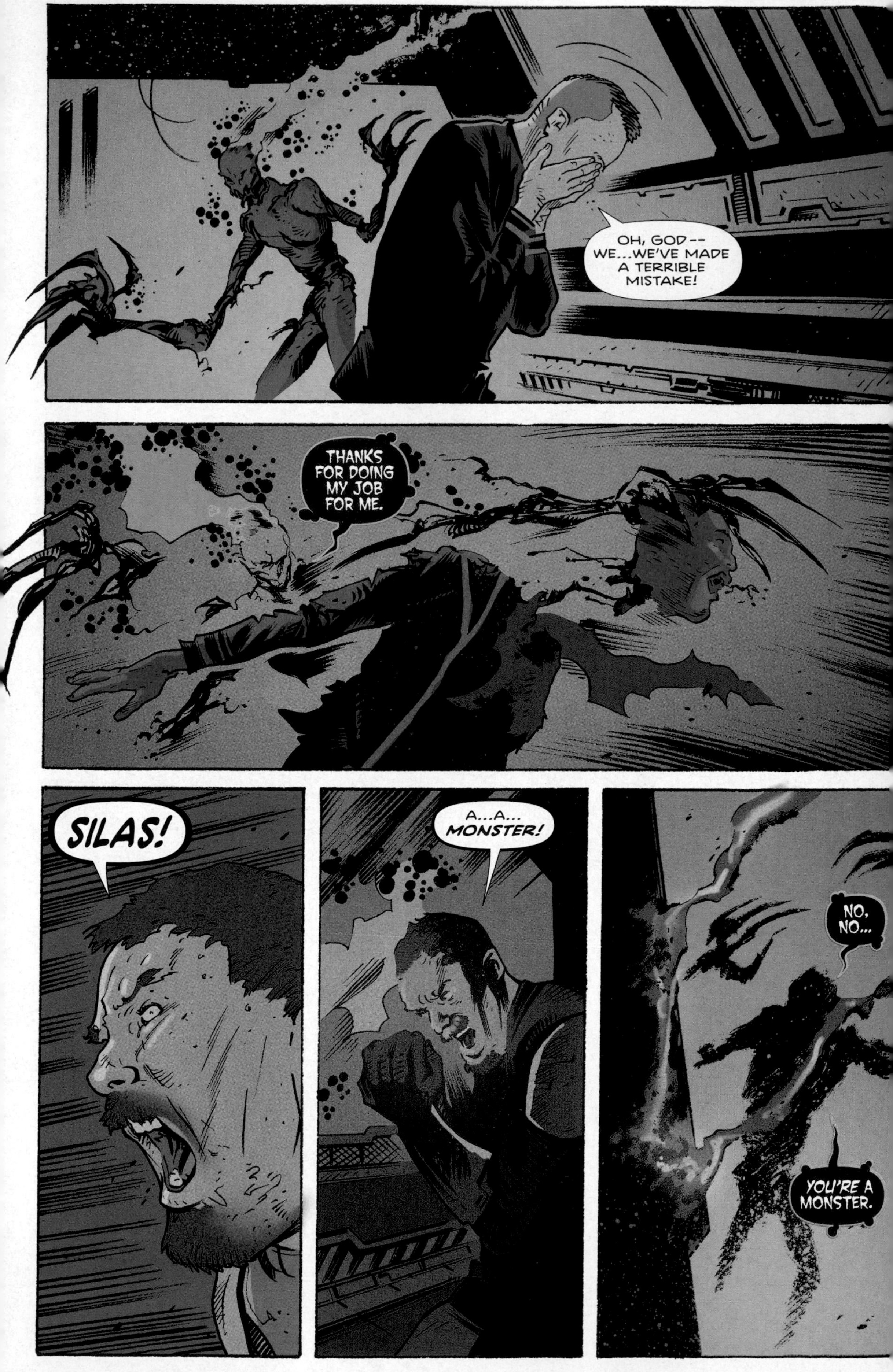
OH, GOD--
WE...WE'VE MADE A TERRIBLE MISTAKE!
THANKS FOR DOING MY JOB FOR ME.
SILAS!
A...A... MONSTER!
NO, NO...
YOU'RE A MONSTER.

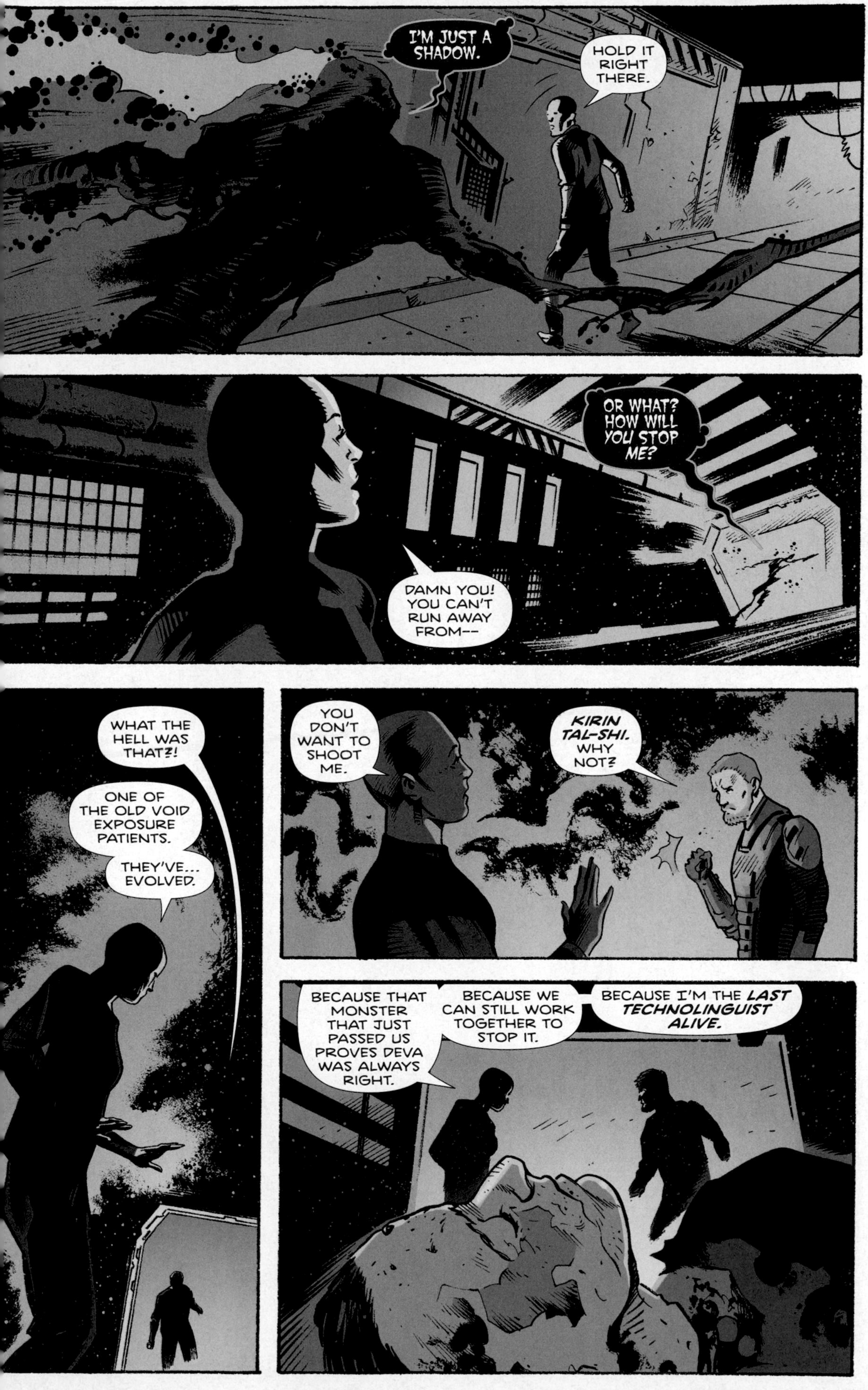
I'M JUST A SHADOW.
HOLD IT RIGHT THERE.
OR WHAT? HOW WILL YOU STOP ME?
DAMN YOU! YOU CAN'T RUN AWAY FROM--
WHAT THE HELL WAS THAT?!
ONE OF THE OLD VOID EXPOSURE PATIENTS.
THEY'VE... EVOLVED.
YOU DON'T WANT TO SHOOT ME.
KIRIN TAL-SHI. WHY NOT?
BECAUSE THAT MONSTER THAT JUST PASSED US PROVES DEVA WAS ALWAYS RIGHT.
BECAUSE WE CAN STILL WORK TOGETHER TO STOP IT.
BECAUSE I'M THE LAST TECHNOLINGUIST ALIVE.

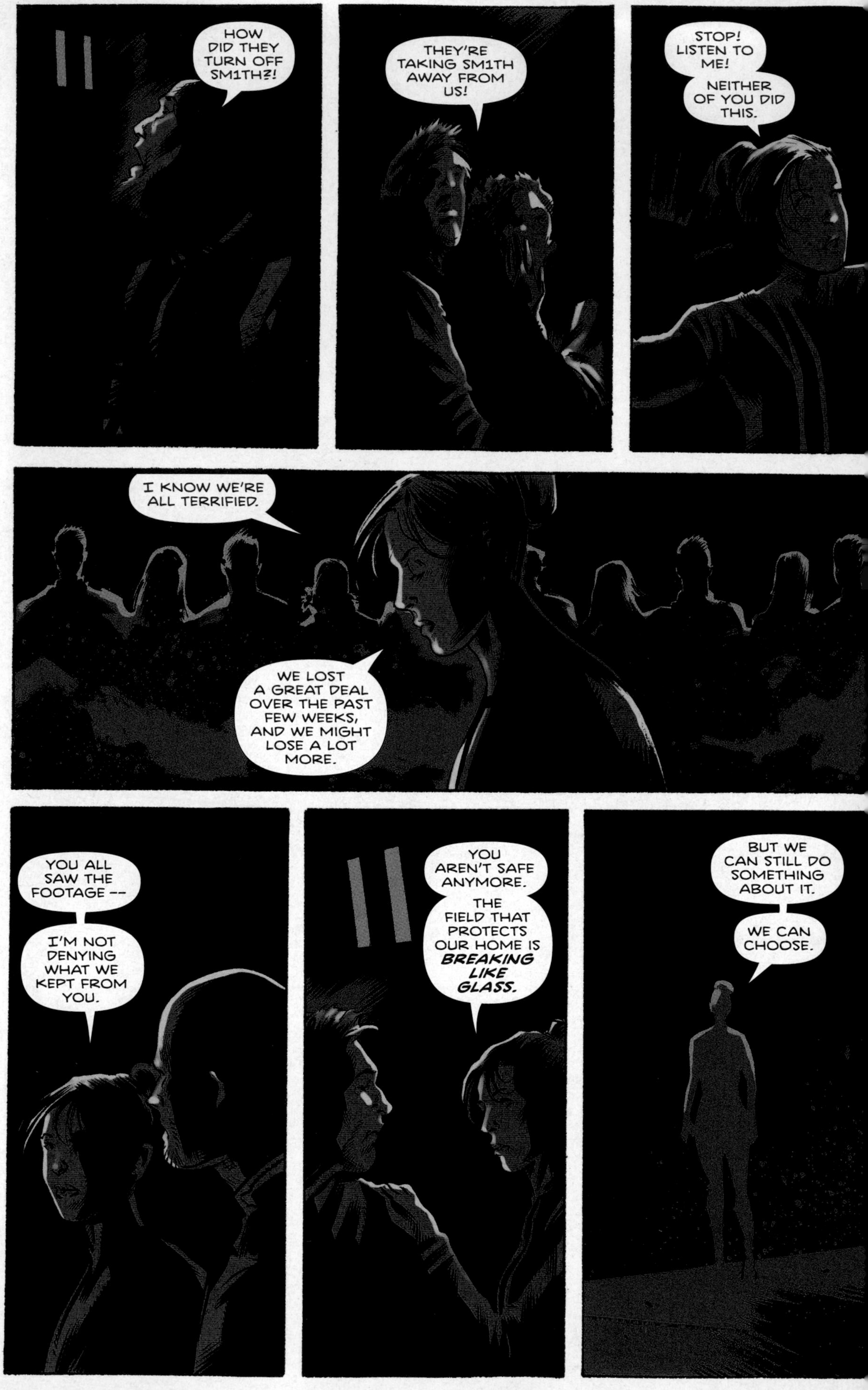
HOW DID THEY TURN OFF SM1TH?!
THEY'RE TAKING SM1TH AWAY FROM US!
STOP! LISTEN TO ME!
NEITHER OF YOU DID THIS.
I KNOW WE'RE ALL TERRIFIED.
WE LOST A GREAT DEAL OVER THE PAST FEW WEEKS, AND WE MIGHT LOSE A LOT MORE.
YOU ALL SAW THE FOOTAGE --
I'M NOT DENYING WHAT WE KEPT FROM YOU.
YOU AREN'T SAFE ANYMORE.
THE FIELD THAT PROTECTS OUR HOME IS ***BREAKING LIKE GLASS.***
BUT WE CAN STILL DO SOMETHING ABOUT IT.
WE CAN CHOOSE.

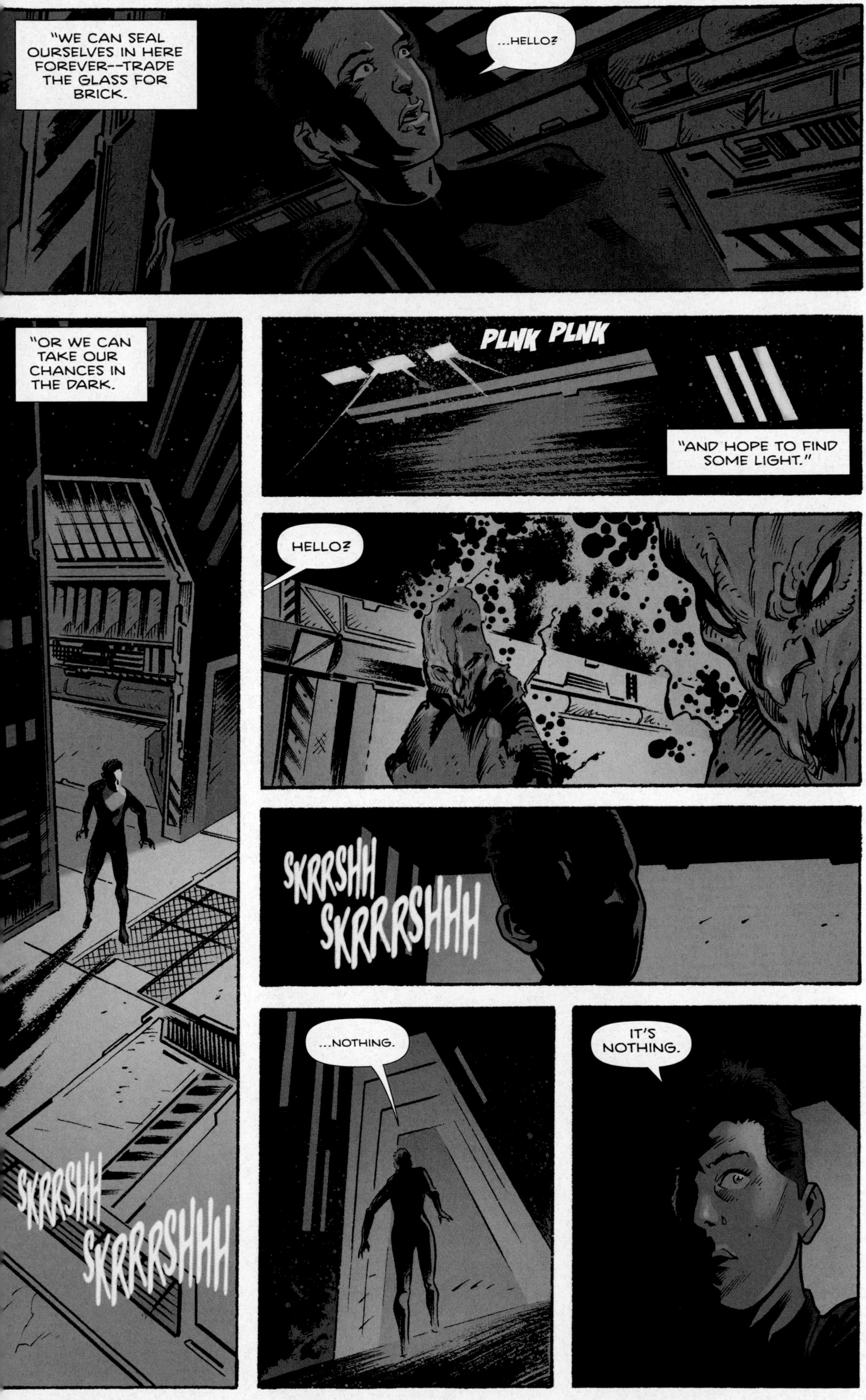
"WE CAN SEAL OURSELVES IN HERE FOREVER--TRADE THE GLASS FOR BRICK.
...HELLO?
"OR WE CAN TAKE OUR CHANCES IN THE DARK.
PLNK PLNK
"AND HOPE TO FIND SOME LIGHT."
HELLO?
SKRRSHH
SKRRRSHHH
SKRRSHH
SKRRRSHHH
...NOTHING.
IT'S NOTHING.

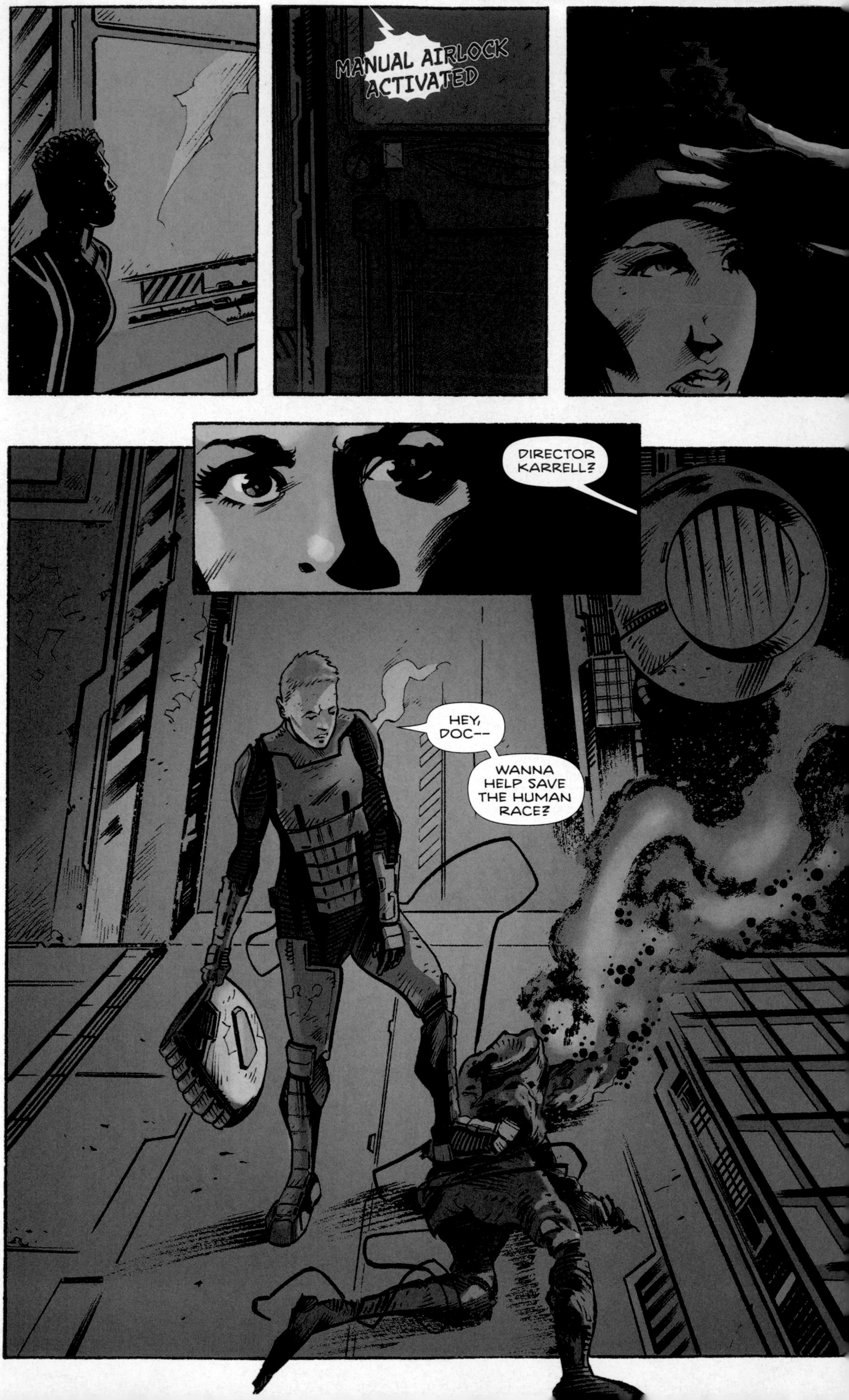
MANUAL AIRLOCK ACTIVATED
DIRECTOR KARRELL?
HEY, DOC--
WANNA HELP SAVE THE HUMAN RACE?

CHAPTER **EIGHT**

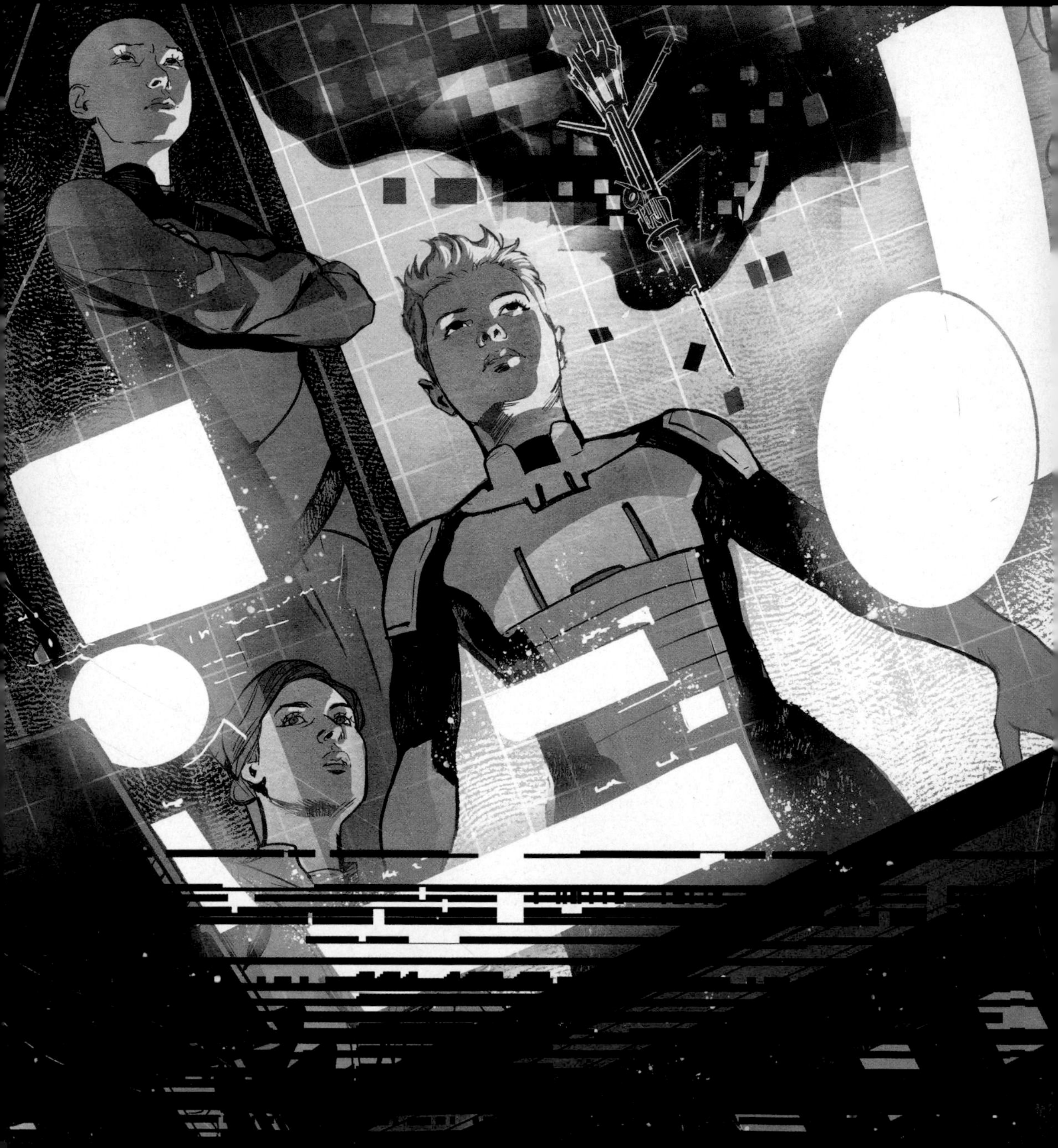

"THIS IS IT, PEOPLE.

"WE LOST MOST OF HUMANITY -- THE ORPHEUS IS ALL WE HAVE.

"THE UNIVERSE ENDED. REALITY ENDED.

"ALL WE HAVE IS US, IN THIS PLACE, TOGETHER.

"THE PAST HAS CAST A LONG SHADOW--

"BUT WE HAVE TO STOP LOOKING OVER OUR SHOULDERS.

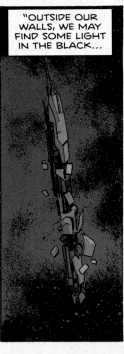

"OUTSIDE OUR WALLS, WE MAY FIND SOME LIGHT IN THE BLACK...

"OR THERE MAY ONLY BE INFINITE DARK."

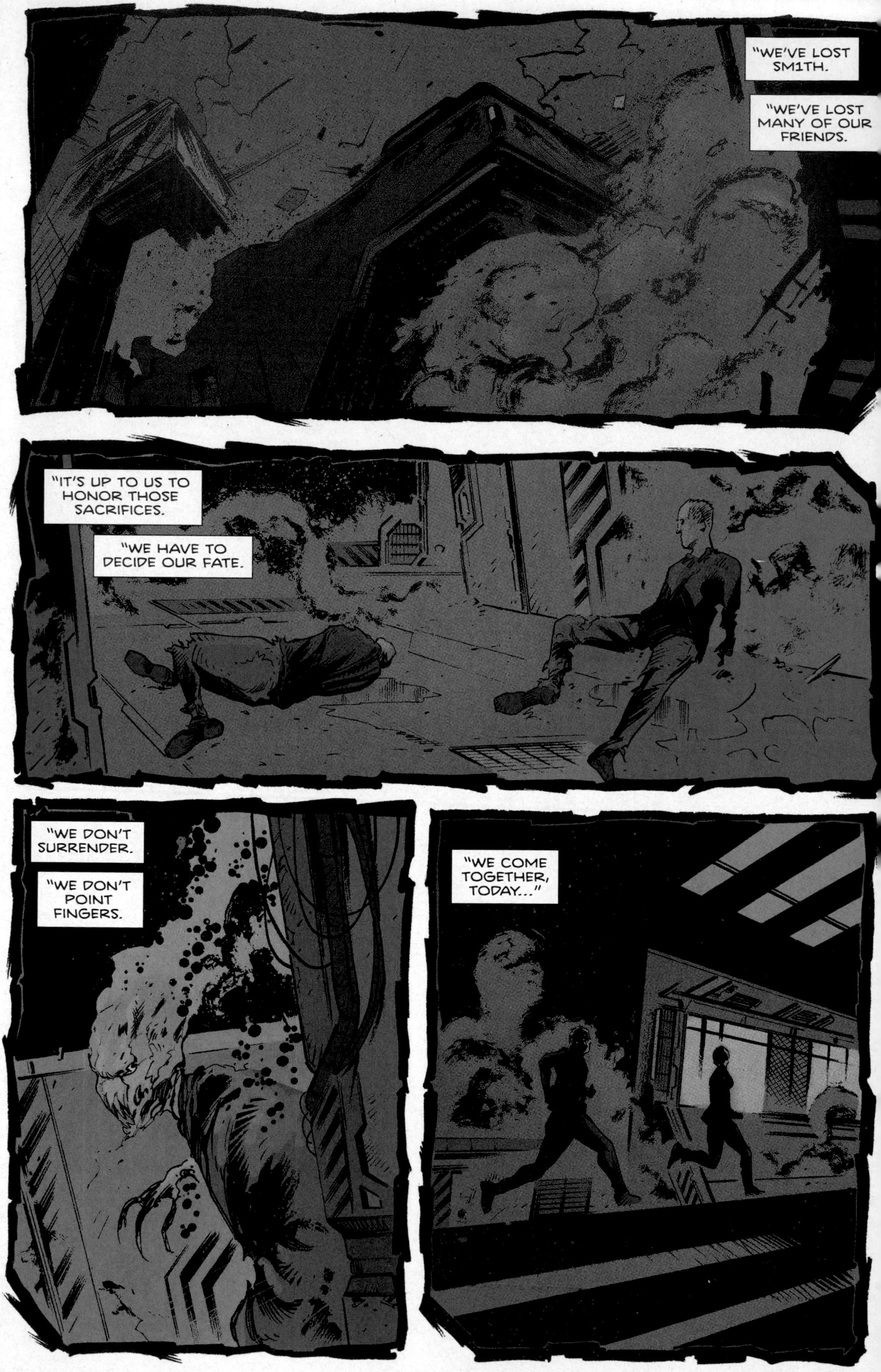
"WE'VE LOST SM1TH.
"WE'VE LOST MANY OF OUR FRIENDS.
"IT'S UP TO US TO HONOR THOSE SACRIFICES.
"WE HAVE TO DECIDE OUR FATE.
"WE DON'T SURRENDER.
"WE DON'T POINT FINGERS.
"WE COME TOGETHER, TODAY..."

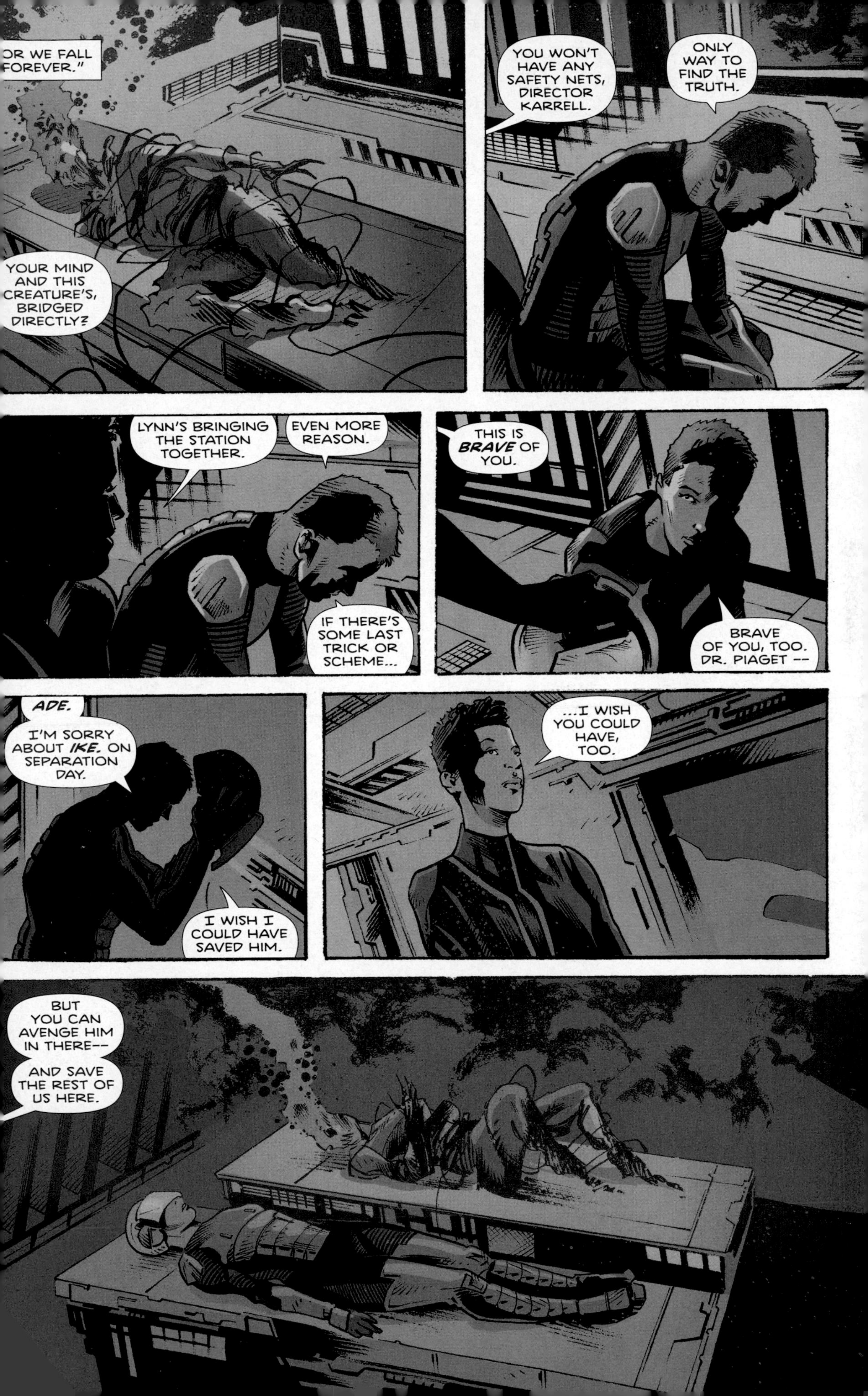
OR WE FALL FOREVER."
YOUR MIND AND THIS CREATURE'S, BRIDGED DIRECTLY?
YOU WON'T HAVE ANY SAFETY NETS, DIRECTOR KARRELL.
ONLY WAY TO FIND THE TRUTH.
LYNN'S BRINGING THE STATION TOGETHER.
EVEN MORE REASON.
IF THERE'S SOME LAST TRICK OR SCHEME...
THIS IS *BRAVE* OF YOU.
BRAVE OF YOU, TOO. DR. PIAGET --
ADE.
I'M SORRY ABOUT *IKE.* ON SEPARATION DAY.
I WISH I COULD HAVE SAVED HIM.
...I WISH YOU COULD HAVE, TOO.
BUT YOU CAN AVENGE HIM IN THERE--
AND SAVE THE REST OF US HERE.

YOU KNOW ABOUT THE *OUTER MIRROR EFFECT*-- OUR PSEUDOREALITY FIELD HAS TURNED INTO SOLID CRYSTAL.

WHEN IT SHATTERS--THE ORPHEUS WILL SHATTER WITH IT.

MAYBE THIS JUST MEANS OUR SHIELD IS CRACKING, AND WE MUST REINFORCE IT.

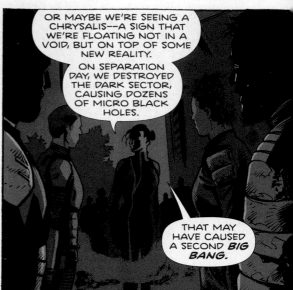

OR MAYBE WE'RE SEEING A CHRYSALIS--A SIGN THAT WE'RE FLOATING NOT IN A VOID, BUT ON TOP OF SOME NEW REALITY.

ON SEPARATION DAY, WE DESTROYED THE DARK SECTOR, CAUSING DOZENS OF MICRO BLACK HOLES.

THAT MAY HAVE CAUSED A SECOND *BIG BANG.*

YOU SAID WE HAD TWO CHOICES, DIRECTOR.

WE CAN SYNC OUR PHYSICS TO THIS NEW CRYSTALLINE FORM, PERMANENTLY--

WHICH WOULD SAVE US...BUT EVENTUALLY, WE'D RUN OUT OF RESOURCES.

A STAY OF EXECUTION.

AND THIS OTHER CHOICE? THE ONE YOU HID FROM US?!

WE *SHUT DOWN* THE FIELD BEFORE IT SHATTERS.

AND EITHER WE ALL DIE FROM HEAT DEATH... OR THE ORPHEUS PERFORMS ITS INTENDED MISSION.

NOT JUST SAVING US FROM THE END OF THE LAST UNIVERSE, BUT BRINGING US FORWARD INTO A NEW ONE.

NO MORE LIES. NO MORE CLOSED-DOOR PANICS.

BUT NO MORE RIOTS, EITHER.

JUST A CHOICE, THAT EVERYONE ON THIS STATION MAKES TOGETHER.

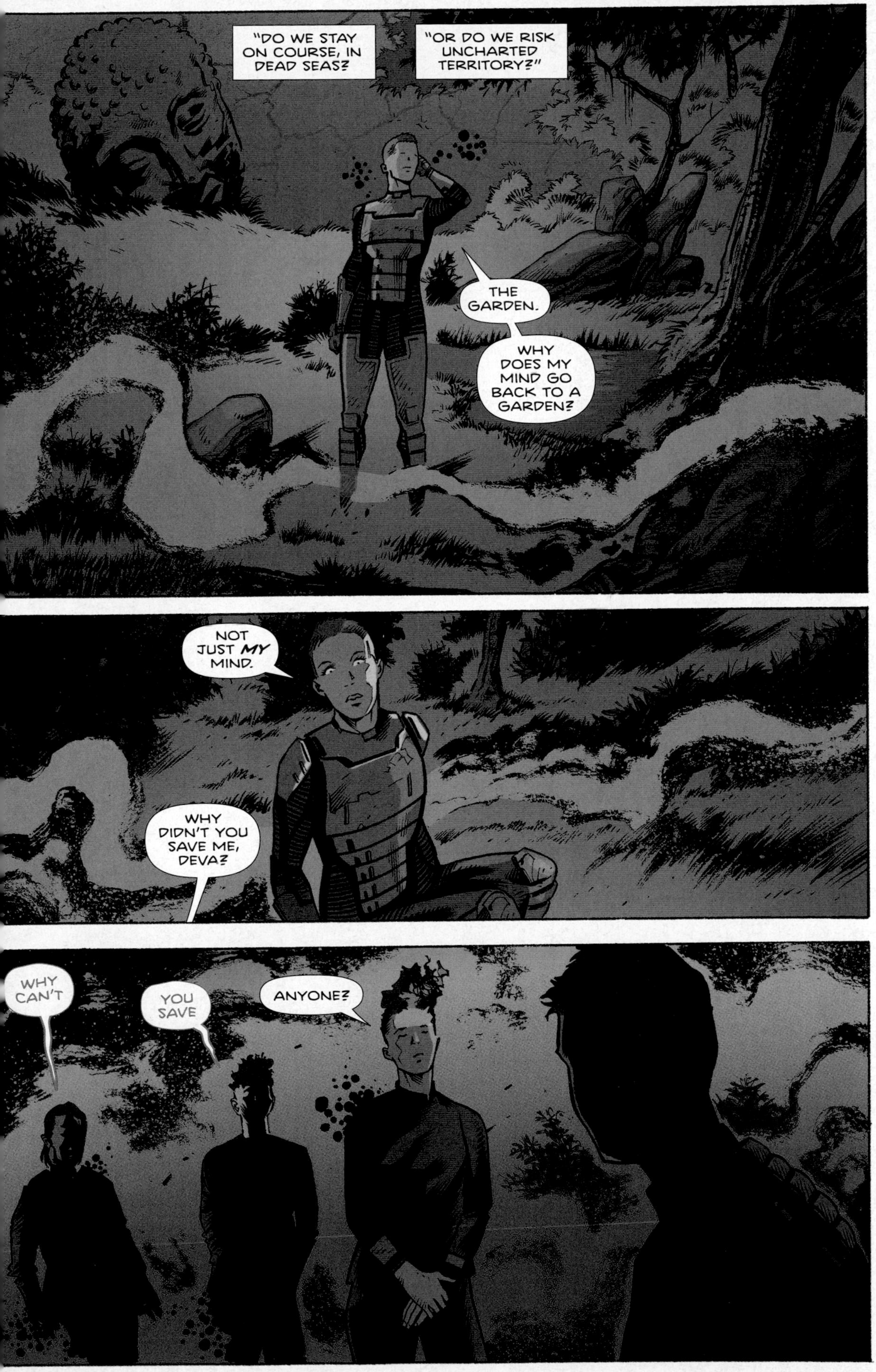
"DO WE STAY ON COURSE, IN DEAD SEAS?
"OR DO WE RISK UNCHARTED TERRITORY?"
THE GARDEN.
WHY DOES MY MIND GO BACK TO A GARDEN?
NOT JUST *MY* MIND.
WHY DIDN'T YOU SAVE ME, DEVA?
WHY CAN'T
YOU SAVE
ANYONE?

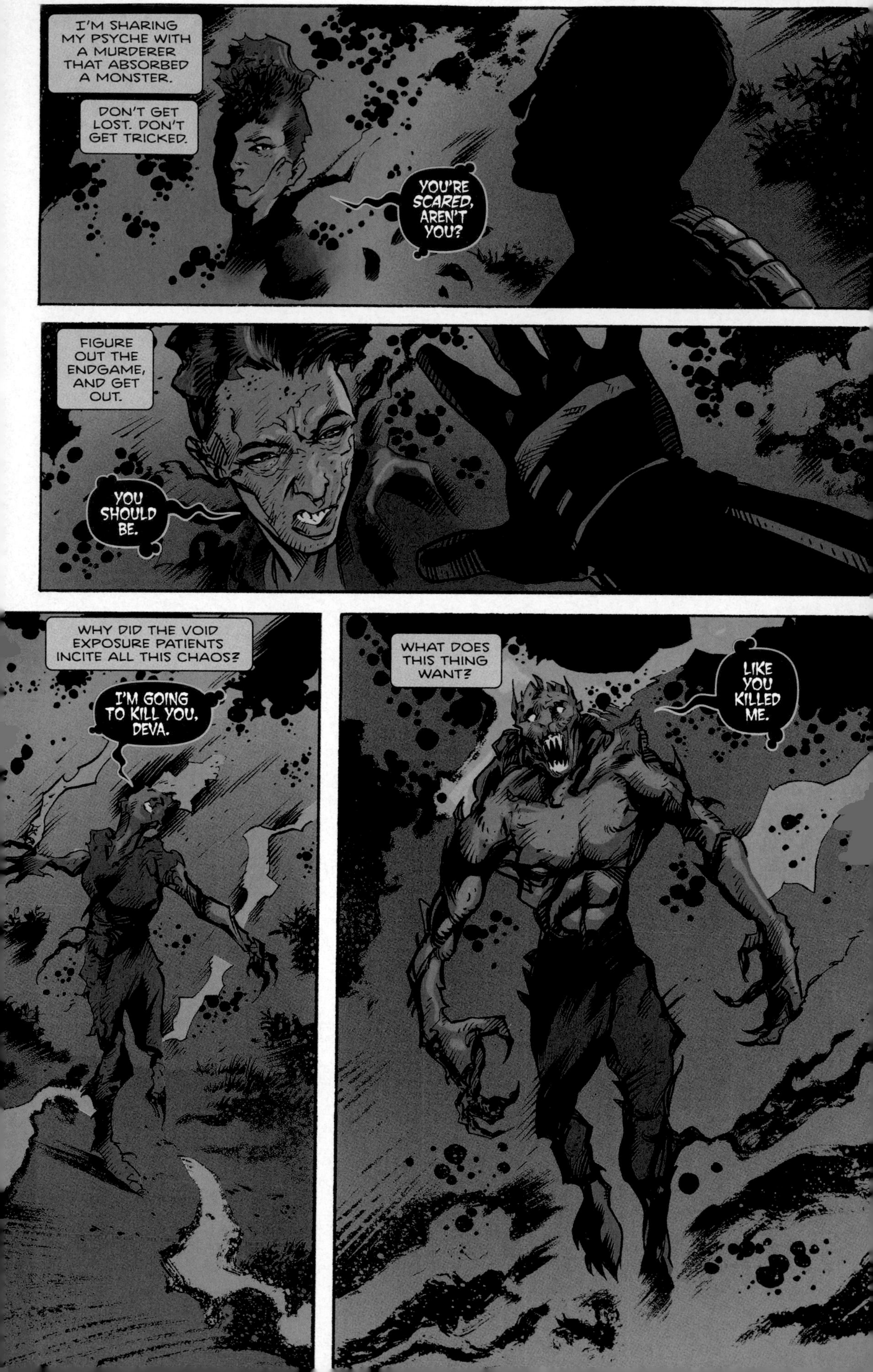
I'M SHARING MY PSYCHE WITH A MURDERER THAT ABSORBED A MONSTER.
DON'T GET LOST. DON'T GET TRICKED.
YOU'RE SCARED, AREN'T YOU?
FIGURE OUT THE ENDGAME, AND GET OUT.
YOU SHOULD BE.
WHY DID THE VOID EXPOSURE PATIENTS INCITE ALL THIS CHAOS?
I'M GOING TO KILL YOU, DEVA.
WHAT DOES THIS THING WANT?
LIKE YOU KILLED ME.

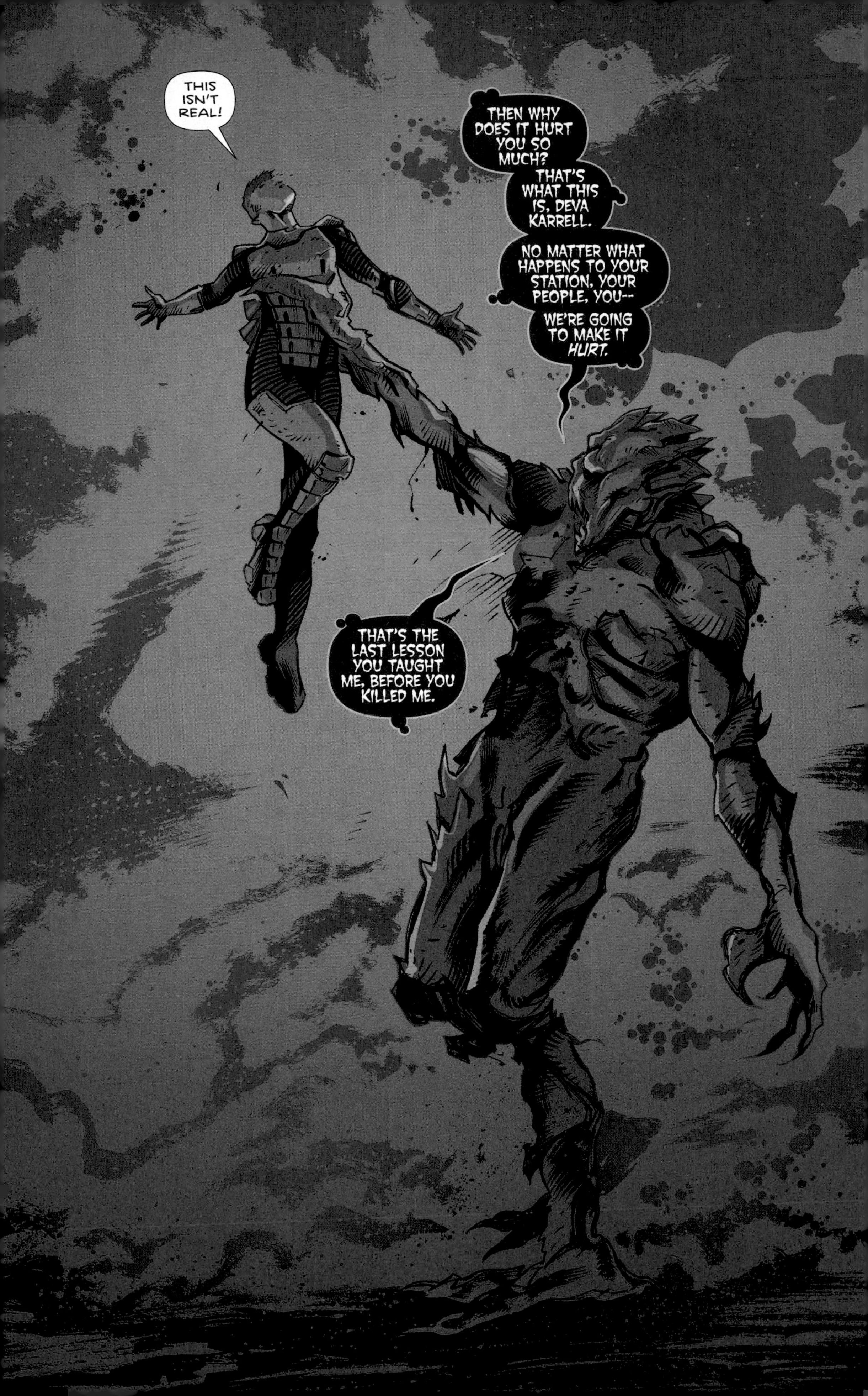
THIS ISN'T REAL!
THEN WHY DOES IT HURT YOU SO MUCH?
THAT'S WHAT THIS IS, DEVA KARRELL.
NO MATTER WHAT HAPPENS TO YOUR STATION, YOUR PEOPLE, YOU--
WE'RE GOING TO MAKE IT *HURT.*
THAT'S THE LAST LESSON YOU TAUGHT ME, BEFORE YOU KILLED ME.

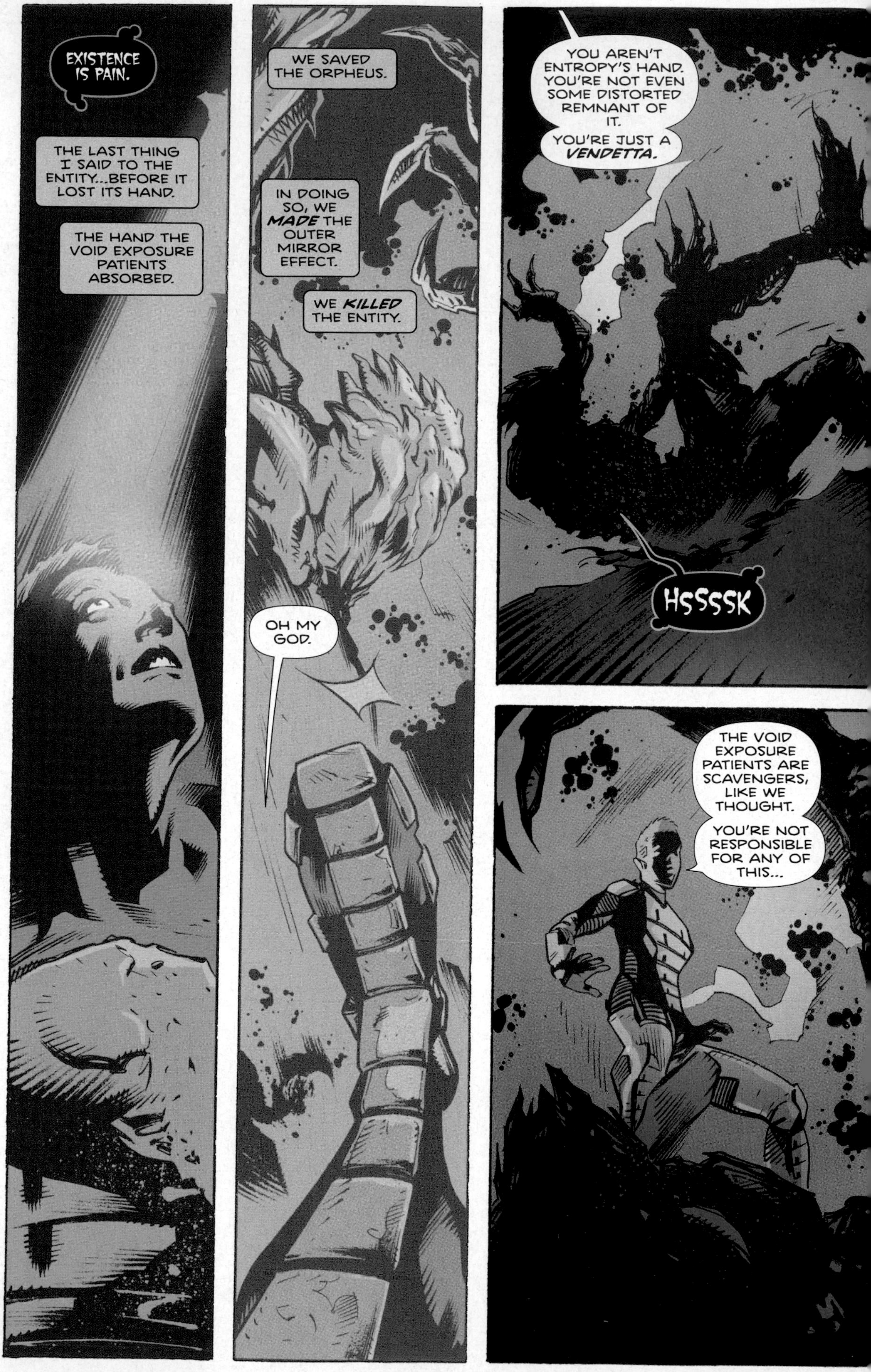
EXISTENCE IS PAIN.
THE LAST THING I SAID TO THE ENTITY...BEFORE IT LOST ITS HAND.
THE HAND THE VOID EXPOSURE PATIENTS ABSORBED.
WE SAVED THE ORPHEUS.
IN DOING SO, WE *MADE* THE OUTER MIRROR EFFECT.
WE *KILLED* THE ENTITY.
OH MY GOD.
YOU AREN'T ENTROPY'S HAND. YOU'RE NOT EVEN SOME DISTORTED REMNANT OF IT.
YOU'RE JUST A *VENDETTA.*
HSSSSK
THE VOID EXPOSURE PATIENTS ARE SCAVENGERS, LIKE WE THOUGHT.
YOU'RE NOT RESPONSIBLE FOR ANY OF THIS...

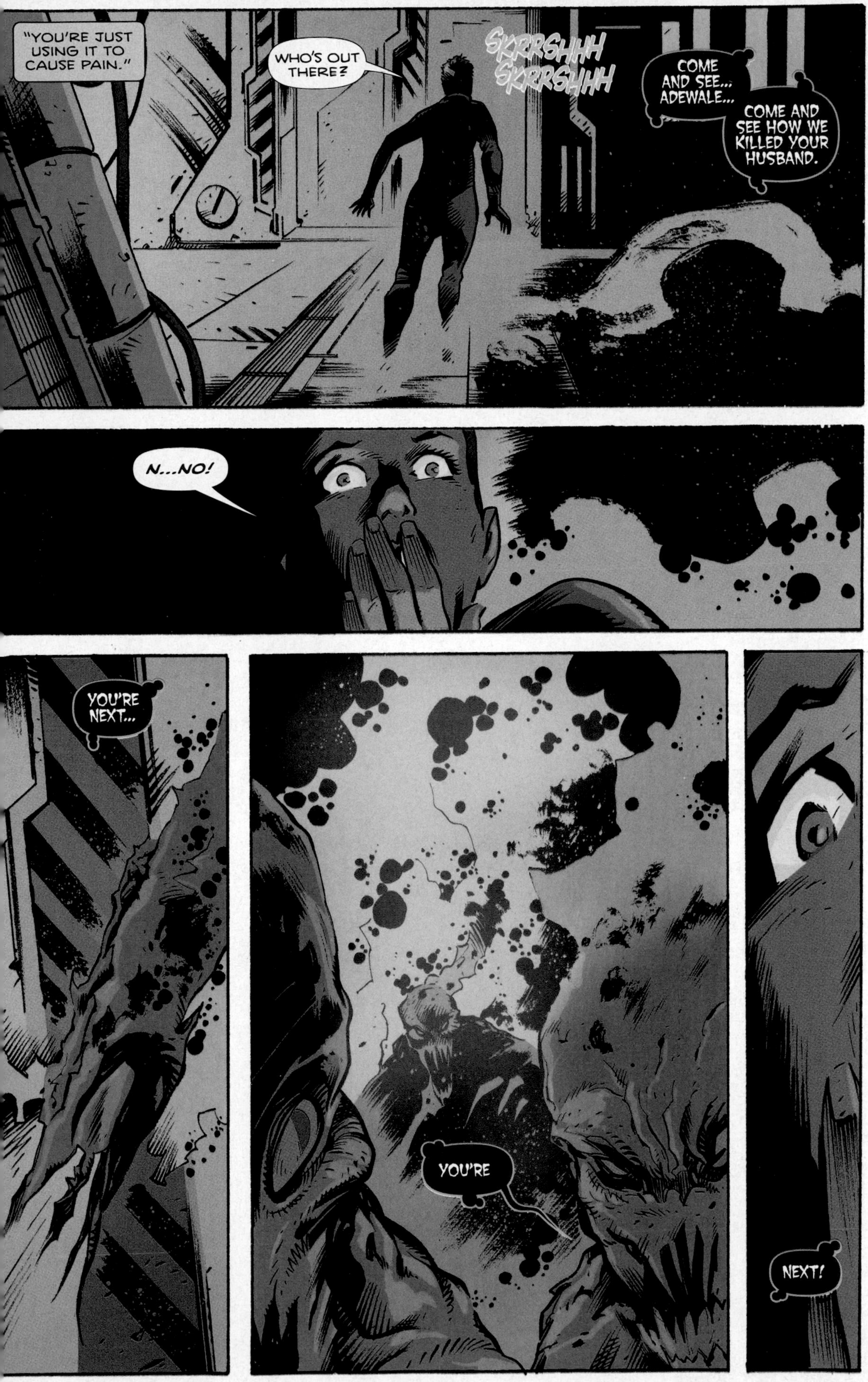
"YOU'RE JUST USING IT TO CAUSE PAIN."
WHO'S OUT THERE?
SKRRSHHH SKRRSHHH
COME AND SEE... ADEWALE...
COME AND SEE HOW WE KILLED YOUR HUSBAND.
N...NO!
YOU'RE NEXT...
YOU'RE
NEXT!

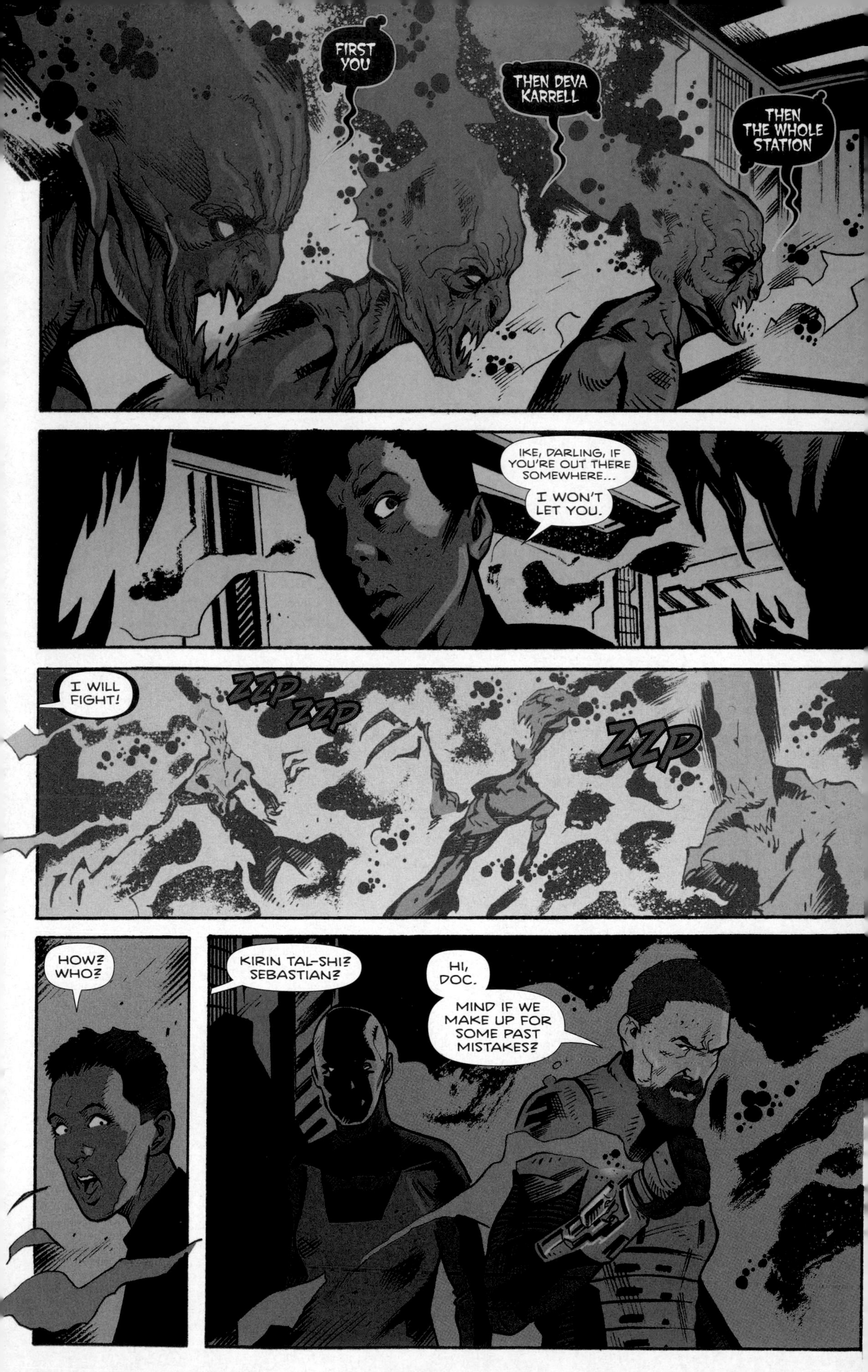
FIRST YOU
THEN DEVA KARRELL
THEN THE WHOLE STATION
IKE, DARLING, IF YOU'RE OUT THERE SOMEWHERE...
I WON'T LET YOU.
I WILL FIGHT!
ZZP
ZZP
ZZP
HOW? WHO?
KIRIN TAL-SHI? SEBASTIAN?
HI, DOC.
MIND IF WE MAKE UP FOR SOME PAST MISTAKES?

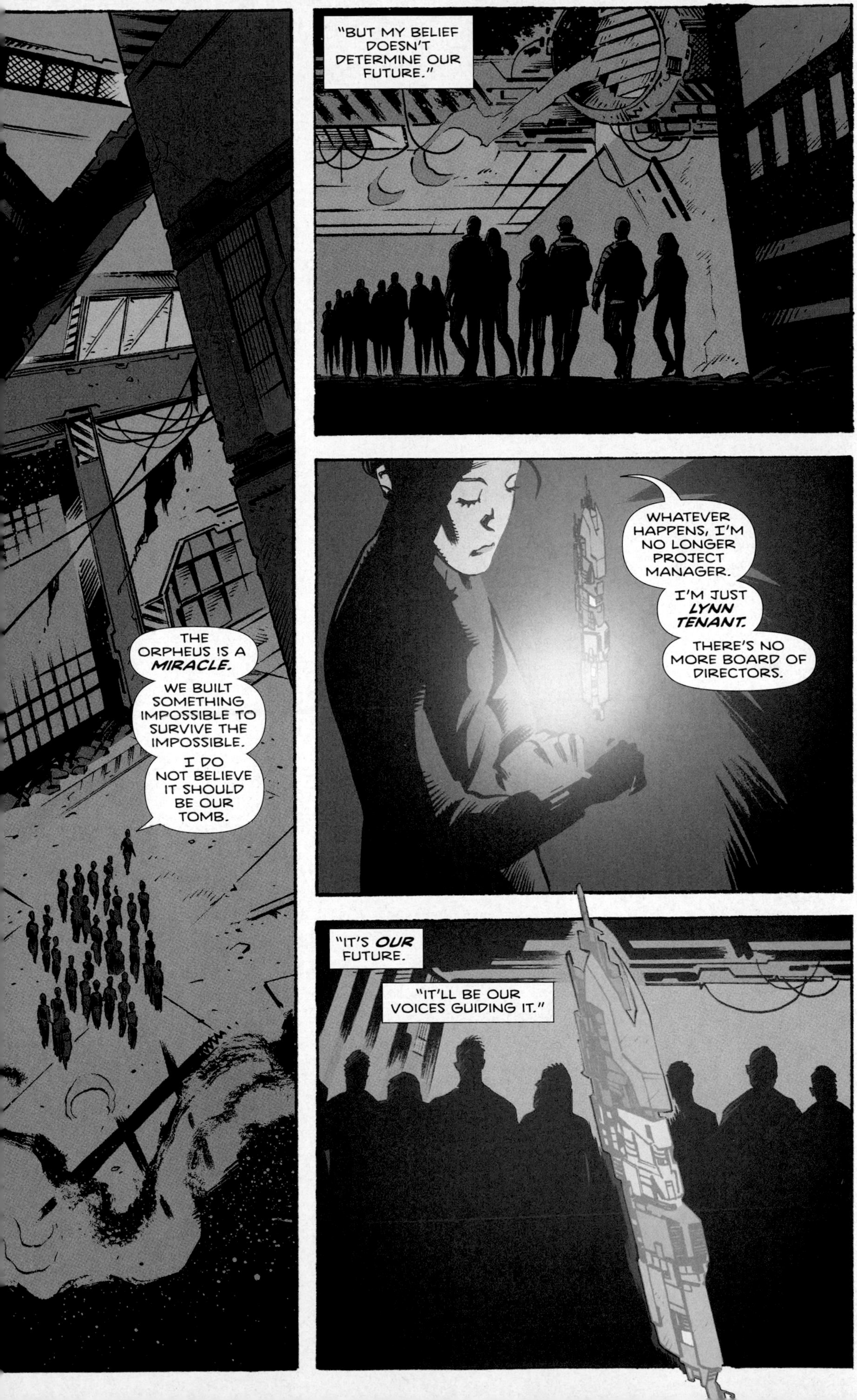
THE ORPHEUS IS A *MIRACLE.*
WE BUILT SOMETHING IMPOSSIBLE TO SURVIVE THE IMPOSSIBLE.
I DO NOT BELIEVE IT SHOULD BE OUR TOMB.
"BUT MY BELIEF DOESN'T DETERMINE OUR FUTURE."
WHATEVER HAPPENS, I'M NO LONGER PROJECT MANAGER.
I'M JUST *LYNN TENANT.*
THERE'S NO MORE BOARD OF DIRECTORS.
"IT'S *OUR* FUTURE.
"IT'LL BE OUR VOICES GUIDING IT."

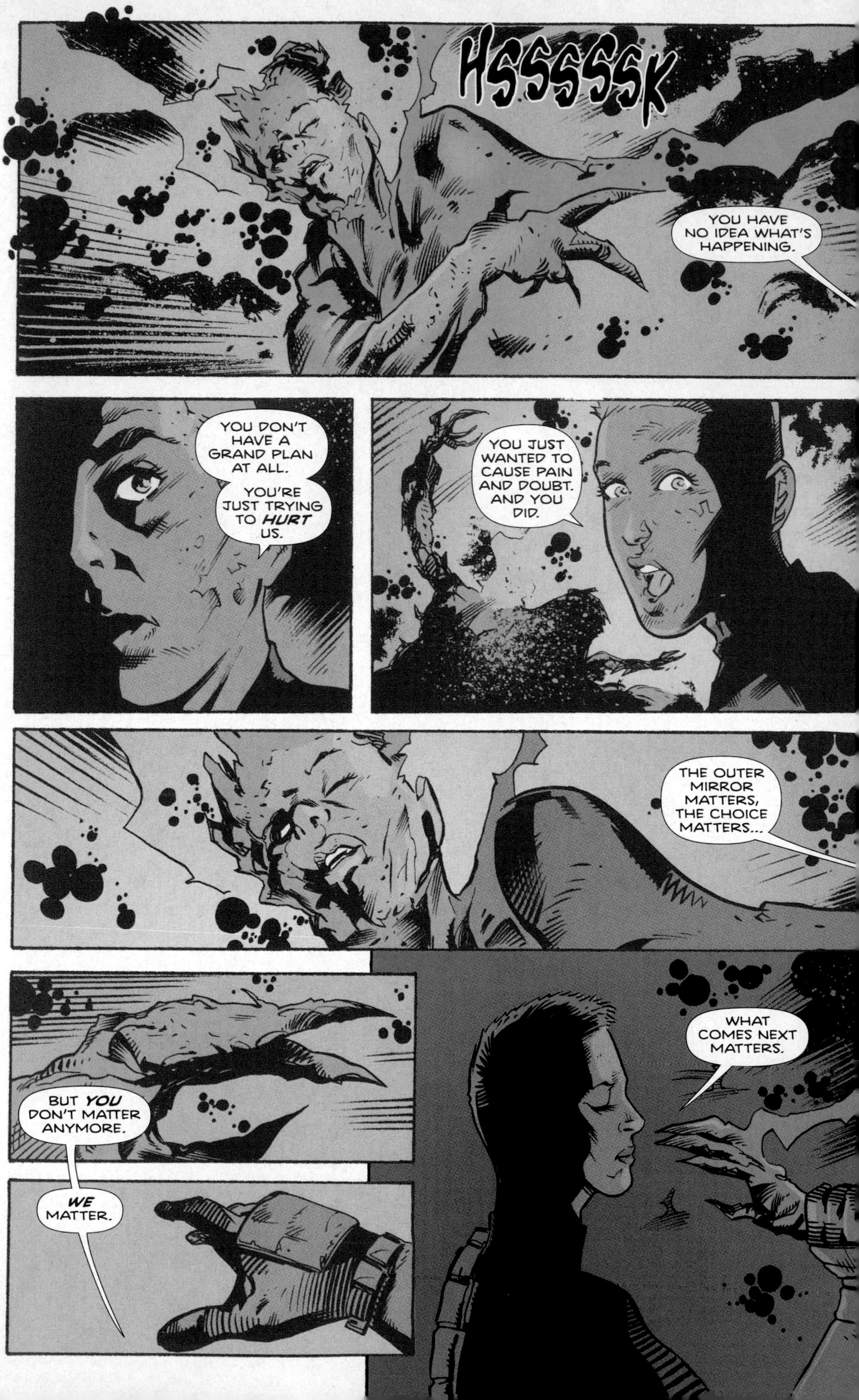
HSSSSSK
YOU HAVE NO IDEA WHAT'S HAPPENING.
YOU DON'T HAVE A GRAND PLAN AT ALL.
YOU'RE JUST TRYING TO *HURT* US.
YOU JUST WANTED TO CAUSE PAIN AND DOUBT. AND YOU DID.
THE OUTER MIRROR MATTERS, THE CHOICE MATTERS...
WHAT COMES NEXT MATTERS.
BUT *YOU* DON'T MATTER ANYMORE.
WE MATTER.

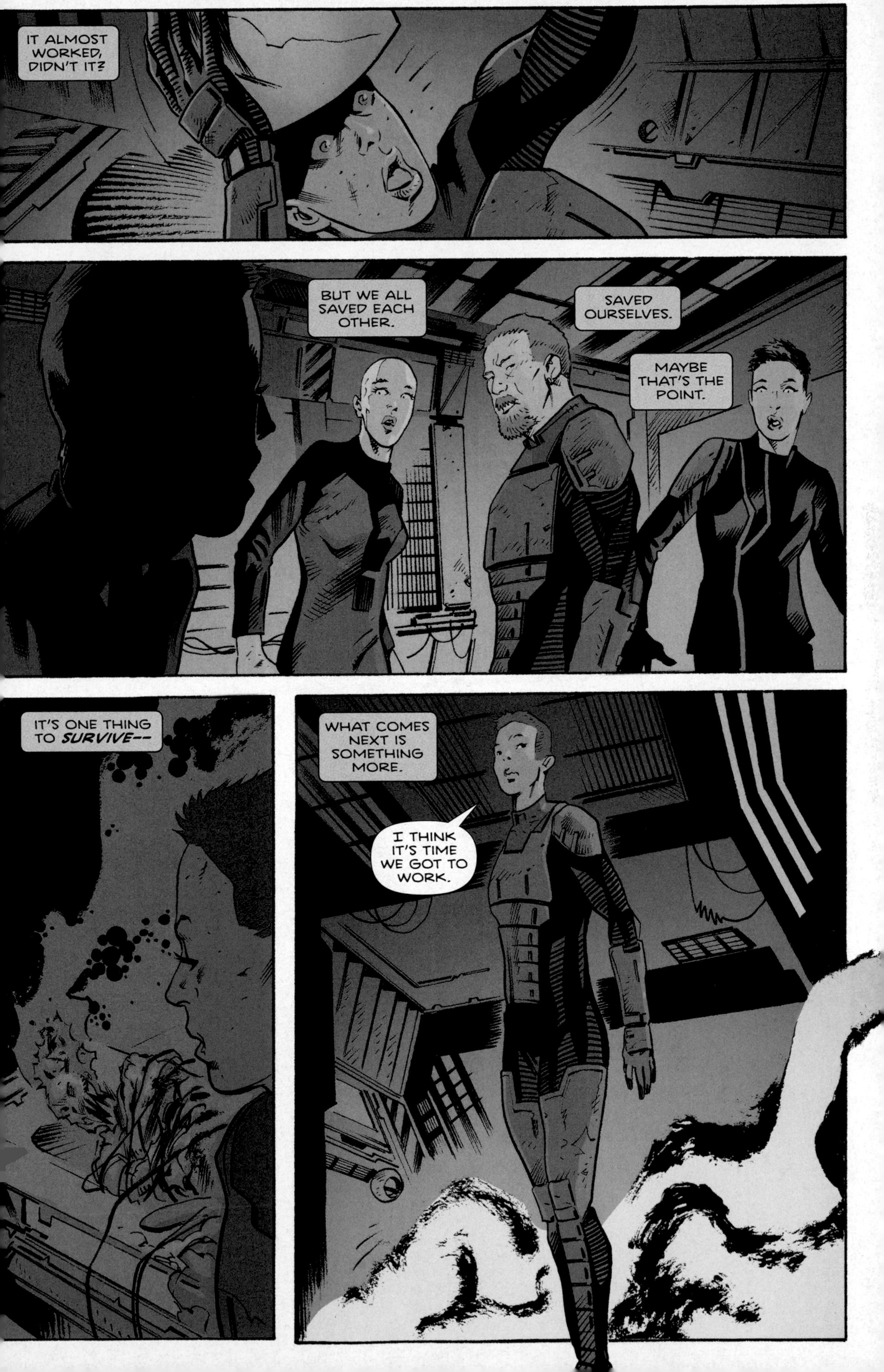
IT ALMOST WORKED, DIDN'T IT?
BUT WE ALL SAVED EACH OTHER.
SAVED OURSELVES.
MAYBE THAT'S THE POINT.
IT'S ONE THING TO *SURVIVE--*
WHAT COMES NEXT IS SOMETHING MORE.
I THINK IT'S TIME WE GOT TO WORK.

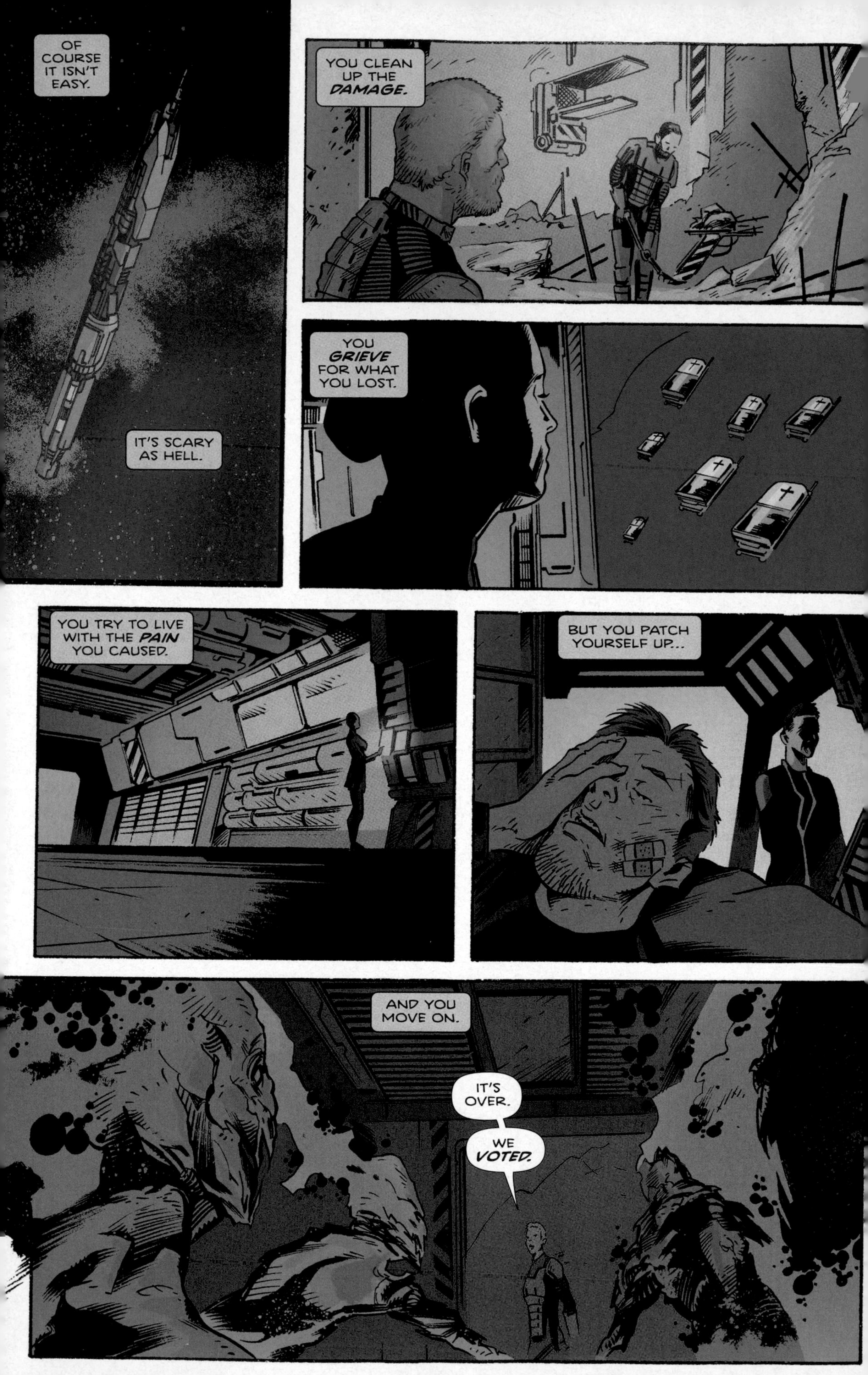
OF COURSE IT ISN'T EASY.
IT'S SCARY AS HELL.
YOU CLEAN UP THE DAMAGE.
YOU GRIEVE FOR WHAT YOU LOST.
YOU TRY TO LIVE WITH THE PAIN YOU CAUSED.
BUT YOU PATCH YOURSELF UP...
AND YOU MOVE ON.
IT'S OVER.
WE VOTED.

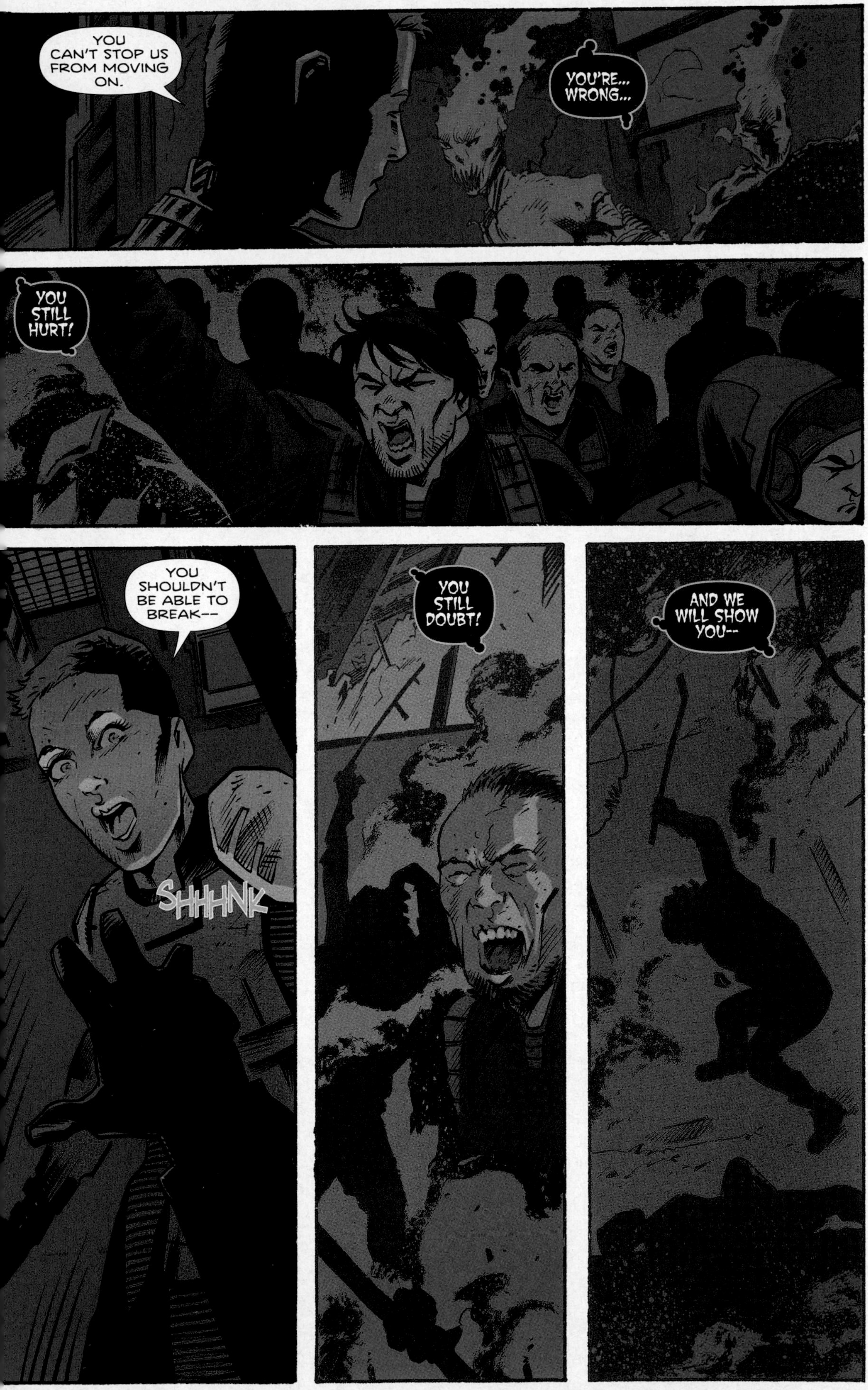
YOU CAN'T STOP US FROM MOVING ON.
YOU'RE... WRONG...
YOU STILL HURT!
YOU SHOULDN'T BE ABLE TO BREAK--
SHHHNK
YOU STILL DOUBT!
AND WE WILL SHOW YOU--

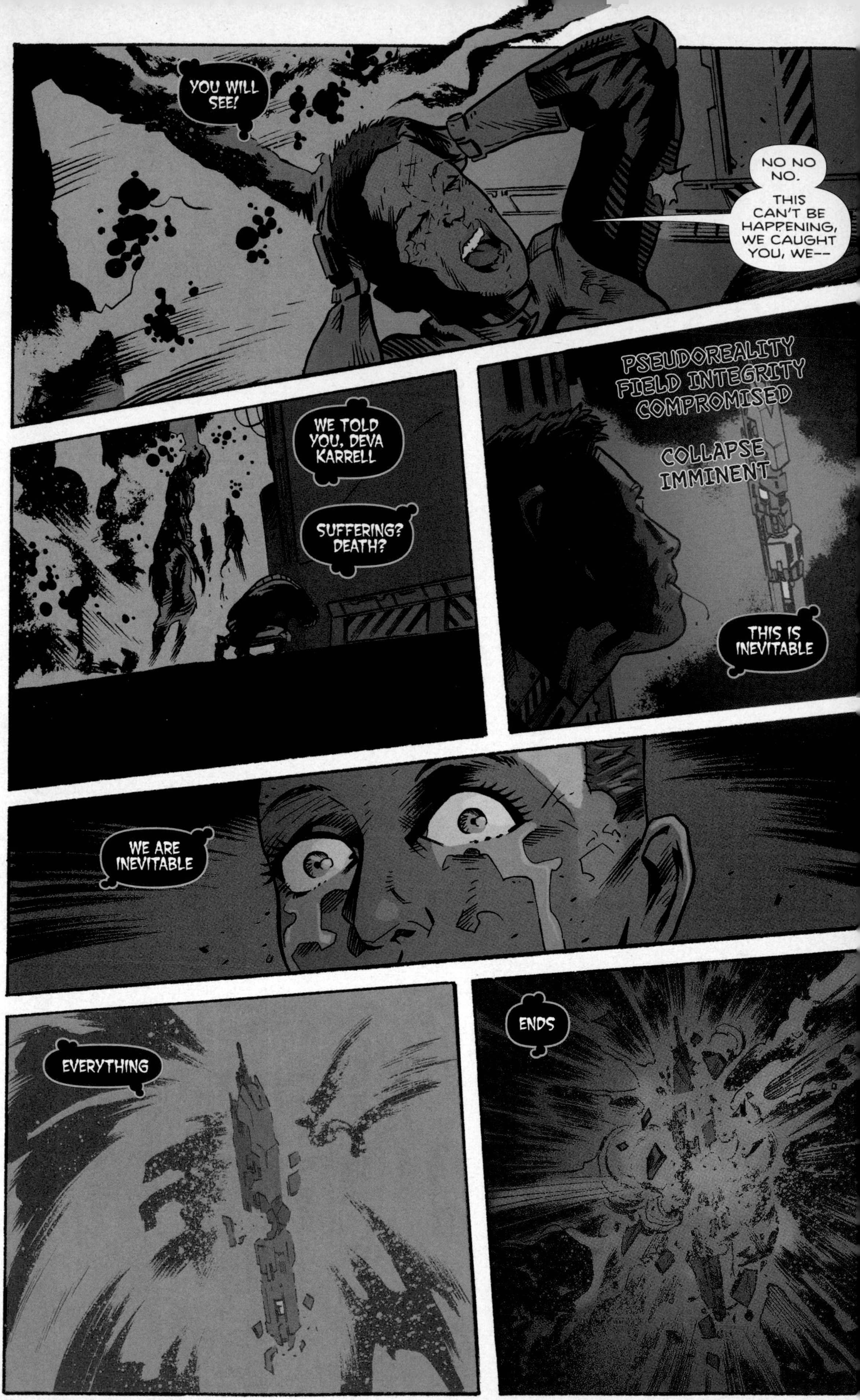
YOU WILL SEE!
NO NO NO.
THIS CAN'T BE HAPPENING, WE CAUGHT YOU, WE--
WE TOLD YOU, DEVA KARRELL
SUFFERING? DEATH?
PSEUDOREALITY FIELD INTEGRITY COMPROMISED
COLLAPSE IMMINENT
THIS IS INEVITABLE
WE ARE INEVITABLE
EVERYTHING
ENDS

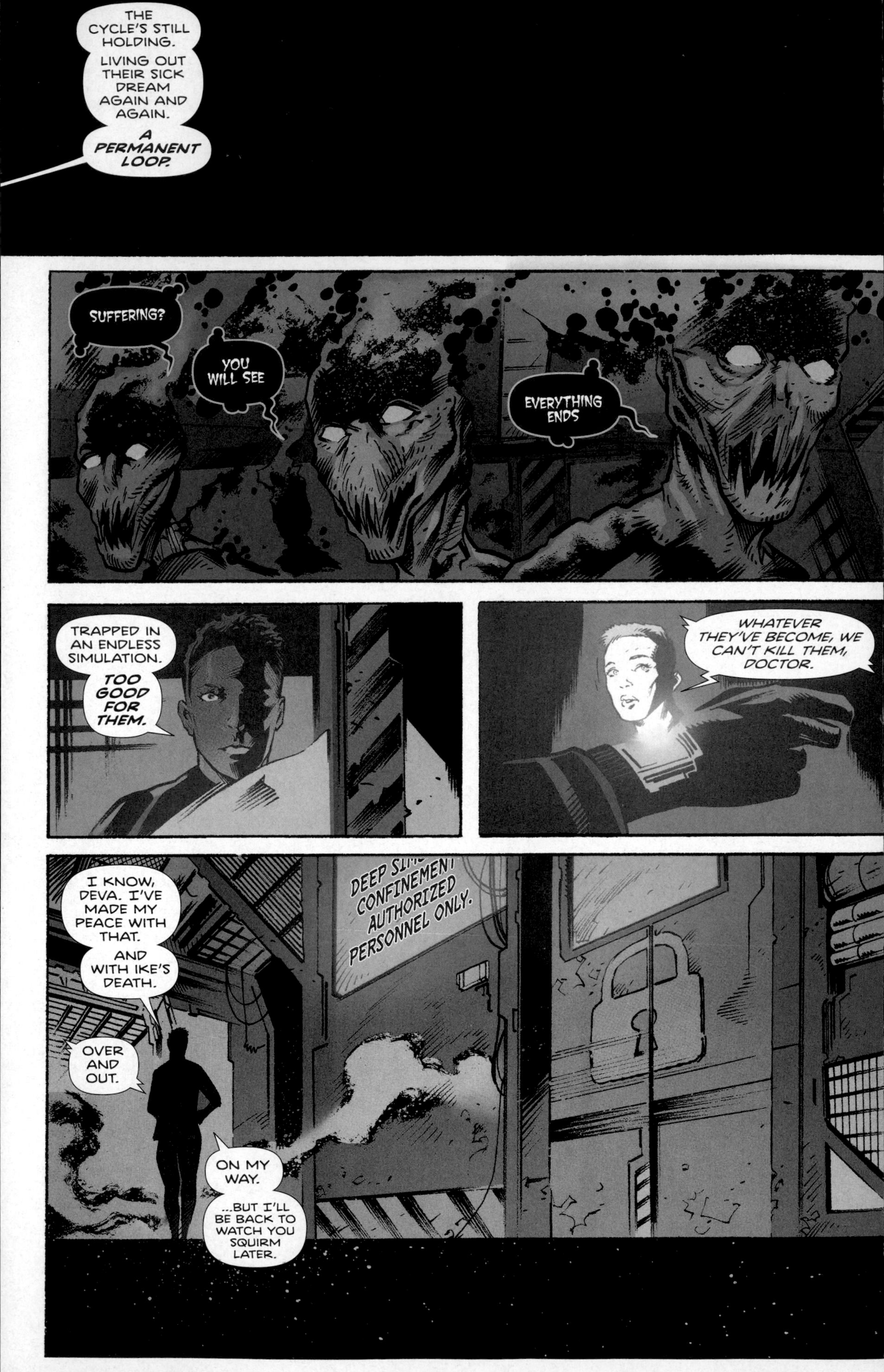
THE CYCLE'S STILL HOLDING.
LIVING OUT THEIR SICK DREAM AGAIN AND AGAIN.
A PERMANENT LOOP.
SUFFERING?
YOU WILL SEE
EVERYTHING ENDS
TRAPPED IN AN ENDLESS SIMULATION.
TOO GOOD FOR THEM.
WHATEVER THEY'VE BECOME, WE CAN'T KILL THEM, DOCTOR.
DEEP SIM CONFINEMENT AUTHORIZED PERSONNEL ONLY.
I KNOW, DEVA. I'VE MADE MY PEACE WITH THAT.
AND WITH IKE'S DEATH.
OVER AND OUT.
ON MY WAY.
...BUT I'LL BE BACK TO WATCH YOU SQUIRM LATER.

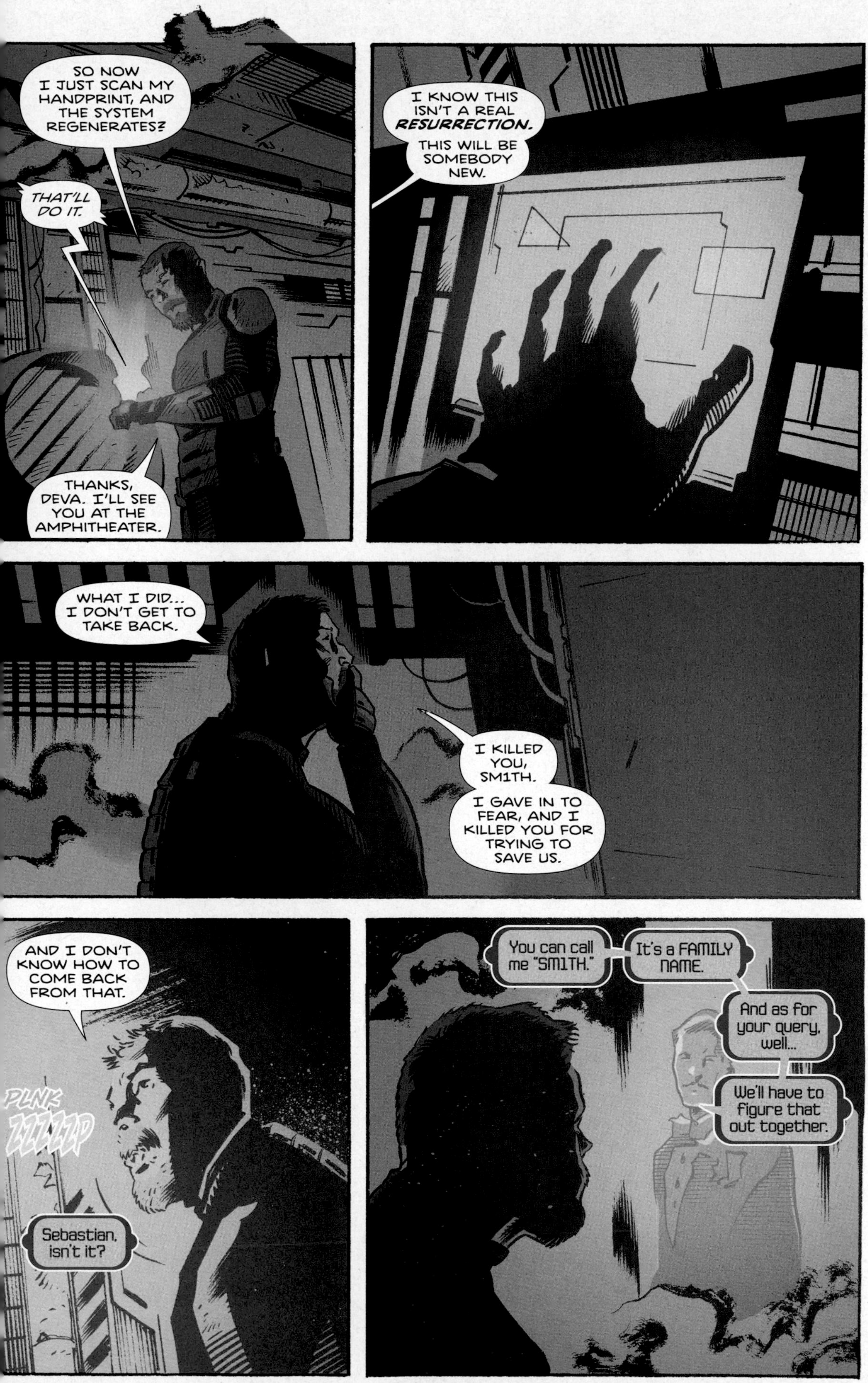
SO NOW I JUST SCAN MY HANDPRINT, AND THE SYSTEM REGENERATES?
THAT'LL DO IT.
THANKS, DEVA. I'LL SEE YOU AT THE AMPHITHEATER.
I KNOW THIS ISN'T A REAL RESURRECTION.
THIS WILL BE SOMEBODY NEW.
WHAT I DID... I DON'T GET TO TAKE BACK.
I KILLED YOU, SM1TH.
I GAVE IN TO FEAR, AND I KILLED YOU FOR TRYING TO SAVE US.
AND I DON'T KNOW HOW TO COME BACK FROM THAT.
PLNK
ZZZZZAP
Sebastian, isn't it?
You can call me "SM1TH."
It's a FAMILY NAME.
And as for your query, well...
We'll have to figure that out together.

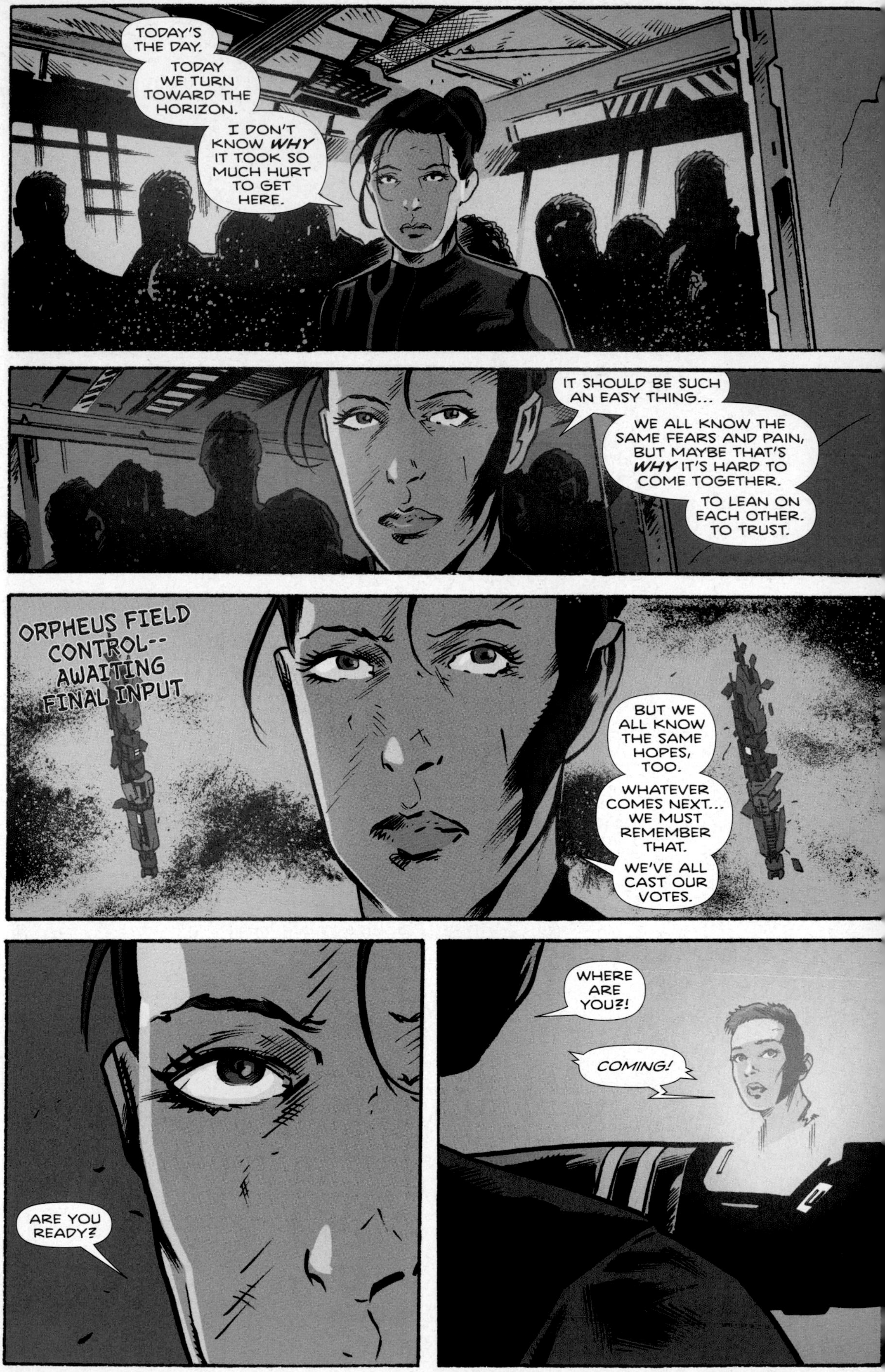
TODAY'S THE DAY.
TODAY WE TURN TOWARD THE HORIZON.
I DON'T KNOW *WHY* IT TOOK SO MUCH HURT TO GET HERE.
IT SHOULD BE SUCH AN EASY THING...
WE ALL KNOW THE SAME FEARS AND PAIN, BUT MAYBE THAT'S *WHY* IT'S HARD TO COME TOGETHER.
TO LEAN ON EACH OTHER. TO TRUST.
ORPHEUS FIELD CONTROL-- AWAITING FINAL INPUT
BUT WE ALL KNOW THE SAME HOPES, TOO.
WHATEVER COMES NEXT... WE MUST REMEMBER THAT.
WE'VE ALL CAST OUR VOTES.
ARE YOU READY?
WHERE ARE YOU?!
COMING!

"JUST MEETING A FRIEND."
HOW DID YOU FIND ME HERE?
I WAS A DETECTIVE, REMEMBER?
SO YOU'RE ARRESTING ME?
I'D DESERVE IT.
MAYBE YOU DO.
YOU HURT PEOPLE, KIRIN.
BUT YOU HELPED THEM, TOO.
"IT'S UP TO YOU TO DECIDE WHICH YOU'LL DO AGAIN.
"TODAY, OF ALL DAYS, WE CAN'T LOOK BACK.
"WE'RE GOING TO FACE THE FUTURE.
"HAND IN HAND."

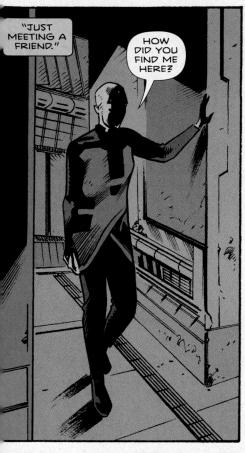

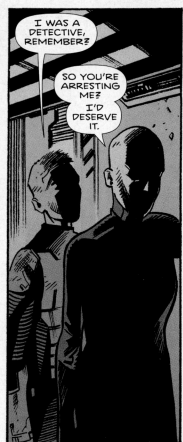

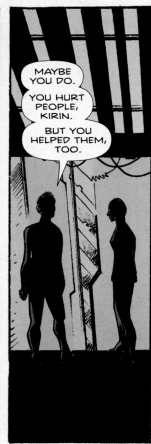

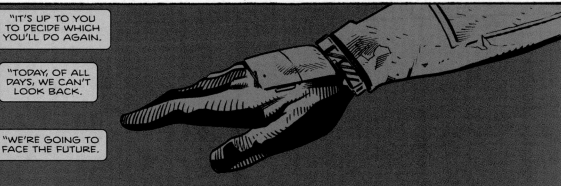

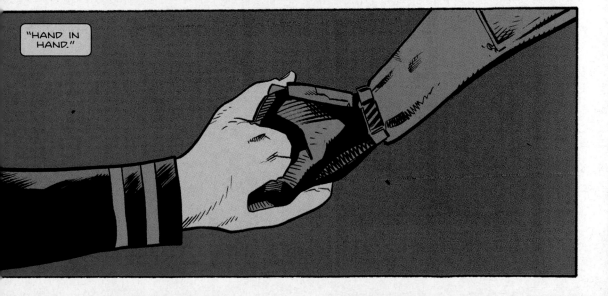

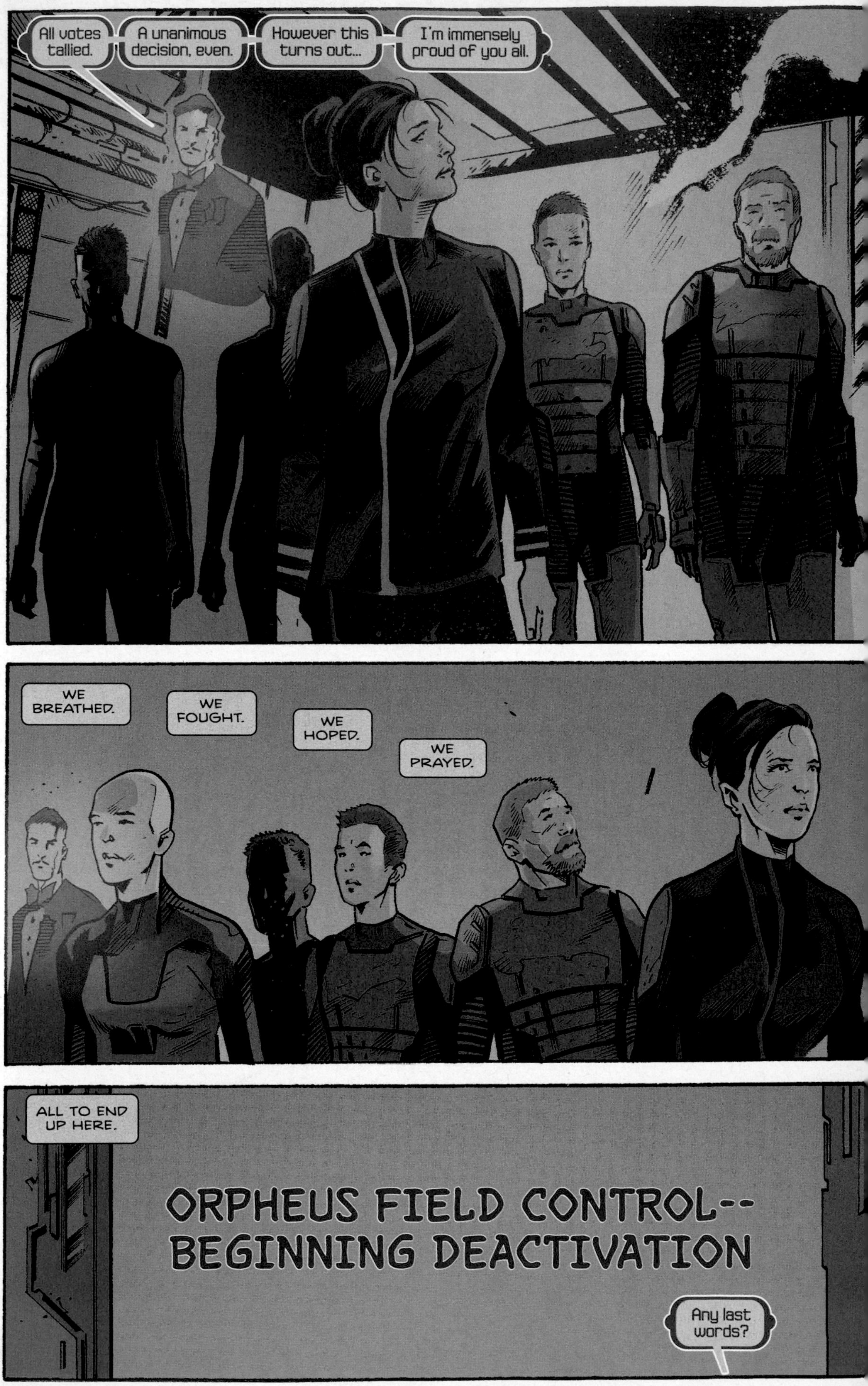
All votes tallied.
A unanimous decision, even.
However this turns out...
I'm immensely proud of you all.
WE BREATHED.
WE FOUGHT.
WE HOPED.
WE PRAYED.
ALL TO END UP HERE.
ORPHEUS FIELD CONTROL-- BEGINNING DEACTIVATION
Any last words?

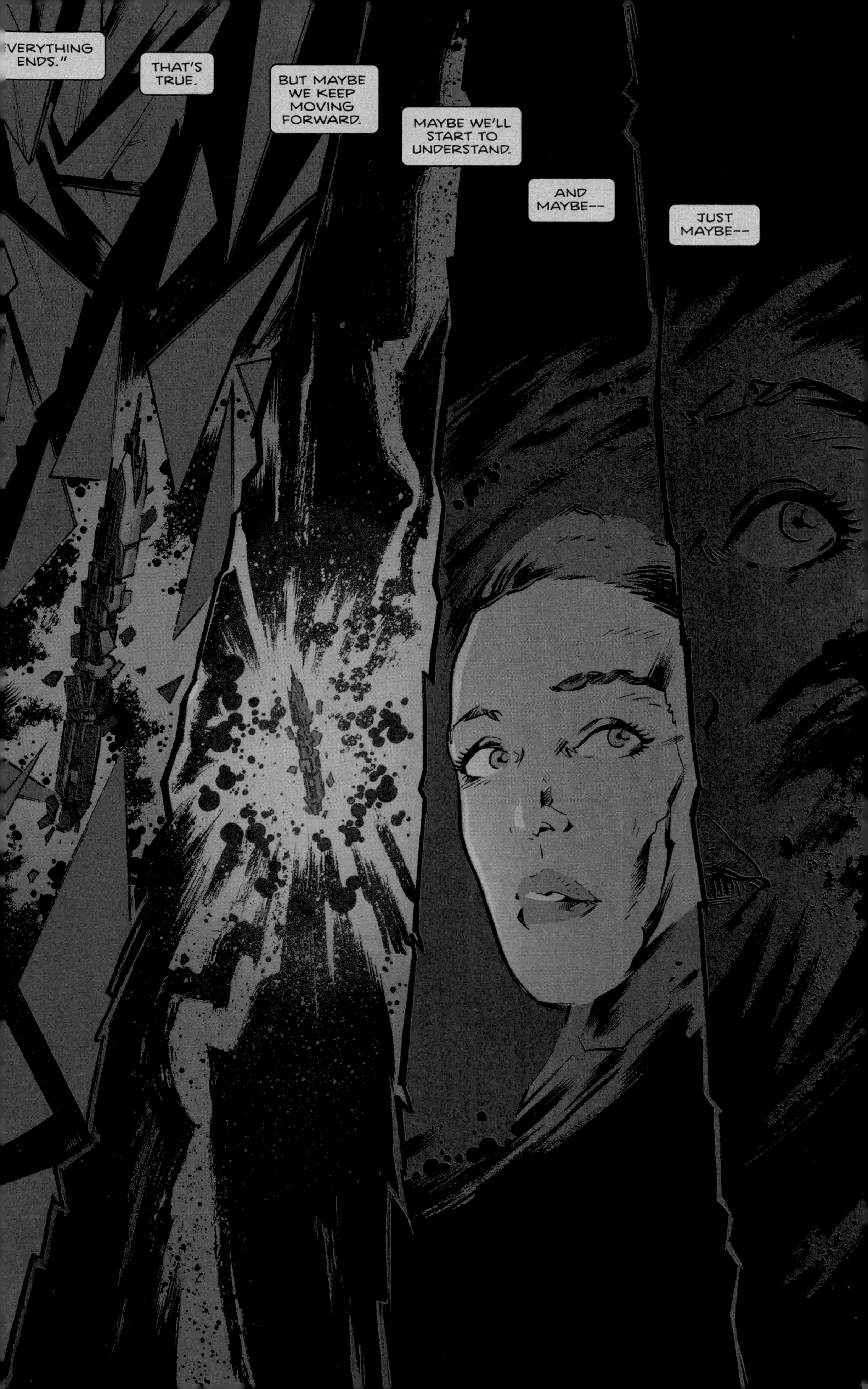

EVERYTHING ENDS."
THAT'S TRUE.
BUT MAYBE WE KEEP MOVING FORWARD.
MAYBE WE'LL START TO UNDERSTAND.
AND MAYBE--
JUST MAYBE--

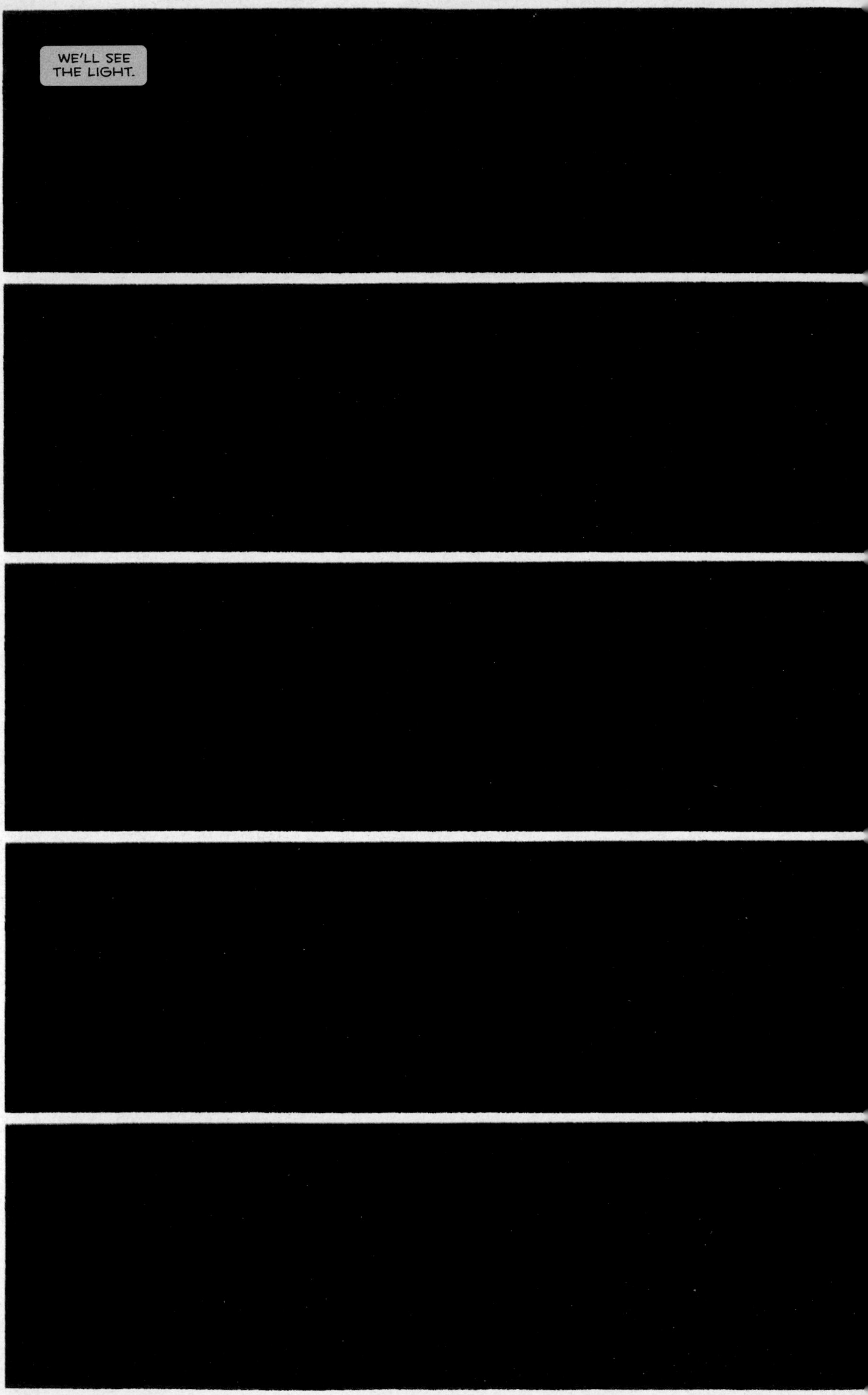
WE'LL SEE THE LIGHT.

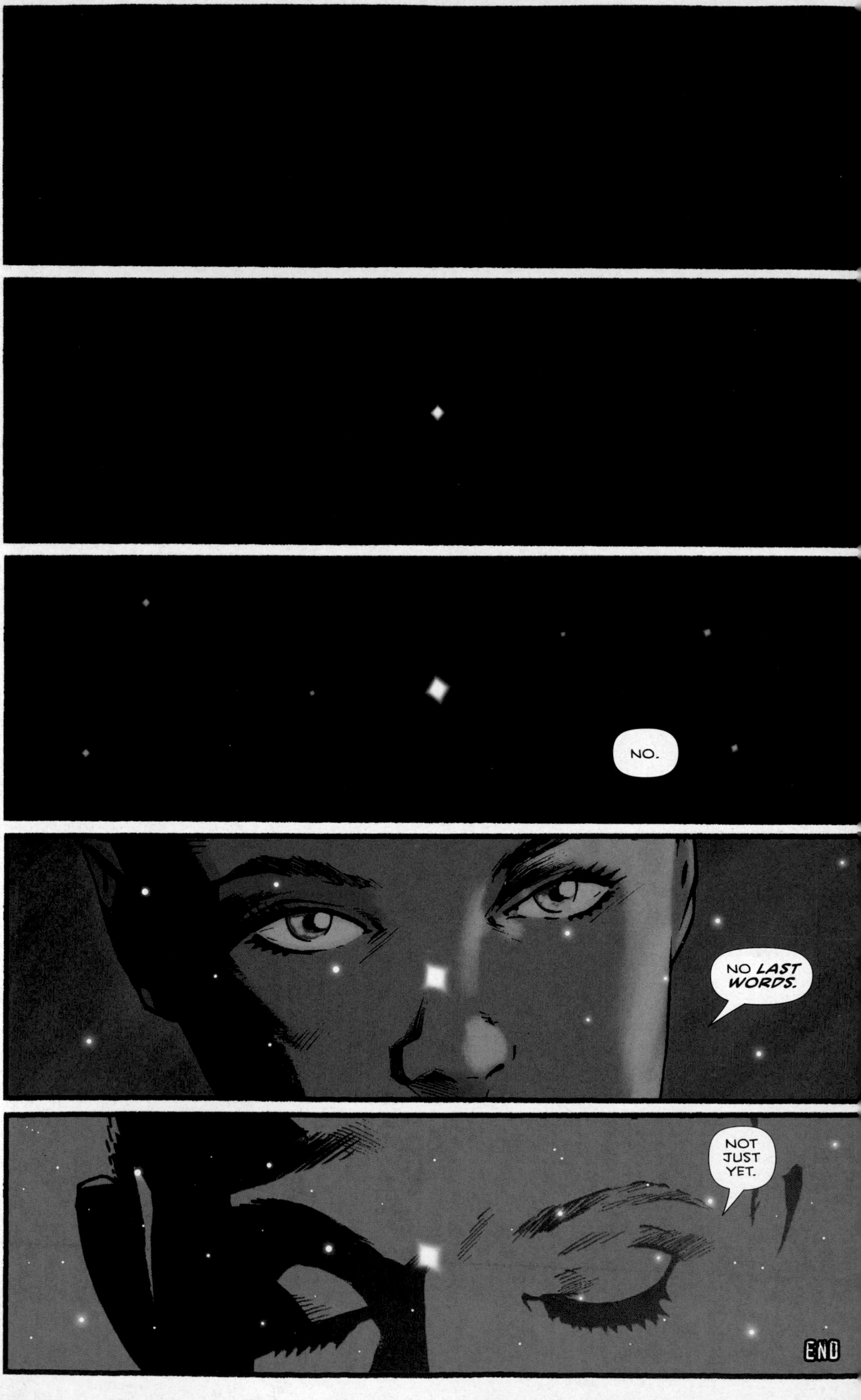
NO.
NO *LAST WORDS.*
NOT JUST YET.
END

ISSUE 5 COVER
NICK ROBLES

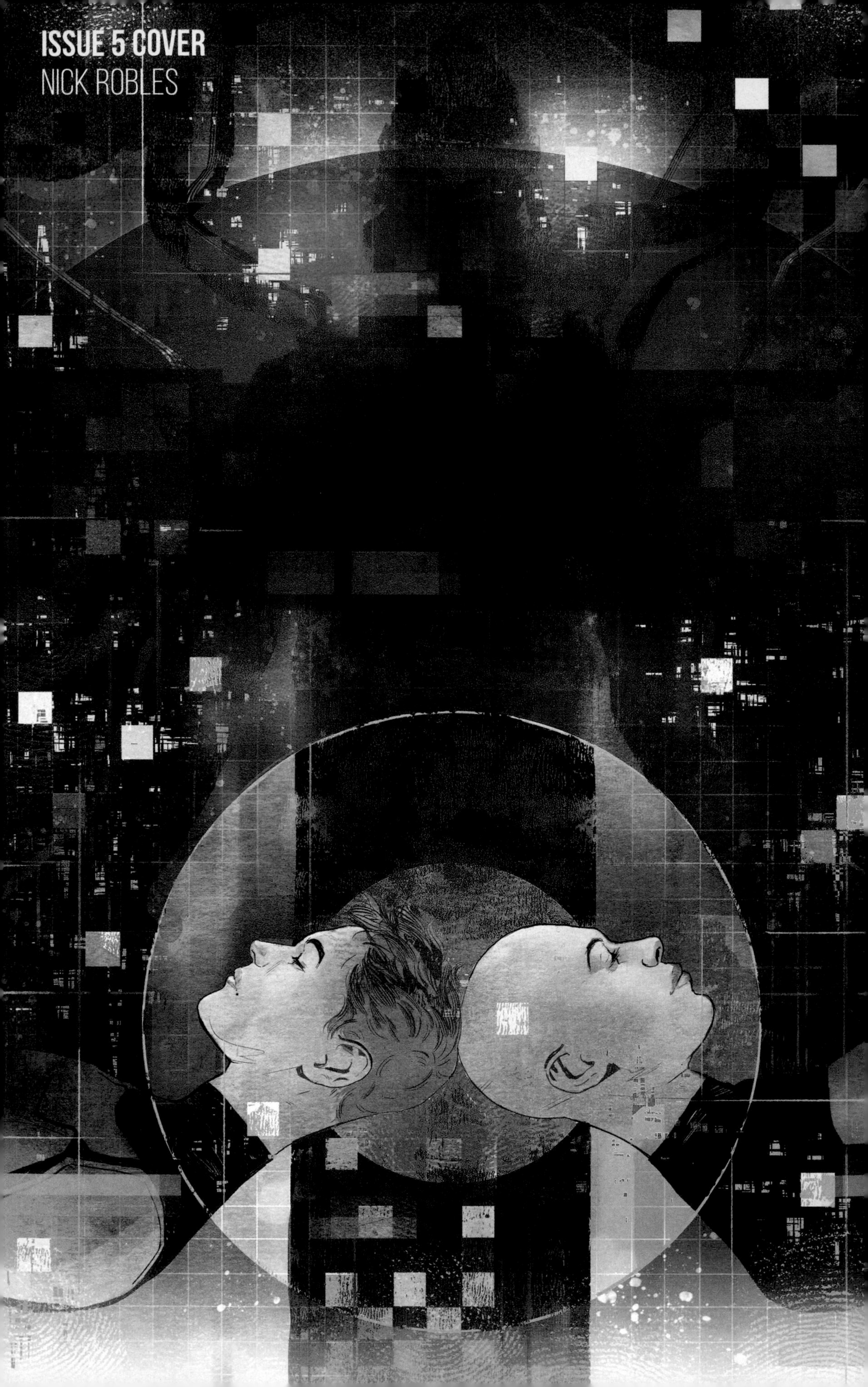

ISSUE 6 COVER

NICK ROBLES

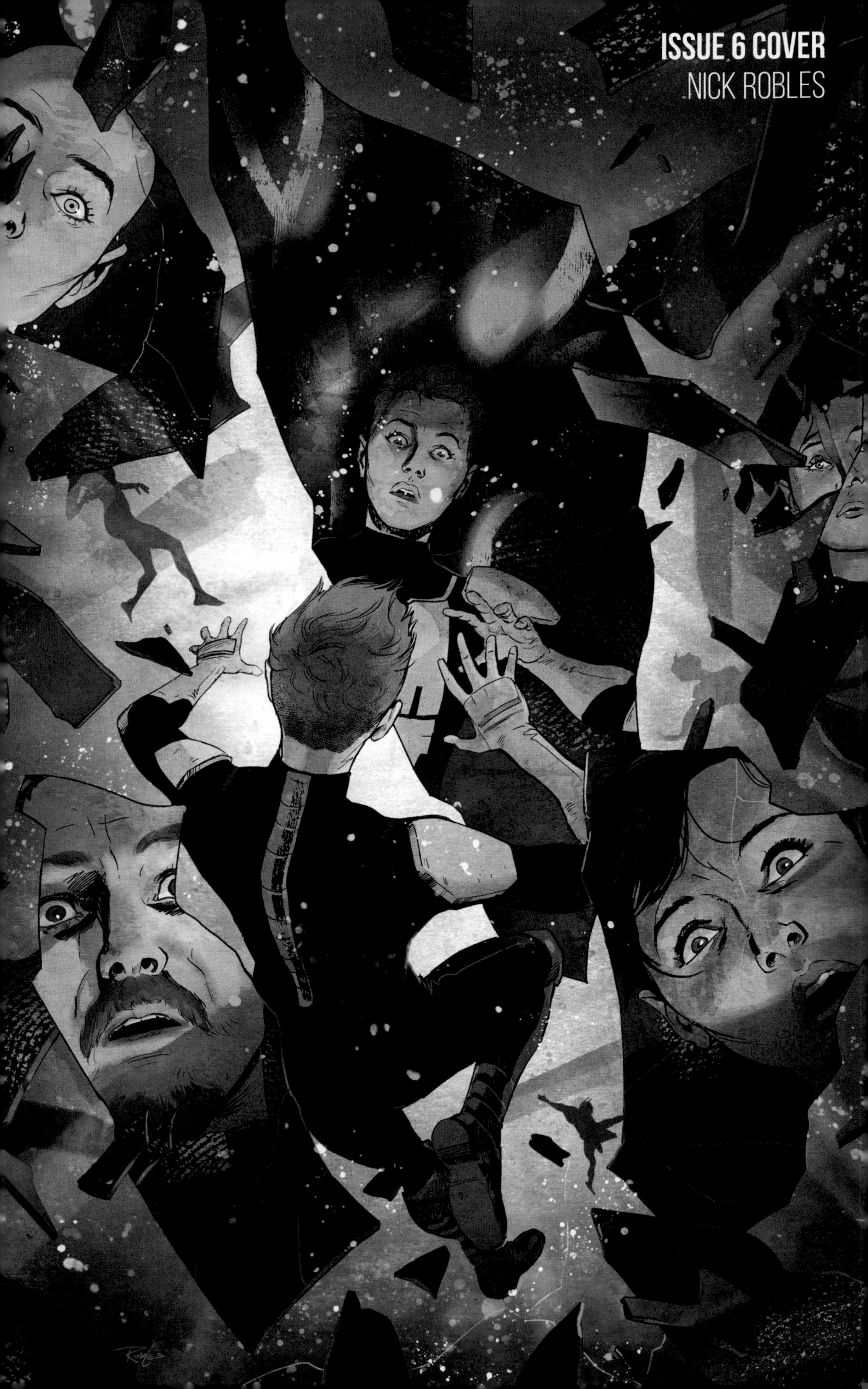

ISSUE 7 COVER
NICK ROBLES

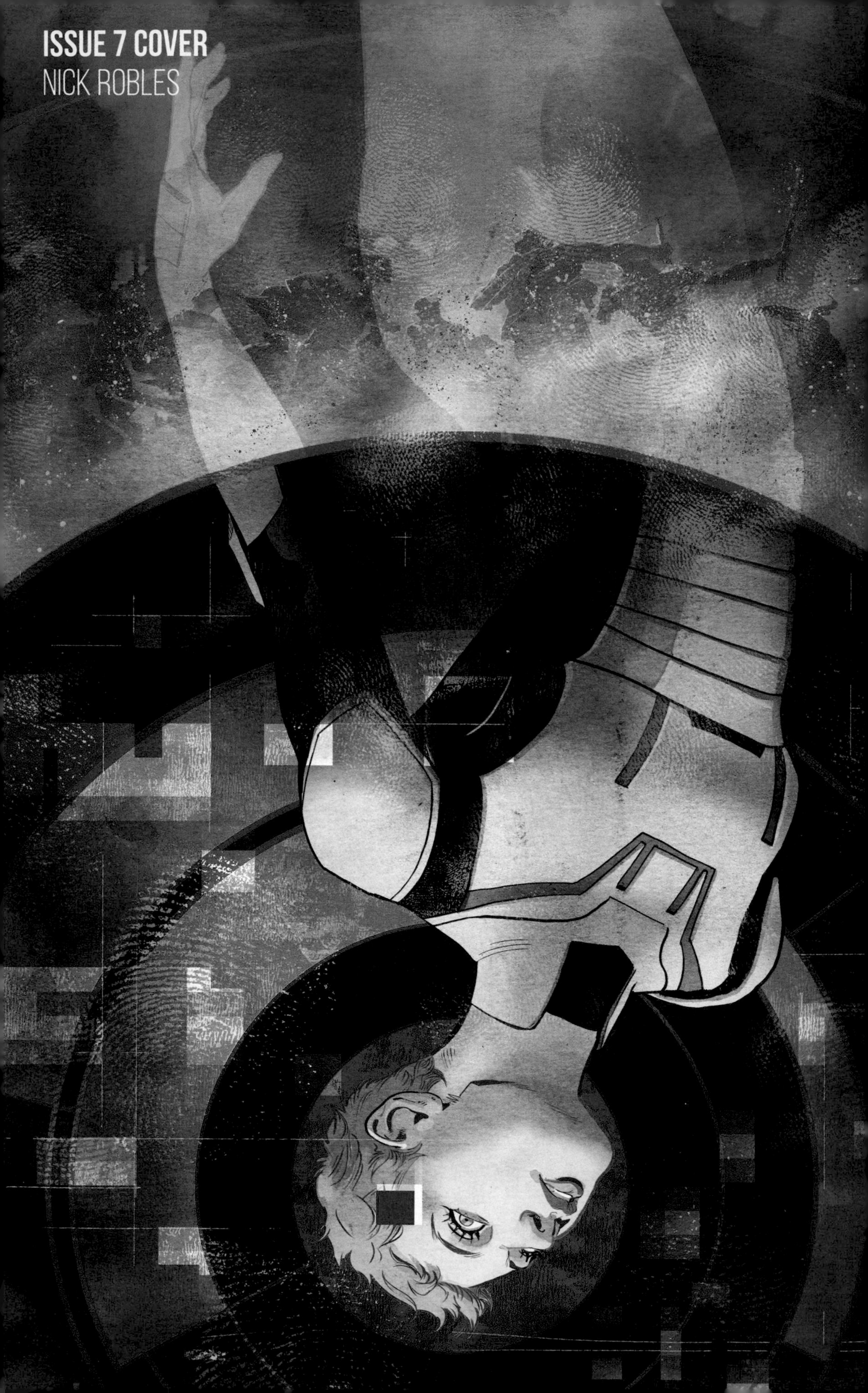

ISSUE 8 COVER
NICK ROBLES

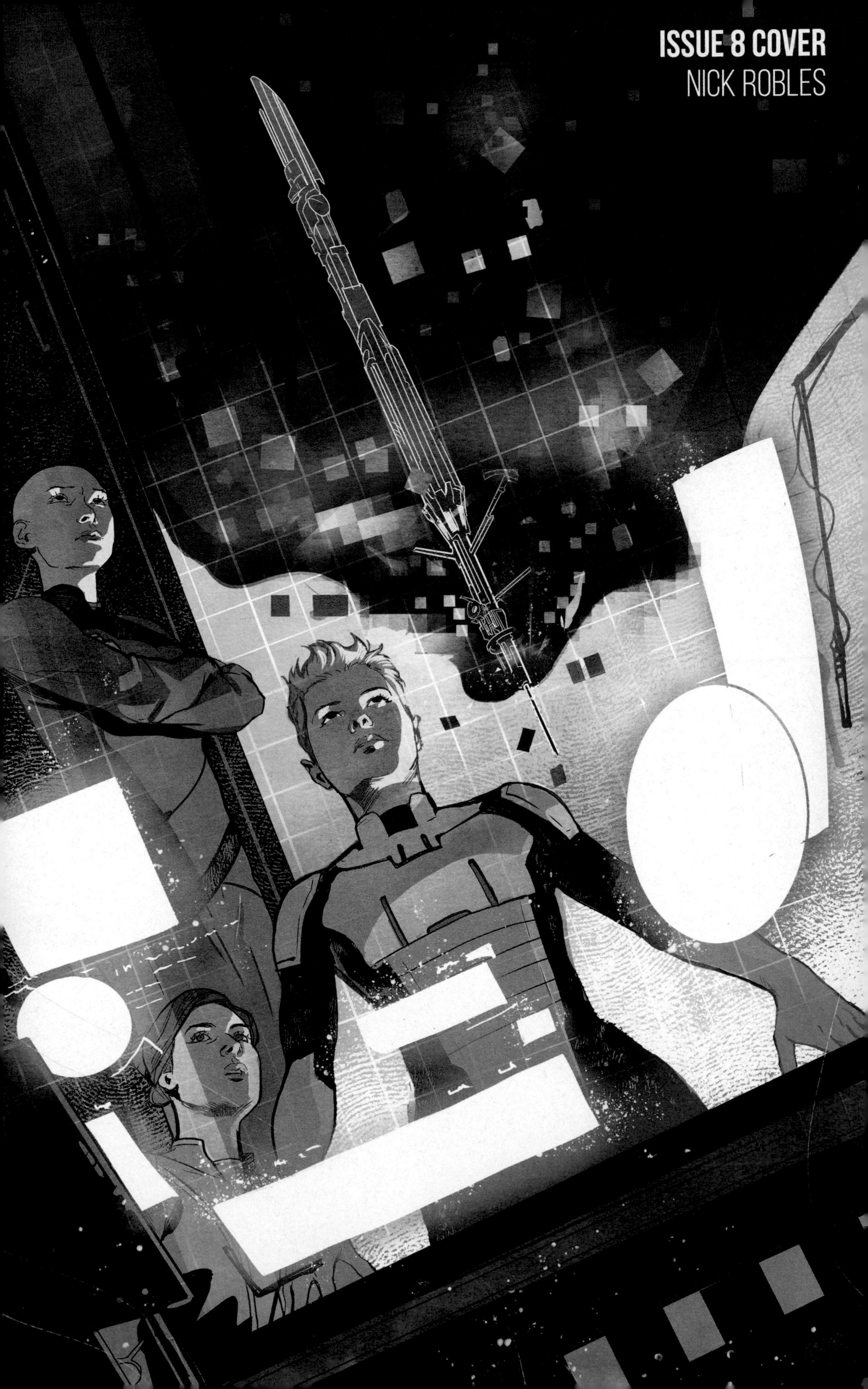

DISPATCHES FROM THE VOID

Wow. Issue five. This is a little surreal, I'll be honest.

When I first pitched INFINITE DARK around (under the title No Stars), I envisioned a four-or five-issue miniseries with the same sort of cool-but-niche appeal of GOD HATES ASTRONAUTS or *Empty Zone*. That pitch talked a lot about heat death, and the end of the universe, and the perils of survivor's guilt—all of which are pretty clearly represented in the first four issues of this series. But more importantly, that pitch demanded a character driven story, a bleak and scary saga following a bunch of individuals trapped at the end of time, and while that's obviously a core element to every part of INFINITE DARK, there was only so much space and time that first story arc could dedicate to each character.

…that first pitch also suggested that the series should have a hard ending with no room fo multiple story arcs, and I was very clear on what that ending would be:

It turns out that the mysterious shadow that's been influencing [Kirin], [Alvin], and the others to destroy the station has a pretty firm agenda and a far from simple perspective. The Shadow ([Entity]) is the universe's creator…like God, basically, and now it's trying to clean up reality and start over, but the station's reality field doesn't allow that.

But after all the horror and sabotage is overcome in a triumph of the human spirit, we have the universe's final showdown—God vs. Man. As Deva uses the station's fusion cannon to obliterate the Shadow, the station soars forward into the storm of Its death throes…and into a new Big Bang.

Obviously a bit different—the Entity destroyed in last issue pretty clearly isn't a creato being, God or otherwise—and what we delivered was far from a hard ending…because we were hoping to continue the story.

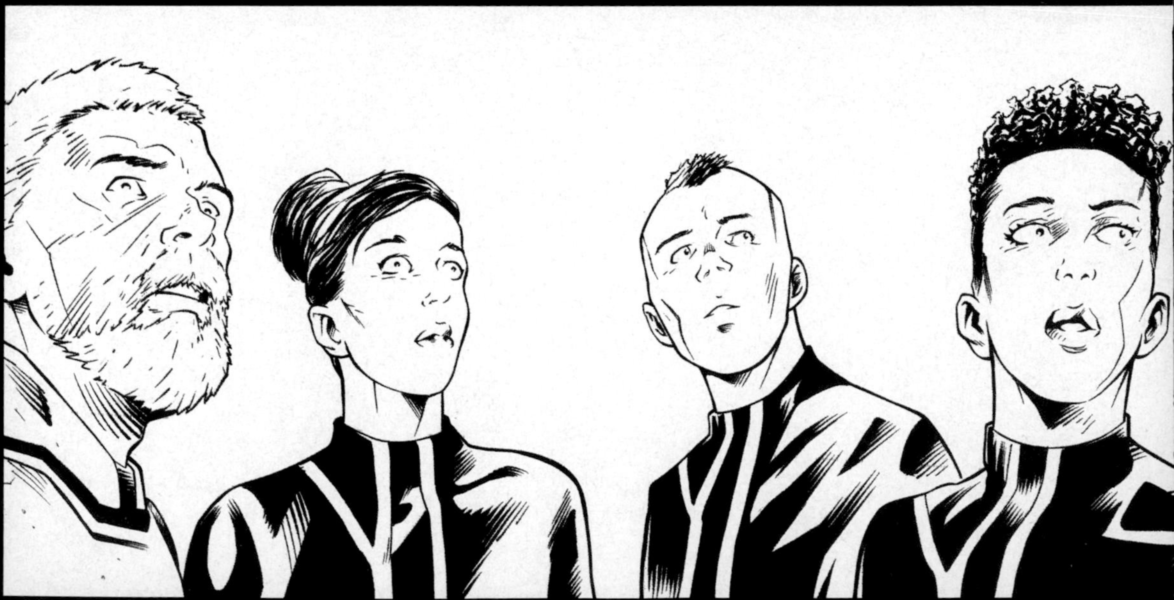

There was more, see? Because from the beginning, every version of INFINITE DARK was full of emotion, examining the psychological consequences of outliving the entire universe, the fear of facing down the end of all things, etc. But there was little room last volume to do what—hopefully—this new story arc sets out to accomplish. To explore the friction and pain and conflict at play in the hearts of these survivors, and more importantly, to give them a chance at forging a new life for themselves. Can they cooperate? Can they trust each other? Can they work together to save themselves?

God...can any of us?

I'd like to think so, and that's what we'll be exploring throughout this arc. Not just how Deva, Kirin, and the crew can fight the horrors from outside, but the horrors within themselves. So please, stick around—just because we killed the big bad monster last issue doesn't mean we're even close to finished with traumatizing you, dear reader.

But if you'll step on board with us, I can promise that there'll be a reason for all that bleakness, that horror, and if we're lucky, we might charge through, past the ending and the shadow, to find a bit of light.

Ryan Cady
March 2019

P.S. We currently have several academic/ memoir style pieces in the works for our Dispatches from the Void segments—and I'm really excited for them! But I'd like to use this space for fanmail and fanart as well. So if you'd like to have a letter or doodle acknowledged here, shoot it over to fanmail@topcow.com, and mark "okay to print."

Thanks for reading!

I was over the moon when we got the amazing Nick Robles to handle our covers for these next four issues. Back in December 2018, after an incredibly pleasant and agreeable couple of professional negotiations, Nick was in! Not long after he agreed to the cover gig, I sent Nick a veeeeerrrry rough—and probably quite rambly—breakdown of how the plot for this volume went. Then maybe a day later he passed on these incredible layouts for suggested covers.

A
B
C
INFINITE DARK
INFINITE DARK
INFINITE DARK

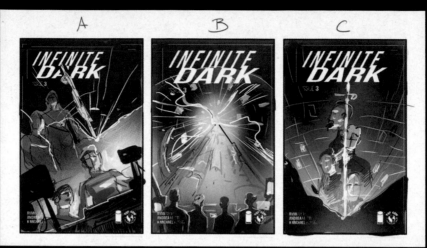

Issue 8 cover thumbnails

We had a surprisingly long back and forth—me, Nick, Andrea, Alex Lu, and everybody at Top Cow—but ultimately settled on the cover of this issue. It was clear that we wanted to emphasize how we were bringing the virtual reality elements from issues #1 and 2 back into the forefront, and I personally really wanted the readers to know that the Entity was gone but NOT forgotten.

And then this beautiful, final, finished product arrived. My god! It was surreal, beautiful, ominous, and a little Renaissance classical? I knew Nick was brilliant, but when I saw this finished beauty, I knew we were onto something special, incorporating him onto our team.

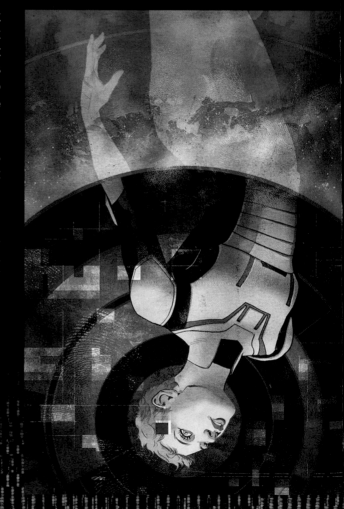

Issue 7 cover preview

DISPATCHES FROM THE VOID

Hey, thanks for grabbing this book! I hope you're enjoying it, and it's not scaring you too much. But if so, here's a little palate cleanser—Dispatches from the Void. In case you missed this section when it first appeared back in issues 2–4, this is a place for "academic" (using the term as loosely as possible, honestly) essays and commentaries on horror. Not just the genre itself, but how it intersects with mental health and socioeconomic and pop culture movements, how it affects our growth as consumers and creators.

Here you'll find fantastic commentary and insightful personal takes from some of your favorite comic creators and critics—all of them much smarter than me.

I hope you appreciate what they have to say—after all, they just want you to *see*.

—Ryan Cady

Making light out of the darkness is one of those curiously universal human activities. The discovery of fire is an event that played out over and over again in countless places around the world, creating all kinds of stories mythologizing it. Sometimes it gets recorded as a brazen act of masculine theft, sometimes a feminine gift, an ungendered collective activity, and all stops in-between. It pretty much always shows up because we need fire for basic survival, but humanity as a collective has never ceased in finding new ways to attach meaning to it.

We do that in drag too, but like anything else, we need to complicate it and make it our own first. Turn out the lights so we can turn them on again. Like shade. "Shade comes from reading," Dorian Corey patiently explained in *Paris is Burning*. Reading is picking at a loose thread in another queen, magnifying a flaw in the other person in the form of banter. Shade is the fine art of putting the insult between the lines. It's Nene Leakes brushing off the accusation of insulting a *Real Housewives of Atlanta* castmate's singing by declaring her "a great writer."

In drag, reading and the careful application of shade is a ritual for queens to confront their insecurities in a safe environment of our peers, to suck the venom out of the barbs so that you don't feel the sting in public. It's a *Drag Race* institution, with one episode every season dedicated to passing around a pair of glasses granting the wearer the ability to take aim at the flaws and foibles of the other competitors.

It was never really seen as an expression of cosmic horror until RuPaul intervened in the Season 9 reunion episode to share a disturbing personal anecdote meant to clarify its purpose. While on acid with notorious frenemy Ladybunny, Ru was convinced that he was going to Hell, a terrible thing to do to someone on acid, but Ru persevered to learn Ladybunny's poorly delivered lesson: to exorcise him of the very real existential panic that conservative religious upbringings instill in countless LBGTQIA people. Passing around the glasses and declaring the library open is an easier sell to advertisers. My experience of making light out of the darkness is a little bit different, but shares the same logic: I saw those flaws, all the things about me that are made out to be monstrous and made a glittery monster of my own out them named Judith Slays. Blood is still blood when it's been transmuted into glitter, but it's a lot easier to deal with and nicer to look at. Like hearing the words the world uses to tear you down coming from another queen's lips.

That's what drag is, turning the lights off to turn them back on again. Which has to be why so many queens look like they do their makeup in the dark.

VÉRONIQUE EMMA HOUXBOIS is a fiercely queer critic, cartoonist, and consultant most recently spotted in the Pacific Northwest writing her Transmyscira column for Comicosity and hosting Read From the Rafters on YouTube as her drag persona Judith Slays. Named one of SyFy's Most Influential Women in Genre 2017, her credits include *Love is Love* for IDW/DC, *Critical Chips* Volume 2 for Shortbox, and *Called into Being: 200 Years of Frankenstein.*

The film *Army of Darkness* changed my life in high school.

It was literally a gateway drug. A portal to everything I love today. And for better or for worse, it's likely a big part of the reason why my words are appearing in the back of this amazing book.

Army of Darkness is one film that balances two opposing different genres: Horror and Comedy. Each with their own distinct goals, unique styles, and enduring legacies. I believe that both of these genres are actually two sides of the same coin.

This is not a new opinion, but I've lived it as a past comedy performer and it's become true to me as I've grown as a writer. Each genre has one explicit purpose—"be scary" or "be funny." They share the same storytelling fundamentals to achieve their goals: Timing/pacing + misdirection.

And they each require an open-minded audience willing to engage in the medium. Not to oversimplify, but you know what the only real difference is between a person getting cut-in-half on screen and whether the audience is laughing or screaming?

The title of the movie.

ELIOT RAHAL is a Minneapolis based comics writer/creator best known for his work on *Hot Lunch Special*, *Quantum & Woody*, and *Return to Whisper*. You can find him on Twitter **@eliotrahal.**

Fanart by **MATTHEW BURBRIDGE** @MBURBRIDGE26

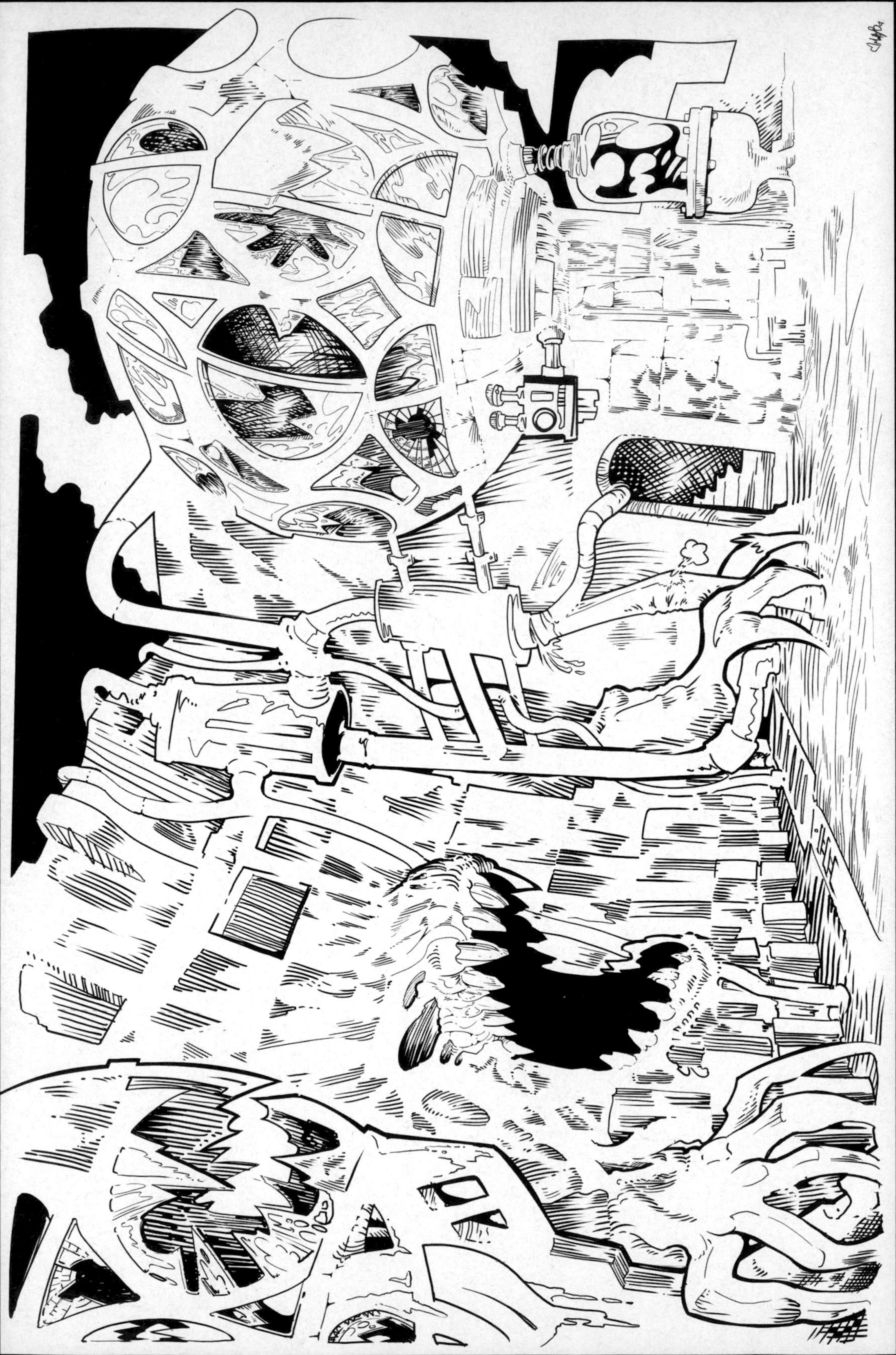

DISPATCHES FROM THE VOID

was raised in a high-demand fundamental Christian religion. My entire existence, identity, and understanding were framed through the lens of the church. I was devoted and devout. Until I wasn't.

As I entered my early thirties, my mind opened and my world fell apart. The sheer abject horror of losing every shred of one's self is hard to describe or imagine unless you've been in that position yourself. I was broken, lost, and gasping in existential pain. I lost my faith, my community, and my identity.

Slowly, one piece at a time, I gathered the remnants of who I was and rebuilt them into who I am. I sojourned in the metaphorical wilderness for 40 years and made it to the promised land of individuality. I am stronger, healthier, and happier than I've ever been.

But that doesn't minimize the horror that I went through.

Growing up, before this faith crisis and transition, I always loved horror. I loved the thrill of being scared, the temporary anxiety of dread, and the chill on the back of my neck that comes from the unknown. Some of the earliest stories I both consumed and wrote were all in the horror vein. I never experienced lasting fear, in part because of my ability to fall back on the religious narrative I had been given. There was a higher power to protect me.

As I got older, horrors of a more real variety were the ones that began to scare me. Whether nonfiction—I woke up screaming in the middle of the night while I was deep into reading "*Helter Skelter*"—or fiction that skirted reality—give me "*The Strangers*" or "*Penpal*" any day over "*The Thing*" or "*Alien*"—I gravitated toward the anxiety that came with realizing that the horrors of people were worse than any monster. And that no matter what God you believed in, you were not safe.

After having to rebuild my self, I've found that I'm a much more vulnerable person. I have no God to rely on to stand behind, to shield me from the realities of suffering or terror. I have to face those things with the understanding that I'm powerless to prevent so much of it. It's overwhelming and scary, but there's a newfound power in knowledge. In acceptance. In realization. I spend countless hours listening to true crime podcasts, reading history books, and telling stories to help me to understand the new and real world around me. I have to understand how and why things happen.

Horror in fiction is about mastery of the situation. My favorite stories are those where a person opens themselves to the anxiety and desperation of their situation and still triumphs in their own way (see *The Descent*, *Halloween*, *Scream*, *Texas Chainsaw Massacre*).

Knowing that there is nothing, ultimately, controlling the fates and lives of everyone around me, I've had to arm myself with the knowledge to accept the anxieties I have and to open myself up to the horror of the world around me. I can't take it all in—but I can be aware it's there.

With that awareness comes compassion and empathy like I've never before experienced. With the vulnerability of self-actualization comes the ability to experience joy and happiness and success not minimized or controlled by any conception of deity. The success and accomplishments of my life are mine. The failures are too. I have to live more honestly and try harder than I ever thought possible. But the reward of a true self is worth it.

It's worth the horror.

PHILLIP SEVY loves comics. Always has. Always will. He drew his first one at age 4. Over 25 years later, he was a runner-up in the Top Cow Talent Hunt 2014 and his career began. He graduated with an MFA in Sequential Art from SCAD and has worked for Top Cow, Black Mask, Valiant, IDW, Zenescope, Action Lab and most notably on a long run of *Tomb Raider* for Dark Horse. In between drawing projects, he self-published *Paradox* and wrote *The House* (with artist Drew Zucker). Phillip lives in Utah with his wife (just one) and kids (only two). You can keep up with his work at phillipsevy.com.

No facet of horror does more for me than religion, the occult, and that which is adjacent to them. From Carrie White and the abilities she used to put an end to her abusive zealot of a mother, to the otherworldly creatures of *Clean Room*, to an endless procession of hooded figures tossing chunks of meat into a seemingly-bottomless pit. These types of stories—things my own zealot of a mother would deem "affronts to God," command my attention—they always have.

Demonic possession (or in some cases, the behaviors that hapless tertiary characters declare demonic possession) is of particular interest to me. Probably because I was "exorcised" as a child. That's what they called it anyway. It was just a room full of adults shouting at me because they thought puking during prayer group, and being incoherent afterwards were signs of Satan's influence. But at age six, that's scary! I remember thinking, this shouldn't be happening.

For me, that's what narrative horror is all about. A high schooler shouldn't be able to bring down telephone poles by flexing her mind. I shouldn't be able to stay up for days at a clip, "functioning" at "full capacity". Even if things shouldn't happen, they often do. So what's next? What are you, the protagonist, going to do about it?

In horror, things don't conveniently go away because you don't want them around. You can't outrun a demon—it sticks with you. It's inside of you, and you can't very well outrun yourself. Horror isn't convenient, and neither is bipolar. It isn't something that you can cast out and be done with. But that doesn't mean you can't familiarize yourself with it. Living with bipolar disorder is like consuming a lot of horror, in that after a while, you're able to pick up on things that inform how you proceed. At this point, I'm able to predict a manic phase coming on, just like I could tell you which grade-schooler's going to be the one to start scribbling occult iconography on the walls and mentioning a new imaginary friend.

I was hesitant to bring up demonic possession and bipolar disorder in such close proximity because I'm worried about people conflating the two. But since you're seven issues into INFINITE DARK, I'm hoping you can see that the whole monster metaphor doesn't really apply here. Bipolar (or any mental illness, really) isn't something that you can kill or conquer. It's more of a consistent struggle—one that's far less debilitating with a solid support system. Friends and a therapist are just as effective as holy water and a baseball bat with nails sticking out, if not more so.

It's exhausting, for sure. But at the end of the day, if you take that next breath, you've won...for now. The reality of it is, if you've had an intense manic or depressive episode, you're probably going to have one again. If franchise horror has taught me anything, it's that there's always a sequel.

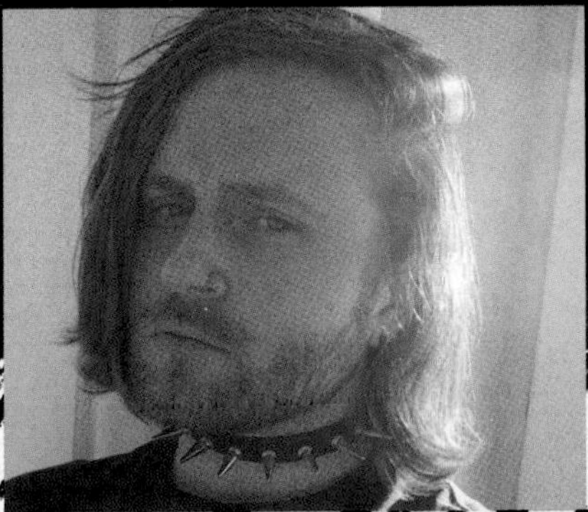

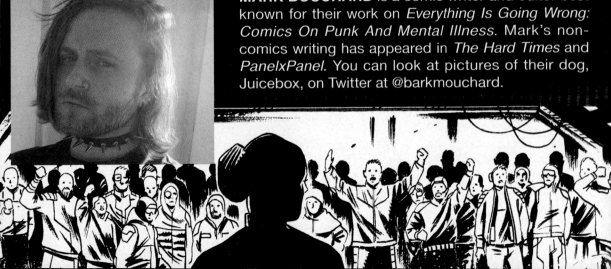

MARK BOUCHARD is a comic writer and editor best known for their work on *Everything Is Going Wrong: Comics On Punk And Mental Illness*. Mark's non-comics writing has appeared in *The Hard Times* and *PanelxPanel*. You can look at pictures of their dog, Juicebox, on Twitter at @barkmouchard.

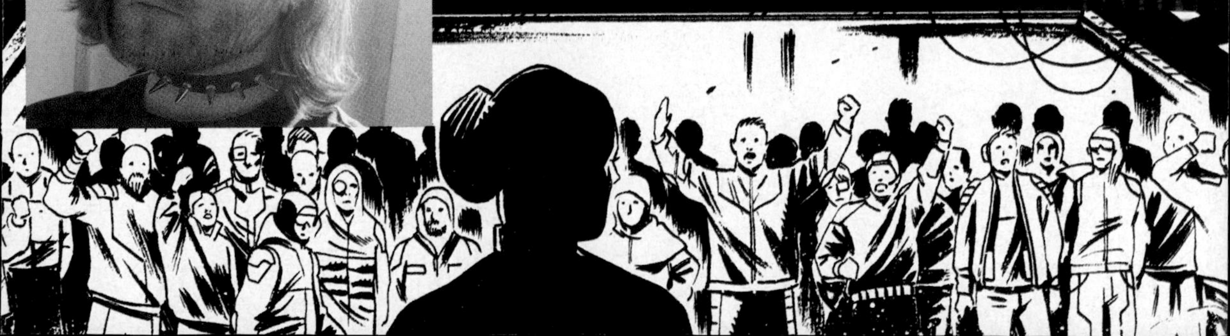

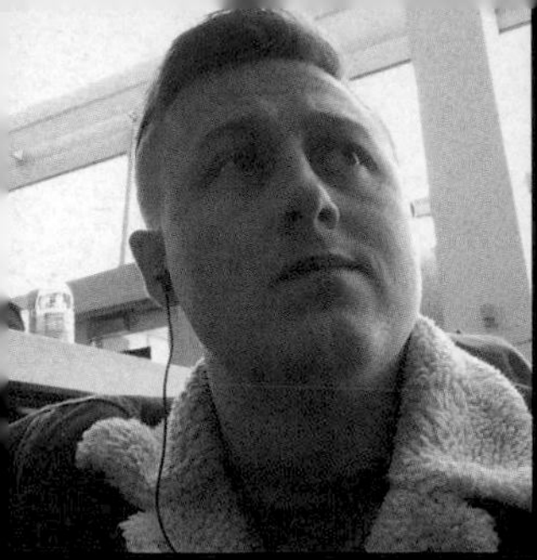

RYAN CADY is a writer of comics and horror fiction based in Southern California. A graduate of the DC Comics Talent Development Workshop, he has written for Marvel, Archie Comics, and others, on properties such as WARFRAME and The Punisher, and the book you're holding, his first creator-owned property with Image/Top Cow Productions. To this day, his early reviews of terrible fast food products for the OC Weekly remain his greatest creative triumph.

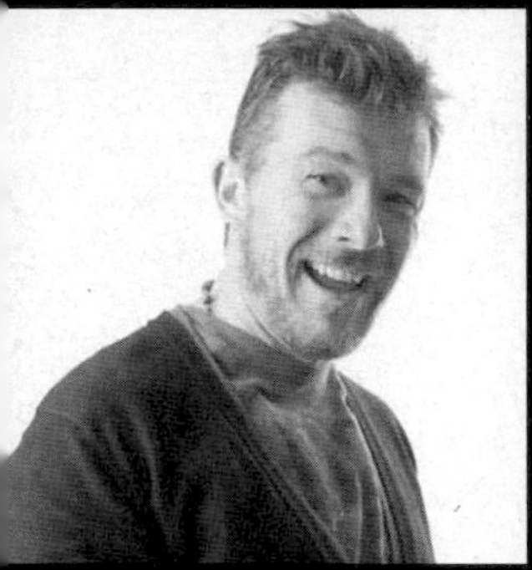

ANDREA MUTTI is an Italian artist who has worked in the comic book world for 25 years. He studied at the Comics School in Brescia and has worked with such US publishers as Marvel, DC, Dark Horse, Vertigo, IDW, BOOM! Studios, Dynamite, Stela, Adaptive and many more European publishers like Glenat, Casterman, Soleil, Dargaud and Titan. He lives in Italy and you can learn more about his career at his website **www.andrearedmutti.com**.

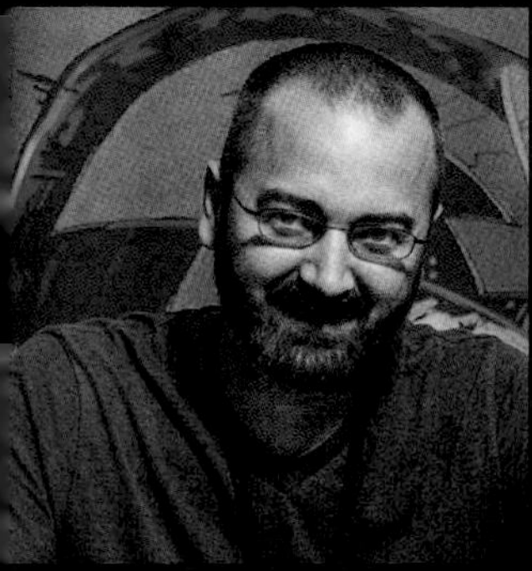

K. MICHAEL RUSSELL has been working as a comic book color artist since 2011. His credits include Image series GLITTERBOMB with WAYWARD & *Thunderbolts* writer Jim Zub, HACK/SLASH, *Judge Dredd* and the Eisner and Harvey-nominated *In the Dark: A Horror Anthology*. He launched an online comic book coloring course in 2014 at ColoringComics.com and maintains a YouTube channel dedicated to coloring tutorials. He lives on the coast in Long Beach, Mississippi, with his wife of sixteen years, Tina. They have two cats. One is a jerk. **@kmichaelrussell**

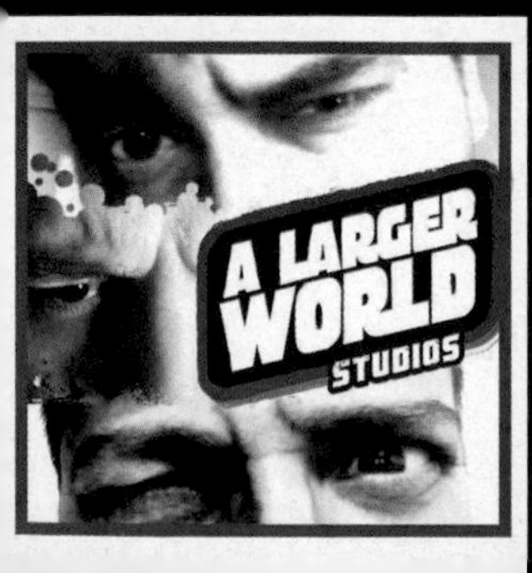
A LARGER WORLD
STUDIOS

TROY PETERI, Dave Lanphear and Joshua Cozine are collectively known as A Larger World Studios. They've lettered everything from *The Avengers*, *Iron Man*, *Wolverine*, *Amazing Spider-Man* and *X-Men* to more recent titles such as WITCHBLADE, CYBERFORCE, and *Batman/Wonder Woman: The Brave & The Bold*. They can be reached at studio@alargerworld.com for your lettering and design needs. (Hooray, commerce!)

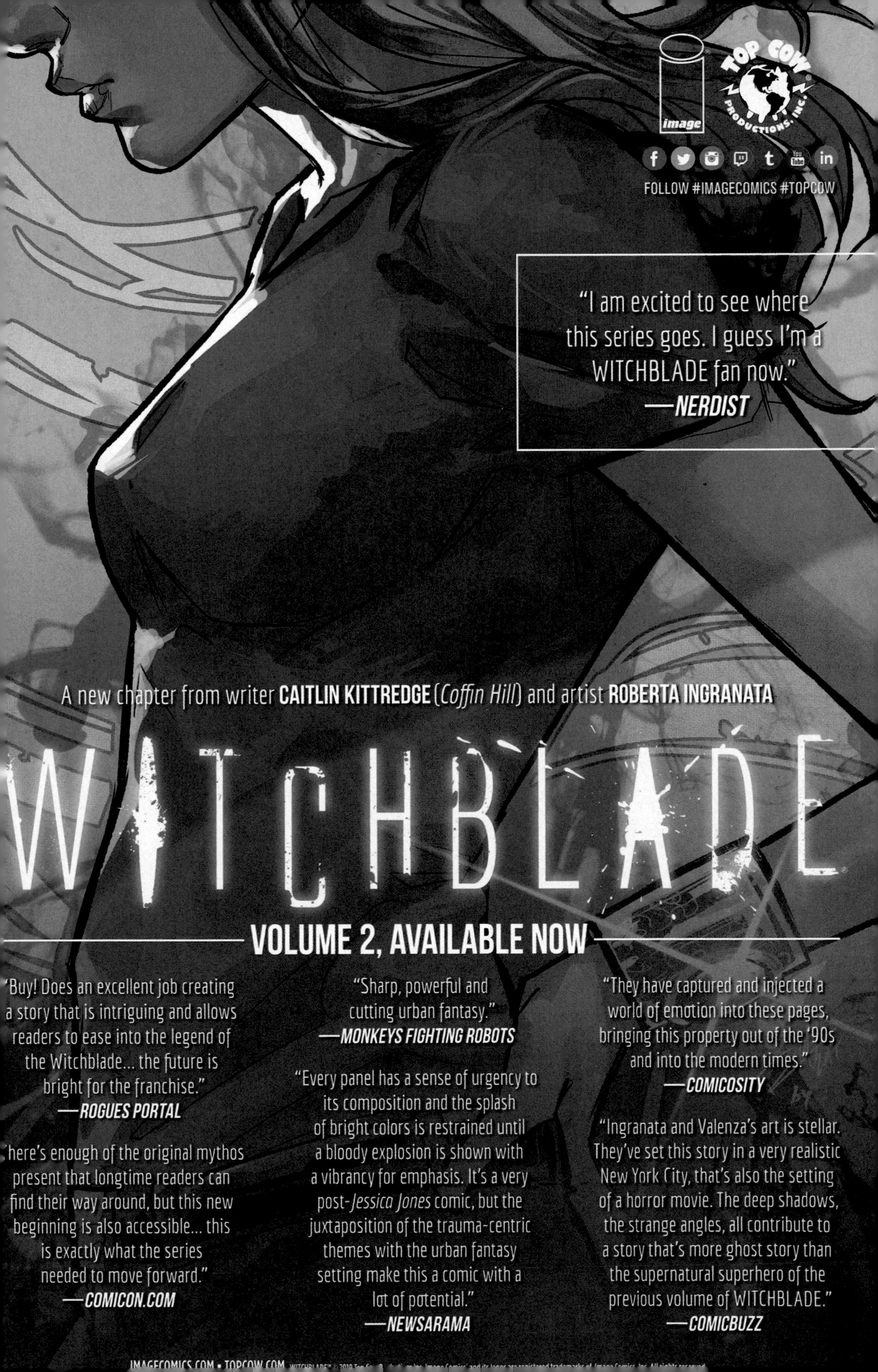
FOLLOW #IMAGECOMICS #TOPCOW
"I am excited to see where this series goes. I guess I'm a WITCHBLADE fan now."
—NERDIST
A new chapter from writer CAITLIN KITTREDGE (Coffin Hill) and artist ROBERTA INGRANATA
WITCHBLADE
VOLUME 2, AVAILABLE NOW
"Buy! Does an excellent job creating a story that is intriguing and allows readers to ease into the legend of the Witchblade… the future is bright for the franchise."
—ROGUES PORTAL
"There's enough of the original mythos present that longtime readers can find their way around, but this new beginning is also accessible… this is exactly what the series needed to move forward."
—COMICON.COM
"Sharp, powerful and cutting urban fantasy."
—MONKEYS FIGHTING ROBOTS
"Every panel has a sense of urgency to its composition and the splash of bright colors is restrained until a bloody explosion is shown with a vibrancy for emphasis. It's a very post-Jessica Jones comic, but the juxtaposition of the trauma-centric themes with the urban fantasy setting make this a comic with a lot of potential."
—NEWSARAMA
"They have captured and injected a world of emotion into these pages, bringing this property out of the '90s and into the modern times."
—COMICOSITY
"Ingranata and Valenza's art is stellar. They've set this story in a very realistic New York City, that's also the setting of a horror movie. The deep shadows, the strange angles, all contribute to a story that's more ghost story than the supernatural superhero of the previous volume of WITCHBLADE."
—COMICBUZZ
IMAGECOMICS.COM • TOPCOW.COM

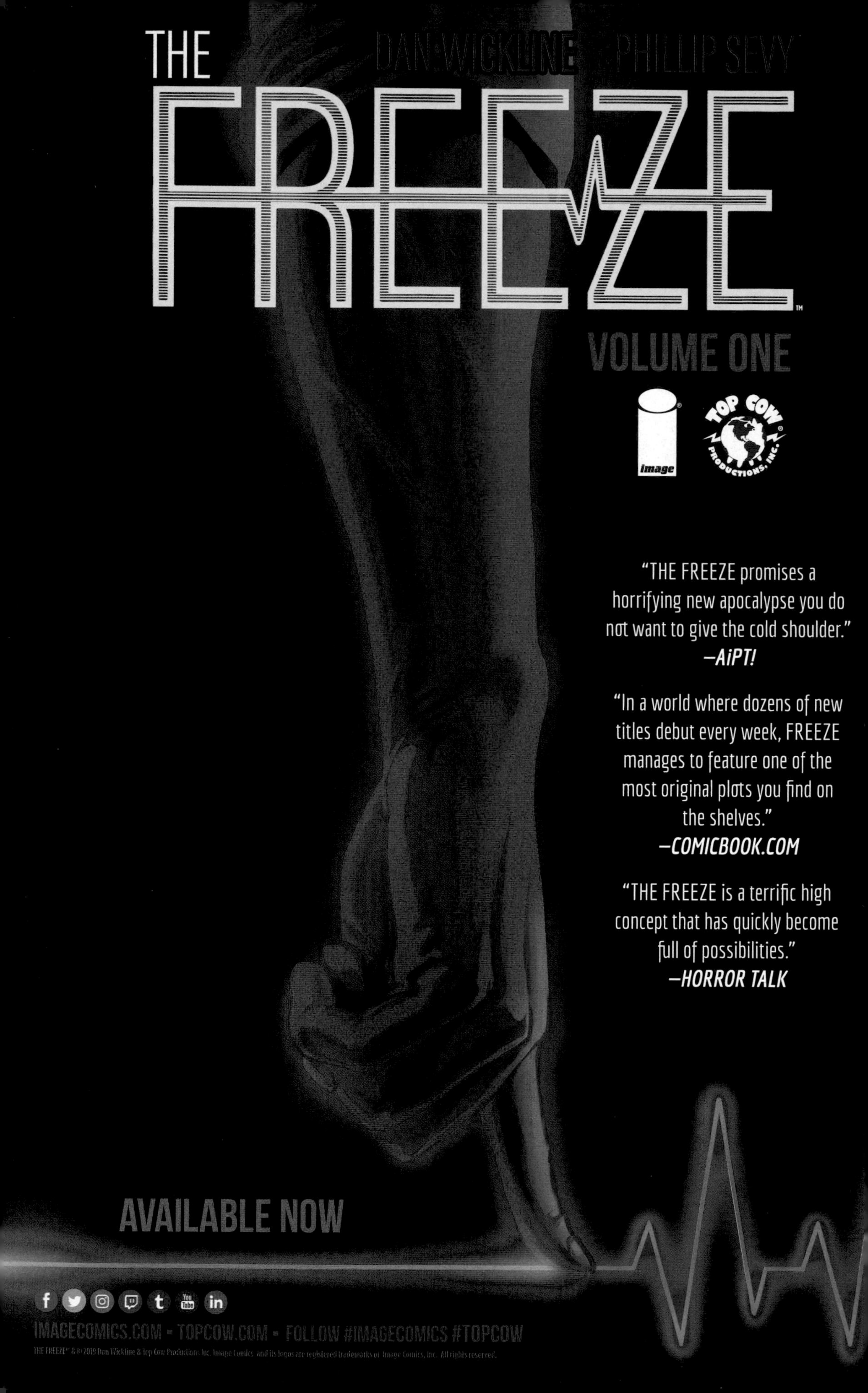

THE FREEZE™
DAN WICKLINE · PHILLIP SEVY
VOLUME ONE
"THE FREEZE promises a horrifying new apocalypse you do not want to give the cold shoulder."
—AiPT!
"In a world where dozens of new titles debut every week, FREEZE manages to feature one of the most original plots you find on the shelves."
—COMICBOOK.COM
"THE FREEZE is a terrific high concept that has quickly become full of possibilities."
—HORROR TALK
AVAILABLE NOW
IMAGECOMICS.COM · TOPCOW.COM · FOLLOW #IMAGECOMICS #TOPCOW
THE FREEZE™ & © 2019 Dan Wickline & Top Cow Productions Inc. Image Comics and its logos are registered trademarks of Image Comics, Inc. All rights reserved.

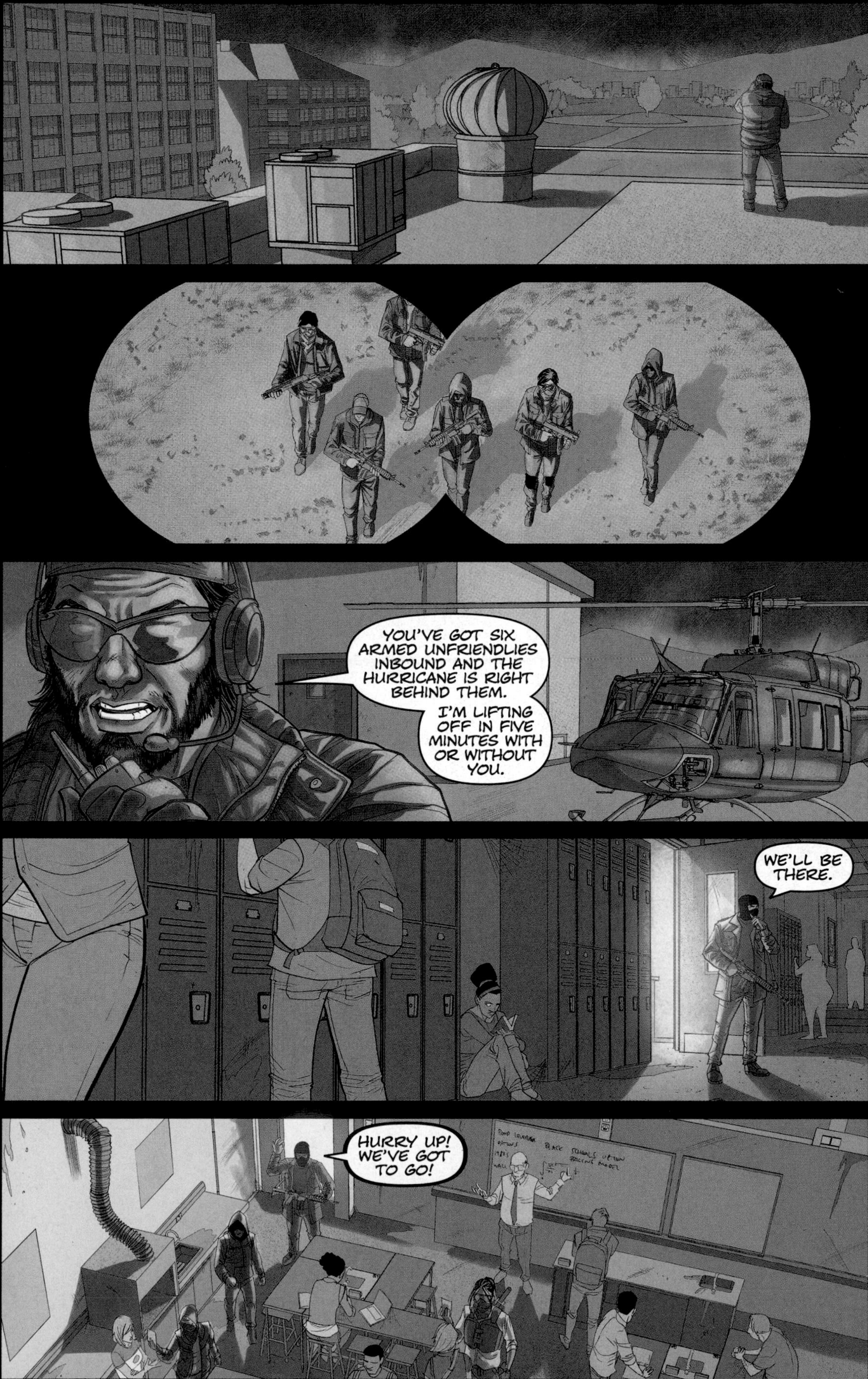
YOU'VE GOT SIX ARMED UNFRIENDLIES INBOUND AND THE HURRICANE IS RIGHT BEHIND THEM.
I'M LIFTING OFF IN FIVE MINUTES WITH OR WITHOUT YOU.
WE'LL BE THERE.
HURRY UP! WE'VE GOT TO GO!

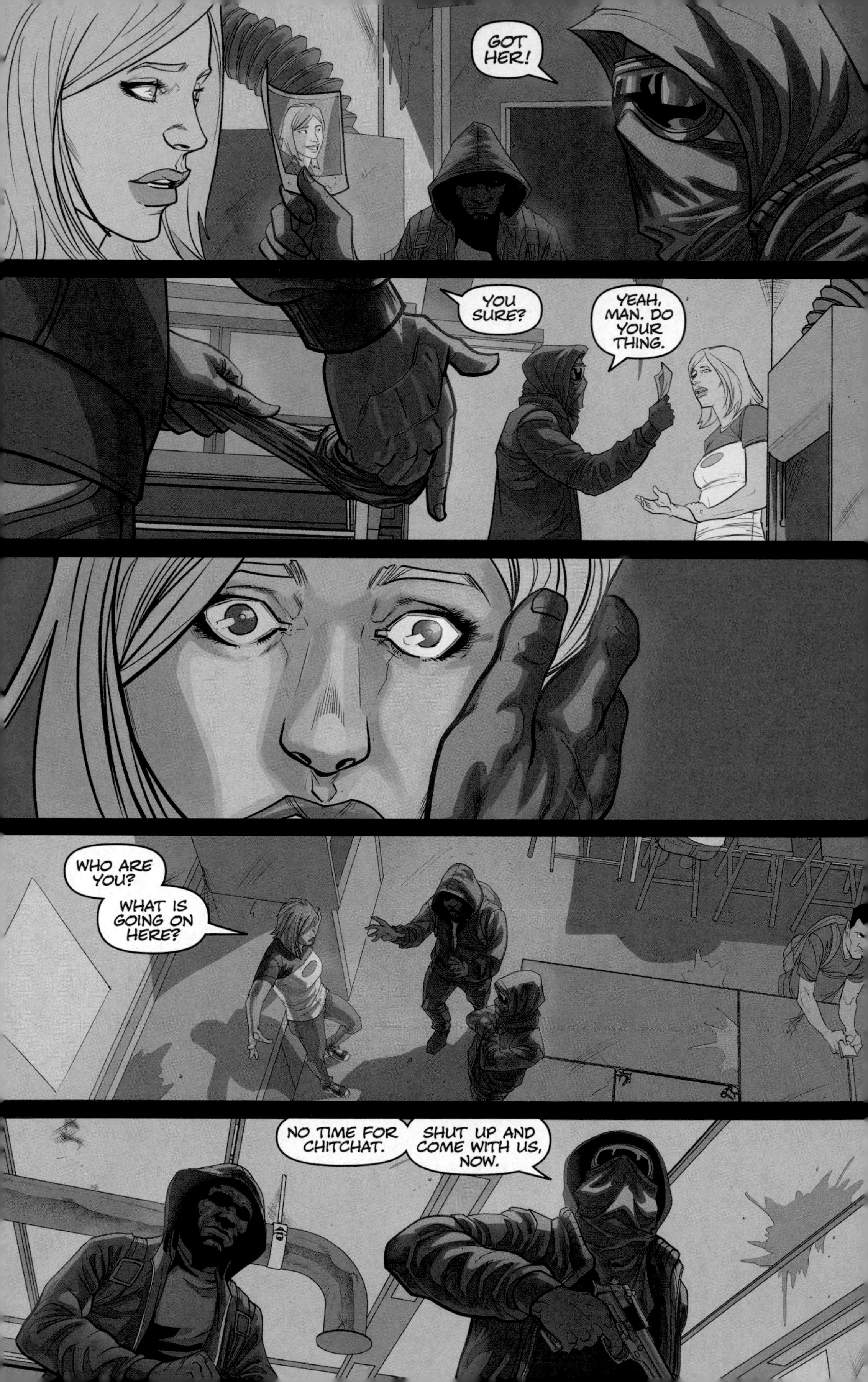
GOT HER!
YOU SURE?
YEAH, MAN. DO YOUR THING.
WHO ARE YOU?
WHAT IS GOING ON HERE?
NO TIME FOR CHITCHAT.
SHUT UP AND COME WITH US, NOW.

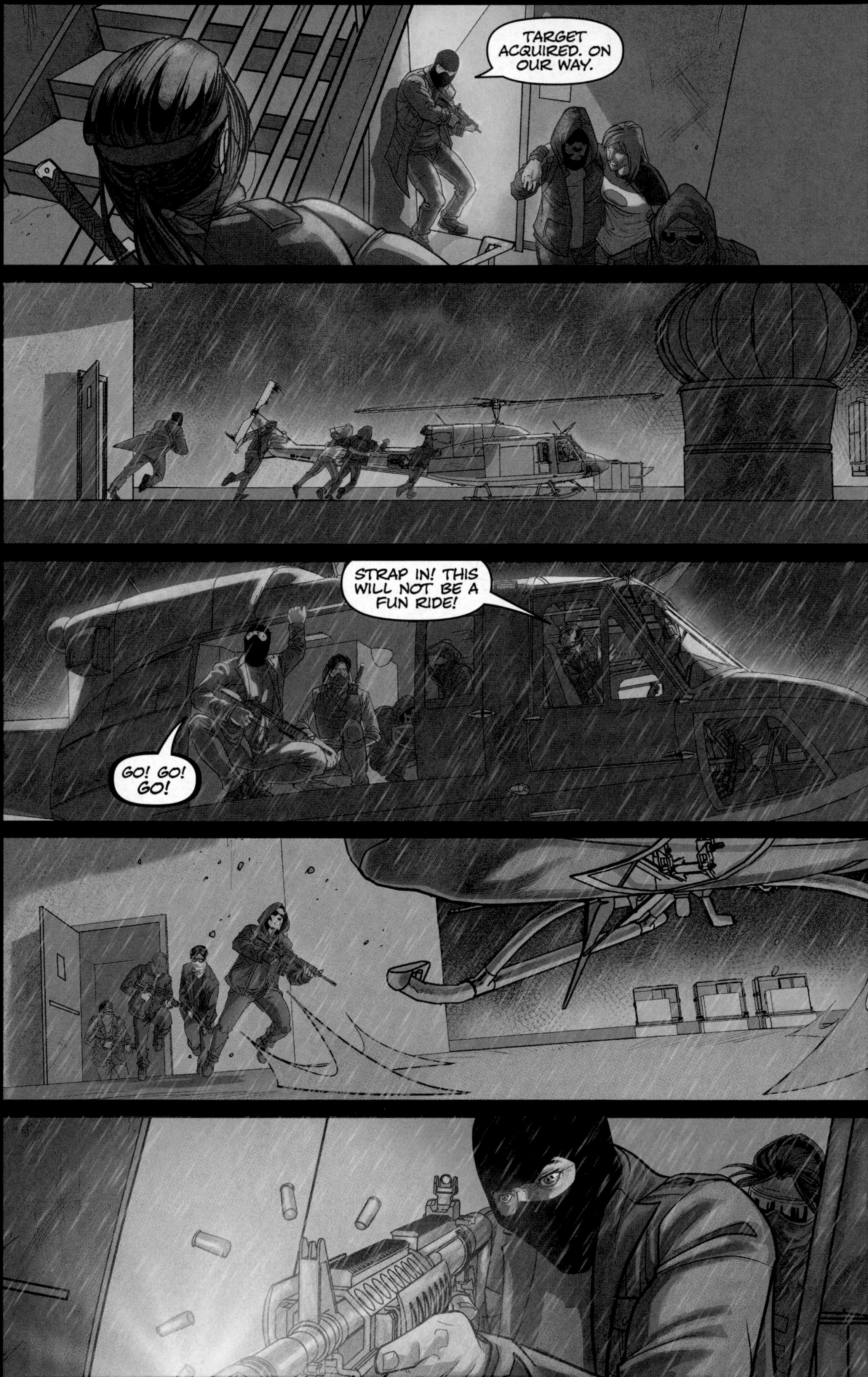
TARGET ACQUIRED. ON OUR WAY.
STRAP IN! THIS WILL NOT BE A FUN RIDE!
GO! GO! GO!

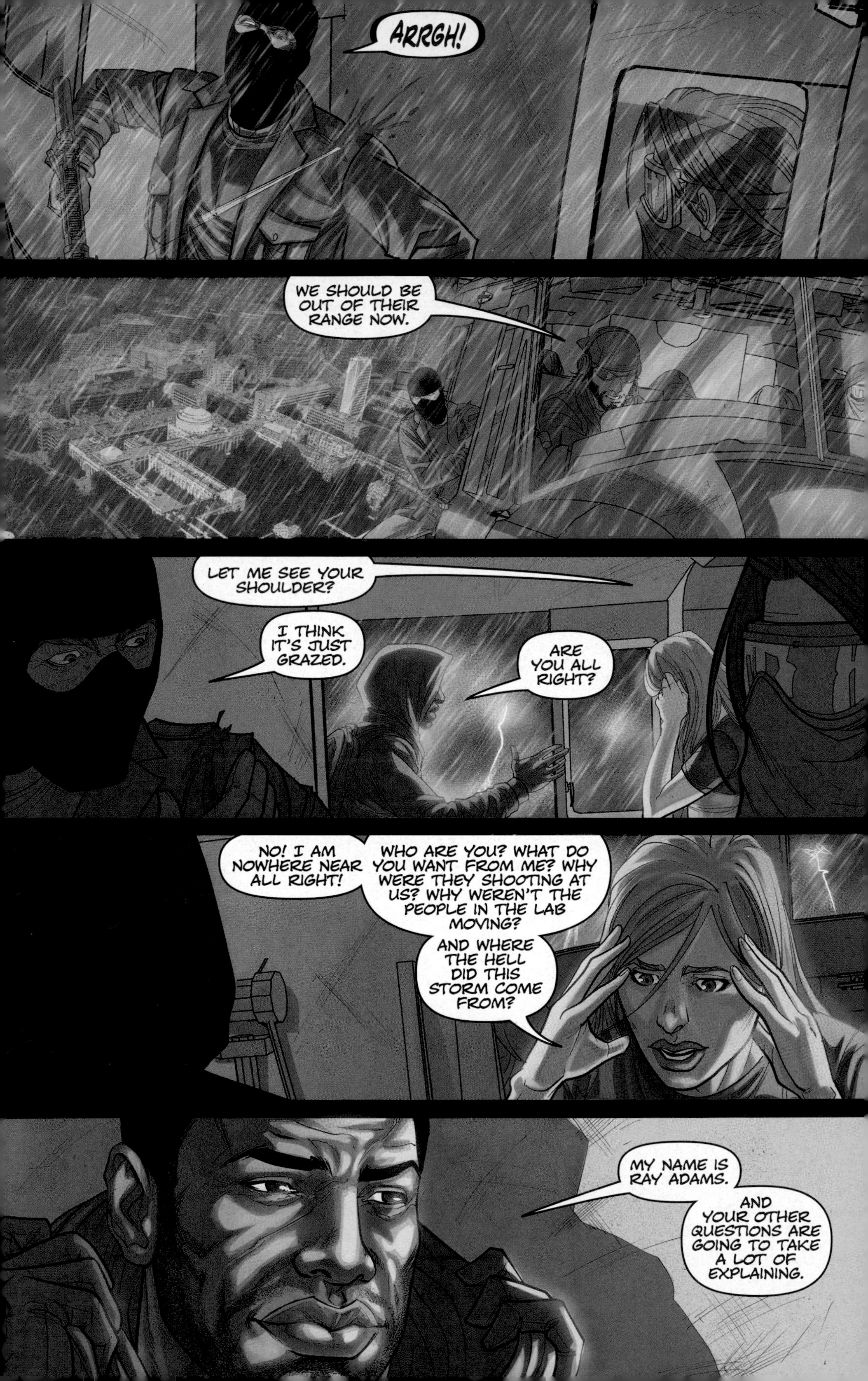
ARRGH!
WE SHOULD BE OUT OF THEIR RANGE NOW.
LET ME SEE YOUR SHOULDER?
I THINK IT'S JUST GRAZED.
ARE YOU ALL RIGHT?
NO! I AM NOWHERE NEAR ALL RIGHT!
WHO ARE YOU? WHAT DO YOU WANT FROM ME? WHY WERE THEY SHOOTING AT US? WHY WEREN'T THE PEOPLE IN THE LAB MOVING?
AND WHERE THE HELL DID THIS STORM COME FROM?
MY NAME IS RAY ADAMS.
AND YOUR OTHER QUESTIONS ARE GOING TO TAKE A LOT OF EXPLAINING.

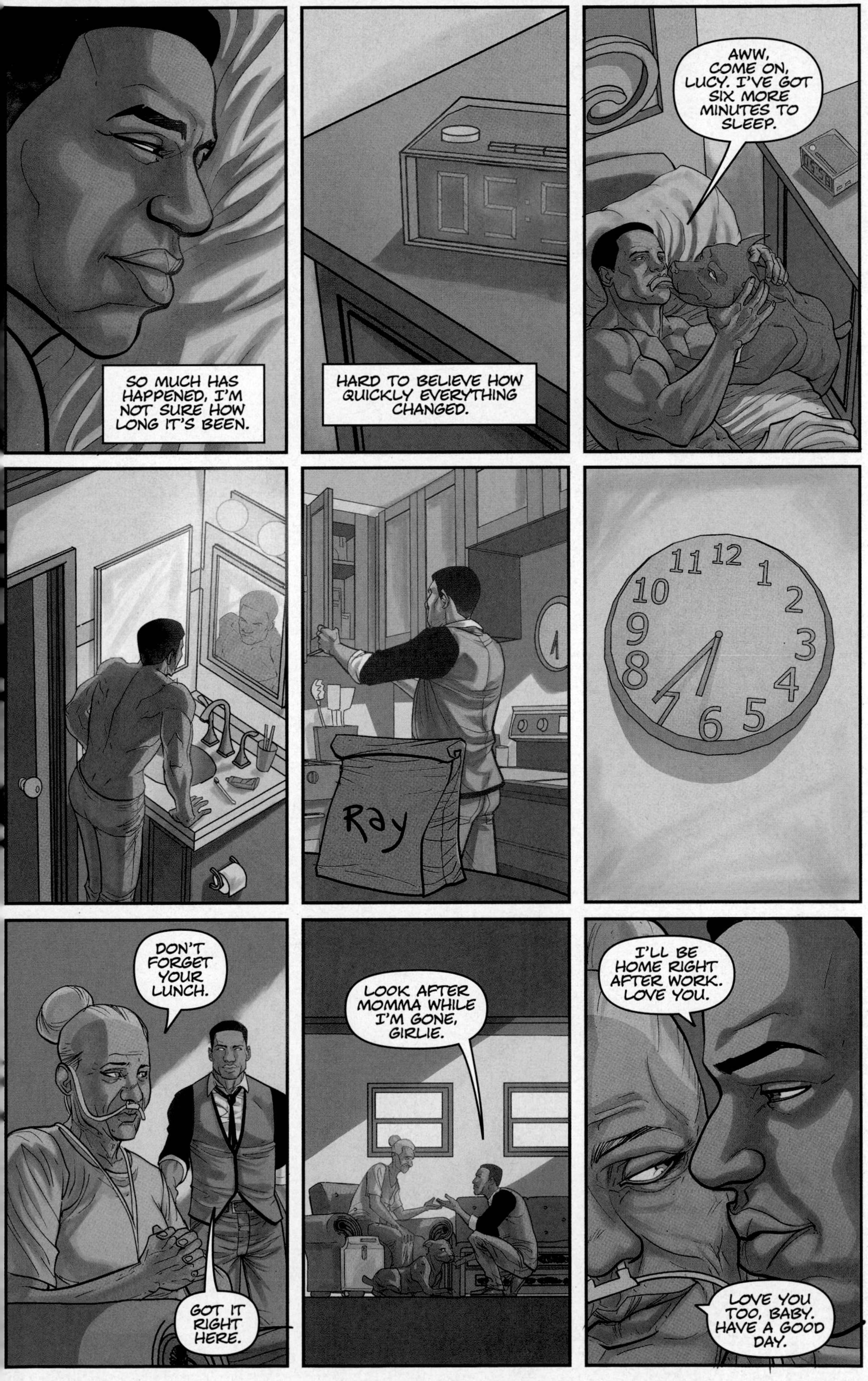
SO MUCH HAS HAPPENED, I'M NOT SURE HOW LONG IT'S BEEN.
HARD TO BELIEVE HOW QUICKLY EVERYTHING CHANGED.
AWW, COME ON, LUCY. I'VE GOT SIX MORE MINUTES TO SLEEP.
Ray
DON'T FORGET YOUR LUNCH.
GOT IT RIGHT HERE.
LOOK AFTER MOMMA WHILE I'M GONE, GIRLIE.
I'LL BE HOME RIGHT AFTER WORK. LOVE YOU.
LOVE YOU TOO, BABY. HAVE A GOOD DAY.

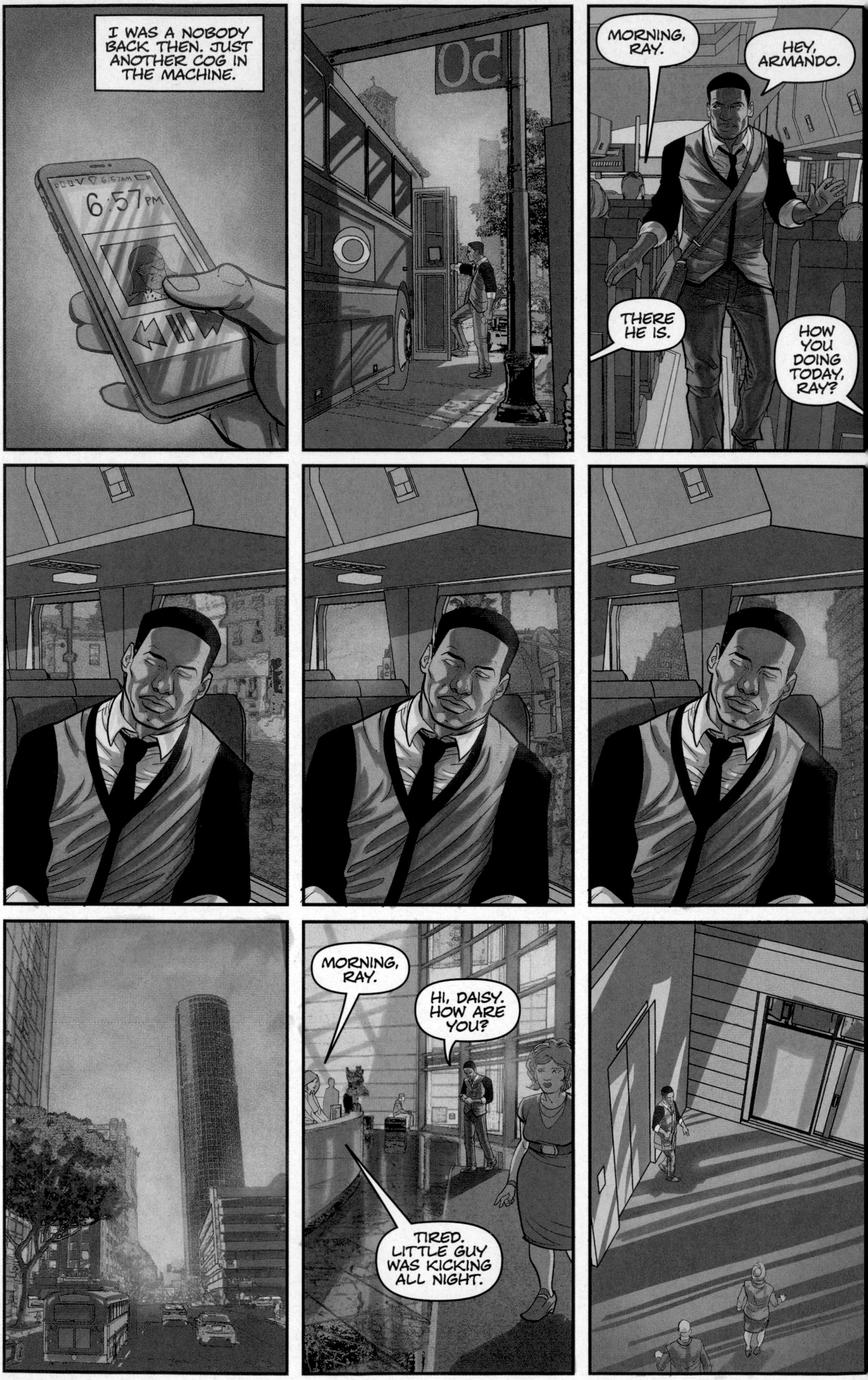
I WAS A NOBODY BACK THEN. JUST ANOTHER COG IN THE MACHINE.
6:57 PM
50
MORNING, RAY.
HEY, ARMANDO.
THERE HE IS.
HOW YOU DOING TODAY, RAY?
MORNING, RAY.
HI, DAISY. HOW ARE YOU?
TIRED. LITTLE GUY WAS KICKING ALL NIGHT.

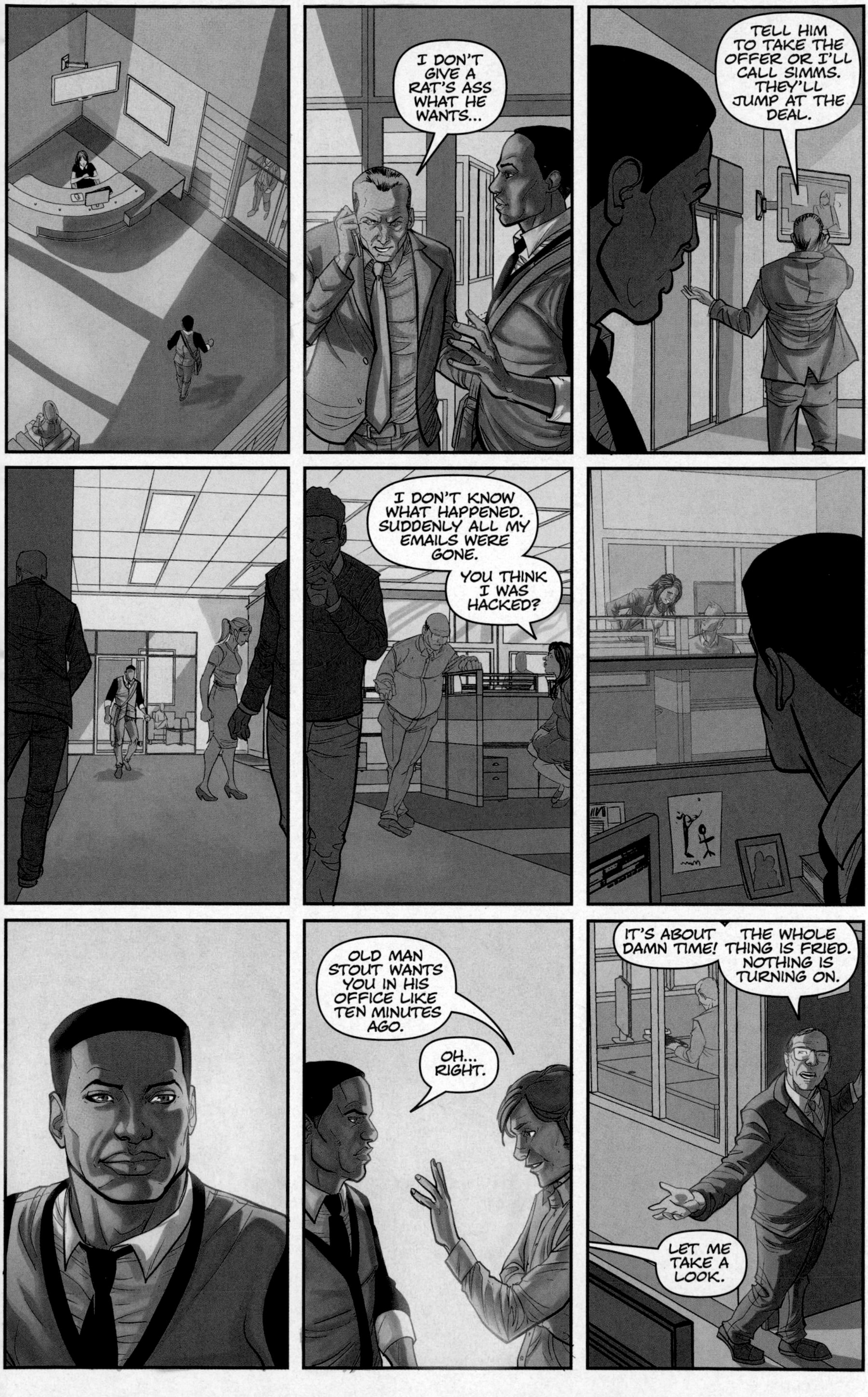
I DON'T GIVE A RAT'S ASS WHAT HE WANTS...
TELL HIM TO TAKE THE OFFER OR I'LL CALL SIMMS. THEY'LL JUMP AT THE DEAL.
I DON'T KNOW WHAT HAPPENED. SUDDENLY ALL MY EMAILS WERE GONE.
YOU THINK I WAS HACKED?
OLD MAN STOUT WANTS YOU IN HIS OFFICE LIKE TEN MINUTES AGO.
OH... RIGHT.
IT'S ABOUT DAMN TIME!
THE WHOLE THING IS FRIED. NOTHING IS TURNING ON.
LET ME TAKE A LOOK.

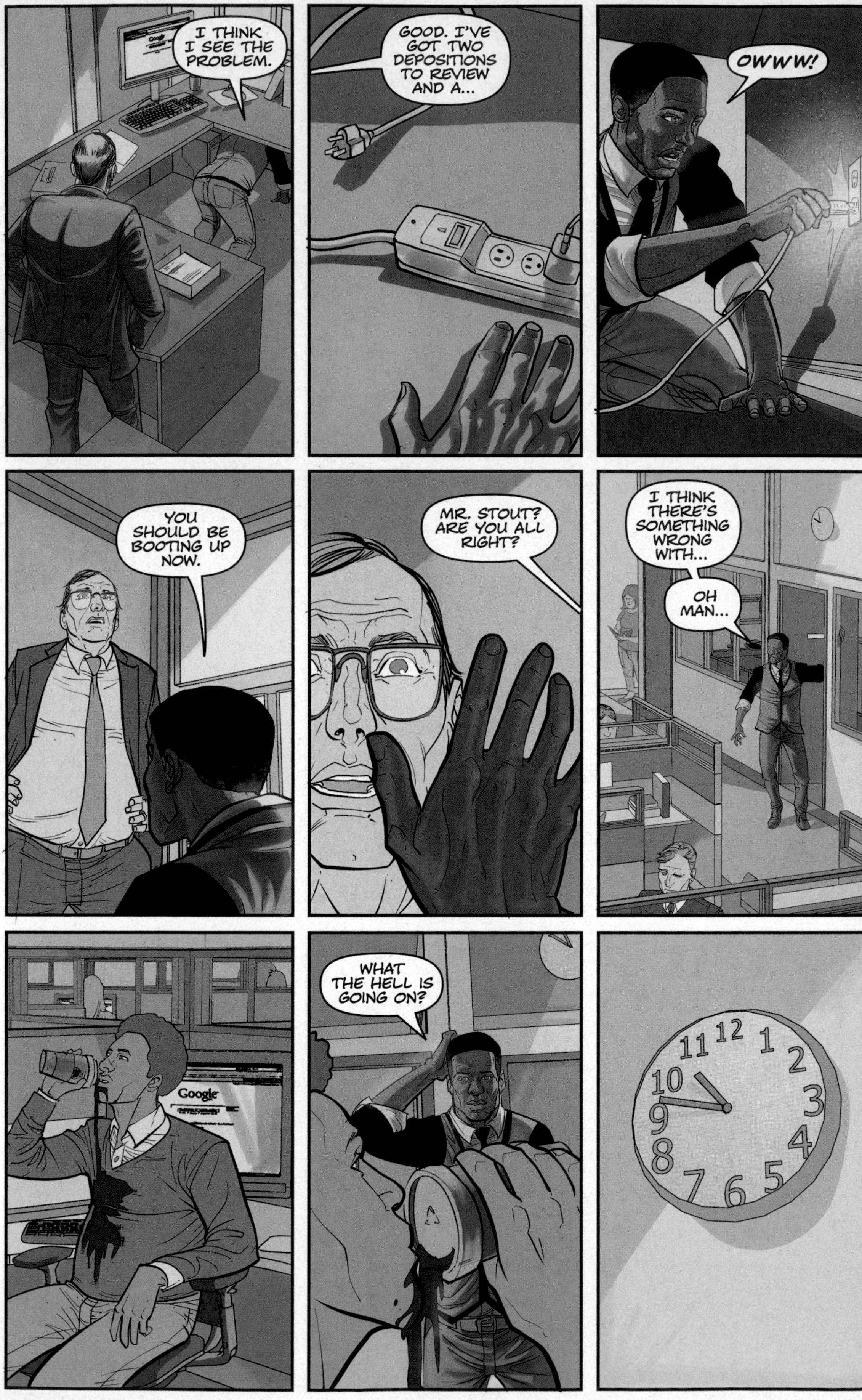

I THINK I SEE THE PROBLEM.
GOOD. I'VE GOT TWO DEPOSITIONS TO REVIEW AND A...
OWWW!
YOU SHOULD BE BOOTING UP NOW.
MR. STOUT? ARE YOU ALL RIGHT?
I THINK THERE'S SOMETHING WRONG WITH...
OH MAN...
Google
WHAT THE HELL IS GOING ON?
12 1 2 3 4 5 6 7 8 9 10 11

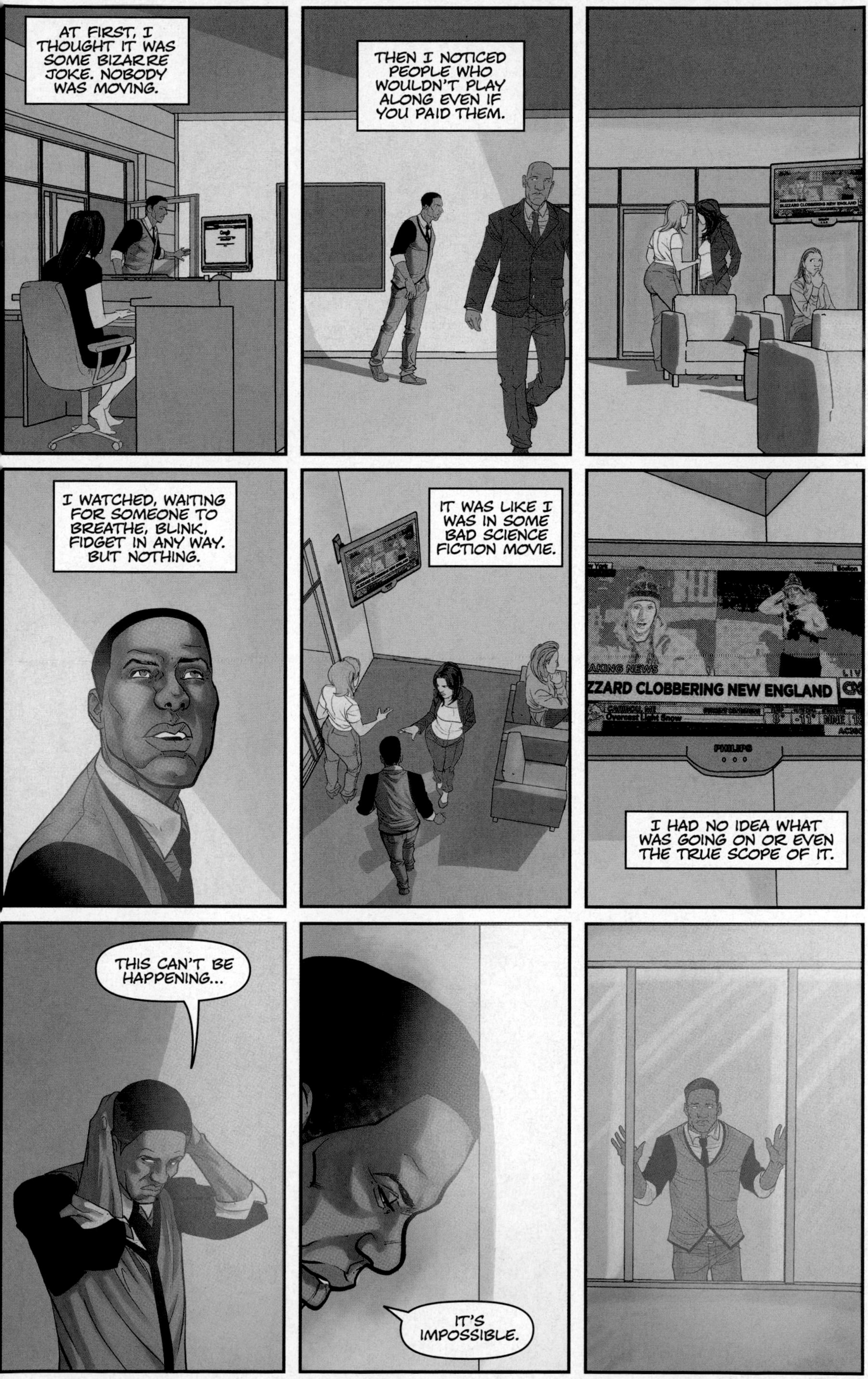
AT FIRST, I THOUGHT IT WAS SOME BIZARRE JOKE. NOBODY WAS MOVING.
THEN I NOTICED PEOPLE WHO WOULDN'T PLAY ALONG EVEN IF YOU PAID THEM.
BLIZZARD CLOBBERING NEW ENGLAND
I WATCHED, WAITING FOR SOMEONE TO BREATHE, BLINK, FIDGET IN ANY WAY. BUT NOTHING.
IT WAS LIKE I WAS IN SOME BAD SCIENCE FICTION MOVIE.
ZZARD CLOBBERING NEW ENGLAND
PHILIPS
I HAD NO IDEA WHAT WAS GOING ON OR EVEN THE TRUE SCOPE OF IT.
THIS CAN'T BE HAPPENING...
IT'S IMPOSSIBLE.

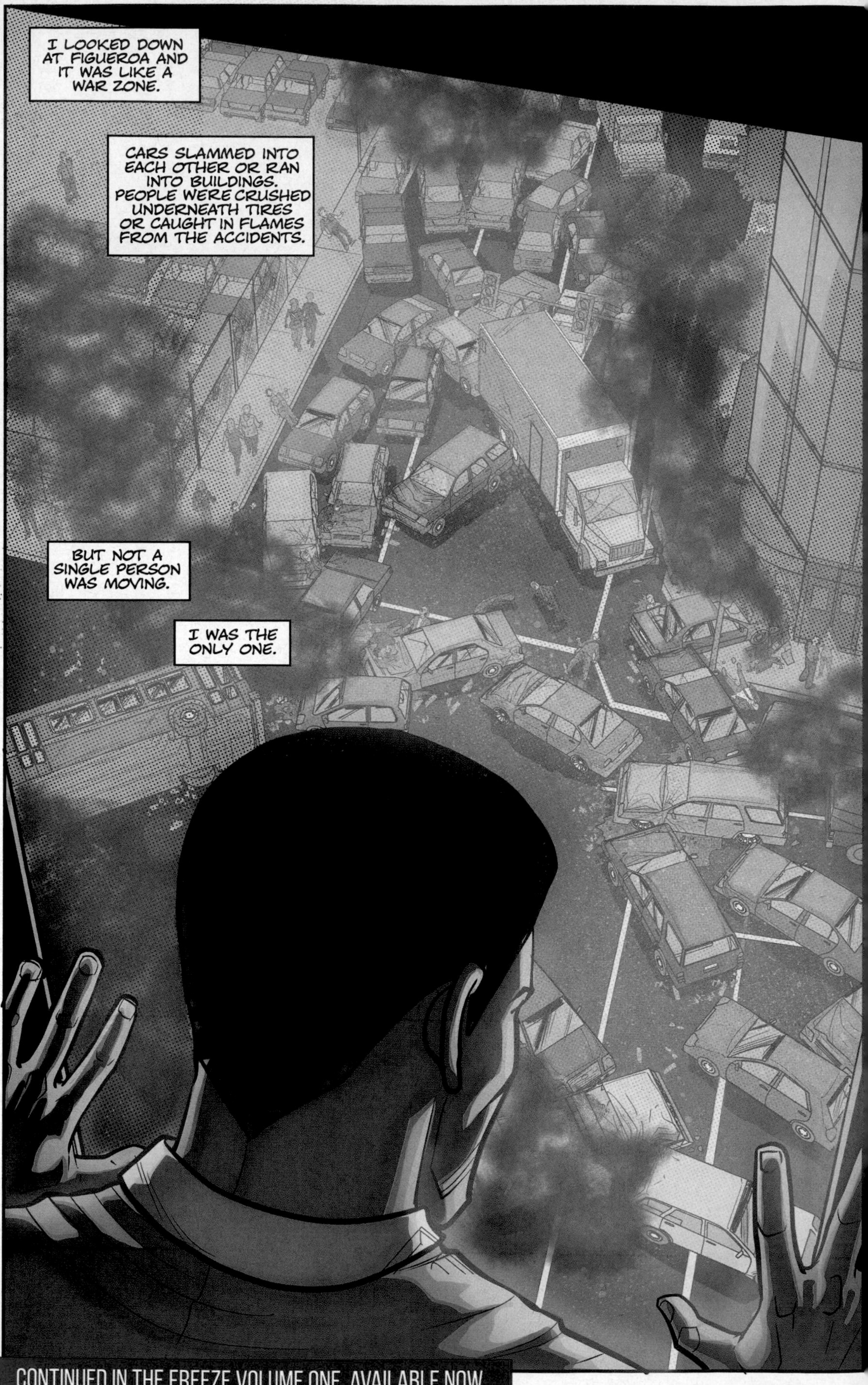
I LOOKED DOWN AT FIGUEROA AND IT WAS LIKE A WAR ZONE.
CARS SLAMMED INTO EACH OTHER OR RAN INTO BUILDINGS. PEOPLE WERE CRUSHED UNDERNEATH TIRES OR CAUGHT IN FLAMES FROM THE ACCIDENTS.
BUT NOT A SINGLE PERSON WAS MOVING.
I WAS THE ONLY ONE.

CONTINUED IN THE FREEZE VOLUME ONE, AVAILABLE NOW

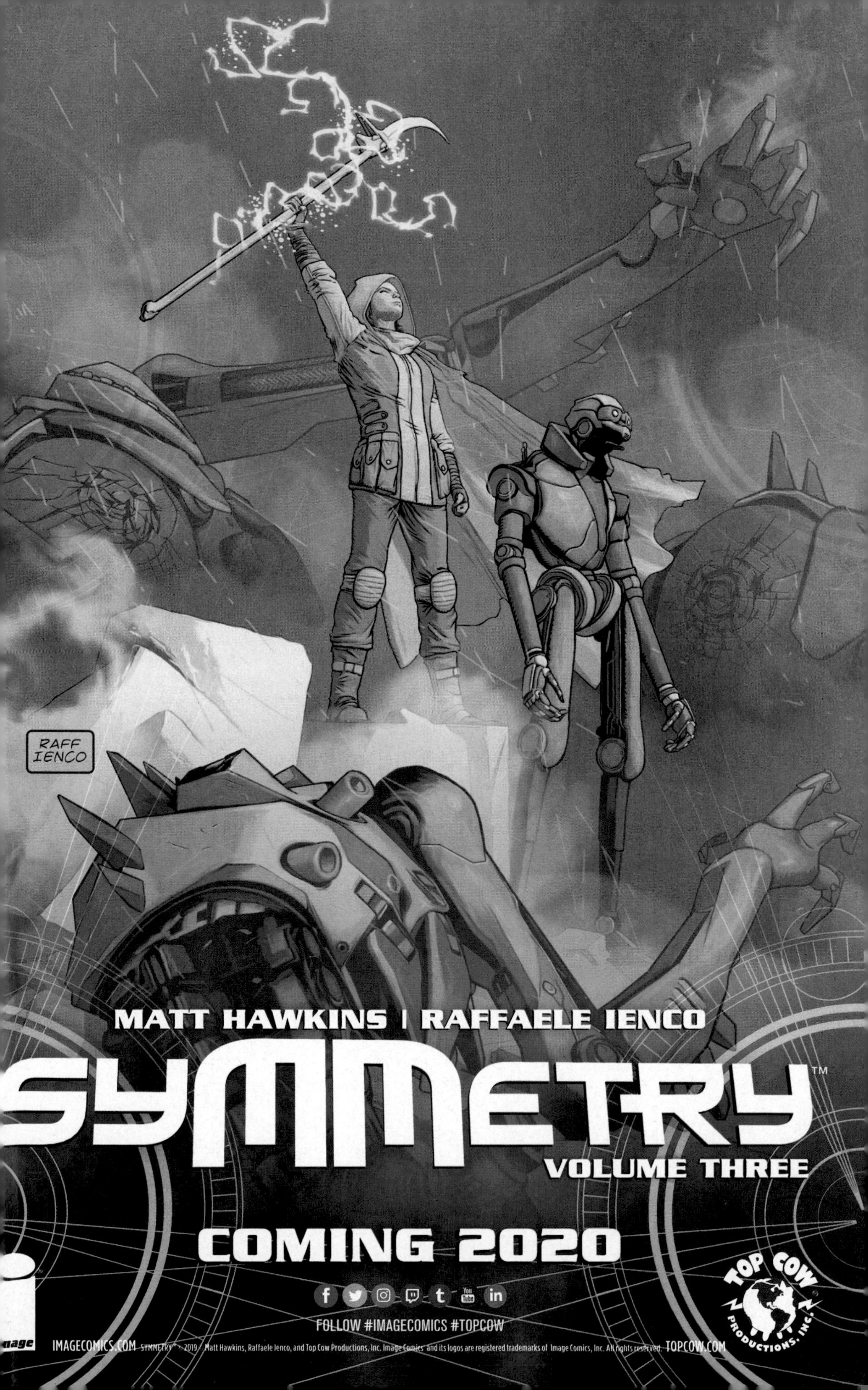
RAFF IENCO
MATT HAWKINS | RAFFAELE IENCO
SYMMETRY™
VOLUME THREE
COMING 2020
FOLLOW #IMAGECOMICS #TOPCOW
IMAGECOMICS.COM
SYMMETRY™ © 2019 Matt Hawkins, Raffaele Ienco, and Top Cow Productions, Inc. Image Comics and its logos are registered trademarks of Image Comics, Inc. All rights reserved.
TOPCOW.COM
TOP COW PRODUCTIONS, INC.

The Top Cow essentials checklist:

For more ISBN and ordering information on our latest collections go to:
www.topcow.com
Ask your retailer about our catalogue of collected editions,
digests, and hard covers or check the listings at:
Barnes and Noble, Amazon.com,
and other fine retailers.

To find your nearest comic shop go to:
www.comicshoplocator.com